# talk flirty to me

# talk flirty to me

## livy hart

Entangled Publishing
644 Shrewsbury Commons Ave
STE 181
Shrewsbury, PA 17361
rights@entangledpublishing.com

Embrace is an imprint of Entangled Publishing, LLC.

Edited by Heather Howland
Cover illustration and design by Elizabeth Turner Stokes

ISBN 978-1-64937-356-4

Manufactured in the United States of America

First Edition May 2022

*For Corey, who carries me through, and Rochele,*
*whose fingerprints are on every page.*

# Chapter One

## PIPER

It's not too late to bail.

In fact, I probably should. My bank account would thank me. If I wasn't rocking a full face of makeup that took twenty minutes to apply and the finest jeans Target sells, I'd probably get right back in the car and drive my denim-wrapped ass home.

Instead, I pace the sidewalk outside McLaughlin's Irish Pub, peering up at the flickering neon sign, questioning my choices. After college, I swore off dive bars. All bars, really, unless they have a full food menu.

But I hadn't yet been forced to move back into my childhood home with my nine rowdy brothers when I made that commitment. I wasn't a perma-babysitter for my pregnant mother back then, didn't have student loan collectors blowing up my phone, and still had single friends to hang with.

My reality is different now. Dive bars are back on the table, as a means for escape.

After spending a rowdy Saturday with my family,

an escape is exactly what I need. The recreational pickings in Roseborough, Massachusetts, are slim at nine p.m., so it was either get in my car and drive to McLaughlin's or get in my car and drive off a cliff.

I drag the last remnants of Ruby Woo Matte across my lips, then push open the door. Warm air immediately spills from the building, and familiarity envelops me. I bump into a couple sucking face and apologize under my breath as I hurry past, keeping my head down.

Avoiding ghosts of my past is why I've steered clear of Roseborough's downtown strip since moving home. No need to risk running into someone I don't want to see, someone who knew me when I rocked scorned-girl bangs and tragically distressed jeans my Nonna called *unbecoming*.

Joke's on Nonna. *Unbecoming* was my goal, just not in the way she meant it. After my life in Roseborough took a turn for the pathetic toward the end of high school and everything fell apart, I wanted to unbecome everything I was.

Six years away in the city helped with that.

I maneuver through the dense crowd. Contrary to my highly specific nightmares, I'm not immediately accosted by people I went to high school with. Victory.

My gaze seeks my favorite chair. Close enough to the fireplace to benefit from the warmth, but far enough that the steady stream of heat doesn't overwhelm. The perfect spot to unwind after the chaos at home.

Except, as the crowd parts, I discover a broad-shouldered man in a knitted Bruins beanie beat me to the punch. After a quick scan, the open chair to his left is the only free spot left in the whole place.

That'll do. As it happens, men who look like they could break me in half are just my type.

I pull my cardigan across my chest as I weave between full high-top tables. My shoulders relax with each unfamiliar person I pass. Anonymity with a side of alcohol—the perfect remedies for a hectic day. The whir of color and noise from a big-screen TV playing the Bruins-Canadiens game catches my attention as I close in on my spot.

The bar erupts in a tide of sports-fueled celebration the exact moment I grasp the worn edge of the wooden chair. An elbow—no, an entire muscular arm—rams into me as the beanie-clad man jumps to his feet, whooping at a scored hockey goal. The force sends me sailing into the nebulous lap region of the man on my left.

"Whoa, sorry!" I scramble to my feet, setting my sights on the assailant as I rub the tender spot on my arm. "Easy does it, Captain Bowflex."

The man whose lap I've vacated slides his arm

across my lower back. "Former Army, sweetie. These guns are locked and loaded."

I squirm from his touch. "Not you." I jab my finger into Captain Bowflex's dense shoulder. "*You.* The guy who knocked me over."

Bowflex eyes my finger, as though a fly has landed on his shoulder. "My apologies, ma'am…" His voice trails away as his eyes meet mine, and the concern melts off his face. "*Piper?*"

My stomach vaults into my throat. The ambient bar noise fades away until my heartbeat thunders in my ears. Eyes the color of celery pin me in place. A sea of memories floods me so hard and fast I need a lifeboat. Maybe an ark.

*Sam.*

Or, as my friends in the city refer to him, Hefty. Because they think he's trash for what he did to me.

"Piper," he repeats. "What are you doing here?"

Even in dim lighting his eyes are bright and tinged with mischief, a sparkler left burning until it singes fingertips. Features once round and boyish are now a case study in lines and angles.

I glance down at my plain black boots, up at waterlogged ceiling panels, anywhere but at my ex-boyfriend as I consider nose-diving behind the bar to escape his line of sight. My heel scratches across the floor as I slide a step back. I'd be all right with a trapdoor straight to the underworld if it meant escape.

Dread lodges in my stomach as he slides off his beanie and runs a hand through his jet-black hair. I drag my gaze to his. "Evening, Sam. I see you're…still alive."

The corner of his mouth turns up. "Try and contain your excitement. This is a public place."

My lips twist into a grimace. *Excitement* is not the correct descriptor for the dread and confusion swirling in my gut. How did I not immediately recognize him? Why did the last few years darken his hair and gift him toned muscles? The only thing the last few years bestowed upon me was debt.

God, as ever, is a comedian.

"Is this guy bothering you?" asks Army Dude, who I had all but forgotten existed until his breath puffs against my face. I recoil at the heavy scent of booze.

"Am I?" Sam asks, cocking his head to the side. The intensity of his stare feels an awful lot like a challenge. Or a trap.

I don't blink. Sam doesn't blink. The only movement between us is the methodical drumming of my fingers against my thighs as I weigh my options. I'm not here to make a scene, but man would I love to give Sam hell right now.

Trapped between a rock and a hard place—two

things that adequately describe Sam's chest in my face—I choose the familiar foe. "No, Sam. You're not bothering me." *Yet.*

Army Dude returns to his beer, and Sam plops down in his seat with a smirk. I drag out my own chair and force myself to sit down.

"God, how long's it been?" Sam asks, coiling his hand around a half-empty pint glass.

This feels like another trap. The last time I was forced to endure Sam O'Shea for an extended period following our breakup was the Hamilton High School Annual Scavenger Hunt. He was a wild senior, and I a tortured junior. He ruined the whole night, and I nearly got him banned from the Catholic church. Many people cope with a breakup by lighting their ex's pictures on fire. I filmed Sam in his drunkest, poorest form as he vomited in a confessional booth at Saint Mary's, uploaded it on every platform, and tagged everyone we knew.

A digital effigy. Whoops.

It's been about seven years since that video went viral, and there's no way he's forgotten. I peek over and find that he's half smiling as he waits for my answer, eyes twinkling.

He knows *exactly* how long it's been, but I'm not taking his bait. "Oh, who can say?"

He lifts a hand to get the bartender's attention,

and I'm hit by his elbow, again.

"Please try to contain that," I snap.

"Contain what?"

I gesture broadly at his well-defined arm. "All of…that. The whole thing. Keep it in your area."

He peeks down at his bulky Popeye bicep and back up at my face before letting out a smug little laugh. "Fine." He raises his arm so slowly I can barely stand to watch. "Let me buy you a drink."

"No thanks."

"My treat."

I am almost thawed by the gesture—the tip of my iceberg slightly sweating—when he adds, "I mean *look* how busy the bartender is. It'd be rude to make him start another tab."

At this point, retreating to my house and watching my giant, Cheaper-by-the-Dozen family demolish a full sheet of ice cream cake doesn't sound so bad. I wanted something to take my mind off my familial stress, yet here I am, bickering with the star of my teenage diary.

I chew the inside of my cheek, seesawing between the external chaos of my siblings and the internal chaos of being this close to my ex-boyfriend after years of pretending he didn't exist. I'm in purgatory, but instead of a cloudy holding tank outside of pearly gates, it's a bar full of fully cocked dudebros in hockey jerseys.

But at least in this purgatory, no one needs anything from me. There are no dishes to be washed or brothers to wrangle. No dinner leftovers to scrape off the linoleum.

This purgatory has beer.

I hang my purse off the back of my chair and shrug out of my cardigan. "Fine. One drink, because I'm already here and my house is a zoo."

"You got it."

I side-eye Sam's fitted jeans, clean white shirt, and the conspicuously formal black peacoat slung over the back of his chair as we wait for our turn to order. Last time I saw him he sported a gnarly old hoodie, basketball shorts, and knee-high socks. Apparently, he's graduated to adult clothing. I look forward to never validating him on his glow-up. "Are you waiting for a date or something? Far be it from me to squat in their seat."

"A date?" He snorts. "You think I bring my dates to McLaughlin's?"

I narrow my eyes. "My mistake. I'm sure you've long cleared the townie roster, so who would be left?"

A laugh-wheeze escapes his mouth. "Guess I'll update my Tinder location to Waltham, then."

"Happy catfishing."

"No, I'm not waiting for anyone." He stretches

his neck slowly from side to side, as though preparing for a workout. "How about I buy you one of those Amaretto Sours you love so much?"

I try to say "Amaretto Sours" and "since when?" in the same irritated breath but wind up sputtering something vaguely resembling "am ass" as the bartender materializes in front of us.

"What'll you have?" he asks, snagging Sam's empty glass.

Sam rubs his chin, eyeing the tap. "Let's go with a Blue Moon—"

"I'll have one as well," I interject before he adds anything undesirable to the order.

Sam snaps his mouth shut as the bartender, a burly Chuck Norris clone with tattoos winding around his forearms, nods and reaches below the bar for two clean pint glasses. He takes turns filling them from the same tap before depositing both on napkins in front of us. The amber liquid glows beneath a low-hanging pendant light.

I reach for a glass. "I didn't know you liked Blue Moon."

He slides both in my direction, his expression cryptic. "I don't. But you do."

*Oh.*

A blush breaks out, bringing heat to my cheeks. He remembered my favorite beer. "I didn't realize you were ordering for me. Thanks." I slide one back to him before adding, "I don't need two drinks."

He slides it back, smiling just enough to flash one dimple. "Don't you, though?"

I take a long swig, mostly to end this game of pint-glass shuffleboard. The glass *thuds* against the bar when I set it down. He orders himself a Guinness before the bartender has a chance to escape.

The crowd around us grows progressively rowdier with two goals in as many minutes. The noise gives me something to focus on other than my proximity to Sam's body as he toys with his glass. His hand keeps inching closer as though it has a mind of its own, like Thing from *The Addams Family*.

"Personal space!" I finally cry when his wrist brushes mine. Sports may have him hypnotized, but I'm still well aware of my limbs. "Forget it. I'll move over."

He drags his attention from the TV when I start squirming in my seat. "What are you doing?"

"I'm scooting."

He leans in, and I'm hit with the familiar scent of Acqua Di Gio. It's like being struck by the memory train at full speed. "You're going to end up in your new friend's lap again if you scoot any farther."

"Only if you push me there. *Again*."

"If you're looking for a wingman, you should have

said so." His voice—husky and engaging—stokes a dangerous sense of familiarity. It's a reminder of how quickly his charm can penetrate the defenseless.

"Very funny." I reach for both pints and slide them toward my chest, cradling them like precious babies.

He plants an elbow on the bar and shifts his torso toward me. His cheek comes to rest against his knuckles. "So, you're back permanently? Caleb mentioned it."

I turn over his question, examining it in parts.

Other than my brother's text warning that he and Sam reconciled a year ago, Caleb and I do *not* talk about Sam. I've lived in town for two months and have asked zero questions, and my brother has offered no information. The state of their friendship is none of my business—and that's where it needs to stay.

Guilt flares in my gut. "Best friends" isn't enough to encompass what they were back in the day. Brothers was more like it. Caleb has always been responsible for me and our siblings, but he got to be fun and carefree with Sam. Their escapades, from sweet-talking their way out of speeding tickets to charming their way into free Bruins seats, were the stuff of legend at our high school.

My and Sam's ugly breakup nearly destroyed their friendship for good. They didn't talk for years because of it.

Because of *me*.

I shuffle the pints of beer in front of me. "Permanently is a stretch, but I'm back for a while." I peek sideways and catch his eye. "Did Caleb have anything *else* to report on the topic of my life?" I don't know exactly where they stand now—the less I know about their rekindled bromance, the better—but I need to know if my brother is breaking the unspoken agreement to keep the me- and Sam-shaped parts of his life separate.

His expression is cryptic. "That was the gist."

So they *have* talked about me.

Equal parts panic and curiosity swell in my chest, and I unsuccessfully try to smash them down. After the breakup, I saw a withdrawn side of Caleb that was not only painful to witness but entirely my fault. In case the pain of my soul-crushing breakup with Sam wasn't bad enough, I had a chronic case of sibling guilt to go along with it because, as my brother, Caleb was forced to take my side. Setting him up with his now wife was the closest I've ever come to righting that cosmic wrong.

Did he and Sam pick up where they left off, or did years apart change things irrevocably?

I mentally shake myself. I'll do whatever it takes to make sure that kind of pain never happens again, to me or to Caleb. And that starts by staying the hell away from Sam O'Shea. No being curious about what he's up to, no fishing for information from my brother, and definitely no asking questions that will lead to a longer conversation. In fact, I should relocate to the other side of the bar immediately.

I pause in the act of gathering my stuff. Who started that conversation about me—him or Caleb? The thought of my name in Sam's mouth makes the inside of my face itch.

*That's the gist.*

What else did my bigmouthed brother have to say? Why is he breaking our Fight Club Rule One that states "you do not talk about Piper to Sam" and vice versa, designed specifically to *avoid* fights? Just how chummy are they nowadays? Should I be worried? If they're super close, there's no way I'll be able to evade him completely.

*Don't ask, don't ask, don't—*

"So, what, you two are still thriving, then? Besties for the resties?"

*Damn it, Piper.*

# CHAPTER TWO

## PIPER

I immediately want to hurl myself into the mass of rowdy hockey fans. What am I doing? Engaging Sam in conversation is *not* a good idea. Ever.

A sideways tilt of his head suggests he's as confused by my attempt to start a conversation as I am. Or he doesn't want to answer.

Probably for the best.

"Never mind." I force an indifferent shrug. "None of my business."

"You're asking if Caleb and I are good?"

Fly, meet sticky paper. I may die in this trap I set for myself. "Sure. I guess. Whatever."

He taps the rim of his glass. "We don't talk as often as I'd like, since we're on different schedules, but yes." His lips threaten a smile. "Thriving. We've got tickets to see the Sox in a few weeks. Fantastic seats."

He seems content to sip his drink and stare at me, so I do the same, attempting to merge my memories of him with what I see. His hair is short on the sides and longer on top, tidier than what High School Sam used to sport. The top shines with product, a new addition to his style repertoire. It tames the waves, and I sort of hate it. His face is clean-shaven, and there's a frustrating amount of symmetry happening in his features. He could do with a broken nose or a scorched brow.

Since Caleb and I specifically do not discuss Sam, per Fight Club Rule One, I'm left to assume he's landed some vaguely corporate job along with a gym membership. When we broke up, he was a few months out from starting college and undecided on a major. If I was a betting woman, I'd bet his smile is plastered on a bus bench ad somewhere. *Ready for financial freedom? O'Shea is the O'Way!*

I wander back to my original point. "Glad you're finding time to bond, what with your schedules and all. Caleb's up all hours of the night with an infant and you're"—I look him up and down, brows furrowed—"a financial advisor?"

He eyes me a beat too long. "You really have *no* idea what I do? Caleb's never mentioned it?"

*Right.* Because my brother regularly takes time out of his schedule to send me unsolicited updates about my ex's career. If Caleb had it his way, I'd forget Sam existed. Or better yet, I never would've met him in the first place.

Can't say I disagree. Life would've been simpler for everyone.

"Real estate?" I press on, shifting in my seat.

"In a manner of speaking."

I roll my eyes. "What's that mean?"

"I'm a firefighter. I see a lot of real estate. Most houses are stripped down to the studs by the time we get there, mind you, but some retain their curb appeal."

I blink. "Is that a joke?"

"Depends. Did you find it funny?"

"I don't know," I hedge, stifling a laugh. It unsettles me that his humor still hits the spot. He always did know how to toe the line between *too far* and *just enough*.

"That tracks." He chuckles into the rim of his beer, fogging the glass. "Decision-making has never been your strong suit, has it?"

My tongue pushes against the roof of my mouth, trapping my rebuttal in my throat. *What an ass.* I reach into the pocket of my jeans and pull out my debit card, sliding it across the bar top. "I'm not doing this with you."

"Was it something I said?" Sam asks, his eyes flashing mingled innocence and mirth.

"I just emerged from three straight days of preparing casseroles and desserts for this weekend. Enough to feed my siblings, my parents, their friends, assorted cousins, aunts, uncles, and everyone they've ever shared a pack of gum with. My battery is drained. I'm not sure how much verbal tennis I can handle tonight."

He points his finger like he's about to accuse me of something, floats it over the debit card, and presses down on the Bank of America logo. The plastic scrapes against the bar top as he drags it to the edge. "Why don't I keep this safe for you until it's time to go?"

I snatch the card and slam it down next to my glass. "That won't be necessary."

"Three days of prep," he says, ignoring my discomfort. "Almost forgot about Bonanza weekend. No one does birthdays like the Bellinis. Your family parties are always more packed than an Olive Garden."

He's not wrong. Our annual Bellini Birthday Bonanza—a weekend filled with meals and birthday shenanigans to celebrate the strange coincidence of three May first birthdays in one family. "Yeah, this weekend is always off the chain. My whole family and Aunt Dawn's clan. Plus, I'm pretty sure Dad invited a few of his coworkers, too. His staff loves sucking up to him, so I'm sure they'll come."

"Principal Bellini and his adoring fans," he remarks with a tilt of his pint glass in my direction. "Your dad's done a lot for the school. High school principals don't get enough respect for how demanding the job is."

My mouth opens and closes. I can't argue with his response, nor do I know what to do with the reminder that Sam's old enough to spew trite (and true) sentiments about high school. None of this computes. He was nineteen and shotgunning cans of Natty Ice, last I checked.

A peek from the corner of my eye reminds me this is no longer the case. He's consuming his beer in a surprisingly restrained way, no slurping, his lips fastened on the top of the glass instead of plugging a jagged hole he stabbed in the side.

I clear my throat. "Giovanni Bellini is good people."

"That he is. So what do you do for work?"

I let out a bit of air at this question. "Is this 'catching up' square dance necessary?"

"I showed you mine," he reminds me, his eyes alight.

"Fine. I work in the entertainment industry."

He snorts. "The *entertainment industry*? And

you moved back here? If this is the new Hollywood, I need to get the hell out."

"Relax, Hallmark. Your little New England suburb ain't all that."

"*My* suburb? Seems you've forgotten you lived here for"—he brandishes his wrist to check his watch—"*two-thirds* of your life."

As if I needed the reminder. "I moved back here specifically because my mother's pregnant, which I'm sure Caleb mentioned to you. With her on the city council and Dad working more than ever before, they could use a little help managing it all."

"Kid number eleven," he says with a low whistle.

I like to think his subdued tone is his way of demonstrating reverence for the miracle of pregnancy, but he's probably just terrified it's contagious. "Right. Anyway, it's a temporary arrangement. After the baby is born, Mom gets her bearings, and the rest of the kids adjust, I'll be on my merry way."

I say this as much for myself as for him, a commitment to getting my own place as soon as possible. No need to mention it financially behooves me to live at home as I try to build my voice-acting portfolio. My student loan debt would bring a boomer to tears.

"Well, congratulations on the baby. Exciting news for the Bellini clan," he offers.

"I— Thanks?" I've never been congratulated on someone else's pregnancy before, but he sounds more sincere than usual. Though it doesn't take much to accomplish that, given he's otherwise radiating snark.

"Entertainment industry," he murmurs, the skin around his hazy, fern-colored eyes crinkling. "That's the last thing I expected you to say. Teacher? Now that would make sense, given…" He gestures between the thick, messy bun on top of my head and the cardigan hanging limply off the chair as a means of explanation. "Or, better yet, a social media manager, since you seemed to enjoy it when your video of me went viral. But *entertainment*…interesting."

Hairs prickle on the back of my neck. "Do you have a point, O'Shea?"

He shrugs two broad shoulders. "I just never would have guessed."

My credit card lays ignored on the bar top, shackling me to this conversation. I sip my beer once. "I'm a voice actress. It's interesting and fulfilling work. Am I not someone who would enjoy interesting and fulfilling work?"

"We all have our calling in life. Calling… phone…voice… There's a voice-acting joke in there somewhere."

"Bartender!" I raise my hand.

Sam reaches over and lowers it to the bar like

he's cranking a slot machine. "I'm messing with you, Piper. The job sounds cool. And I told you, the drinks are my treat."

I'm about to inform him that treat is too strong a word when he changes course. "That *does* clear up something I've been wondering."

I watch two red-and-blue-clad hockey players collide on the nearest TV screen. "Oh yeah?"

He reaches into his pocket and pulls out his phone. A few keystrokes later, my face fills his screen. "Stumbled across this sometime last year. I see why you've made a career of this. The talent jumps out."

Mouth agape, I turn to him. He is a ball of pure, unbridled glee as my emotions cycle through embarrassment, anger, and irritation. His hands tent together like a cartoon villain's.

My eyes narrow. "How do you *stumble* across my YouTube makeup tutorial from three years ago?"

His smirking face is supremely punchable. "Algorithms are a funny thing. I guess YouTube thought I'd enjoy a Boston content creator. We support our own."

I mute the phone, silencing my ramble about the merits of eyeshadow primer. "YouTube tutorials aren't the same as voice acting."

"I mean…you were talking. You used your voice. And unless you *really* love blush, there was an element of acting. So much excitement over the shade. Orgasm, was it?" His eyes twinkle.

I tap my glossy bottom lip. "Yes, Orgasm by Nars is a popular blush. What an oddly specific thing for you to remember from a video you caught in passing. Also, the blush part comes last. You watched a fifteen-minute video of me applying makeup?"

He plucks his phone from the bar and slides it into his pocket with a gentle shake of his head. His lack of response is perhaps the best response of all.

I want to revel in the victory of rendering him speechless, but the idea of him not only watching my video but also remembering key details upsets my understanding of the space-time continuum a little. I swirl my glass, considering the admission's implications. We don't keep tabs on each other. That's not a thing we do.

*Is it?*

His silence is short-lived. He crosses his arms, and I catch the sheen of a dark red scar circling his right wrist. "Your YouTube videos really have nothing to do with your job?"

"You assume there's more than one?"

His exhale is a huff. "We've established I saw your channel."

"It's all related. Voice acting, like everything these days, is about building your brand. It's not enough to have a compelling and versatile sound. If you want to be successful in the type of voice acting I'm interested in, you have to look good doing it. They film voice actors in the studio and use the footage for publicity and publishers' YouTube channels. We're selling ourselves like any other actor, headshots and all. So my channel is just another way to brand myself."

He waits a few seconds before responding. "And how's the Piper Bellini brand working out for you? Are you booked and busy?"

I purse my lips. The truth would curb stomp this conversation. My work schedule has been a barren wasteland since I wrapped a project last December, but the idea of telling Sam makes me shame-sweat. "My turn to ask questions. A firefighter? After swearing up and down you'd never give your dad the satisfaction?"

He shifts positions and catches my eye. "I know this might be hard for you to believe, but people can change their minds, Piper."

Mingled irritation and curiosity surge through me as I hold his gaze long enough to challenge him back. "Why would that be hard for me to believe?"

His voice pitches low—almost too low for this loud bar. "Because you're still as angry at me today as you were seven years ago."

My stomach churns, but I don't even have time to respond because he immediately turns away and raises an arm to get the bartender's attention. "Can I get a cup of beer-cheese soup? And whatever the lady wants."

"I don't want— I'm not angry with you, that's—"

I snap my mouth shut. This conversation is like a dog off a leash, quickly escaping me. I thought I buried frazzled, reactive Piper in college, yet it seems he has revived her. And for what? Bar banter?

The bartender bounces on the balls of his feet, glancing over his shoulder at the computer. "Dewar's. Neat," I add hastily.

Sam's eyebrows climb. "*Scotch?* When you could have *soup?*"

"So?"

"I'm impressed, is all."

"Lucky me," I mumble as the bartender's tattooed arm pours my poison into a tumbler and passes it over.

I close my eyes and throw back a sip. Maybe if I funnel my focus on the warm liquid sliding down my throat, I can effectively drown out my other senses. Sensory deprivation. Sam deprivation.

"Is that your phone, Pipes?"

His voice jerks me back to attention. *My phone.* In the upheaval of running into him, I almost forgot I'd promised myself I wouldn't check the job board for five full hours. The alarm beeps to congratulate my restraint.

I yank my phone from my purse and navigate to the VOICE-FX website—saved as a shortcut on my home screen for obsessive revisiting—to scan for new opportunities. I drink it all in, orienting myself to the influx of new posts, from both job seekers and those looking to hire.

Sam leans toward me. "Found yourself a Tinder date?"

I jerk my phone to the side. "Work stuff, thank you very much."

Nice of him to *assume* I'm single. I mean, I am, but it's not like I'm advertising that fact.

I refocus on the job listings and try not to let disappointment play out on my face as I check my personal stats. My "Seeking Opportunities" post from this morning has zero bids or saves.

*Piper Bellini, American vocal actor seeking opportunities in literary narration, voice-over, or commercial work. Work sample attached.*

I wish I could see how many downloads my sample had, if any. It would help tremendously to know if it's my voice that's the problem, my lackluster work history, or my headshot (because life is a circus of superficiality, even in off-camera work.)

I scroll down to the help wanted ads.

*Seeking male to narrate billionaire shifter series. Baritone preferred.*

*ISO female with **authentic** Australian accent to narrate audiobook. Priority given to Australian natives.*

*Need an auditorily pleasing podcast cohost; must be experienced in discussing stock market from client and advisor perspectives—*

My eyebrow twitches. Nothing stokes my anxiety faster than a list of gigs I don't qualify for. Save for a body-swap scenario with a male baritone or "auditorily pleasing" stock market drone, looks like I'm out of luck. My thoughts fast-forward to Christmas and beyond, when I'll undoubtedly still be living at home because I can't afford a security deposit—or anything—if I don't secure another gig.

"You all right?"

Sam's voice snaps me from my spiral. I lean back, still clutching my phone. "I guess. Sometimes I just—" I peek over at him and abruptly stop talking. His brows are furrowed, creating a tiny ridge in an otherwise smooth forehead, and his glance darts between my phone and my face. If I didn't know any better, I'd say he's genuinely concerned.

But Sam is not my friend, and the survival of his version 2.0 friendship with Caleb will depend on all of us upholding our firmly established roles. He is not my confidant, nor will I ever be his. I feel the hot hand of guilt squeezing my stomach even talking to him at all without Caleb around. "Nothing."

He scratches his smooth jaw. "I'm not sure I believe you."

I fiddle with my bun, tucking in rogue hairs. "Such is your prerogative. Listen, this little run-in has been the thrill of my life and all, but now that we've gotten it out of the way, can we agree to shifts with this place? I'll take days ending in Y, you can have the rest?"

He taps out a beat with his thumbs on the bar, saying nothing. I twist the gold ring on my right ring finger over and over.

When he finally responds, his tone drips with diplomacy, like we are striking a business deal. "An alternative idea for your consideration: Instead of blacklisting me from the bar, we could accept we're going to run into each other and play nice. Especially with Caleb as a common denominator. I'd rather not avoid you and your family for the rest of time."

"Play nice? When have I ever *not* been nice to you?"

"Uh—do I need to roll the tapes? I can't attend a Catholic mass in all of Merryfield County because of you. If those tapes resurface…" He trails off, his expression icing over. "That wasn't your nicest moment, is my point."

Acid rises in my throat. If he's baiting me into a who-messed-up-more battle, he'll go down in flames. Fireman pun intended. "So, you threw up in a church. Big deal. Who among us hasn't faced public embarrassment?"

"Good point. I had my church video; you talked about orgasms in a YouTube tutorial—we've all been there."

I slide down in my chair a little and raise my glass to my lips, which gives me something to do besides pout. "Fine, I'll play nice. You said it yourself—you and Caleb are thriving. All the more reason for us to uphold the status quo. You two stay in your lane, limiting your hangouts to your apartment or whatever cave you live in, and I'll stay in mine. Barring me spontaneously combusting and the fire station coming to my rescue, I don't see us crossing paths."

There's shuffling as he procures a tube of ChapStick from the coat slung over his chair. "I'm seeing you tomorrow, actually. At your house."

The scotch burns a path down to my lungs as I choke. "*What*?"

"Sorry, let me be more specific: *Bellini Birthday Bonanza Brunch*. Caleb invited me. I assume that's okay." He rings the tube around his lips as he stares me down. "Unless you still have some…unresolved anger you'd like to discuss?"

I force myself not to look at his mouth, but my gaze insists on wandering there as he goes for a second pass. His lips look perfectly fine, completely hydrated. Healthy.

They twist into a smile, and he pops the cap back on the tube. "Well?"

"God, you're relentless. I'm not mad at you, all right? Come to brunch, don't come, whatever."

Admitting I'm mad would mean acknowledging I still have an opinion about us, or what we used to be before The Incident. I can't let him know I care in the slightest; that'd be serving him the upper hand on a silver platter. I draw in a deep breath to quell the heaviness in my chest.

With Sam, I always cared too much. A debilitating amount, even after we broke up. Heck, that's why I asked for a break in the first place. The too-muchness of it all. He was beloved at school and my house, hot, kind, driven, and worst of all—graduating a year before me. He was moving forward in life. Meanwhile, I was wayward, planless, and self-conscious in his shadow. I thought he was too good to be true, and better off single when he went to college so he could live his full experience and find someone worthy of him. I didn't want to be the hometown girl holding him back.

Turns out I was right.

It wasn't until I went to college a year later and met other people with complicated stories of first-relationship heartbreak that I realized Sam and I were doomed from the start. First boyfriends are *never* The

One. I welcomed my initiation into the sorority of the heartbroken, Phi Beta Scorned and moved on.

What's done is done—but, when family and sibling friendship is involved, never fully forgotten. Which is why I itch to call Caleb right here and now to ask what the hell he was thinking, inviting Sam without warning the family. How do we uphold Fight Club Rule One if we're all going to be together, at the same place? Do we acknowledge how weird it is, or that Mom and Dad still haven't forgiven him for breaking my heart?

The man beside me seems keen to pretend it's not weird at all, but it's my brother's feelings I'm trying to understand.

I release a long breath. If Caleb wants an afternoon of fraternization, I guess it's my job to suck it up and smile. It's just one event. I owe him that.

No matter how miserable it sounds.

Sam's gaze flits down for a fraction of a second before turning toward the television. "Excellent. Glad to hear you aren't mad."

"No beef here." I flick my hair over my shoulder and direct my attention to the Bruins' goalie, where it should've been all evening.

He leans back in his chair, crossing his arms as a celebration erupts at the other end of the bar. "Then I guess I'll be seeing you at brunch."

# CHAPTER THREE

## SAM

A few weeks before Christmas 2006, I delivered a slam dunk of a speech to my parents outlining all the reasons why I, nine-year-old Sam O'Shea of 10 Hartford Lane, deserved a brand-new PlayStation 3.

I've written a hundred or more speeches since then—even some for money, in high school and undergrad—but that PlayStation production still feels like my best work to date. It wasn't about how badly I wanted it, though I would've robbed a Best Buy if I thought I would've gotten away with it.

No, it was the thrill of putting my accomplishments on display. Of convincing my parents I deserved something they didn't want to give me. Of holding their undivided attention, for a change.

I cross the sloping front lawn, carefully avoiding patches of mud, as I recall the way Young Sam laid out his case with confidence.

*I get A's and head pats from teachers.*

*Never been in a fight, not even once.*

*My chores are always done early.*

I could tell by my mom's body language that my talking points were greasing the wheel. She did the bottom-lip-out affirmative-head-shake move. Dad wasn't actively cutting me off, which is as good as it gets with him. I saw my opening, and I stated my request.

Christmas morning, I woke up to a hunk of brand-new tech. The PlayStation of my dreams became the PlayStation of my messy bedroom. Asking yielded results.

Tonight, I'm prepared to put that theory to the ultimate test. I'm going to ask Piper Bellini for something big. A favor of epic proportions.

Only one problem: despite what she said last night, she can't stand me. And neither can her parents.

As I close in on the Bellinis' front stoop, sweating bullets despite the cool breeze, I remind myself of bold words spoken by nine-year-old Sam.

*I work hard, and hard work should be rewarded.*

I could use a hit of his confidence right about now.

Catherine and Gio Bellini's three-story brick

colonial looks like a suburbia stock photo. My legs feel heavy as I hover at the door. Through the glass of a huge picture window, I track the blurring shapes of hyper kids ping-ponging off one another in the living room. Some of those kids weren't even born yet the last time I was here.

Caleb and I have only been back in contact a year, but for most of my life, the Bellinis' house was my second home. Gio taught me how to fix up my first car, a beat-up Saturn my dad won off another firefighter in a game of gin rummy and passed off to me when he discovered it didn't work. It took Gio and me six Saturdays to get it running, but he never once made me feel like it was a chore. Catherine made sure I always had a place at their dining room table and hung a Christmas stocking for me every year (though she probably torched it after the breakup). Caleb has always been like a brother to me, which means a lot, since I have no siblings.

Basically, I was an honorary Bellini, until my breakup with Piper changed everything. I haven't felt welcome since.

Being here again, as scary as it is, also feels… right.

Armed with casseroles in a thermal bag I bought specifically for this occasion, I swallow my nerves and ring the doorbell. I haven't even crossed the threshold and tension already creeps into my shoulders. This is the very definition of Piper's home turf. Our hatchet is big and bloodied, and if her demeanor at McLaughlin's is any indication, she has no interest in burying it.

A flicker of irritation pulses in my gut. She can be moody all she wants, but it doesn't change the facts. I'm not the bad guy, despite what she seems to think. If we're keeping score, Piper Bellini didn't just break my heart in high school—she left it in the cold and never came back to claim it. She ended our relationship out of the blue and shut me out of her life. All I did was kiss another girl a few days later, trying to survive the brutal breakup any way I could. But according to Caleb, Piper and her parents see me as public enemy number one.

Great.

I've long since moved on. Piper doesn't have to like how I behaved in high school. But if I'm going to get what I came here for, I need to find a way to earn her respect.

I startle when the door swings open, revealing Caleb, a freckled, gangly teen trapped in an adult's body. He appears completely at ease.

That makes one of us.

"It's about time!" He reaches for my hair and promptly fucks it all the way up. "Were you out there primping in the car?"

"Had to look good for you."

"You look as mediocre as ever." He studies what I'm wearing and chuckles. "Oh, this should be good. C'mon in."

I glance at my clothes. "Wait, what—" But Caleb is already heading inside. I suck in enough air to last me a month or two. Air has a distinctive smell in the rainy season, like leaves and pine sap. It's pleasant, but the savory scents escaping through the door are even more enticing.

He pulls me into a hug as soon as I cross the threshold and slams my back three times with an open palm. "You good? You and Piper settle your differences in a bar brawl?"

I wince as he releases me. He may have told me where to find her last night, but that doesn't mean I feel good about tracking her down. "I wouldn't go that far. But we talked."

"You didn't tell her I ratted on her location, right?"

"No," I say sharply. "And neither should you."

He grunts. "Believe me, that was my last meddling act. Anyway, you wanted to warn her you were coming. You did. Mission accomplished."

I tug at my collar as we pass through the Bellinis' living room. New couches, same plaid wallpaper and dark red curtains. The plaid always reminded me of pajama pants. Can't unsee it, even now. "It's fine that I'm here, right?"

"It has to happen eventually. I'm tired of tiptoeing around all the time. It's time things get back to normal."

*Normal.* Whatever that is. I still remember the exact moment I broke Caleb's and my "normal" the first time, when Piper walked into the kitchen wearing shorts so short and tight, I found religion. I fell out of my barstool watching her bend over to get a frying pan out of a low cabinet. The knot on my head after I hit the edge of the counter wasn't nearly as uncomfortable as the look Caleb gave me when I surfaced.

I rub the spot, searching for the long-gone bump as we enter the very same kitchen.

Piper grinds to a halt, a pitcher of foamy orange juice in one hand and a bottle of cheap champagne in the other, lips parted in horror. My gaze travels up and down her body.

Yellow and black.

Number 37.

We *match.*

I glance down at my jersey, faded in similar spots to hers. Our jeans are the same dark shade. We couldn't match harder if I'd called her up and asked for a picture to study. Only real difference is the way she looks in her jeans, like they were custom sewn for her legs.

A laugh catches in my throat. With her wild hair falling out of its high ponytail, Caleb's daughter slung across her back in a complicated baby contraption, and her hands full with party prep supplies, she looks like an aunt on steroids.

"*Seriously?*" she whispers.

I bite back a smile at the way this coincidence seems to bother her. As if this isn't Bruins country at the height of hockey season. "Great minds, eh Pipes?"

She prods Caleb with the top of the champagne bottle. "This has *you* written all over it."

Caleb shrugs. "What, you think I checked your outfit and texted him? I don't have time to prank you. I have an eight-month-old."

Kat coos on Piper's back, confirming the alibi.

"The jersey looks better on you," I offer, sweeping my gaze up and down her body. I check myself before I linger too long on any one spot. Or any two spots. "You know, other than that stain on the bottom."

Her nose crinkles in a *fuck you, Sam* sort of way. I'm not proud of the sick thrill it gives me to piss her off, even though I'm here to do the exact opposite. She just makes it so easy, with the world's most readable brown eyes. The irritation is magnified, like a book with huge print.

Caleb kicks me in the shin. "What's in the bag?"

I glance down at the fabric sack bleeding warmth into my hip. "Breakfast shepherd's pie and corned beef hash."

Baby Kat takes a hard tug at Piper's hair, who doesn't even seem to notice. She blinks at me, expression neutral. "Oh?"

"Oh?" Caleb asks, throwing a wary look at his sister. Like he's afraid we're going to break into an argument over a couple casserole dishes. "What does *oh* mean?"

"Just…" Piper shifts her weight as she eyes my bag. "Tell Clodagh thanks."

Abruptly, a memory hits me upside the head. The two of us scarfing corned beef hash at my kitchen table, courtesy of my mom, who'd cook for us before she left for her Sunday shift at Dillard's. Piper forcing me to eat a second helping so I'd have energy to study. Suppressing the urge to touch her as she licked her fork clean.

I clear my throat. "I made them, actually."

Her eyes widen. You'd think I poisoned the damn things.

"I'll take those," Caleb offers, yanking the strap off my shoulder. He springs to action, unbagging the dishes and popping off the lids. "Since my sister clearly can't be bothered."

Piper grumbles under her breath—*is your dad this annoying at home, Kit Kat?*—as she scoots past Caleb to get to the drink station off the counter. I watch from the corner of my eye as she mixes a vat of mimosas and, fittingly, Bellinis. The Keurig blinks green, though there's already enough coffee in two jumbo thermal pitchers to power a small town. Her family *could* be a small town, if we're talking numbers. A fair number of relatives have trickled in over the last few minutes.

She catches me staring as she soaks up tiny brown puddles on the counter with a paper towel. I let her subsequent glare bounce right off me. I'll snuff out her flame by depriving it of oxygen.

I angle my body toward a Bellini who can stand the sight of me. "So, where's your much better half, CB?"

Caleb shoves a serving spoon in the shepherd's pie and frees a crying baby Kat from Piper's back. When Kat stops her sobbing immediately at his touch, I marvel not for the first time that the same kid who used to strap mattresses to the back of my truck for road surfing is a *father* to an entire human being.

"Jane's upstairs pumping," he replies. "It's the only private spot in this madhouse."

My gaze travels through the open archway framing the living room and lands at the base of a rickety, narrow staircase. "Right. Piper's room," I mumble, recalling the creaky steps. Three and five always sounded especially loud after midnight, when I would sneak upstairs.

When I turn my attention back to Caleb, he's watching me through narrowed eyes.

*Right.* Should've just screamed *been there, bought the T-shirt!* and saved myself the time.

Getting back to normal means pretending none of *that* ever happened.

Before I can joke the awkwardness away, the oven timer sounds. Piper drops what she's doing and snatches thermal gloves off a hook. I follow her toward the stove, lured in by the thickness of the smoke barreling from the basin.

I squat to get a better look and point toward a charred mound. "Got some food gathering on the base there, beside the coil. I can clean that out for you after brunch if you'd like. About a third of oven fires—"

"I can take care of my oven, Sam," Piper snaps. She sets the dish down with a little too much force, throws the oven mitts aside, and grabs a pie cutter from a drawer.

I shrug. "All right. I guess technically it's your

mom's oven, anyway."

Judging by the hostility radiating from her body, this was the wrong thing to say. Getting in her good graces may be a bigger uphill battle than I anticipated.

I inch a little closer.

She presses her eyes shut and throws her head back, flashing a long stretch of delicate neck. Her sigh is long and measured, and she follows it with a flat, "What can I do for you, Sam?"

"Let me help you with something. I can cut the pie." I gesture at the burned pie tin.

"It's quiche," she corrects. "And I got it."

"Then why does it have a crust on top? Shouldn't you see the eggs and stuff?"

She stabs the quiche with a level of dramatics usually reserved for Shakespeare. "Nonna's recipe. Would you like to tell her you find it unacceptable, or should I pass that message along?"

"And risk offending the woman whose passion in life is cooking for her family? I'm all set."

The crispy crust doesn't cooperate as she tries to saw a path down the center. Her ponytail bobs with exertion.

I hover a hand over her forearm. "Are you sure—"

"I wouldn't get that close to her when she's wielding a weapon," Caleb warns from the other side of the butcher block kitchen island.

"It's a dull pie cutter—how much damage can she do?"

Piper bats her eyelashes. "Anything can be a weapon if you believe in yourself."

Shielding my chest, I back away slowly.

As I sidle up to Caleb, the noise level in the kitchen seems to ramp up all at once. A bunch of Bellinis congregate on the other side of the massive room. Children set up camp at Giovanni's feet as he holds court, regaling the room with stories and wildly gesticulating. Glad to see he's still the life of every party. My lips threaten a smile. It's been a long time since I've been in a room like this, filled with family. This doesn't happen in my world. Hasn't since the last time I was here.

I turn away and catch Piper watching me, big brown eyes sad. She startles, yanks a pitcher off the counter, and pours herself half a mimosa. *Half.* I stifle a laugh as she takes a tiny sip.

"Hope you aren't driving after all that—"

"—where's the rest of it?" Caleb says at the same time.

We point a finger at each other.

Piper's gaze flits between us. Her irritated mask snaps back into place. "You two share a ghostwriter, or is it a hive-mind situation at this point?"

Caleb throws an arm over my shoulder. "Happy

to share a hive mind with you, my dude. Funniest jackass in the game."

"Get a room," Piper mutters.

"You're awfully cranky today, sis." Caleb releases me and extends his arms toward his sister. "Does someone need a hug?"

"Stop. I'm not cranky."

"Oye, Piper," Aunt Dawn calls across the kitchen, her sharp voice cutting through the noisy hustle and bustle with alarming clarity. A dog whistle is somewhere quaking at the competition. "How's the audiobook game? I listened to the *best* memoir last month about a female pilot. Her voice was so soothing. Though now that I think about it, that probably wasn't even her voice, was it? I don't know how any of it works, but surely you could do something like *that*."

Piper's face falls. "Oh, I don't know. My job is... complicated."

Dawn ambles our way. "How so? Don't you just record yourself talking?"

Piper cups her hand around her ear. "Did you hear that, Dawn? I think the baby called your name." Piper's tone takes on the erratic pitch of someone avoiding a conversation. "There—did you hear it?"

The baby says nothing. Not a damn sound exits her mouth.

Until Piper steals Kat from Caleb and places her in Aunt Dawn's bony arms. Then the waterworks start in earnest.

Piper's eyes feign remorse. "Oh no! She's fussy. Better bring her up to Jane. Thanks, Auntie."

Caleb shoots his sister a look as Dawn disappears from the kitchen. "You're acting weirder than usual. What's going on with work? You never did text me back when I sent you that listing last week."

"The listing was for a singing audition."

"The post said it was for voice work. Don't you want *voice work*?"

"I appreciate the thought, but I'm fine finding jobs on my own. I have job boards I monitor." She reaches into her pocket and types furiously. "See, I…"

Her eyes widen from quarter-sized to a slightly bigger quarter-sized.

"See *what*? What's wrong?" Caleb snatches the phone. His eyes dart across the screen. "I don't get it."

Piper gasps. "*Darla and Damien Gentry*. Coming to Boston for an open casting call. They're the head honchos of the audiobook industry."

Caleb brings the phone closer to his face and squints. "Ah. So it's a gig."

"It's *the* gig, Caleb. You have *no* idea how long I've waited for something like this to come up. The Gentrys practically invented the type of narration I'm trying to break into. And they're holding an open audition, which rarely happens because producers normally headhunt their talent. This is a once-in-a-career kind of opportunity." Her voice shakes. "It's the dream."

"Hey, that's great. Right here in Boston, too!" He glances back down at the screen. "What does M slash F mean?"

"WHAT?" She snatches the phone back and reads the posting again. "No. *No no no*. It means the audition is for a male and female team. *Fuck. Me.*"

"Piper," Gio yells across the room as he makes a T with his hands. "Not in front of the kids."

I stifle a snort. Piper tosses me a wilting glare. I raise two hands in surrender.

"Here's what we're going to do," Caleb says, taking back the phone. "I'm going to skip my class, and I'll go to the audition with you. If we get the job, we can work out some kind of schedule. Problem solved."

"Absolutely not. You are way too busy for this." She extends a grabby hand toward the phone.

He dangles it out of reach.

"Caleb. Give me the phone."

He tosses it my way. I catch it in my right hand and peek at the post.

*M/F.*

"Let's see here." I scroll, and it doesn't escape my notice that I am very much an M to her F.

Piper lunges in my direction, a red flush creeping up her neck. "M-Y-O-B, O'Shea."

Her feistiness lights a fuse inside of me. It's too easy to rile her up. "Caleb, go long!"

Caleb darts behind me and lifts his arms high. The phone flies over her head, and Caleb barely manages to catch it before his body slams into the refrigerator. Several magnets fall to the ground as freed artwork floats lazily through the air.

Piper swivels, digs her hand into Caleb's hair, and takes a fistful. "Give me the phone."

He buckles at the knees. "Let me audition. I'd be *great* at voice acting."

"Thank you, but no. You have nurse practitioner classes, clinical rotations, a baby, and a wife. I'll figure this out on my own."

"What, afraid I'll upstage you?"

I snort. "Oh, did the listing specifically ask for a congested Mark Wahlberg?"

Caleb spits out air and, coincidentally, spit. He kicks a magnet in my direction. "We can't all have your deep voice, Mr. February."

*Fuck.*

I glare at Caleb and make an axe gesture at my neck. Ixnay. *Ixnay.*

Piper turns toward me. "Mr. February?"

Caleb either doesn't notice my silent pleas or

doesn't give a shit. I'm guessing the latter. "Yeah, this asshole made Mr. February last year on the Merryfield County Firefighters calendar. Holding a heart-shaped box full of puppies or something. Or was it kittens? Sold out in like twelve minutes."

Piper drags her eyes from the top of my head all the way to my boots. I heat three full degrees under her critical gaze. "Is that true, Sam?"

I grasp for the nearest distraction, stroking a cabinet. "This real wood? Nice quality."

She cocks her head to the side. "Puppies?"

"Valentine's Day. It was for charity, all right?" I tap the nickel handle with the pad of my pointer finger. "Can we not talk about this?"

"Why? Does it bother you, discussing how your photo lives rent-free in some suburban housewife's She Shed?"

"What the hell is a *sheshed*?"

Caleb whistles for our attention. "All right, chill. What are you going to do, Pipes? You going to let me help you?"

Her shoulders fall. The fight seems to leave her all at once, riding out on her exhale. "No thanks. I'll figure something out."

An impulse seizes me, sinking in its teeth.

She's giving me the perfect opening. The opportunity to show her—and, by proxy, her family—

that I'm not some villain. I can help her in her time of need. She may want to broil me in her dirty oven, but she can't deny she wants this gig. I saw it in the arch of her smile, the thrill in her eyes. I'll make her an offer she can't refuse.

"Or, instead." I lean back on my heels, crossing my arms. "You could let me help you."

# CHAPTER FOUR

## PIPER

Somewhere in the distance, an 18-wheeler comes to a screeching halt. Birds fall out of the sky, and Earth starts rotating the opposite direction. I try to read his expression, but I find myself emotionally illiterate from the shock. "*Pardon?*"

"Yeah, *pardon?*" Caleb echoes.

Sam chews the inside of his cheek for a second, perhaps using this time to search for the punch line to his intended joke. "I said, 'I'll help you, Piper.'"

A black stiletto crosses the threshold between living room and kitchen, followed by another. "Help Piper with what?" Mom struts toward us looking like she's fresh from a boardroom as she pulls an AirPod from her ear.

Sam straightens his preposterously tall frame. "Mrs. Bellini. Hello. You look very nice today. I wouldn't even know you're pregnant if I didn't already know. I mean, well, I would *know*, because of the"—he gestures at his own mockingly flat stomach—"but it barely shows! In...the rest of you..."

The birds that fell from the sky earlier rise up for the chance to die again. My father's head whips our direction as a hush falls over the kitchen. Even the children pause in their heated game of "pinch one another until blood is shed" to stare at my mom.

Sam's face goes scarlet as multiple sets of eyes bore into him. My lips curve. Watching him squirm under my mother's powerful gaze might be my new favorite pastime.

"How...kind of you," Mom states, her face blank in a most dangerous way.

Sam steps sideways into Caleb's shadow. "Thank you for having me."

Her steps echo as she passes behind him, grabs a single yeast roll off the counter, and inspects it for approximately thirty-seven years. "Anytime, Sam."

As soon as she disappears from the room, Caleb shoves Sam's chest. Sam doesn't move an inch but flinches nonetheless. "Dude, what in the ever-loving fuck? You never comment on a pregnant woman's *anything*. Them's the rules."

Sam shrugs, eyeing the doorway my mother left

through. "I don't know, man. Your mother is terrifying. I was trying to be nice, and I think I blacked out."

A tense silence settles between the three of us. Is it amusing to see the bravado melt from Sam's body and pool into a miserable heap at his feet? Absolutely. But the genesis of it all—the years of history behind my mother's icy mood toward Sam— are a stark reminder of where we've been. Mom hates Sam because of me.

I hate Sam because of *Sam*.

But he and Caleb didn't talk for six years because of me.

A lump of hot guilt lodges in my stomach in place of all the casserole I didn't get to eat.

The discomfort is alleviated only slightly by Jane bounding into the room with Kat in her left arm, her pump in her right hand, and a bright smile on her striking face. "Hello, Bellinis. And Sam." Her thick lashes flutter as she shoots me a brief but meaningful look.

One bonus to setting your brother up with your wonderful college roomie? She becomes legally bound to you and is privy to all your business—past, present, and future. AKA she knows Sam being here is awkward as hell for me. But on all Sam-related matters, Jane became Switzerland the day she married my brother. Neutral.

"Caleb, help your bride," Dad calls across the island. He points his overflowing champagne flute toward Jane. "She's got her hands full."

Caleb extends his scrawny arms. "Yes, my beautiful bride! Let me help you with something."

Jane's laugh is a warm breeze. "We've been married three years, babe. I hardly qualify as a bride anymore."

"I still call Catherine my bride," Dad counters.

I snag Jane's pump and set it on the counter. "Your wedding was one for the books. Nonna *still* talks about how that hot bartender danced with her. Pretty sure it made her life complete."

Jane giggles. "I love how drunk Luca and Enzo look in all the family portraits."

"They looked drunk because they *were*," I clarify. "They snuck wine all night! Teenage amateurs."

Sam's smile is a dull impression of the real thing as his gaze falls to the floor. "Bellini men and open bars. Bet that ended in a few hangovers."

Silence settles over the group.

*Shit.* Awkward alert.

Why the hell did I bring up the wedding? That's the last thing we need to wax poetic on right now. Sam should've been an integral part of Caleb's experience as Best Man, and though I wholly believe that the words *best* and *Sam* don't belong in the same sentence, it's not about my opinion.

Just another reminder of how epically I screwed over my brother by dating his best friend. If only the consequences of bad decisions fell off the record after seven years, like credit card debt.

I grasp for some kind of out to this conversation that doesn't involve me inserting my foot farther into my mouth.

"Is that, uh, my phone?" I reach for the silent, definitely-not-vibrating cell on the counter, and it slides over the edge before I can secure a grip. It falls at a speed that defies gravity, and the screen shatters as soon as it hits the floor.

A cry leaves my mouth, but it's too late. Sam plants his shoe on top of a few glass shards as I drop to my knees. "No, no, no—"

"Careful, Pipes. There's glass everywhere."

I don't see glass. I only see hundreds of dollars of damage to an uninsured phone. Hundreds of dollars I don't have.

This day is Satan-sent. I'm sure of it.

I retrieve a hand broom and dustpan and drop to my knees next to the mess. Mere minutes have passed, and already I'm plunging from the high of seeing that Gentry job right off the top of Kilimanjaro into my very flat reality.

Every day I'm confronted with hundreds of reminders that money is essential, and that I lack it. This broken phone is yet another problem to add to my growing list. It seems like a cruel joke from the universe that I'd drop it just seconds after hearing about another unattainable gig.

The audition is in four days, and there's no way I can pull it off. And Sam offering to help makes my stomach uneasy. I can't have him feeling sorry for me. My pride is like a Bengal tiger: nearly extinct. In need of protection.

And even if I were entertaining the idea of accepting help, I couldn't accept Sam's. Today is an exception to our avoidance rule. As was last night. Shunning resumes tomorrow.

My six-year-old brother Nico bounds into the kitchen and shoves his way between Caleb and Sam.

"Sam! Do you want to play video games? We have an old PlayStation 3 in the basement."

My Spidey-senses tingle. I throw the broom into the pantry and slam the door shut. "What did you say, Nico?"

He cups his hands around his mouth and shouts, "I said, *Sam, do you want to play video games*?"

"How do you even remember Sam? You haven't seen him in years."

Nico's confused brown eyes meet mine. "Sam comes to Caleb's house all the time. We play *Uncharted* and *Borderlands*. And when I'm older, they said I can play *Grand Theft Auto*!"

A siren wails in my head.

*Caleb's house.*

*All the time.*

So much for my assumption that Sam and Caleb *only* hang out at Sam's lair.

Sam is suddenly very busy pecking at his phone.

I usually feel in control in my own house, even amidst the chaos. But today, with Sam apparently hell-bent on encroaching on every area of my life, my control grows slippery at the edges.

"Game nights, eh?" I say, staring daggers at Thing One and Thing Two. "Interesting."

"What's your point?" Caleb asks.

*I didn't know*, I want to yell. But why would I? Fight Club Rule One—a rule *I* followed.

It's one thing for Sam and Caleb to maintain their friendship. But I thought it was universally understood that their friendship was to be kept separate from our family. Did I miss the part where the rest of my brothers attached themselves to Sam, too? *No mixing Sam and family*, that's how this was supposed to work. Or so I thought.

I take a fortifying breath and regroup. If my

brother wants to invite Sam to a few game nights and include the whole herd, so be it. I can be civil for Caleb's sake. "Nothing. Sounds…fun."

"Rain check on the games, kiddo," Caleb informs a sugar-addled, vibrating Nico.

"Please?" Nico repeats the word on a loop, hopping up and down, gaining steam. Imminent meltdown posturing. "Pretty please? Just for a little while?"

Caleb spins Nico's tiny, hyper body toward the door. "Not today. It's a party. Go find Raf or someone else to play with."

Nico wails as he runs out of the room.

Oh, what a party it is.


Brunch segues into a rowdy game of Bullshit in the dining room, which lasts until midafternoon. The sound of my father yelling the word "malarky" at top volume every single time someone takes a turn during the card game is a creature comfort to me. He yells extra loud during Sam's turns.

We retire into the living room when the game concludes. Nico and Raf wrestle and crash into the walls while my other brothers hedge bets on who will bleed first, making the space feel like a WWE ring. Dad eventually orders the younger boys to their basement lair, and the room calms down considerably. I lean against the living room's doorway, biding my time until everyone whose names rhyme with Fam leaves.

Sam is cozied up next to Caleb and Jane on The Pit—a couch so named because it sucks you in—and fawns over baby Kat while Caleb studies from a large textbook. Jane is passed out with her head against Caleb's shoulder, a curtain of black hair obscuring her face.

Sam bounces Kat on his knee. "Say it. Say *Sam. Sam.*"

Her tiny hands grip the logo emblazoned on the front of his jersey, and she flashes him the gummiest little grin, enamored by his high-pitched babble.

Kat is a traitor.

"Miss Piper," Dawn says, smacking my ass as she stumbles through the doorway beside me. As is tradition at Bellini parties, she's transcended drunk and is basically a bottle of booze in a sweater dress. "I'd kill for your body. What's your workout plan?" Champagne sloshes out of her flute and splashes down my arm.

I squeegee off the liquid with the side of my hand. "I chase around my siblings, mostly."

Across the room, Kat lets out a coo that could charm a corpse to life.

Dawn rushes over to the couch. "Look at my perfect angel!" She attempts to sit on the armrest but misses, landing next to Sam. It's a tight fit, but she's a twig and doesn't seem to mind. In fact, she burrows farther into the cushion as she looks Sam up and down. "You have a way with babies, don't you?"

"Kat makes it easy."

"Take the compliment, Sammy," Dawn insists. She sips her drink once before adding, "There's plenty more where that came from."

*Sammy.* My spine stiffens as I watch her unsubtle wink. It lasts so long I wonder if her eyelashes have become fused. Drunk, single aunties need to be saved from themselves.

"Can I get anyone anything?" I offer. "Dawn, a soda? Ice water?" *Perhaps a cold shower?*

Dawn reaches over and rakes fuchsia-painted nails through Sam's hair, making my own hair stand on edge. "I'm fine with *this* tall drink of water. I swear, Piper, if you don't marry him soon, I will."

My shoulder slips off the doorway, and I slam into the side of a bookcase. "*What?* No. Gross."

"Jeez, Piper," Dawn says with a shrill laugh. "Have you always been such a lousy flirt?"

Sam's gaze falls to the ground. For a second it feels like we are coconspirators, stuck in Dawn's sticky conversational web.

Until he laughs. A dimple-popping slow chuckle, at my expense.

"Jesus H Christopher," I mumble, turning on my heel. I crash into Dad. He jumps sideways, surprisingly lithe in his attempt to protect his plate of birthday cake.

"What'd I miss in here?" Dad saunters past me into the living room.

"Didn't miss much, Gio. I'm just joking with Ol' Sammy," Dawn says. She burps into the back of her hand and then adds, "Though, I better get out of Piper's seat—don't want to make her jealous."

Dad's sardonic laugh fills the room. He plops down in his La-Z-Boy and rests his plate of food on his stomach. "Don't be ridiculous. Those two broke up *years* ago. Ancient history."

Dawn sighs. "Kids these days are so picky, I swear to God."

Dad points his fork at his sister. "Shouldn't swear to God, Dawn. He has a long memory."

"Speaking of the mystical man, woman, or creature in the sky." Caleb elbows Sam. "Have you given any more thought to the dedication dates I texted you? Kat's not getting any younger."

Sam fishes in his pocket. "Let me look again now that we've got our June work schedule."

"It's the last two Saturdays. For the child

dedication services. Obviously we want to do a day
when you're off work and off call, so whichever date
of those two—"

"Child dedication?" I interrupt. "What are you
two talking about?"

"Sam is Kat's godfather," Caleb says, as if it's
the most obvious thing in the world. As if it's not an
earth-shattering declaration. "Anyway, we just need
to hammer out which day and time works for the
baptism. Well, it's not technically a baptism—not a
Catholic one, anyway—but the same general concept."

Dad perks up in his chair. "Nonna will be thrilled
to hear this. She'll want to have a christening party."

Pressure blossoms behind my closed eyelids.

Sam, Kat's *godfather*.

Sam, linking himself to my family in a way even
more binding than his eternal bromance with Caleb.
This is for life. Longer than that, if eternity is a thing.
Godparents have a fast pass to the best parts of the
afterlife. Probably.

And here I was stressed about tolerating him for
the length of a brunch.

"Why didn't you tell me, Caleb?"

The look he gives me is somewhere between
*what's it to you* and *stand down, soldier*. "I'm telling
you now."

I pivot to Sam. "And while we were shooting

the breeze at McLaughlin's, you also didn't think to mention it?"

Sam ignores this, attention fixed on his friend. "First Saturday works for me. This is huge, buddy. I'm *honored* to be Kat's godfather."

Caleb beams. "It's going to be great. And hey, if Nonna wants a christening party, I say let's go big. A cake, barbeque—the whole nine yards. We'll do it at my house; Jane's parents will fly in. I'll need to get the yard ready—"

"I'll help you with the landscaping. We've got time."

What in the Home Depot hell? The thought of those two landscaping steals my last straw and snaps it. "Caleb, are you sure about this? You do have *nine* brothers to choose from."

"And I also have a sister," he replies evenly. "Which is why it has to be Sam. You are already her aunt. They are uncles. That holds its own kind of weight."

"And who will be the godmother? Sam's lady du jour?"

Sam bristles. "Hey, now—"

"Does the titleholder change annually, like Miss America?"

"Whoever he marries," Caleb interrupts. "Can you chill, please? You're harshing our otherwise nice moment."

I offer the fakest smile I can muster, despite the rage fire ravaging my insides. "My apologies. Congrats to all parties involved. And Caleb, if you and Jane could refrain from dying, that'd be outstanding. I'd rather not wind up in some kind of spiritual custody battle for my niece."

Caleb massages his forehead. "Don't be ridiculous, sis. That's not how custody works. At least I don't think so."

"Yeah, don't be ridiculous, Pipes," Sam adds. "I'll gladly go halfsies with you on raising Kat, should my best friend and his wife drop dead."

"Can we stop talking about death? It's my birthday," Dad interjects.

"It's everyone's birthday!" I cry. "Wait. Why am I yelling?"

"I don't know!" Caleb yells. "Sit down and relax!"

"It's fine. I'm going upstairs."

"Here," Sam says, standing as I march past. "You stay. Take my spot."

Amazing he can see me at all, since I'm fairly sure I've descended to the seventh circle of Hell. I point to the dozing baby in his arms. "You stay. Godfather duties."

Nico shoves past me as he barrels into the room. "Sam, look what I've got!" His arm is aloft, clutching a tube.

A tube with a *lit fuse*.

"Nico, no!" I lunge forward, hands outstretched.

A loud pop cracks through the air. Then another. Nico shrieks and lobs it across the room. It arcs through the air and lands in the lace overlay of the drapes, penetrating the layered fabric like a torpedo. The curtains spit white sparks until they catch fire. The flames gobble up the gaudy gold and red layers, spreading the blaze with remarkable efficiency.

Dad falls out of his chair sideways like he's been tased, and the contents of his plate scatter across the ground.

Wooden clogs strike the floor as Dawn tears across the room. Sam catches her in a few loping steps and thrusts Kat into her arms. "Take her away from the smoke."

Caleb struggles to free himself from The Pit. "Jane, the house is on fire! Up!" He lunges forward and snakes his arms beneath her shoulders. One pull and he ends up falling in a heap at her side. "Are you dead? Get up!"

"*Nico*," I shout over panicked cries. "What were you thinking?"

He turns to me, his eyes wide with horror. "I thought it was a sparkler!"

Dad army crawls away from the chair, stopping only to yank Nico down by the wrist as black smoke billows. "On your elbows, son!"

Sam jogs past Dad and Nico—who are inch-worming their way to safety—and exits to the kitchen.

Mom rushes into the room with the four-year-old twins trailing her like ducklings. Nova and Davie shriek with excitement, like they've stumbled upon a game. Mom lunges for their hands to pull them back. "What the hell is hap—"

"Run, Catherine! Take the twins. Get everyone out!" Dad roars.

Sam returns with a rusty fire extinguisher. "Coming through!" He vaults over my father, pulls the pin from the extinguisher's neck, and aims the nozzle at the curtains.

Nothing happens.

Sam's eyebrows twitch. He tosses it to the ground and takes off at a run toward the front door.

Dad elbows toward the discarded extinguisher. "What's wrong with this one?"

Mom clutches her stomach as she hacks out a cough. "If it's the same one from the oven fire, it's probably empty. Raf's first Thanksgiving, remember?"

The blaze climbs higher and wider as smoke clogs the room. Dark soot spreads across the ceiling. "It's moving too fast. We have to get out."

Before I can take a step, Sam blasts into the room with a shiny new extinguisher. He tears out the pin and douses the curtains in a steady stream of white powder. We watch in collective awe as he sweeps the nozzle back and forth. Halon dust shimmers in the air like snow.

Finally, when the fire is out and the charred curtains are covered in gunk, he lowers the extinguisher to his side. He stares at the window for a moment before turning to Mom. "That ought to do it."

Several mouths hang agape. The first one to speak is Jane as she blinks open her eyes. "Caleb?" Her words are muffled by Caleb's body, draped across her like a weighted blanket. "Why are you on top of me?"

Caleb rolls off her. "Tried to wake you up to save you from a *fire*, my apologies. Oye, Sam, where'd you get that thing, anyway?"

Sam glances at the extinguisher in his hand and gives it a little twirl. "Oh, this? I always keep a spare in my truck."

Of course he does.

"Will someone google if the white stuff is toxic before the twins bathe in it?" Mom asks. Her eyes flutter closed for a second, and she lets out three quick, controlled breaths.

"Sit down, Catherine. You're going to stress out the baby." Dad pats the floor beside him.

"Catherine, I have a blood pressure cuff in my

truck. Let me get this area cleaned up and I'll grab it," Sam offers. "And Piper?"

I wrench my gaze from the extinguisher now tucked under his arm. "Yes?"

He leans in so close the hairs on the back of my neck stand up. "Kat threw up on your shoulder. It's dripping down your back."

I march in defeat to the top of my staircase before ripping the jersey off. I throw it in my open hamper with too much force. I'd like to throw the entire day away as easily, ridding myself of every frustrating memory.

My brother sprung this godfather business on us like it's no big deal—now I'll never escape Sam. My pitiful bank account is about to take a further beating at the phone store. An impossible-to-get gig taunts me.

The audition details play in my mind, as does Sam's smooth baritone.

*I'll help you, Piper.*

Maybe the mimosas and the cocktail of emotions from seeing him again are working together to grease the hinges of some kind of time portal. Suddenly I'm traveling back and forth, comparing the way he sounds now to how he sounded when we were younger.

I hate that I can hear his voice so clearly, the smokiness of his tone. I can't pretend I don't know his usual cadence like the back of my hand, all the layers and inflections distinguishing his from any other. I'd notice these qualities in anyone because voices are my job, but I remember—etched-in-my-brain-forever remember—everything about his.

I can still hear the way he said my name the first time I caught him asking Caleb about me. I was snooping outside what is now the twins' room but was then Caleb's, fueled by my insatiable interest in the hot Model UN nerd whom I'd known most of my life but suddenly couldn't stop thinking about. I had a monumental crush on my brother's best friend, a tale as old as time. I had my ear to the door, and Sam said my name like the word itself was a question, upwardly inflected at the end. *Piper?*

Then there was the blueberry-picking incident, when he backed me into a bush and fed me my name like he was leveling with me. At that point we were unbearably close to breaking out of the friendzone and every conversation felt like we were one correct word away from unlocking something inevitable. *Piper.*

But few memories are as salient as the sound of him growling my name in my ear the night he snuck into my bedroom the first time. My name fell like rich velvet from his mouth. The "P" was a whisper on his lips, melting into a long vowel "i" that lasted forever and ever as he hovered his mouth around my ear. The end of my name had fallen away as he pressed his lips on my neck, just above my pulse point. *Piiiiii—*

I throw myself face down on my bed.

So what if he put out a curtain fire without breaking a sweat or offered to do a nice thing for me. I still don't trust him as far as I can throw him. Which, to be clear, is no further than an inch. But he's obviously not going anywhere, and if I'm going to tolerate him, maybe there's something in it for me.

I can still hate Sam O'Shea and recognize, by all objective measures, he's got a pretty great voice. A much better voice than my bill collectors. And if I don't secure a gig soon, they'll be the ones in my ear.

# CHAPTER FIVE

## SAM

Fact: the last six times we got a call at the station, my laptop happened to be open.

Another fact, obvious to anyone with a brain: my laptop being open does not prompt spontaneous fires across the city of Roseborough.

Correlation does not imply causation—we get calls because we're a *fire station*, not because I own and operate a MacBook Air. But my squad, despite their various talents and credentials, rejects logic.

"Open that fucking laptop, and I'll cut your dick off." Forrester throws me a menacing look across the lounge. "Not that you're using it."

I drag my backpack's zipper even harder. He's all bark, no bite, and even less of a blip on my worry radar right now. "Not using my laptop or not using my dick? Clarity is important in a debate."

He pushes back in his recliner until he's horizontal. "Both. Shut up. I'm not in the mood for a call, O'Shea."

"No one wants a call. But I've got work to do."

"What are you talking about?" He gestures at the semicircle of chairs and the coffee table full of empty water bottles, his tone reverent. "*This* is your work."

I choose to ignore him, and he forgets he asked the question within five seconds of *Deadliest Catch* returning from commercial break.

*Good*. What Forrester doesn't know won't hurt him.

I pull up the file that has taken up every split second of my free time the last few weeks. The bold header gives me a little hit of adrenaline. In two days, this thing will be in the hands of the City Manager, along with my petition for mayor.

### *Roseborough Improvement Plan*

The plan has come a long way since last year. It's the embodiment of what I've been working toward, my blood and sweat poured into a Google Doc. No tears, though. The only crying has come from my father, big fat crocodile tears that I would dare step outside the walls of his station, even though my plan poses no conflict to my job here at RTFD.

As chief, he's approved my new schedule with reduced hours to take effect Monday. But as my dad, he urged me away from city hall on multiple occasions. His warnings, tinged with anger and bitterness over years of budget disputes and public scrutiny, sometimes worm their way into my thoughts.

*Make no mistake, son—my job is political. And in politics, you belong to everyone but yourself. They'll turn on you in a heartbeat.*

With Monday's deadline so close, I can't worry about his opinions. We may work at the same station, but we are very different people.

Above the TV, the massive security flatscreen flickers with life as a car pulls into our lot. An old Ford Fiesta crawls at a geriatric speed and parks near the front door. My stomach twists. It's the same car I spotted outside McLaughlin's, and then again yesterday in the Bellinis' driveway.

*Piper.*

I snap the laptop shut and push away from the table, grinding chair legs against linoleum.

The four of us watch the monitor as she swings her legs out of the car. When she stands, her high-heeled black boots hit above her knee. Her coat is tied with a bow at her waist, and her hair is loose and wavy. She holds a cup in each gloved hand and uses her hip to bump her car door shut.

*Jesus*, those boots.

My brain flickers with momentary panic, like I left a tab open on my computer I don't want anyone to see. She doesn't know what a pair of high-heeled leather boots does to me—and she wouldn't care, even if she did—but judging by the way she struts across the lot, she knows how to work them.

I swallow a lump in my throat.

What is she doing here? She made it clear how she felt about my presence at brunch with all her eye rolls and sassy comments. Overall, Operation Earn Respect was not the success I'd hoped for.

Needless to say, my workplace is one of the last places I'd expect to see Piper thirty-six hours later.

I scrub my cheeks with my hands. Whatever the reason, she's *here* and dressed up like she's about to execute a will.

Forrester livens, lifting his head a few inches off the leather headrest. "Look at the legs on her. Shit, look at the everything on her. Two-syllable *day-umn*."

"Calm down," I snap, my eyes still glued to the monitor.

He crunches to get a good look at me, straining the buttons on his shirt. "Wait a minute, is this a *special* buddy of yours, Sam? Of the fuck variety?"

The urge to smack him in the mouth brings a surge of heat to my hand.

He swings a leg over the side of the recliner. "No? Well, it seems rude not to greet our guest, so if you're not going to, I guess I should—"

"I got it."

He hums like he's accomplished something. "Ah. Who is she?"

"She's my…"

I turn over the phrase ex-girlfriend in my head, but it doesn't feel broad enough. Friend? That's laughable. I don't see us kicking it at Caleb's anytime soon.

"That's my best friend's sister," I finally say. "From back in the day. And from now, I guess, since they're still related—*doesn't matter.*"

I cut myself off. Thank God the Roseborough Improvement Plan is mostly written, since I can't seem to form a damn sentence.

All three of the men in the lounge snicker as I jog to the front foyer. When I open the front door, Piper jumps sideways, sloshing coffee from two *Beany Business* cups onto her white gloves. "*Shit.* Um. Hi."

"Shit-um-*hi*," I echo, removing both cups from her hands.

"You surprised me."

My lips curve into a small smile. "You're *surprised* to see me? At my place of employment?"

"Surprised you opened the door when I just so

happened to be standing there," she clarifies with her pointer finger raised.

I hold the door open and invite her in with a nod of my head.

A fruity scent hits me as she passes. She pulls off her stained cotton gloves one at a time and shoves them in her coat pocket as she studies the space.

Doomsday scenarios start playing in my head. Her parents sick or injured. Something wrong with Caleb, her other brothers, Jane, or Kat. My stomach lurches. "Did something happen? Is everyone all right?"

Surprise flashes in her eyes. "Oh no—nothing like that. Everyone's fine."

"Cleanup going okay at the house? Did you call the company I recommended for the smoke damage?"

"Yes, all of that is under control. I was actually hoping we could talk."

"Oy, O'Shea, aren't you going to introduce us?" Forrester calls from across the lounge, crossing his arms behind his head like the king of the La-Z-Boys. Far be it from him to mind his own damn business, even for a second.

I lower my voice when I turn back to Pipes. "Let's go upstairs, yeah? It's quieter."

She nods and beelines it for the staircase, stopping only to check for me when she's on the third step. It's not like her to shy away from a crowded room. The Piper I knew is the polite and chatty type, so long as the topic of the conversation isn't her actual feelings on an important topic. For example, she'll tell a stranger ten ways to roast a turkey and where to stick the baster, but won't tell her boyfriend of two years why she wanted to end a relationship.

My grip on the paper cups tightens as I follow her upstairs. We reach the second-story lounge, and she perches on the arm of an old leather couch and folds her hands in her lap.

I lower down on the chair opposite her and raise the drinks. "Double fisting it today?"

She rolls her eyes. "Obviously one is for you. They're the same. Take your pick."

I hover one beneath my nose. Peppermint coffee. I smile and place them both on the old wooden table between us. "Thank you."

"Don't you like peppermint lattes?"

"I like generous gifts."

She arches a brow. "Fickle tastebuds, Mr. February?"

Heat creeps up my neck. Fucking Caleb had to run his mouth about that dumb calendar.

Truth is, if I have another drop of caffeine I will probably suffer a cardiac event. We've been awake the better part of thirty-six hours, surviving on espresso pods from the expensive machine a local company donated last year. But it'd be rude to tell her that when she made a special stop, so I divert by gesturing at her coat and fussy posture. "You can't be comfortable like that."

If possible, she straightens her spine even more. "Says who?"

Stretching my arms overhead, I lean back and extend my legs before me, demonstrating what relaxation looks like to a woman who's apparently never heard of it. "Fine. Have it your way."

Her gaze travels slowly down my body, stalling briefly on my RTFD button-up, eventually landing on my black boots. "That tight uniform is comfortable?"

The question hangs between us as my eyes catch hers. I drape my arms over the back of the couch, sighing contentedly to further my point.

"All right, you win." With a huff, she shrugs out of her coat, revealing a dark red dress underneath. It's fuzzy like a sweater but tighter. She lowers herself from arm to couch cushion and crosses one leg over the other. The hem of her dress slides up, flashing smooth skin.

A flash of heat pulses deep in my core. It's been months since I've seen or touched that part of a woman, where the back of their leg segues into the danger zone. And *much* longer since I've touched

Piper there.

I blink away. That's the last thing I should be thinking about. Her body is enemy terrain.

"You're probably wondering why I'm here," she says, calling my attention back to her face.

I cross my legs at my ankles. "Nah, I know you're here to coordinate jerseys for Kat's christening. I'm thinking Marchand, unless you have a preference."

Her eyes narrow. "We made it through brunch. Barely. Let's not tempt fate."

I lift a hand, giving her the floor to speak. "What can I do for you?"

A few seconds pass as she wiggles in her seat, crossing and uncrossing her arms. Her lips pull in a tight line like she's bracing for bad news. "Um…"

I zero in on her fingers as she spins a gold ring on her right hand, over and over. She breaks a few seconds later to pluck her coffee cup off the table. "Just wanted to say thanks. For what you did at the house. Who knew curtains were so flammable? Anyway, glad you were there to take care of it."

Rich, considering she could barely look at me all of brunch. But curiosity gets the better of me. I mirror her, grabbing my own cup and swirling it in my hand in slow circles. "You came all this way just to say thanks?"

She winces. After a steady inhale, she continues. "There's one other thing. I've been thinking about something...interesting you said the other day."

I know it's wrong, but damnit if I'm not enjoying watching her sweat after I had to endure her attitude at the bar and brunch. "I say many interesting things. Can you clarify?"

Her cheeks flush pink. "You offered to help me. With the audition."

*The audition.*

I lean forward and prop my elbows on my legs, staring down at my cup while my brain rapid fires. The audition she freaked out over just seconds before adamantly refusing my or Caleb's help, for a gig she clearly wants. The last time I'd seen Piper that excited about anything was when she scored high enough on her SATs to apply competitively for Penn. She never would've strayed that far from her family in a million years, but it was a dream of hers to get into at least one Ivy.

I peek up. "I remember you rejecting that very kind offer I made, yes."

She chews her bottom lip like it wronged her. "Yes, you offered to help, but I don't think you realize what it requires."

My blood pumps fast and hard. I've been searching for a way to get back in her good graces, and she's basically dropping one in my lap like a packaged gift.

But knowing Piper, the fact that I *want* to help will make her suspicious. Our last two run-ins have shown me her skittish side. The P in her name might as well stand for *proceed with caution*.

I stroke my jaw. "I'm a smart guy. Surely I can handle a little audition. I have a voice. How hard could it be?"

An offended huff leaves her mouth as she jumps to her feet. "Never mind. You clearly think my job is a joke. This was a mistake."

I lunge for her hand as she turns to walk away. "Okay, okay. I'm sorry, and I'm listening. Tell me more, Bellini."

Her gaze falls to where we touch before she rips her hand away and shakes it out. "I thought *maybe* you could *perhaps* consider coming to the audition with me. But it's more than that. If we book it, you'd have to work the gig with me. This wouldn't be a favor to me specifically, as you'd take half the money."

"So it's like an ongoing project?"

"Yes."

Hesitation clouds my brain for a second. I just cut back on my hours at the station, and what she's proposing sounds time intensive.

She cracks every one of her knuckles individually as she watches me. I worry she may pop a blood vessel if this goes on much longer. I wave at her couch. "Please sit. I need more information."

Relief softens her expression as she lowers back onto the cushion. "It's a recorded audition. They film our lines and ask us a few questions. Then, if they pick us, we'd work out a schedule of home and studio recording. It's pretty flexible, and we'd mostly work at home, so we could accommodate your schedule. That's the gist."

"*Home?*" I practically hear her brothers' screams echoing off the walls. Miniature Bellinis clawing at her legs as she records.

"I have a home recording setup. Insulated sound panels and all. In my closet."

"Ah. And will there be video footage involved, like you mentioned at the bar? Your closet seems like a weird place to film."

"We would film publicity footage in the producer's studio." Her mouth opens and closes once before she adds, "I'm surprised you remember the video stuff."

She acts like it's been a lifetime and not, in fact, three days since we talked about her job while tossing back drinks at McLaughlin's. "I have a long memory. Especially when it comes to videos. For example, St. Mary's—"

"*Anyway*, the audition is a cold read, since

much of the job is cold reading. I have some practice dialogue we could run ahead of time, if you agree."

"What kind of story would we be reading?"

She tilts her head toward the clock. "Genres are so limiting. Like why put a label on it, you know?"

"Maybe *one* label, to help me get an idea."

"Probably a thriller. Thrillers are hot right now. Murder and lawyers duking it out in the courtroom, stuff like that?"

The way she says it, light and flighty, makes her sound unsure. "Was that a question or a statement?"

"Statement." She engages in a staring contest with the lid of her coffee cup. "Could be a fantasy, though."

I study her for a moment, starting with her bright lipstick—did she wear makeup just to come here?—and then her face—unmistakably flushed, like we've been running laps instead of talking—before landing on her leg bobbing up and down. "Fantasy? Like that vampire stuff you used to read?"

Her gaze shoots up. "Irrelevant. But yes, vampires, fairies, that sort of thing."

"Fairies," I murmur. "Fascinating."

She huffs out a breath. "Look. It would be nice if we could get along. Be civil, at least. For Caleb's sake. You audition with me, and I'll make sure he knows there's no bad blood between us. Heck, if we land this gig, I'll even sing your praises."

*Bad blood between us.* If I were driving, I'd slam the brakes and circle back around to that statement. I'm not the one with a grudge, even though I easily could be.

But not when I'm this close to a peace treaty.

I hit her with a wide smile. "Praises, eh?"

She wrinkles her nose. "I'll tell him I find you tolerable. That's the highest form of praise you'll get out of me."

I hem and haw for a second, pretending to think it over. Pretending like I wasn't prepared to give her whatever she wanted when she sat down simply to move this train forward.

"Please, Sam." Her tone is pleading. "I hate to ask, but this…" She drops her head into her hands for a second before peeking up through her lashes. "It means everything to me."

My pulse skyrockets. I couldn't even get eye contact out of her at her house, and now she's looking at me like I'm water in the damn desert.

I *should* be stating my terms. She's given me the perfect opening. I could ask her right now for exactly what I want—what I tracked her down to get—and use it as a bargaining tool. She has her goals with this voice-acting thing, and I need to tell her mine.

The words gather on the tip of my tongue, ready

for deployment.

*I'll help you, but in exchange I need your city councilor mother to drop her grudge and publicly endorse my campaign.*

And most importantly: *It has to be you who asks her. Caleb's opinion won't mean anything. After everything that happened with our breakup, Catherine will never support me unless you convince her to.*

But instead, I freeze.

Freezing in my line of work is a death sentence, yet here I am, choking on my words. Something in the way she's looking at me, with her brown eyes wide and fearful and her full lips pinched together, makes my stomach riot. Like she's genuinely scared I'll say no after she's all but begged me. Like my answer could break her.

How cold does she think I am? It's never been clearer that she doesn't trust—or even really *like*— me at all.

I knew it logically, but it sucks to see the proof splayed across her face. If I drop the mayor news now, she'll think I'm helping her to get something in return. And as true as that may be, I can't bring myself to pull the trigger and confirm it. If we audition and don't get chosen, it'll feel unbalanced, like I messed up her dream while still expecting her to support mine.

And then there's the other side of the coin—she could outright refuse to talk to her mom and call the whole deal off. She could double down on her anger and tell Catherine that I wouldn't help her when she needed it most.

I let out a slow hiss of air, buying myself time. Nothing between Piper and me is *ever* simple.

But I know myself, and I'm not a halfway guy. If I do this, I'll give this voice-acting thing 100 percent. I have a few days before my mayor petition is due. That gives me a few days to show her how committed I'll be to the gig before my candidacy hits the local news. I'll research voice acting and all the tips and tricks and blow up her phone with questions to show how seriously I'm taking this.

*Then* I'll broach the mayor topic.

We can both get what we want. And I'll work like hell to make it happen.

A smile tugs at my lips. "Let's do it, Pipes."

# CHAPTER SIX

## PIPER

I bury my face in my hands, and my hair falls forward, shielding Sam from view. A joyful cry escapes my mouth. I can't care how pathetic I must sound—my brain is too full processing the unfamiliar feeling blooming in my chest.

Hope.

Sam agreeing to help me beyond the audition was a long shot buried in the Marianas Trench that I thought I'd have to dig out by hand. His quick agreement and easy smile feel too good to be true, but then I should've guessed he'd do anything to secure his friendship with Caleb. Those two are a modern-day Bonnie and Clyde, but instead of robbing banks they commit petty arson in *Grand Theft Auto*.

Whatever the reason, the audition is on. Maybe, if the stars align and the sparring with Sam doesn't kill me, this could be my shot at a career-making gig.

My mind races with to-dos as I stand up and flatten the front of my maroon sweater dress. First up: a deep dive on the producers to research their past projects more extensively. I'm halfway to the stairs, already kneeling at the Google altar in my brain, when I throw him a look over my shoulder. "Thanks again, Hefty."

"What?"

His confused tone hits my ear like a record scratch. "I said thanks."

"You called me Hefty."

Icy panic washes over my skin. How did that word exit my mouth without my consent? He can't know the origins of his nickname, because then he'd know I told my friends about our past in enough detail to warrant a nickname. The North remembers, but the North doesn't need the South to know that.

In the interest of keeping up the "you've been dead to me for seven years" charade, I shrug coolly and play it off. "You call me Pipes. I decided—just now—you need a nickname, too."

He cocks his head to the side. "And you landed on Hefty?"

"Is that a problem?"

He stretches his arms lazily overhead, and his shirt untucks. My eyes are magnetically drawn to the exposed strip of torso poking out beneath his hem. There's skin and abs, and now I need eye bleach. "Nah. I'm glad you associate me with *size*."

If I had a match, I would burn this fire station to the ground, celebrate the irony of the moment, and run over the ashes with my car. "Whatever. I'll text you the studio address. Better make it email, actually. Where can I reach you? Narcissus at Gmail dot com?"

He waits until I reach the top of the staircase to reply. "Where are you going?"

I pivot on my heel. "Um—home? To live my life?"

"Aren't we going to practice?"

"Now? Don't you want to watch *Deadliest Catch* with your team?"

He waves a broad hand. "I spend plenty of time with those guys. What do we need to do to get ready? Do you have an old script or something I could look at?"

Nerves simmer in my gut. With only three days until the audition, the need to prepare is strong. Stronger than my desire to get out of this station, unfortunately. My shoulders slump as I return to my seat for the third time. I've never felt more tethered to an inanimate object in all my life as I am to this hunk of leather. My traitorous fingers navigate to the browser open on my phone. I airdrop him sample dialogue from the producer's website.

He perks up at the sound of his text tone.

"Let's go through a few lines and see how it goes. My lines are in blue; your part is in black."

"Sounds like a plan."

I clear my throat and put on my best acting voice.

"*I've never seen so many cyborgs—*"

"You're just going to jump in, vocally raw? No warm-ups?"

I lower my phone. "What?"

"You know…do re mi fa so—"

"What *exactly* do you think we're about to do? Sing opera?"

He gives me a wicked little smile. "I think we're tracking down a murderous cyborg."

"No pre-reading! You've got to encounter the text for the first time when we run it together. It's like the opposite of regular acting in that way."

A smarmy smile slithers across his face. "Sorry. My mistake for getting ahead of the game. Let's start again."

I clear my throat and cross one leg over the other.

"*I've never seen so many cyborgs in one brothel. Do your clients know what they're paying for ahead of time, Mr. Buxley? The companionship of a machine can't possibly compare to the real thing.'"*

Sam blows out air. "Awfully pretentious little excerpt, wouldn't you say? Cyborgs have feelings, too. Probably."

My fingers grip my phone, and I fantasize about lobbing it at his head. "They intentionally choose dialogue with genre-specific words so you can get a feel for the author's writing style. Shall I further explain any of those terms for you, or can we proceed?"

Taking the hint, he jumps into his lines.

*"The detective's upturned nose lets me know exactly how she feels about my establishment. But I have nothing to hide.*

*"'Of course they know what they're paying for, detective. My patrons are looking for an escape, plain and simple. Cyborgs make fine companions. Hell, I've met humans who are more robotic in the sack.'"*

He looks up at me and purses his lips together like he's biting back an epic cackle. I want to fault him for it, really I do, but I giggle the second "sack" leaves his mouth.

My turn. Time to show off my skills.

*"I watch Mr. Buxley for a tell or a twitch, a hint he knows what's happening behind closed doors in his own establishment.*

*"'Cyborgs make fine companions until they*

*start slicing and dicing, Mr. Buxley. Autopsy reports indicate clean knife slices on both victim's femoral arteries. I trust you know where that particular artery is located, or dare I be more specific?'"*

I look up to find Sam staring at my crossed legs. When he glances up and sees I've caught him, he mumbles a quick, "Makes sense, anatomically," before stumbling over his next line.

"'*So the dead guys were cut up. What's that got to do with the price of tea in Tahiti?*'"

I cringe as I deliver the next line.

"'*It's the groin, Mr. Buxley. Both victims died in your establishment from lacerations to their groin. Seems your cyborg "companions" go in for the gold and stay for the kill.*'"

Silence falls as Sam tosses his phone aside. "Granted, I mostly read political biographies, but this book seems strange."

Not that I'm defensive over this practice excerpt I have no particular attachment to, but I do respond a little sharply. "How so?"

"It just…goes back and forth between the two of them? I don't know. Maybe I need to read more books. It feels like a script, but all the characters say all their stage directions."

"It's called Head-hopping Immersive Fiction, and it was basically created for the audiobook genre.

It's the ultimate fusion of acting and audiobook-ing. You get insight to the characters' thoughts but lots of dialogue, too. It's all the rage now, hence why the market is so hot for high-quality voice teams."

He crosses his arms, and his navy uniform sleeves strain around his biceps. "Fads these days. I wonder what'll be popular next."

I'm about to mount my "pop culture is supposed to be a moving target, reflective of the era" high horse when a piercing siren sounds. My heart skips a beat, and I almost bring my hands to my ears. It's like being in a fire drill at school.

But this is not a drill.

Sam pushes to his feet. I expect him to take the fireman's pole in the corner, but he hits the stairs at a brisk walk, his boots echoing as they strike the ground. I follow behind, my pulse hammering from the siren's howl.

His voice cuts through the racket. "Thanks for stopping by. Text me the studio address."

"I will."

He pauses for a fraction of a second at the foot of the stairs, and I crash into his back.

I steady myself with the banister. "What's wrong? Did you forget something upstairs?"

"No." He glances over his shoulder and meets my eye. "Just—send me more sample dialogue. Or send a link to a voice actor you like. Something I can study on my own, all right?"

By the time I collect my thoughts enough to respond, he's already halfway through the lobby.

I sit in my car for a long while as I wait for the truck to exit the parking lot. Curtain fires suddenly feel like small potatoes. Someone's house could be leveled by the time the truck arrives. Medical emergencies, car accidents…anything is possible.

The big truck rumbles onto the road. Flashing lights pierce the dark night. He has a full-time job, and now I'm adding to his workload.

He could've said no to me, but he didn't.

I can still hate Sam O'Shea and recognize, by all objective measures, he's an overachiever. And not as awful as I once thought.

• • •

The morning Bellini circus begins promptly at 5:30 a.m.

If I'm going to live at home and help my parents, I'm going to help the crap out of them. This intrinsic motivation to be useful lures me out of bed and into a fluffy bathrobe. Caffeine alone could never do the trick.

My brothers materialize from the basement in reverse-age order: Nico first, with a sweater hanging off his head like a cape, followed by eight-year-old Raf (faux-hawk on point), Georgie (cranky tween), Max (thirteen going on thirty with his slicked-back hair and bow tie), and Enzo (glued to his phone like any self-respecting high school senior).

Luca, a college sophomore who scored his own bedroom on the main floor and schedules his classes to conflict with sibling drop-off and pick-up duty, is notably absent. Getting Luca to agree to help with errands is my life's work, my Everest. I will likely die without the satisfaction.

Mom ambles out of her bedroom with both hands on her stomach, still not dressed for work. I do a double take at her lack of pantsuit.

"You all right?" I ask as I shove six loaded bagels into six tiny Tupperware. "Can I get you anything? Your Zofran?"

She eyes the coffee pot wistfully, her eyes the same color as the brew. The slow nodding of her head suggests she's on the verge of hurling.

Nonna shuffles into the kitchen, decked out in a puffy trench coat and bucket hat. "I'm early for the changing of the guard. Where are the twins?"

"Still sleeping, thank God. I'm about to run the boys to school, and Mom is"—I am interrupted by Mom's guttural groan as she plops down in a rickety kitchen chair—"unwell."

"Where is your breakfast, Catherine?" Nonna demands. "How can you feel well without a proper breakfast? Remember what the doctor said: *high-risk pregnancy*. My grandson needs protein."

"It might not be a grandson," I point out.

Nonna tosses her head back, and her windburned cheeks glow with laughter. "Oh, preferita, you make an old bird laugh."

"Protein isn't going to make me any younger, Julia. I'm forty-four years—" Mom's voice falls off as her phone rings, a sound so common I barely notice it. She snatches it off the table. "Catherine here."

Ears trained on her conversation, I distribute to-go breakfasts to the boys as they barrel out the door.

Mom grips the table, her mouth hanging open a full three seconds before she responds. "*Yesterday?* How on earth did he manage that?" She moves an elbow to the table and drops her forehead to her hand. This tenth pregnancy to produce her eleventh child, only four years after having twins, has nudged her closer to looking her age. "I cannot believe it. This news is going to cause a stir. Thanks for the heads-up."

"Who's she talking to?" Nonna asks as she pours a splash of coffee into a full mug of creamer.

I shrug. "Probably Cecily Hare."

Nonna clicks her tongue. "More city council business? Your mother needs *rest* and four square meals, not more of this stress."

"You know Mom survives on a steady diet of adrenaline and antacids, Nonna."

Mom flicks a dismissive wrist. "Thank you for calling, Cecily. Talk soon, okay?"

Georgie flies through the kitchen and snatches the breakfast baggie out of my hand. I prod him in the back of his calf with my toe. "You're going to miss the bus."

"*Am* n*ot*." He drags the vowel sounds out.

I shoo him away so I can indulge my curiosity. I take a seat beside Mom and tent my hands under my chin. "Spill it. What's the gossip? Did Dorothy finally decide to retire? Is Roseborough getting a petting zoo?"

Mom continues to stare at her phone, her expression a mix of curiosity and irritation. "Sam is running for mayor of Roseborough."

If she wanted to shock me, a toaster into the full, sudsy sink could've achieved the same effect. I lean back in my chair and cross and uncross my arms twice as the news penetrates. "*What?*"

"Can you believe it? *Why?* Where'd he get the idea he could run for mayor at his age? Wait a second—is that why he was at brunch?"

Her words sound like they're coming at me underwater. "Hold on." I pump air brakes with my hands. "Are you sure?"

"Cecily heard it became official yesterday morning. Apparently, he rolled into City Hall with his petition straight from his shift, still in his RTFD uniform."

Nothing about this makes a lick of sense. "I can't believe he didn't…" I trail off, trying to connect the dots. This seems like awfully big news for Sam to keep to himself, given we've now spent a large chunk of time discussing my work.

Something stirs in my belly, the gross heat reminding me of what it felt like the last time I discovered one of Sam's secrets. Him showing up at brunch three days before handing in his petition—knowing *damn* well my mother is a city counselor and colleagues with Paul Stine, the shoe-in candidate for mayor—feels intentional. Slimy.

"Caleb's friend? Your ex?" Nonna asks from across the kitchen, where she's scrambling eggs Mom won't eat.

Mom nods. "One and the same. Wonder if Caleb knows?"

"I have to go get ready." My voice barely has enough pizzazz to travel the tiny space between me and Mom. I push away from the table, my mind reeling.

I make it a whole three steps before Mom lobs another dart. "What's Sam's phone number?"

I wheel around. "Why?"

"I'm going to call and talk some sense into him." She closes her eyes and rubs a hand absently over her stomach. "God, I hate him for what he did to you. I'll never forget when we found him in the back of Sidney Conway's minivan."

I lose air from her sucker punch. "No need to remind me. I was there."

Nonna raises a wrinkled finger. "Hate isn't good for the baby, Catherine."

Mom ignores this. "You know, I did think it was nervy for him to show up here all these years later, but I was polite because Caleb still cares about the guy."

"Understatement," I snap. "They're closer than ever. Sam is Kat's godfather."

Mom turns up her nose. "I don't like that. I don't trust him. He never even apologized to you."

"That was years ago," Nonna points out. "Things change. Maybe we're overreacting."

"Uh, *I'm* not overreacting. Piper asked for a break in their relationship, so Sam hooked up with her friend. Pretty terrible."

I wince. "Mom, enough."

Finding Sam and Sidney fogging up the windows of her old minivan—while I was accompanied by my *mother*, to snatch up Caleb from an out-of-control house party—is not the kind of memory I want to relive before noon. Or ever.

"Everyone fights in high school. Maybe the boy has changed," Nonna offers. "Shouldn't we give him a chance, for Caleb's sake at least?"

Mom's face twists in disgust. "I appreciate the sentiment, but Sam was with another girl a few days after having a falling-out with Piper. What does that say about his character?"

Nonna cuts Mom off with a wave of her spatula. "You must forgive and forget in this life. I dated a lot of men before Giovanni Senior. A *lot* of men. Were they all saints? No. But was it a roaring good time?" She cackles wickedly, her eyes foggy with nostalgia. "*Yes*. At one point I dated three at the same time. Perks of living in a port city!"

Mom's forehead falls to her palm as the ghosts of a hundred 1950s soldiers on leave dance on the kitchen table.

"Don't call Sam," I finally say as the silence stretches thin. "I'm supposed to see him today, and I want to feel him out, get the scoop from him."

"Why the hell would you see him today?" asks Mom.

"He's helping me with a work thing. Technology related." The half lie slips out, and I know she won't question it. Catherine Bellini knows even less about technology than she does about birth control.

"Don't let him near your studio," she urges as she slowly rises up out of the chair.

A twisted little laugh slips out of my mouth. "What's he going to do, light it on fire? And then call himself to put it out?"

"You sound awfully defensive."

"I'm *not*. I need his help, and he offered. If he wants things to be civil between us so he can crack on being Caleb's thunder buddy, I might as well get something out of the deal."

"I think it's all a ploy. If he's looking for my endorsement for his misguided mayoral run, tell him to check Sidney's back seat."

# CHAPTER SEVEN

## SAM

Piper beats me to the studio. Back perched against her car, she clutches a folder to her chest and watches as I pull into the parking space beside her. She looks like a dirty librarian fantasy come to life in her work ensemble and fake glasses. Interesting how someone shouldering such a heavy grudge can still maintain such rigid posture.

Her hawkish stare prompts me to check the dash to make sure I'm not late. I hop out and circle the front of my car, ready to get down to business. "Hey Pipes, how's it—"

"Why didn't you tell me?"

I blink twice, recalibrating. "What?"

"You're running for *mayor*?"

Awareness trickles in slowly and settles like a lead weight in my stomach. I feel the smile slip off my face. "How did you know?"

"I've got moms in high places," she mutters.

I rest my hand on the hood of my 4Runner, warm from the engine beneath, and immediately snatch it back. *Smooth.* "Didn't realize we were in the business of sharing our five-year plans with each other. Nice to hear you care so much about my life. I'm flattered."

She stomps clumsily through the tunnel between our cars, struggling in her tight skirt and heels. "Is that why you came to brunch? To schmooze my family and suck up to my mom? A little campaign pit stop?"

"Caleb invited me," I say carefully. Which is *true.* After I said I'd like to come, he gleefully extended an invite. "I'm sorry if that upsets you."

She jabs a finger into my chest. Her gaze flicks upward, and I catch hold of the anger in her expression. Once I see it, I *really* see it, etched in her eyes. "Dishonesty upsets me, in all its many forms."

"I wasn't dishonest."

She presses harder into my chest. "Then why'd you come to my house for brunch, of all the days, months, years? Why come around now?"

Heat spreads outward from the point of contact, quickening my pulse. The dull pressure works its way into my core. Or maybe it's the pressure of her question, the insinuation that I've done something wrong. "We have an important person in common. Which means we can't ignore each other forever."

The fiery look in her eyes suggests she would've happily done just that.

I could've told her my mayor plans from the start, at McLaughlin's. I could tell her *now*, before it encroaches on withholding territory. A quick, simple explanation.

*I want your mom's official endorsement for my candidacy.*

My thoughts feel as scattered as the dead leaves floating in the breeze. One mistimed admission or one wrong omission, and I could lose her trust irreversibly.

Finding the right words was never an issue for me, until now.

My gaze flits to her copper eyes. Two very pissed-off pennies. A cold breeze hits, whipping her hair up and into my face, dousing me in apple and vanilla. It smells like pie à la mode and overwhelming familiarity. It hits me like the whole fucking apple tree fell on my head.

Her tone cuts right to the quick. "If you're being honest—if you really didn't come to brunch to play Mr. Mayor and schmooze my family—why's your heart racing like you've been caught in a lie?"

I turn away, and a tight laugh escapes my mouth. I return to our staring contest with renewed intensity.

"Got a big audition coming up." I hook her tiny wrist with my thumb and clasp two fingers over her pulse point. "Better check yours, for comparison purposes."

She wriggles out of my grasp. "No need. My pulse is fine. Just…don't be shady, all right?"

I gesture at the cloudless sky. "No shade in sight."

She returns to hugging her folder. "Politicians are always slimy and fake."

My stomach roils. "*Slimy?* That's not fair. What about your mother?"

"That's different. She's not a *politician*-politician."

"I see. Since you're such a wealth of knowledge on the topic, maybe you can teach me the difference between politicians who are fake, politicians who are not actually politicians, politicians who are secretly magicians—"

"Forget it. This conversation will have to wait. We've got to get inside."

I whip my head in the direction of Studio 7. A new kind of adrenaline flares—one that has nothing to do with Piper invading my personal space and everything to do with the task at hand. "Right."

"Remember: calm, cool, collected. Don't rush while you're reading. When I'm saying lines, look at me as much as you can until your turn is approaching. And a smile goes a long way, even when the camera is off."

I plaster on a determined smile. "You got it, Bellini. Let's track down some cyborgs."

Her nose scrunches, and she turns away. "Save the dimples for the camera."

I let her set the pace, and she charges toward the building. Her hips do that sashay thing that's impossible not to watch, no matter whose hips they are. It's hypnotizing.

Scientifically speaking.

"How am I beating you to the door when I'm in five-inch heels?" she calls over her shoulder.

I scrub my jaw as I catch up beside her. We step onto the curb, and she halts abruptly.

"What's wrong?"

She gulps, and it's visible in the smooth line of her neck. "The waiting room is packed. There must be like six other teams in there."

"You're nervous." I brush my hand along the small of her back, ushering her toward the door. "That's good. Means you really want it. Use it to fuel you."

She peers over at me, eyes wide. "I do want it. More than just about anything I've ever wanted."

I nod. High-intensity situations are my life's work, and the pressure to not fuck this up for her is at an all-time high. I can see how badly she wants it in the way she watches the crowd through the clean glass, sizing up everyone who stands in her way with a competitive tilt of her chin.

A small smile tugs at my lips as I open the door. "Okay then. Let's make it happen."

After Piper signs us in, we file into the only open plastic standard-issue lobby chairs remaining. She's a bundle of jittery nerves beside me, wiggling around in her chair and smoothing her hair with jerky slides of her hand.

The other teams reek of ruthless professionalism, especially the man and woman who are wearing matching charcoal-colored power suits and aviators—indoors. Both have their laptops out, and both machines are beefed up with bulky cases that appear indestructible. They look like they're here to do my taxes and then promptly murder me.

Piper leans in and whispers close to my ear. "You see that pair who look like GQ models?"

"Which ones?"

"Millennial Fabio over there. Windswept chestnut hair, tattooed chest, unbuttoned white shirt? He and his partner—the stupidly hot one in the white jumpsuit next to him—narrated one of my favorite series last year and made a splash."

"Hey, that's pretty cool—"

"*Not* cool, Sam. Opposite of cool. I can't

compete with that."

I turn my head toward her, and she shirks my gaze, blinking down toward the folder in her hands.

"Pipes. You are a professional. You have no reason to believe you won't walk in there and wow them." I poke her in the arm. "And since I'm *me*, you are doubly protected. My innate talent for blowing hot air into a mic will bring them to tears."

Her lips curve into a tentative smile that disappears as quickly as it comes. "I can't believe we're doing this. I should have married rich so I wouldn't have to work at all."

"It's not too late." I jerk my head toward Millennial Fabio and mouth, *how about this guy?*

"No thanks."

Curiosity stirs as I watch her for a beat. The phrase *mind your business* comes to mind, but I ignore it. "Seeing someone, then?"

"I'm seeing a full Bellini household, seven nights a week."

I search my brain for a return joke and come up short. She angles away from me, closing her eyes as she does vocal warmups like the other teams.

As the lobby clears out one team at a time, restless energy works its way into my body. When we're the last couple left, Piper throws me a look somewhere between distress and resignation. "Thanks for doing this. If—and probably when—it goes south in there, just know I appreciate the effort. I know this isn't exactly a bucket-list item for you, and you didn't have to offer in the first place or agree. It was a surprisingly…nice offer." She tucks a strand of hair behind her ear. "So…thanks."

The softness in her tone sucker punches me right in the chest. *Fuck.* Guilt doesn't discriminate based on time or place. Now is definitely *not* the time to clarify why I offered to help in the first place, or that I really was hoping for something in return.

But damnit, I wasn't banking on soft Piper. Vaguely annoyed Piper, yes. Sarcastic, absolutely. But this girl with hope in her eyes who looks like she's on the verge of actually trusting me again? It nudges me off a cliff I didn't know I was standing on.

Omission doesn't feel right. If I don't say something now, I'll regret it.

"About that nice offer—"

"I already told you—you're getting half the wages. Don't try to nickel-and-dime me now, Mayor O'Shea."

My gaze trips on her playful smile before flitting up to the ceiling. "Right. About the mayor stuff." I rub the back of my neck and peek back at her. "Perhaps there's some truth to what you said in the parking lot."

She stiffens. "What do you mean?"

"I mean, yes, I wanted to come to brunch because Caleb asked me. That's true. But I also came hoping to get your mom's endorsement. I know it's a long shot, and I know how your family sees me...but I'd be lying if I said I didn't really want it."

I watch her cycle through several emotions before she lands on gap-mouthed shock.

"Are you *kidding* me? I asked you in the parking lot to be honest with me about why you came over! You acted like I was ridiculous for assuming it was connected to the mayor stuff."

On the lobby's far wall, a loud silver doorknob turns. The door to the back of the studio creaks open, and a woman in pink cowboy boots bids Millennial Fabio and his partner a quick goodbye. She turns her attention to the clipboard in her hand. "Bellini, O'Shea, you're up."

"That's us!" I affirm loudly, grabbing Piper's clammy hand to help her out of the chair. I lean in and feel her body tense as I speak in a low voice: "I'm being honest now. All I hoped was that you'd put in a good word with your family."

She speaks through gritted teeth as she pulls her hand from my grip. "I can't believe you're putting me in this position."

"Is it really that big a deal?"

"*Yes.* What do you want me to do? After everything that happened, my mother is more likely to endorse a tattoo on my forehead than your run for mayor."

*Everything that happened.* The words wash over me like ice water.

"Welcome to Studio 7." The woman arcs her arm, and her wrist-bangles make music. "Thank you for coming."

"Thank *you*," Piper and I say in unison, like polite robots. For the first time ever, we appear to be on the same page about how to conduct ourselves: as fakely as possible, until we can duke this out in private.

The woman gestures at the wall of windows. "The sky is so blue today. You'd never know it's colder than a mother-in-law's love out there. I'm Darla."

I scan the clipboard she's clutching to her chest, noting the engraved text. *Darla Gentry.* Must be the producer.

"It's so nice to meet you," Piper gushes. "I'm a huge fan of your work."

Darla beams. "It's nice to meet you, too, Ms. Bellini. Are you two ready?"

Piper's eyes turn on when she smiles, warm and eager. "We're *so* ready."

Darla steps aside, waving us forward. I stretch my neck and shake out my arms. *Game time.*

I throw Piper a cautious look, signaling for her to walk first. But she doesn't need my concern. As we step into the dimly lit hallway, a transformation happens. Her nerves seem to slip away as she struts with confidence at Darla's side. She leads the small talk, professional and charming in her delivery. They speak in code, industry lingo I barely understand.

A foreign sensation overtakes me. Something that feels a lot like nerves. The hallway is so quiet, so insulated with thick carpet to catch our footfalls. My unsteady breathing is loud in my own ears.

This is fully Piper's domain. The closer we get to the door at the end of the hall, the more Piper comes alive, brightening the dim space. In her element, she shines.

Sure, I've made a ton of speeches in my day and will make plenty more in my campaign, but the magic in public speaking comes from being authentic in front of an audience. Here, I'll have to be someone else. An actor.

I have to get this right. More than one career depends on it.

# CHAPTER EIGHT

## PIPER

The hallway leads to a single door with a neon sign centered above it like a crown. We enter the sound studio, and familiarity washes over me. The equipment, the setup, the muffled acoustics that almost feel like pressure on your eardrums…*this* is what I needed to get in character. In this environment, I'm no longer Piper, gateway to Councilwoman Bellini. I don't have to care that Sam has an agenda the size of his ego.

I'm Piper Bellini, professional voice actor. And I'm ready to prove it.

The camera operator, who is sitting on the other side of a glass panel, presses a button on his dashboard. The glass slides down into a sleeve like a car window.

"Good afternoon. I'm Damien Gentry, Coproducer of Studio 7." He points up at the elaborate robotic arm holding the sleek black camera. "This is E.T., my right-hand man. He'll be moving around you as you perform, grabbing footage. And you've now met my wife, Darla Gentry."

"Mr. Gentry, thank you for having us. And Mrs. Gentry, thank you for getting us situated. Fantastic space you have here," Sam says, slathering on the charm.

"Thank you kindly, Sam," Darla coos. Her accent screams Tennessee, southern and honeysuckle sweet.

Damien boasts a similar drawl. "Is that an RTFD logo on your sweater, brother?"

Sam glances at the patch on his chest. "Yes, sir."

"I have a firefighter cousin over in Dorchester and two others out of state. Y'all do a hell of a job. Thank you for your service."

"Just doing my job. And DTFD, great guys. Don't let them fool you—those rivalry rumors are mostly false."

"It's those PD dogs you gotta watch out for, eh?"

Sam's laugh is that of a frat boy on steroids. "You got that right!"

The tension of wanting to murder his pandering ass while also wanting to hug him for handling the small talk is at an all-time high. "He's not wearing a sweater on camera, though," I blurt. "Take it off, Sam."

For once, he has no snarky retort. He pulls off the fleece to reveal a dress shirt underneath, mussing his hair in the process. His black, short-sleeved button-up is buttoned all the way to the top, collar button included. This look traps him somewhere between "Ryan Gosling on a brisk evening stroll" and "youth pastor recruiting for bible camp" territory.

It's not a terrible sight, especially with his broad shoulders and arms. Definitely camera ready.

"Are y'all ready for the lowdown?" Darla asks, stepping into the room. "Dames, the glass?"

Damien jumps to action. "Darla will take it from here. Pay no attention to the man behind the curtain. Best of luck." Damien presses the same button on his dash, and the glass panel rolls back up. It locks into place with a rubbery sort of snap. The whir of the robotic camera arm—or E.T., apparently—makes Sam jump. Sounds are so crisp and clean in here they almost sound threatening.

Darla nudges a dimmer switch on the wall. "Today we will be auditioning with actual material featured in Untitled Project 72, the project you are auditioning for. If you'll each sign this NDA"—she frees a paper from the teeth of her clipboard and hoists it in my direction—"we'll jump right in."

Sam and I take turns signing. I don't even

bother reading what's on the page. I know the drill well enough. *Don't talk about projects until they are released* is pretty much the cardinal rule of audiobook narration. This just takes it a step further, as we will get to glimpse the material sooner in the process.

She tucks the papers away and nods her head toward the closer of two podiums. "Piper, you'll be at Station A. Sam, Station B."

We shuffle to our spots, two podiums that look like they're squared up for a debate. A crystal chandelier dangles overhead. Condenser microphones are mounted low but angled upward, less conspicuous than my home microphone.

"Are you two ready?"

Sam smiles. "Yes, ma'am."

"Ma'am is my mama, sweet thing. Please call me Darla," she croons. This woman is lemonade on a hot day. "In a moment, I'll exit through this door. The sign will light up as soon as the cameras start rolling. Your job is to sell us an experience. Good luck, folks. I'm rooting for you."

I run my fingertips over the smooth podium as my limbs buzz in anticipation. Darla slips a black plastic sleeve in front of me that houses the script. She does the same for Sam.

"Scripts out," Darla commands. "Piper, your lines are in red. Sam, yours are in blue. Remember, begin when the light above the door turns red." The sound amplification intensifies as she shuts the door behind her.

And then there were two.

Sam gives me a reassuring little wink, and despite how much I wanted to pummel him five minutes ago, I cling to this little gesture like a lifeline.

The neon sign above the door, identical to the one hanging in the hall, flickers to life.

NOW RECORDING

We slide our scripts from the sleeves in unison. My eyes drift to the cover sheet. I wonder what the Gentrys have cooked up for this project. Gnomes inciting an underground rebellion against evil leadership? Siblings taking each other to Judge Judy–style court over a familial murder?

*Untitled Project 72*

*Chapter 4: The Creek*

The script's first lines are blue.

Sam's.

"*Princess Victoria's eyes are normally a crystal blue, but right now all I see in her stare down is fiery red. She tries to yank the reins out of my hand, but I hold firm on my grasp.*

"'*You act as though sharing a horse with a commoner like me will be the death of you. I shouldn't be surprised; you've been uptight since the day we met. Tell me one thing, princess: When was the last time you were well and truly—'"*

His voice falls off, and two desperate green eyes find mine, ivy searching for a place to cling.

"*'—fucked?'*"

My heart hammers an erratic rhythm in my chest as his voice echoes in my ear.

Well. And. Truly.

Well. And. *Truly fucked.*

I scramble to find my first line as the camera circles overhead.

"*For a stable boy so beneath my station, he certainly has nerves of steel.*

"*'I'm taking this horse across the creek alone whether you like it or not, Lazarus. You can wonder all you want about who has well and truly fucked me. Just know it'll never be you.'*"

Sam looks like he's about to have a stroke, his eyes bulging out of his head as he watches me. His jaw hangs down, and I resist the urge to reach over and slap his mouth closed. The only thing bridging the seconds between our lines is my determination to look like a professional, even if it kills me. I stare at him like "Princess Victoria" would, face contorted in sexy camera-ready anger.

It isn't a thriller or sci-fi.

Not even a gnome or fairy fantasy.

This is a romance novel through and through.

Sam's gaze falls to his page.

*"I may be a lowly commoner, but I'm no fool. She can't hide her attraction to me; she merely funnels it into rage.*

*"'You and I both know that's not true, princess. It's just a matter of how long you pretend not to want me. Now, mount the horse and let me ride behind you before someone spots us.'"*

I gobble up the chance to look away from Sam's face and back at my script.

*"It's a long ride across the river, and he and I both know what lies beyond the creek is not only dangerous but deadly.*

*"'Fine. But if I so much as feel you behind me, I'm knocking you off the horse.'"*

E.T. brings the camera low and holds tight on Sam's face. His gaze catches mine, and I wage a silent war with my eyes. *Do it for the cameras, Hefty.*

*"I mount the horse behind her and feel her hair against the hollow of my neck. I may be kicked off yet, because with the princess in front of me, the temptation to inch forward is dizzying.*

*"I want her to feel* me."

He pauses again.

*"To feel how much I want her."*

Minutes bleed together as our characters fight

their way across the creek. Sam spouts so much filthy inner monologue I fear I'll pass out on the podium.

We did a *lot* when we dated, but we never had sex. It was the final frontier I was terrified to cross, even though my body was desperate for his. It was the worst Catch-22 of all time: couldn't have sex because I didn't want to complicate things, complicating things by not having sex.

And now, here we are. Throwing phrases like *throbbing core* and *steely member* like it's standard fare.

I am fucked. Well and truly.

My heel snaps in half as I chase Sam across the parking lot. I hobble on uneven feet for a few seconds before pausing to strip off the other one. "Slow down!"

He stops but doesn't turn around. "What was *that*?"

My inner defense squad assembles. "An audition."

"That was *not* cyborgs."

"It was dystopian romance." Heat prickles my skin. "Guess I didn't mention that was a possibility."

"Guess you didn't."

I catch up beside him so we can stomp side by side in the direction of our cars. "First of all, I didn't write the script, so you can cut the attitude."

"I don't have an attitude. I just need time to process whatever the hell that was."

"Oh, you need *time*?" I spit the words like a poison dart as high school Sam's face comes into view. Ancient feelings spill out, wild and unstoppable. "I didn't realize you understood the concept. Because when I asked *you* for time, our relationship ended."

He runs tense fingers across his scalp and pulls on his hair. It stands straight up even when he lets go. "I knew it. I knew you were still mad about what happened between us."

"I'm mad about a lot of things. Presently, you asked for my mother's *endorsement* precisely twelve seconds before the most important audition of my career. You should've been honest and up-front."

"You weren't honest, either. I didn't know we'd be reading a book like *that*."

"I didn't know! Listen, I understand this isn't ideal. The scene had some challenging content. But if the idea of narrating romance with me is so disgusting to you, then I'll march right back in the studio and tell them to forget the whole thing."

"*Challenging content?*" he splutters. "When Lazarus was on the horse—with his—" He gestures dangerously close to his belt region as a blush creeps up his neck.

"I know, all right?"

"Right. Then obviously *we* can't…" He trails off, gesturing between the two of us. "It would be…"

My temper flares as each of my vivid career dreams slips through the porous concrete beneath us. "So you're backing out on me?"

A rustle in the distance catches both of our attention. Damien and Darla are exiting through the studio door, heads bent together. Darla's laugh drifts across the parking lot.

"Piper." His voice drops to a hair above a whisper. "Stop yelling or they'll hear you."

I look between the Gentrys and back at him twice, fire and flames dancing in my periphery. "Are you quitting, yes or no?"

"Get in before they notice us." He opens the passenger door to his 4Runner.

I knock it closed with my hip before stomping to my own car. In my brain, I'm smashing the knife emoji on my keyboard as I slip into the front seat and toss my shoes and folder in the back.

Sam is in my face before I have a chance to think. He hinges at the waist, clutching the top of my car for support as he takes up the whole doorway, eclipsing the sun. "Fine. You want to have an honest conversation?"

"Yes. For the love of God, yes."

"I went to McLaughlin's the other night to find you."

"*What?*"

"That's it. That's the rest of the truth."

"Let me make sure I understand: You came to McLaughlin's to ambush me but then pretended it was some coincidence you were there?"

"I asked Caleb where to find you. I wanted to talk things out before brunch. To make things less awkward for everyone."

I grip the steering wheel until my knuckles turn white. Red-hot embarrassment wraps around me like vines and squeezes until my voice comes out strained. "Caleb knew about this? What, am I a political liability to you? Something to be handled?"

"Piper. It's not like that. Please. Caleb doesn't know about the endorsement. He just wants us all to get along."

"I'm done with this conversation." I hate how my words come out in a strangled cry. The vulnerability in my tone makes me almost as angry with myself as I am with him. I should be better at controlling my voice. It's my job.

Here's the thing about broken trust: it doesn't matter what happens the next day, the next month, or even seven years later. Every little breach from the moment of the first break feels bigger than the last. It's a virus that lays dormant, waiting to flare up again.

I realize his mayoral ambitions have nothing to

do with me and that they demand a political finesse. Of course he wants my mother's endorsement. She's a city councilor in a small town. That's part of the game.

But I refuse to be a pawn.

He squats, his left knee poking into my car and butting up against my leg. I inch away from him.

"How can you be so angry when you're the one who broke up with me?" he asks, voice nearly a whisper.

And there it is. The topic I didn't want to talk about, or even think about, laid bare between us.

"We were on a break. We were *not* broken up. I asked for time. You then went and hooked up with our mutual friend at a party. I *saw*..." My voice breaks, and I can't get it together to finish the sentence.

His shoulders and arms tense as he grips the doorframe. "You said, '*I can't do this, Sam.*' Those were your words. That's the definition of a breakup, Piper."

"I said, '*I can't do this right now. I need time.*' And within a matter of days, you'd moved on."

*Confirming my worst suspicions about whether or not we could last when you were at college*, I don't add.

He blinks away from me. "I know I messed up. Breakup or not, that night was a mistake. I never should have even talked to her, let alone anything else. But Sidney *told* me you were done with me.

What was I supposed to think? You two were friends, and you weren't talking to me, so I put two and two together and concluded you'd fully moved on."

A new betrayal pricks my skin. "Sidney told you that?"

"*Yes.* Which I would have explained to you sooner, if you had let me. I tried multiple times to talk to you. Do you know how frustrating it is to be pushed away?"

"It wasn't over for me. Sidney lied to you. How could you think I'd moved on that fast, even if we were broken up?" My palms grow slick with sweat.

"I never would have touched her if I thought there was still a chance for you and me. And it *sucked* that you think I would."

"Well it *sucked* seeing you having sex with someone else."

He sucks in a gust of air. "What? She and I didn't— I would never; not after you and I..." He pauses and squeezes his eyes shut. "Sidney never should've happened, but it wasn't sex."

This declaration hits like rain on a tin roof, heavy and loud. Slow.

*It wasn't sex.*

Does it matter?

I dare a look over at him, determined to ignore the relief mixed with unease rippling down my spine.

"The fact is, you were still half naked in a car with her. It was so fast. Do you know how replaceable that made me feel?"

"*Replaceable?*" His eyes widen. "The fact that you said that tells me you *still* don't understand—to this day—how I felt about you. Or how much it hurt me when I thought you ended it. People do stupid shit when they're hurt. I can't take back what I did, and there are no words to say how sorry I am about Sidney. If I could turn back time…" He rakes his fingers through his hair. "The point is, I never intended to hurt you. And I take full responsibility for my side of what happened."

My heart beats in double time, a frenzied rhythm that leaves me breathless. He's taking responsibility for his side.

Is he implying that I should take responsibility for mine?

What *is* my side?

*It wasn't sex.*

All this time…

"But you hurt me, too," he adds. "You could've talked to me. You didn't fight for us before the breakup—*break*—or after. You threw in the towel. Of all the ways we could've ended, that one was the worst for me. Being fully shut out."

He's right. I didn't fight. Because as much as it

hurt, I'd believed he'd moved on, and I wasn't going to stand in his way.

The part of me that wanted to end the break and try to fight for what *I* wanted for once died when I saw him in that car.

Something inside my chest crumples, and a dull pain radiates outward.

"I have to go." I shove my key into the ignition. "Forget all of this ever happened, all right?"

"Forget *what*? The audition?"

"Yes. This was a terrible idea. I'll call and retract our application."

"Don't you dare." He pushes against the car door with a strained smile as I try and close it. "Think of the enchanted forest, Piper. What the fuck are Victoria and Lazarus running from? How will we know if we quit?"

I let out a strangled groan and slap the steering wheel. "You are impossible."

"Don't drive off upset," he says, his voice softening. "Too many accidents happen that way."

My head falls forward, and hair spills around me as I lean my forehead on cold vinyl. "I think I've got all the facts now. You want my mother's endorsement. You want my big ol' Italian family singing your praises across town. And you find romance novels horribly offensive to your delicate sensibilities. Does that about cover it? Can I go now?"

I can't see him with my face buried in the wheel and my eyes closed, but I hear his gruff words as clear as day. I feel them in my chest.

"Goodbye, Piper."

# CHAPTER NINE

## SAM

The long drive home from the studio is still not enough time for me to calm down. My body is still a knot pulled tight, one of those bowlines that's hard to untie as I alternate slamming breaks and stomping the gas.

The situation with Piper is worse than I thought. She's been walking around for years thinking I cheated on her, that I seduced and fucked a girl in our friend group without a care in the world mere days after we broke up. All while I've been twiddling my thumbs on the topic, confused at why she was so mad.

I operated under the fundamental belief that *she ended things*. I made out with another girl to distract myself (the wrong girl, and took it a little too far, but still); I respected Caleb when he said he didn't want to talk about Piper *ever*; I moved on with my life and never really understood. But I accepted it.

Now I have all this new information clogging up my headspace and no idea what to do with any of it. Everything feels unsettled. I highly doubt Piper is going to skip on home to talk to her mom about the endorsement, and we certainly aren't getting the gig — my awkward audition made sure of that.

Electricity shoots down my spine. I know what we did in the studio was acting. But it was a jolt to my system to hear Piper talk like that, to see her smolder fixed on me. She's one hell of an actress and could weaponize that voice if she was so inclined. How anyone can sound so sweet and so wicked at the same time is beyond me.

But she's also still *her*, I'm *me*, and it was fucking bizarre.

I should drive home, eat dinner, and drown myself in campaign work. Acting as my own treasurer was my first and maybe worst political decision yet, but I'm a small enough one-man operation to swing it. At least I can get lost in a budgetary spreadsheet and put the disastrous confrontation with Piper out of my mind.

Home is the right call. And yet, I itch to make a different one.

"Hey Siri, dial Caleb Bellini."

He answers on the third ring. "O'Shea! What can I do you for?"

"Already with the dad jokes," I mumble miserably.

"When you produce your own loin fruit, you'll get your shot at comedy."

"Where are you? We need to talk."

"*Ouch*. We need to talk, eh? Is this a breakup?"

I scowl. *Breakup* is the most loaded word he could've chosen. "It's about Piper."

His reply is wary. "Oh. Is she all right?"

"Yes. Where are you? Is that screaming I hear?"

"I'm on the corner of Fifth and Fowler, at Little Gym."

"I'm five minutes from there. Can I come by?"

"Sure. Can you swing by Spuckies down the block first? Jane is hangry. She'd like an Italian Baller with extra sauce."

"She should've married differently, then."

"Thank God you're pretty, Sammy. See you soon."

Fifteen minutes later with a fat sandwich in hand, I enter the gym and spot about a thousand tiny humans visible over a half wall. Or twenty, at least. Their shrill cries of joy and/or sorrow echo off blue mats.

A few employees seem to be leading them in baby games. Some jump up and down inside hula hoops while others play a crawling version of hopscotch. Many roll around with blissed-out smiles on their chubby faces. Parents form a large, loose circle at the edge of the mat, watching their baby Olympians.

Kat sticks out in the herd in a poofy outfit that has Jane's name written all over it. She'd send that kid to Mars in frills.

I check in with a girl at the front desk. Caleb meets me, and after a quick ID scan I'm cleared to enter.

"Shoes!" the clerk yells as I step toward the half door.

Caleb snickers as I toe off my loafers and arrange them in a cubby. "Overdressed for godfather duty, eh? Where were you?"

My stomach plummets. "Piper and I had the audition this afternoon."

"Ah," is all he offers as he guides me to his and Jane's spot in the circle.

One of the babies does something that elicits great fanfare from other parents. Caleb claps politely as he takes a seat on the ground. With some effort — okay, a *lot* of effort; my formal audition clothes are tight for floor sitting — I squat slowly until my ass hits the ground. My ankles poke out as I cross my legs. Two feet ahead of us, Kat does a ninja roll, almost colliding with another baby. This place is pure anarchy. She's far and wide the cutest munchkin in the bunch.

Jane leans forward to look past Caleb. She clocks the sandwich in my hand, and her eyes grow three sizes. "Hello, Sam."

I extend my arm and hand it off like a baton, elbowing Caleb in the face for good measure.

"You are now my favorite of Caleb's friends," she squeals.

"Virtually no competition," I note.

She scoots backward off the edge of the mat and creates a barrier with her diaper bag and purse, does a sweep of her surroundings to see if anyone is watching, and proceeds to peel open the wax paper. The scent of oregano wafts my way.

I turn my attention back to Caleb. "So, I learned something of great interest. Namely that Piper didn't intend to break up with me, never thought we were broken up until she caught me kissing Sidney while thinking it was more, and that I was magically supposed to know this without her *ever* mentioning it. Care to comment?"

Caleb watches me, guarded. "What happened to our rule? No Piper-relationship talk?"

"We talked about Piper last week."

"Yeah, so you could find her and get the awkwardness out of the way now that she's home for good. So you could come over to my house without being a paranoid freak about getting caught. Not to open Samdora's Box of ancient history."

"All that time senior year you knew damn well"—I lower my voice, even though the shrieks of babies drown it out—"*darn* well that Piper and I were massively misunderstanding each other. You didn't think it was important to tell me she saw us as being on a break, not broken up?"

"Hey, I've seen that episode of *Friends*!" Jane chimes in before hoovering another bite. "Ross and Rachel were on a break, *not* broken up," she adds, but with a mouthful of food it sounds like an alphabet being gargled and spit out. "Or were they?"

Caleb shoots her a quelling look over his shoulder. "Too soon, babe."

"I'm just saying, there are similarities between that situation and this one. But Sam isn't nearly as bad as Ross, and poor Piper misunderstood what went down—"

"You know what my favorite part of that episode was?" Caleb interjects. "When the other four friends stayed out of it. Ross's own *sibling* stayed out of it, which is what I wanted to do then and what I'm trying to do now."

Jane's eyes narrow. "Are you getting snippy with me?"

"Sorry." Caleb's tone takes a dramatic shift for the

sweeter. "Just—can we get on the same page, please?"

"Same page." Jane takes another bite. "I'm Joey Tribbiani, just trying to enjoy my sandwich, staying in my lane."

I clear my throat. "I'm not trying to cause a marital spat, here. I'm just annoyed you didn't think that pertinent information was worth passing along, Caleb. Do you know how much drama that could've saved us all?"

"I had one rule. *One*. We don't talk about you and Piper as a couple. It wasn't my place to meddle. There are two sides to every story, and how was I supposed to know what was right? You said the relationship was over, and she said…nothing, because it's Piper. Then when the Sidney thing happened, I was kind of relieved because at least she'd stop crying in her room if she knew you'd moved on. I didn't expect it to spiral into the Bellinis Shit on Sam parade it became, but you and I both left for college a few weeks later anyway. I've apologized for taking her side without fully understanding yours—"

"It's your sister, I get it."

"—and everyone did their best. And most important, *it's in the damn past.*"

"She was crying in her room?" The words slip out, sounding more sad-sackish than I would like. But I'm not a monster—of course I feel a twist of pain in my gut hearing that. The thought of Piper upset, laying around crying about what happened between us, is another surprise in a long list of surprises. At the time, I thought she barely cared at all.

From the corner of my eye, I see Jane's brows climb into her hairline. I squirm in my seat to avoid her gaze.

"Sam. Tell me this is in the past." Caleb's warning tone is sharp enough to nick glass. "Tell me you aren't going to go there again. Not after last time."

My jaw tenses. "*Obviously*."

"Boys," Jane says, stern teacher voice on full display. "Why don't we recalibrate? Sam, are you and Piper going to work together on this project?"

"No way we're going to be cast after the awful performance I put on." I throw my hands up, the universal symbol for *Fucking A, Man*. "Safe to say I ruined that job for her."

"And you called *me* a congested Mark Wahlberg," Caleb mutters.

On my right in the circle, a woman lifts her hand to get my attention. In my scuffle with Caleb, I barely noticed her sitting two feet away. "Excuse me. Are you the O'Shea boy?"

I study her briefly. She looks my mom's age, if not a little older. Kids' music swells through the speakers, and I raise my voice to compete. "Er—yes ma'am. I'm Sam O'Shea."

"You're the firefighter boy running for mayor! I saw you in the paper. Your dad's the captain, right?"

A surprised *oh* catches in my throat. I've never been recognized before, and it didn't occur to me that the black-and-white thumbnail photo included with my candidacy announcement in the Roseborough Post would lead to it. I want to be excited at this development—an underdog will take what he can get in the PR department—but the phrase *firefighter boy* balloons in my brain until it pops. It reminds me of being young and trying on my dad's boots. I smile anyway. "Yes, that's me."

"So exciting. Love to see a young man with good family values running for office. You'll be a great role model for the up-and-coming generation. It's not often you see young guns interested in civil service."

My smile falters a little. *Family values.* She clearly thinks I'm here with my child.

"Thank you for your kind words," I manage. "I have a lot of ideas for how to make Roseborough a more desirable place for young families. I'll be speaking on that next week, at the library. What's your name?"

"Claudia Higgins."

"Thank you, Claudia. I'm thrilled to share my plans, most notably a rent subsidy for—"

"So which one of these cuties is yours?"

*Right*. Rent subsidies aren't as interesting as chunky babies.

Jane crawls past us on her hands and knees, yoinks Kat off the mat mid-tumble, and thrusts her into my lap. "Sam, the baby is ready for snuggles!"

I fumble for a second before pulling her tight to my chest. Her head falls reflexively against my shoulder as she babbles close to my ear. The sound soothes me as I pat her back.

"Sam is *so* good with her. The baby whisperer." Jane looks at Claudia and then back at me, oozing affection I'm almost positive is left over from when I handed her the sandwich. "Family values are a huge part of his campaign."

Claudia waggles a finger between Jane, Caleb, and me. "How are you all related?"

Caleb squeezes my shoulder. "This guy is like a brother to me. Godfather to my daughter." He flashes a sincere, closed-mouth grin, and adds, "He's going to make one hell of a mayor. No question."

I swallow a dry lump in my throat. Hearing him say that out loud when no one else has, and with such confidence, ignites my sense of purpose.

"So *precious*!" Claudia cries. "That's my grandson, Owen." She points at a baby boy locked in a staring contest with his shoes.

Our conversation ends at the sound of an

employee's whistle, signaling some sort of wrap-up song ritual. After a very cultish few minutes filled with lots of hand dancing and increasingly cranky babies, we gather our things and start for the door.

Jane passes Kat to Caleb. "Will you take her to the car? I need to tie my shoelaces, and she's about three seconds away from a meltdown."

Caleb nods, mocks my clothes once more for posterity, and struts out the door.

"Wait." Jane yanks my loafers out of the cubby before I can get them. "Sit with me for a second."

I follow her to a padded bench. She drops our shoes on the ground. Hers are decidedly lace-free. "Wait, you said you had to lace —"

"Caleb has had about three hours of sleep the last two days; he's not going to notice my shoes. Now, let's get down to business."

"Business?"

"You and I both know Caleb would commit a murder for Piper. If you want to talk to an impartial party on the topic, I'm your girl. What's really going on?"

I exhale. "That's a nice offer, but Piper is your friend and sister. Impartial is not the word for you, Janey."

"Listen. I get that Caleb feels a mafia-style duty to protect his sister from the perils of relationships.

But she and I were best friends for three years before I married into the family, and as her friend, I just want what's best for her."

The word *protect* pitches a ball, and the word *relationships* fouls it dramatically. "Whoa, whoa. Let's back up a few steps. Piper and I aren't in a relationship. She doesn't need protecting from me."

Jane laughs under her breath. "Oh, I know. Piper needs protecting from herself."

I side-eye her. If she's baiting me, it's working. "What do you mean?"

"Just that our girl has a difficult time owning up to her feelings until they have her in a choke hold. Love her to pieces, but she can be a little…closed off. She either hides her feelings and opinions or cloaks them in sixteen layers of sarcasm. Every time you come up in conversation, Piper gets in a mood but won't talk about it."

My skin prickles with uncomfortable heat. "Allow me to speak for her, then. She can't stand me."

"That's not what I'm suggesting. But I want to know how *you* feel."

I slip my feet into my shoes. "I feel like I need to get home and get busy with campaign stuff. I appreciate the chat, but my reason for coming here was simply to give Caleb shit for holding out on me. He had an opportunity to make things easier for everyone involved, and he didn't. But I'm over it." I smooth my hand over my shirt as I stand. "It had nothing to do with Piper, specifically. Just a flare of my temper. All good now."

She narrows her eyes. "Oh yeah? It had nothing whatsoever to do with Piper?"

"Nope. Probably won't even see her again."

Jane's laugh could be heard across the gym. "Nice try. It's a small town, and our family is everywhere. If your strategy for managing Piper is avoidance, I'd suggest revisiting your plan."

# CHAPTER TEN

## PIPER

I snatch the flannel footie pajamas out of Caleb's hand. "On a scale from one to divorced, this monstrosity is a nine."

"What's wrong with this? Jane likes cozy stuff."

I raise a dubious eyebrow. "You wanted my advice on anniversary presents, did you not?"

"Yes, but—"

"My advice is don't buy your wife anything with a trapdoor on the ass."

Traffic congests every aisle of Macy's. Caleb's offensive pajama selection is snapped up by a nearby shopper mere moments after he returns it to the rack.

I scan the women's section for something pretty and practical, like a silk robe. My eyes catch on something two racks over, a display so gorgeous it tugs on my purse strings. I weave out of the pragmatic pajamas section and land squarely in front of the impractical.

The tag hangs from the garter, inked with frilly calligraphy.

*Dark red underwire plunge bra adorned with sheer tulle.*

*Delicate lace cups lined with soft, silk sweeps.*

*Satin bows decorate center and both apexes for an added touch of romance—*

Settle down, Agent Provocateur.

I entertain the idea of robbing a bank and buying it for kicks. If I lived alone, I'd pour a glass of Shiraz and wear it just to feel desirable. Warm colors do wonders for my skin tone. I peek at the tag again.

*Fire engine red.*

I release it like it is, in fact, on fire.

Caleb's irksome voice cuts through the aisle. "Hilarious. As if I'd buy my wife lingerie recommended by my *sister*."

I swat him away when he pulls up beside me. "Not everything is about you. Maybe I'm also shopping for myself."

Mature as ever, he gags so loud a middle-aged woman comparing two thongs throws us a dirty look.

"Can you be cool for even a second?" I hiss.

"Why would you need this crap, anyway? You're single."

Now I'm the one gagging. "I'm not talking about my love life with you."

His eyes narrow. "Wait a minute. You aren't…"

I turn up my chin. "I'm not what?"

"Nothing. Just had a moment of panic that you and Sam… Never mind; sounds even more outrageous out loud. As if that'd ever happen again in a million years."

I pick up a pair of slippers from an adjacent display and shove them into Caleb's hands. "Outrageous. As if."

"He told me about your audition, by the way."

Sam and his big mouth strike again. My fingers run up and down the length of a fugly green bathrobe. "Oh yeah? What did he say?"

"He said it didn't go well."

"So glad he immediately called you to tell you all about it."

"Who else is he going to call?"

"I don't know, how about anyone else? Someone not related to the person he auditioned with? Surely he could bore other firefighters with that kind of thing."

"We talk about everything. It's what we do."

My eye roll is audible at the way he drags out the word *everything*. "Cool, so happy for you two.

Hey, maybe for your anniversary you can buy two plane tickets to Maui!"

He cocks his head sideways. "Maui?"

I pluck a frilly nightgown off a rack and drape it over his shoulder. "This will help soften the blow when you tell Jane she's not invited."

"Piper. Sam and I are finally in a good place. For years, I didn't think we'd get there. I'm not going to pretend I'm sad the audition sucked. You two clearly can't work together without it ending in disaster, so it's better you don't try."

His warning tone kindles my fight-or-flight instincts. Caleb has always been my ride or die. I am not keen to relive the saga of Sam or how much it hurt Caleb when I tried to make him choose.

I stare holes into the mud-colored carpet. "Did he say anything else?"

"That he did a shitty job during the read and ruined it for you."

Tires screech to a halt in my head. He can't possibly think *he* ruined it. It was doomed from the start.

He nudges me in the back with his pointy elbow. "Just saying, if you'd have let me audition, you would have gotten the job on sight."

"On sight," I echo numbly. It sounds like Sam told him the audition happened without mentioning the romance factor.

But why bring it up at all?

I map a familiar constellation between Caleb's freckles as I watch him check price tags. Maybe Sam withheld the truth because he doesn't want to make things weird between them again. Mentioning romance would've been a surefire way to do that.

I corral him toward the nearest cash register. "I need food. Or wine. Food cooked in wine. Let's get out of here."

"So I'm getting Jane this dress, the slippers — what else?"

"Make a dinner reservation someplace fancy. Date night. I'll watch Kat."

He watches me for a second as we take our spot in a massive checkout line. "I'm sorry about the gig, Pipes. I know you wanted it. But everything happens for a reason."

"Oh yeah? And what's the reason this time?"

"Now you don't have to work with Sam."

• • •

Nine pregnancies, and not once has my mother wanted a baby shower. But three days ago, while splayed out on the couch between conference calls, she claimed there is something about this pregnancy that "just feels different" and she'd feel "cheated" without a "small get-together."

My dad and I had exchanged a look at this, because obviously there is no such thing as a small get-together in our world, but otherwise I was thrilled by her declaration. I have been dying to do something productive that doesn't involve searching for new gigs.

At yesterday's sonogram, Mom's ob-gyn prepared a sealed envelope with the baby's sex written on an index card inside. The envelope is nestled inside my purse, cozy and safe, and it's my job to deliver it to Georgina at The Rolling Pin before noon today. The temptation to spoil the surprise is eating me alive, but I will refrain because I can't keep secrets from Mom.

Except for Sam's endorsement request. I have no problem keeping that from her.

Sam and I may be incapable of getting along, but I see no need to shore up more drama by mentioning his campaign. Mom already thinks Sam is untrustworthy; adding "political opportunist" to the list will incite fire and flames—the kind even he can't put out. Since Caleb is determined to keep Sam around, I'll keep my mouth shut and pretend the last week never happened.

A clean slate. Onward to new opportunities.

Discomfort swirls in my gut as I rifle through my dresser for my favorite jeans and a T-shirt. My gaze snags on my cream-colored cashmere sweater at the bottom of the stack. Maybe a touch of luxury is the thing I need to distract myself from the idea that Darla Gentry could be offering Millennial Fabio and his perky partner my dream job right this minute.

Nonna is at our house for her shift with Davie and Nova. The couch comes into view when I'm halfway down the stairs. She leafs through a newspaper, her legs crossed at the ankle like she's the queen at high tea as the twins play on the carpet.

I hit the base of the stairs, and she attempts a whistle. The sound is muffled and spitty but all the more endearing for it. "Hot tottie! You look beautiful. Are you meeting someone?"

"Georgina at The Rolling Pin. I'm off to drop off the sacred envelope for Mom's reveal cake."

"In my day the 'reveal' was when the baby came out with or without a—"

"I know, Nonna. But Mom asked for this. Even though the whole 'pink or blue' concept is antiquated, it's what she wants."

She watches me walk in the direction of the foyer. "You've always looked good in ivory, you know."

"Thank you."

"You know what else comes in ivory?"

I try to laugh as a tinge of sourness shoots across my tongue. I've heard this one time too many. "A wedding dress?"

"A *wedding* dress," she echoes, misty-eyed.

"But alas," I reply, lobbing my words across the chasm between where I am in life and where she wants me to be. "Just the sweater for now."

"Of course." A crooked little smile plays across her lips. "For now, you'll stun the whole bakery in that fancy sweater. I love the way it hangs off the shoulders."

"Thanks, but I'll be gross in my raincoat. These shoulders won't see the light of day."

"You're stunning even in a coat, love. Beauty is deeper than the skin."

Her words are a salve I didn't know I needed, smoothing something dry and brittle inside of me. "Anything from the bakery? If you don't tell me what you want, I'm getting you tiramisu."

"If Georgina has the black and white zeppole, buy the lot. I'm about to ask your dad to change my oil later. I want to be good and ready with payment."

My mouth salivates. Zeppole with fresh custard is selling-you-naming-rights-to-my-firstborn-for-a-bite good. "You don't have to tell me twice. All the zeppole in the bakery is coming home with me."

I'm not even out of the driveway yet when DJ Eagle Eye's voice chirps through the car speakers.

"You're listening to ninety-seven point nine, The Eagle. Local news coming up on the seven: Does

Sam O'Shea, son of Roseborough Township Fire Department Captain Gregory O'Shea, have what it takes to follow Mayor Flory's thirty-five-year legacy in Roseborough? Our thoughts on this week's *shocking* mayoral candidacy announcement after the break."

My appetite, so strong seconds ago, fades to nothing as I grip the wheel.

*Clean slate.*

*Pretend last week never happened.*

*But be prepared to encounter Sam at every turn.*

An hour later, when I turn back on my street, there's a Toyota 4Runner in my driveway.

Not even the box of zeppole buckled into the seat beside me could sweeten the bitterness I feel at the sight of Sam's vehicle.

"What now?" I mutter under my breath, throwing the car into park. He wouldn't dare come sniffing around the house to talk politics. He'd take care of business at City Hall.

I have the nonsensical thought that maybe my house is on fire, but I (unfortunately) know his work schedule. Also, firemen don't pull up to house fires in their SUVs.

I park in the street, giving Sam ample space to back up and get lost.

Nonna's laugh fills the house like helium as soon as I step into the foyer.

"Oh, Sam. You are too much! Here, let an old pro show you how it's done. You must chop the onion *very small*, see? Almost diced, but not quite…"

I storm into the kitchen and confront Sam's broad back. "What are you doing here?"

He turns to glance at me for a second before returning his attention to his cutting board. "Smaller cuts than this, Julia?"

"Perfect."

I clear my throat. "*Hello?*"

Nonna looks up from the head of garlic she's mincing. She wipes her hands on a dish towel. "Preferita! You're back so soon. How was the bakery?"

"What's preferita?" Sam asks, still not turning around.

I spot the delicate strings of my apron tied around his waist. Nonna knitted me that apron herself, and the sight of the tight knot at the base of his back makes me seethe.

Nonna turns to Sam and raises a coy shoulder. "Oh, it means *favorite*. But we don't tell the others."

I pretend not to be flattered, as I always do when she uses my nickname. "I'm your favorite of Dad's *girls*."

"Right. Of course." She winks and gestures at the sink with her elbow. "Wash up and help me shuck the corn, would you? Do I spy a treat box in your hand?"

"The zeppole," I mumble, thrusting it into her arms.

I have no choice but to circumvent the island to get to the sink, allowing me to glimpse Sam's expression. His brows are screwed up in concentration as he stares down at the cutting board.

"Are you going to acknowledge me?" I ask.

"Good afternoon, Piper!" he says, too brightly to ever be construed as natural.

Nonna flutters her eyelashes in Sam's direction. "Sam's helping me with the meatballs. And would you believe he got the twins to nap?"

"Sure," I grumble. "He puts me to sleep all the time."

Sam finally meets my eye, and I'm whacked over the head with a sense of déjà vu. The two of us staring each other down with only a podium between us, not unlike the kitchen island.

*Well and truly fu—*

"Just thought I'd stop by and visit my friend Julia." He peers over at Nonna. Sunbeams shoot straight through the kitchen window, funneling light onto the planes of his face. Accentuating his long, dumb lashes. "Enjoying her company."

"Sounds like a totally reasonable thing for you to do out of the blue."

"I thought maybe we could have a chat when

I'm done here in the kitchen."

I scoff. "Why? Need another favor?"

He slides his finger down the chef's knife's blunt side to remove clingy pieces of onion and places it on the cutting board. With unnecessary gusto, he lopes past me on his way to the sink, pausing only to whisper in my ear. "Nah. Because I have it on pretty good authority you didn't do the *first* favor."

I elbow him in the ribs. "Excuse you. I was about to wash my hands."

He turns on the faucet and lathers up with lemon-scented dish soap. "Schoolyard rules. I was here first."

"You're a child."

He rinses, turns off the faucet, and shakes his hands dry right next to my face, hitting me with flecks of cold water.

"That's what this—*my*—apron is for." I grab a handful of the knitted fabric around his waist and yank it hard. He lurches forward, tethered, and grabs the counter's edge for support.

His glare sends a thrill down my spine, like maybe I'm bothering him as much as he's bothering me.

"If you want me to take it off, just say the word," he whispers, nudging hair out of my eye with a lazy flick of his clean hand. "No need to undress me in front of your grandmother."

I pull harder, but he's too grounded now to falter. He doesn't even flinch. "Don't touch me."

He glances down at my fingers still gripping his apron, and he doesn't stop looking until it feels like my hand is going to catch on fire. "Then I suggest you let me go."

Nonna coughs lightly. "I'm going to check on the twins."

Her voice is like a rubber band snapping my wrist. I release my grip as she pads out of the kitchen. "Way to go, Hefty. You made Nonna uncomfortable with your attitude."

"Me? *You're* the one—"

"Forget it. I've got corn to shuck." I hold his gaze as I drop to my knees and pry open the cabinet below the sink. He jumps out of harm's way in time to spare his shins from a mighty bruise. After pulling out two plastic grocery bags, I rise back to my full height, daring him with my scowl to say something else. "I'll be in the living room. This kitchen feels small."

He watches me with his arms crossed as I shove corn into bags, which takes a full minute or longer. Good thing I can hold on to anger for a long time. A biblical amount of time.

I'm still grinding my teeth as I stalk off toward the living room.

"Hey, Pipes?"

I stop, my shoes catching on the linoleum. The bags slip out of my hands, and corn rolls in every direction as I wheel around. *Damnit.* "*What*, Sam?"

He takes three tentative steps in my direction, his eyes glinting mysteriously as his lips pull into a weak smile. "We got the gig."

# CHAPTER ELEVEN

## SAM

Piper's face turns ghostly white. "What?"

"That thing we auditioned for a few days back? Turns out we weren't half bad."

Her eyes—very much like a Milky Way bar, rich chocolate brown with swirls of caramel—flash pure suspicion as they catch mine. "You're joking."

"I wouldn't joke about something like this."

I wait and watch as an entire show plays out on her features. The dawning of understanding, the grand sweep of surprise, the hasty shift to disbelief. It's all right there on the surface, like she can't put words to the feelings fast enough. My desire to rile her up fades away. I can't bring myself to mess with her when she's so overcome. I peel off her apron and toss it aside.

This means too much to her.

"I didn't get a call or email. They would've tried to contact me." Her voice is barely audible, a bunch of breaths with the occasional consonant sound.

"Did you ever set up voicemail on your new phone?"

Her eyes widen. "Oh. I guess I didn't."

"Darla called me this morning. They want us for a three-book deal."

She opens and closes her mouth three times before letting anything out. "They offered you a three-book deal?"

I drop to my knees, holding her gaze as I sweep the fallen corn into the bag. "No, Pipes. They offered *us* a three-book deal."

"It was a contract for one, with series potential."

I deposit the bag on a chair. "She said they loved the footage, they loved the audition, and they enjoyed us. *Raw talent.* Those were Darla's exact words."

Her hands fly to her face to cradle her cheeks. "I can't believe this."

"Why not? You nailed it."

"You don't get it, wunderkind. This kind of stuff doesn't happen to me. You get calendar spreads, groupies, votes. Everything you've ever wanted, you've gotten. I'm not— I haven't had the best of luck. A few gigs here and there, but never something this big. This was all starting to feel like a dead-end dream."

An odd sensation settles in my chest. I push her twisted view of me aside—*groupies?*—to argue my point. "Do you have any idea what you sounded like in that studio? How you commanded the whole audition? The way you—" I stop myself shy of saying looked. Of course she looked incredible, but it was more than that. It was all of her on display that day, inside and out, stepping into a sphere tailor-made for her talents. "It was fucking impressive. Why *not* you?"

The sound that escapes her mouth is soft and fragile. "I sounded good?"

I reach into my pocket and pull out my phone. "See this 212 number in my call log? That's Darla. It wasn't just a yes, Pipes. It was a *hell* yes."

The number is some kind of linchpin. As soon as her eyes land on those ten digits, a dam behind her eyes bursts and a sob escapes her mouth. All the hostility from before melts away as she buries her face in her hands.

The rebuttal on my tongue dissolves at the sound of her cry. A primal urge to comfort her, to pull her into my arms and stroke her back until she calms, knocks the wind out of me.

She wouldn't want that. But it seems like something she *needs*. I war with myself for a moment before scooping an ear of corn from the discarded bag. Before I can listen to my brain shouting the reasons why I shouldn't—a potential knee to the groin is high on the list—I coil an arm around her, reeling her into my chest. Her body is tense but warm. Timid. Her forearms lay parallel on my torso like train tracks as she continues to cry into her palms. I tap her on the head with the ear of corn. "There, there."

She tilts her chin upward and spreads her fingers. My arm freezes, and the ear of corn hovers above her head.

After staring at the vegetable for three full seconds as if it's the first one she's ever seen, she rolls her eyes with Piper-level ferocity, which is to say her ocular muscles are at risk of sprain. "*Really?* Sam, you are just so…"

But what I am is unclear, because she gives up. Her face falls against my shirt as her mangled crying resumes. But it's softer now. Tinged with something I can't decipher.

The sound spurs panic in my gut. "I'm sorry; I was kidding—*hey*. It's okay. You're okay." I drop the corn and pull her tighter. My chin comes to rest on top of her head, and I get a noseful of her trademark apple and vanilla. Summer scents in a chilly spring. "You rocked the audition. This is well deserved."

She fully surrenders, sinking into my chest as her arms fall to her sides. We stand together, swaying lightly as her crying subsides. My body registers hers, the feel of her hips notching below mine, the rise and fall of her chest. Her face pressed against me. I can't feel her mouth specifically, but I'm suddenly so aware it's there.

"Thank you," she murmurs into my shirt, the whiskey-rich sound vibrating my pec.

Longing rips through me, hijacking my better judgement, pumping heat in every direction. My hands itch to slide across her back until they find the curve of her waist.

*Shit.*

We pull away at the same moment. I shift uncomfortably as she drinks two gulps of air and wipes moisture from her cheek. "Anyway, it wasn't just me in that studio. You did the whole 'no big deal, but I'm a fireman' bit. Nice work, wearing something with the RTFD logo. They ate it up."

"I didn't wear it on purpose."

She shoots me a wink. "Sure thing, Mr. February."

The residual heat of her closeness lingers. Attraction to Piper may be biologically founded, but I can't entertain it. Not even for a second. I can practically hear her brother's portrait on the wall, telling me to back the fuck up.

I find an excuse to reset in a box of tissues across the room. As I retrieve them and shove the box into her chest, I remember something the Gentrys mentioned on the call. "They want us in the studio on Friday to sign the contract. Something about onboarding, verifying our documents, giving us a crap ton of pages so we don't have to print them ourselves?"

She paces circles, talking under her breath. "I can't believe this is happening. *Friday.* That's so soon, and the day of Mom's party—it's fine. That'll be earlier. I'll need to pick something to wear." She throws me a look. "You'll have to dress up. Photos on contract signing day are a rite of passage on Instagram, plus they'll need a photo for our records at the studio."

I lift a finger. "Well, *if* we do it. Let's back up a step. We still need to talk—"

"*What?*"

I wince at her sharpness. "I was just saying, if we do this—"

"Why do you keep saying *if*? We got the job. We're going to do the job."

"Piper..." I scrub my chin. "I think we need to at least have a conversation about this."

She books it toward the staircase. "I'll show you my studio."

I follow, matching her step for step. We make it halfway up the staircase before I reach for her hand. "It's not a done deal. What about the...complicating factors we discussed? The content of the books?"

She pivots on her stair. "Sam, you aren't really

suggesting you came here to tell me I got my dream job, only to *then* tell me I can't have it because you changed your mind. That would be a jerk move."

"*Jerk?*" I grip the banister on either side of the staircase, shoulders tensing. I'm two steps below her, which gives me an eye-level view of her glaring face. Frustration spikes hot and demanding as I lean in and glare right back at her. Just when I think we are turning a corner for the friendlier, she whips out the attitude. "Really, Piper?"

She blinks toward a family portrait hanging on the wall. "If the shoe fits."

"I'm a jerk for acknowledging the painfully obvious? This isn't a normal situation, Piper. I'm running for mayor. Voters will have *opinions* if they find out I'm recording romance."

"So record it under a different name. People use stage names or pen names all the time. Besides, the first book won't be released until the election is over. Problem solved."

"That's only Point A. Point B: the fact you and *I* used to—"

She makes a halting noise before I can finish. "That was a long time ago. It's been, like…seven years. We're adults now. This is work—a professional arrangement."

The ghost of her body pressed against mine not

five minutes ago passes through me, leaving me cold. After our fight in the parking lot, I understand why she was mad. But now she's going to overcorrect by pretending we never touched, all while we spend our time together verbally discussing *people touching*? We're just going to act out romance like we never had one? Like it won't stir up *anything*?

I've got news for her. "We're adults" doesn't stop me from remembering she's most ticklish right below her hip bone, especially when I nip her there with my teeth. "A professional arrangement" doesn't mean I forget the way her mouth used to feel on mine, devouring me with hot and hungry kisses when I'd sneak into her room. That mouth is skilled at *way* more than just voice acting. And "like…seven years" is not long enough to forget the desperate little sounds she makes when she's worked up and needy, all because of *my* mouth.

But apparently, she's deeply comfortable denying we ever touched. Pretending this is normal.

*Fine.* Two can play at that game.

"Look at me," I demand.

She snaps to attention, her knuckles white as she grips her own forearms. "What?"

"You don't want to talk about this; I get that. I'll make it simple: just tell me the audition didn't bother you at all, that the job won't be weird. Tell me you have no problem hearing the words 'well and truly fucked' out of my mouth—and every variation on that theme— every time we enter the studio, and I'll let it go."

Her cheeks flush pink. "Seems like *you're* the one who can't handle the content."

"Say it," I whisper.

A huff leaves her mouth. A small empire rises and falls in the time it takes her to speak. "It won't be weird."

"Fine. If you're good, I'm good."

Her gaze flicks between my hands and my face. "Then why does it look like you're about to break the banisters?"

I glance at my hands, which are death-gripping the old wood. "I'm not." I release my hold and put on my best politician smile. If she wants to pretend this is a professional business transaction, I'm happy to oblige. "Okay, Piper. You win. I'll do it."

She pauses a beat, watching me as I stretch my arms overhead. "Really? You're in?"

"And you'll talk to your mother for me. About the campaign endorsement."

She stiffens. "Sam, I can't just—"

I back up a step, putting distance between us.

Her body shifts forward, just enough to betray her panic. "Wait."

"This is your dream, isn't it?" I take another

step backward, and the old wooden stair groans underfoot. "Worked toward it your whole career?"

She steps. "Of course it is."

"So you understand why I need the endorsement. For *my* career."

"I have no control over my mom's opinion of you!"

"You and I both know that's not true. She'd cut off my balls if you told her to."

"Don't say balls."

I arch a brow. "Thought you were fine hearing me talk about any and all—"

"Fine!" She throws up her hands. "You win. I'll talk to my mother. I'll do everything I can to get her endorsement for you."

My shoulders relax. "Really?"

"Yes. *God help us all*, but yes."

Air leaves my lungs like it's been trapped for a century. This was always a long shot. It's still a long shot. But I was able to make Piper see—I think— that the Sidney fiasco wasn't what she thought. Piper now knows she and I were *broken up*. Maybe she can make Catherine understand.

I clap my hands once to clear my head. "All right, then. Let's go."

"She's not even home yet. Relax."

I point over her shoulder. "I meant the studio.

Aren't you going to show me the setup?"

Something shifts in her expression, and she glances over her shoulder. "On second thought, I want to rearrange some things up there to make it more comfortable. Friday afternoon is Mom's baby shower. Not that you'd be interested in *that*, but you could come over right after it ends and take a look before we go to the signing. We'll ride together."

My lips pull into a smile. More face time with the family is *exactly* what I'm interested in. Plus, brunch was more fun than I'd admit to Piper. After a lifetime spent in an empty house—my parents worked all hours of the day when I was younger, and I've lived alone since—the chaos is addicting. Another Bellini party wouldn't be the worst thing.

Her sweater and my shirt create static electricity as she brushes past me, like the crackle of a fleece blanket fresh out of the dryer. I watch as she walks, momentarily distracted by the bounce of her wavy hair. And all right, the way the ends of her hair skim her mid-back, which invites my eyes lower.

I shake off the impulse to stare with a few clomping steps after her. "Will there be cake at this party?"

"There will be a cake the size of a small house, fresh from The Rolling Pin."

"Time?"

"Noon."

"Attire?"

"Wear black. I want it to be a classy affair. But if you're coming to the party, bring a different-colored shirt for the signing. I don't want us matching in our studio picture, and I'll probably wear black to that, too. Bring some different pants options, too, to be safe."

"Fine." I clear my throat. "What about Caleb?"

"Don't worry. Your bestie will be in attendance."

"The only person whose attendance I worry about is Nico's. Be sure to hide the fireworks so we don't have a repeat of brunch." I land beside her, sensing the end of this conversation in the way she guides us to the foyer. "What I meant was, what are we going to tell Caleb? In regard to our project."

Our eyes lock, and she gives me a little shrug. "The truth. That we're working together."

"Nothing else?"

She throws open the front door and pins it with her body. Humid air fills the tiny space. When I meet her eyes, I catch a flicker of guilt. Or maybe it's a reflection of the guilt in mine. Which is silly, because work is work. There's nothing wrong with it, and it has absolutely nothing to do with Caleb.

"Nothing else," she affirms. "The details are under contract, anyway. We'll have to keep it a secret."

# CHAPTER TWELVE

## PIPER

Caleb offers to pick up the cake on his way to the house, saving me an errand. When he struts into the kitchen holding the buttercream creation, it's every bit as decadent as I expected. Georgina decorated the three tiers with sugared flowers. Edible pearls dot the center of each bud.

"This is nicer than my wedding cake," Caleb huffs, lifting it onto the island. He unrolls the sleeves of his black thermal.

Jane is a few steps behind with Kat in her arms. In keeping with the theme, she's in a flowy black dress, sheer tights, and Doc Martens. She unwraps Kat from a blanket, and fluffy black tulle explodes out in every direction. "Our cake was good. The honeymoon room-service chocolate mousse was better."

"*Jane.*" A flush spreads across his cheeks. "Not the mousse."

"I said we ordered it, never specified what we did with it."

He squeezes her at the hip, coaxing her hoarse laugh. "How do I get you to stop talking?"

They continue being gross and in love, so I turn away and snap a picture of the cake with my phone. With so many brothers running around at all times, I learned at a young age to immortalize nice things before they are accidentally trashed. "I'm going to go put on my dress. Don't let the heathens near this perfect cake while I'm gone."

As if on cue, Nico's scream pierces the house, followed by Raf's maniacal laughter.

My brothers and I could care less about the sex of baby number eleven. A Bellini kid is a Bellini kid, and we will love and endlessly tease them either way.

But my brothers *will* trash that cake if it's unattended, and Mom *will* cry.

As I climb the stairs, I daydream about shoving through the frosting and yanking out the colorful innards to spoil the surprise to get it over with. Curiosity could kill the cake today.

I stop in my pantry-sized bathroom at the top of the stairs and pluck my favorite black bra off the hook behind the door. Nothing says *fancy* like a lacy La Perla splurge no one but me will ever see.

The dress I've chosen is draped over my bed. I strip down to nothing and re-dress with the efficiency of a party planner on the clock. My hair is half done when the staircase creaks. Based on the frequency and intensity of the steps, it's Caleb running up. Has the cake fallen victim to my brothers so soon?

"Howdy, partner."

Sam doesn't knock so much as barge into my room, bringing palpable energy and a draft of air from the landing right along with him. He has a Beany Business coffee cup in each hand and a bag slung over his shoulder.

I stare at his reflection in my clawfoot mirror as I hold a curl tightly around my iron. He's in a crisp charcoal polo and a pair of dress slacks that defy my understanding of the human body. How can a garment fit so well? Did he get dressed, or was he artfully poured into the fabric? I clear my throat as I release the coil of hair from the hot wand. "What's in the bag?"

"Change of clothes for the signing, as instructed. Turns out my business partner is picky as hell about what I wear." He sets the cups on my dresser and rids himself of his duffel by chucking it on the bed.

"Make yourself at home," I mutter. "And maybe I just wanted you to have a backup shirt, for when you inevitably spill cake down your front. You're welcome."

He laughs in mock scandal. "I think you have me confused with someone else—a messy eater. Perhaps Caleb, who recently used two slices of pizza as utensils to scoop sticky wings into his mouth."

"Surprised you didn't just feed him the wings yourself. Some best friend you are."

He smirks as he pulls two tiny airplane bottles of Baileys Irish Cream out of his pocket. They look comically small in his big hands. "Brought you a little something. Happy signing day."

My heart skips a beat. *Signing day.* Outside of *we got the gig*, those are the most exciting words I've ever heard. A warmth spreads outward from my core. "Thanks. Surprisingly thoughtful of you."

"I aim to please." His reflection shifts in the mirror as he angles toward the dresser. He pops the lids off the coffee cups and pours a shot in each.

My last curl holds its shape nicely before I switch off the iron. As I play with my hair in the mirror, running fingers through the strands to get them to sit right, Sam's reflection grows larger until he's right next to me.

I watch his movements in the mirror as his hand brushes past my shoulder. "Here you go. For the brains of the operation."

The cup is warm in my hand, even through the

cardboard sleeve. "Does that make you the muscle?"

Light from my bedside lamp hits his face as he cracks a smile, carving out his dimples. "Perhaps."

I wait for him to say something else—to crack a joke about how he's muscles *and* brain or something similarly bigheaded. Instead, his gaze travels up and down the mirror's length. Twice. He takes his time and doesn't even bother to be discreet about checking me out. The brazenness makes my skin flush. "So by wear black, you meant *all* black, huh?" he asks in a quiet murmur.

"Yep. All black," I repeat, because I am the poster child for original thought.

We sip our cups in unison. The silence between us makes me want to crawl out of my skin.

This is the first time we've been in this room together since *back then*. The intensity of this realization washes over me about as delicately as a wave crashing overhead and dragging me through sand. Before I can stop myself, I glance at my bed.

*Crap*. His gaze tracks mine, and now *he's* looking at my bed.

He blinks a few times and turns back to our reflections, his jaw tense.

"Let me show you the studio." I step away from the mirror and throw back another long sip.

"Excellent idea."

I gesture toward the closet door. "That's my closet."

"I remember."

*Right.* I try not to wince as this simple statement hits me like a Mack truck. Of course he knows where my closet is. He's hidden in there more than once, when my parents came a-knocking.

He crosses the room, somehow looking a thousand feet taller than he used to in this space, and ducks down to let himself in.

His voice carries through the open doorway. "Aren't you coming?"

My nose crinkles. "I'm good."

"I don't bite, Piper."

Mostly because I feel compelled to defend my studio equipment, I follow him into the closet. The first thing I do is flip on the light—he was just standing there in the dark, staring at the lone rack of dresses on the far wall—and get as far away from him as possible.

"So, this is my setup. Computer on a tiny table. A stool. One condenser mic and mount, so we'll have to share."

"A practical setup," he offers, crossing his arms.

"For long monologues, we can take turns in here. I'll handle all the computer work—saving, storing, styling, sending—on my own."

"The Four S's."

"How'd you know?"

An amused smirk dances across his face.

"Ah. You just...deduced it."

"This'll be an adventure."

I can't tell if he's being sarcastic, but my default is to assume he is. "I'll try and make it as painless as possible for you."

"I'm a big boy, Piper. I can handle hard work."

Caleb's distant voice echoes up the staircase. It's barely loud enough to pick up in here. "Pipes, where are you? Is Sam up here? His car is outside."

"Caleb!" He trips over the stool in his haste to get out. "Just checking out the studio."

The anxiety in his tone makes me want to hide under my covers for a few minutes.

I would not like to unpack that impulse.

One thing becomes abundantly clear when the party picks up steam and guests crowd the downstairs: All-black attire and "classy" decor was *not* the move for a baby shower.

I thought if everyone wore dark colors, the pop of color when Mom cuts the cake would stand out. I had visions of sparkling water in champagne flutes and Mom wearing her heirloom diamond necklace. An extravagant cake dished out on fancy silver (but still disposable) plates.

It looks like a damn funeral.

I wind through family and friends and track down Sam. He's leaning against the wall in the corner of the living room, eating snacks off a tiny plate.

"I messed up. I need a favor."

Sam's predictably amused by my distress. "What's the rub, Bellini?"

I gesture to a gaggle of people chatting nearby. "All this black. It looks like someone died. This is a disaster. I overheard Dad explaining to his coworkers that everyone is, in fact, alive and well and the theme was merely *his daughter's idea of a good time.*"

He pokes me with a salami-and-cheese roll-up. "This is what you wanted."

"Well, it's depressing."

"What do you want me to do about it?"

"I can't leave." My hands squeeze into fists. Why is this so hard? I should be able to ask him for help, considering our entire working relationship is premised on helping each other. "Anyway, I'd be eternally grateful if you could make a quick run by the store and grab a bunch of colorful stuff. A tablecloth, streamers—whatever they've got. I'll give you my card."

He cuts off mid-laugh when he realizes I'm serious. "Okay, boss. You got it. I'll run to the store. In the meantime, may I suggest a paintball fight? Enzo's been talking about paintballing the last three guys' nights."

"Don't even get me started on guys'—*wait*. That's actually not a bad idea." I bob up and down on the balls of my feet, scanning the room for Enzo. "The paintball thing, not you and Caleb tainting my innocent little brothers under the guise of male bonding."

He chokes on his roll-up. "*Innocent?* Have you *met* your brothers?"

I brush past this, envisioning how paintball could work in our favor. "We can have them make guesses with the paintballs. It'll add much-needed color."

"When will you accept my genius?"

I remove the plate of snacks from his hand. "Store, please."

Once Sam leaves, I track down Enzo and inform him of the plan. Word spreads through the brothers like wildfire. In record time, they're rolling up the basement stairs in more tactical gear than anyone outside the armed services has a right to own.

Aunt Dawn and her children arrive at the party right as my brothers march through the living room, which forces a dramatic about-face so the boys can march back downstairs to get their extra equipment for the cousins. Finally, when everyone who wants to participate is suited up, I corral the growing party to the back porch.

Mom—looking stunning, if not a tad forlorn in a crushed black velvet romper—points at the paintball gear when I drag her onto the porch. "What is this about, Pipes?"

I clap my hands three times and bring them to my mouth, creating a hand megaphone so I can explain to everyone at once. "Shoot one another with green or blue if you think it's a boy, yellow or red if you think it's a girl!"

"Why not pink paint for a girl?" Dawn shouts between noisy slurps of her drink.

"Bellinis, do you have pink ammunition?"

"No!" they shout in proud unison.

I shrug by way of explanation.

They line up at the deck's edge: my brothers who look hell-bent on destruction, several of Dawn's kids, and a few other cousins on my mom's side. Dad's coworkers stay as far away from the porch's edge as possible, whispering to each other while he chants, "Give 'em hell!" To whom that's directed, I'm not sure. Caleb steps onto the porch in time to watch.

I put five fingers in the air and count them off. "Five—four—three—two—"

I don't make it to one. Georgie leaps off the wooden deck and does a dramatic tuck-and-roll. Nico trips on his way off the porch but recovers quickly.

Enzo and Max are whispering conspiratorially as they take off in a slow march. Raf flails his gun wildly around, loudly daring anyone to approach him. Luca takes off without the dramatics of the rest and books it straight for the thick oak tree on the far end of our one-acre backyard. I'm *certain* he's only playing this game as an excuse to peg Enzo for stealing his AirPods.

My cousins share looks suggesting they've miscalculated how seriously my brothers would take this. When Raf points a gun their direction, they scatter like loose change on a dashboard.

Mom snakes her arm behind my back and rests her head on my shoulder. She's a good four inches shorter than me, which has always pleased me. Height is the only thing I have on this superhero of a person. "Clever idea."

The sun shines bright overhead, unobscured by clouds. I start to sweat in my tights. "It was…" I seal my lips. If I tell her paintball was Sam's idea, it may color her opinion of the game—pun intended. "Yeah."

"Thank you for throwing a party. I needed this," she says, giving off a rare hint of sentimental energy. I peek over and find her eyes glassy. Mom is always warm, but it's a businesslike warmth, as in "I will do the absolute most for you because I love you, but also *you're welcome* and if you put one toe out of line, I will ship you to Aunt Dawn's house to clean."

I wrap my arms around her. "I would have thrown a party for the other ones, if you'd have let me."

"I know. You're an angel. I don't know what I'm going to do if this baby is a girl. She's going to have impossibly big shoes to fill."

A lump lodges in the center of my throat. I've thought about this moment a lot—what it would feel like if and when Mom finally had another girl. Each time it didn't happen, she became more convinced it never would. I stopped bringing up the idea of a sister three boys down the line because it didn't matter to me anymore; I love my stinky, annoying brothers. It's wild that at forty-four, she's reckoning with the possibility of another daughter.

Meanwhile, at twenty-four, I am nowhere near where Mom was at my age. She had three kids, a Doberman, and a house to her (and Dad's) name. I've put jobs over dating, singularly focused on building a portfolio and making ends meet. A career and money are crucial variables in the success equation, and when you have debt like I do and no partner to shoulder the bills, they are non-negotiables. But while I've been busy trying to grab a foothold in a vaporous field, the other variables in the success equation have evaded me. A house and family, in this economy?

Had I taken the fast track to domestic bliss like half of my graduating class, I could be married and nearing motherhood. Many of the girls I grew up with are already hitched and popping out babies of their own. Sam's question from the studio lobby rings in my ear. *Seeing someone, then?* Energy crackles inside me.

Competitive energy. I think.

At least he's not married, because if he was...

I shake my head, trying not to indulge the thought. But it's hard to shake the visual of him and some rando planning their Park Plaza wedding, taking a honeymoon in the Caribbean. Smiling like idiots with streaks of sunscreen on their cheeks, clutching colorful cocktails in their hands. The idea of it makes me nauseous enough to clutch my stomach.

Nico races up to the porch's edge with a wail, his face and neck covered in blue paint. "Piper, Raf is cheating!"

I let go of Mom and hop down to the grass. "Where is he? I said no head shots."

"This way." Nico takes off at a speed I don't feel inclined to match. I shield my eyes with my hands and scan the backyard. Kids and teens blur together as they whoosh past. Clouds of paint haze obscure my view. Raf is nowhere in sight. I'm about to give up and let them destroy one another.

That's when the first shot hits me, squarely in the ass.

# CHAPTER THIRTEEN

## SAM

I was aiming for the grass and *not* Piper's ass. Or at least that's what I'll tell her.

It was just too tempting. Hitting her, I mean. Not her ass. Although if we're looking at it objectively, hers is—

"What the hell?" She wheels around, searching for the shooter.

I bite the inside of my cheek. She's been running around this party like a chicken with her head cut off. I figured a paintball break will do her good—put her in the right mindset for our contract signing later. Or, alternatively, it will piss her off so much she'll sulk in her room. Either way, she'll get time to relax before we make a forty-five-minute drive.

Based on the inhuman screech that leaves her mouth, it'll be the latter. She runs her hand through the red paint on the back of her dress. "Who has a death wish?"

I step out from behind Dawn—a terribly ineffective hiding place; she's the size of a string bean—and hop off the porch. "Bold of you to threaten the person with a weapon."

The look on her face when she figures out it's me should be framed and mounted in a museum. Portrait of an enraged Italian. "Sam, what were you thinking? You ruined my dress!"

The scowl on her face is epic. It fuels me. "You haven't even seen it from the back. How do you know it's ruined?"

"I'm going to—"

*Bang.*

I skirt her leg without making contact. Flecks of paint settle on her tights as the ball explodes on the ground beside her.

She flails for a second, cursing under her breath. When she stops scoffing, she sticks out her arm as her brothers zip past. "Luca! Give me your gun."

Luca slides to a stop and barks out a laugh at the sight of her dress. He glances between the two of us, and a smile tugs at his lips as he tosses her his weapon. "This ought to be good."

"Still feeling brave, Hefty?" She aims right at my chest.

She's bluffing. I can see it in her mouth, in the way her full lips twitch. A shot of adrenaline floods my veins. "You don't have the cojones to shoot me, Bellini."

She pulls the trigger and lurches backward at the recoil. Blue paint splatters across my shirt. The blast stings like a bitch. For a brand of gun designed for beginners and sanctioned for kids ages eight and up, I didn't expect it to pack such a punch. Flecks of paint land on the yellow crepe-paper bow tie I made when I was decorating her house with my grocery store haul.

"Not my new bow tie," I gasp, clutching my chest. "How will I go on?"

With a victorious laugh, she points the barrel of her gun at my leg. "Should we call it a day, or should I make it an even two for two?"

I step forward and place my barrel against her chest. My gaze snags there for a few seconds. Her dress fits like a glove, and I'm only human. After too much time has passed, I pull my eyes up to her face.

Her lips twist into a smirk. A Piper smile has always been dangerous. But this wicked half grin on her face, this caught-you-ogling look screams *power*. I tighten my grip on the gun and prod her lightly, right below her collarbone. Right above the swell of a place I'm trying not to notice.

"You wouldn't dare," she whispers sweetly.

I stroke my gun. "If I were you, I'd run."

A squeal leaves her mouth as she darts across the yard. I let her gain speed, knowing damn well I could catch her in seconds flat. Ten, twenty, thirty feet come and go underfoot as I jog, pretending to give it my all. I fire a few strategic shots. One grazes past her arm, one hits her calf—I wasn't trying to make contact, now that I know how badly these "kid" guns sting, but she swerved to change course—and two coat the ground with color.

She turns to shoot me, and I fire reflexively, coating her entire right arm.

*Whoops.*

Her hair is the last thing to disappear as she whips behind a tree.

We are equidistant from the safety of the porch in our current positions. All I have to do is wait her out. Luckily, I know my opponent. She's too impatient to hide for long. My heart drums a wild rhythm in my chest as I watch for her. For being relatively fit, my body is acting like it's never exerted itself a day in its life.

Leaves crunch underfoot as she sprints to safety. She's fast.

I'm faster.

I skirt her ass with another shot as she closes in on the porch. She clutches her side, and her pace slows. Not trying to send her into cardiac arrest, I slow mine as well.

"Wow, Sam and Piper chasing each other and screaming. Where have I seen this before?"

Piper skids to a stop at the sound of Caleb's voice. "What?"

Caleb shrugs. "I'm just saying it's awfully familiar."

She glances over her shoulder, and we lock eyes as red paint blasts the side of her head. Her hands fly above her ears, and she lets out a blood-curdling scream.

"I got her, Sam!" Nico yells.

"Nico, *no*!" I shout.

But it's too late. Piper coughs so hard I worry she'll sprain her ribs. Dust and liquid around her face obscure my view of her. I race to catch up. "Are you all right?"

Caleb lets out a frustrated groan. "Nico, you know better than to land a close shot like that! Especially on the head. You okay, sis?"

I circle Piper's wrist, orienting her to my proximity. Her eyes are pinched shut, and her face is screwed up, like she's crying without tears. "Pipes, can you see me?"

"You had to chase her, didn't you?" Caleb goads. "You two can't be cool for five fucking minutes."

"Not now, Caleb," I snap.

"Stop fighting!" Piper cries, yanking her arm away as she takes a sudden step sideways. Her shin rams into the jagged edge of the porch. She falls, and her right arm catches the brunt of it, scraping wood.

Catherine rushes over, clutching her stomach. "Piper? Oh my God, is that blood? Paint? Both? How can I tell what's blood and what's paint?"

She yelps, her voice shot with pain. "I'm fine, I just can't *see* anything. *Ouch*, my arm. I think I caught a nail."

My gut is rock solid in any emergency, but seeing her in pain sends my gut into a nosedive. A quick plan of action forms in my head as I survey her damages. "Caleb, can you get my medical bag out of the car and throw it on Piper's landing?"

Piper sways sideways when she tries to take a step. "What bag?"

I catch her, winding my arm around her waist and lifting her from the ground. "Oh, just my arts and crafts bag. May do a needlepoint later."

"Put me down! You're so dramatic, I don't need a fireman's carry— *GOD it's like someone is trying to gouge my eyes out!*"

"Yes, please tell me more about how dramatic *I'm* acting."

"Jesus," she groans into my neck. "This is so embarrassing."

"You can't even open your eyes, Piper. We need to flush them out and check your arm."

"*Oh God*, my arm is gushing blood, isn't it? It stings so bad."

"Eyes first. Then arm."

I weave through her house and take the stairs at a jog. Her feet bang against the banister.

Her whimper is as angry as it is sad. "I think they're about to fall out of my head, and you slamming me around doesn't help."

"Sorry, I've got a lot of baggage. A buck twenty of it, at least."

She snorts into my neck, tickling my skin. "You've got baggage, all right— Wait. Are you trying to guess my weight?"

I hit the top landing and attempt to navigate us through the narrow bathroom door. Her ass hits the doorframe.

"My God, you're trying to kill me," she cries as I step back and attempt another angle of entry.

"Sorry, miscalculated the *width*."

"Of my *ass*?"

I lower her into the porcelain bathtub and steady her when she slips on an old puddle of water in the basin. Her eyes flutter for a second, but she keeps them closed. I fumble the handle until water jets out of the showerhead and hits her neck. A nearly feline noise leaves her mouth as she stumbles sideways. "It's pure ice!"

I restrain her under the water. "It's not that cold. We need to get this paint off your injuries."

"It's *freezing*, Sam!"

I grip her waist and reposition her so less of her body is in the water. She blindly gropes overhead until she wraps her hand around the showerhead. "This thing c-comes off. Not trying to freeze to death on top of everything—"

"Okay, okay." The dramatics of this woman. She'd rather bleed out than be cold.

I yank the showerhead off the wall and grasp the nape of her neck. I work my hand through her thick, wet hair so I can get a good grip and apply pressure until she bends at the waist. "You'll feel water only on your head, now. I'm rinsing where Nico shot you," I inform her, aiming the stream carefully.

She stills as the water cascades down her cheek. Red paint swirls with water as it pools in the white tub. I shut the water off when her face is free of paint. "Okay. Let's stand up straighter."

Eyes still shut, she surprises me by actually obeying. I position her so she's facing me and study her splotchy cheeks, quivering eyelids, and red lips. I linger on her lips, making sure they're her usual color. For medical purposes.

As gently as I can, I slide the pads of my thumbs over her eyelids. She trembles at my touch. A flash of unease bubbles in my stomach. "Do they hurt?"

A slow exhale forces her lips to part. The first two words come out in a whisper. "Not as bad as before."

Surrender plays across her features as my thumbs run down her cheeks and lower over her neck. For a brief blip in time, her body is signaling trust. Trust that I'll take care of her in this small way. I'm suddenly desperate to earn it.

My gaze falls to her arm. "Shit. Your sleeve is soaked with blood."

"That explains the burning."

"No it's—it's really covered. Fuck." Visions of past injuries I've seen in the field spark me back to life and fill me with dread all at once. Her hurt arm faced the wall while I rinsed her, so I didn't note the depth of the cut. Eye injuries are always a priority, but I should've moved faster to get to her arm.

Won't make that mistake again.

"This needs to come off. Now. I need to check your cut."

"So dramatic," she grumbles. "*Fine*."

After fighting with the seam of her dress where shoulder meets sleeve, I give up on trying to rip it apart.

New strategy. I grasp the hem of her dress and tear it up and off her body.

"*Wtck Fneig*." Her words are muffled by fabric. When she's finally free, she adds, "How embarrassing for you, struggling so much to get a girl's dress off."

"Please, Piper. That was…" My voice trails off as the chilly air sends goose bumps rippling across her skin.

Her smooth, soft skin. My gaze roams over her perfect chest, full and almost busting out of a bra so revealing I stop breathing for a second. The black mesh fabric shows every inch of her in tinted perfection.

Now would be the perfect time to look away.

But I can't. The image of her hard, perfect nipples sears my brain. To know I've touched them before, taken them in my mouth heats my skin. Would she taste the same as she used to if I ran my tongue across the peak, sweet like that apple soap sitting on the shower's ledge?

*Fuck*, she's delectable.

And I'm an asshole for even thinking about this right now.

I force myself to look at the ground to reset my thoughts. My mind is deep in the gutter at a terrible time. I'm here to clean her up, not check her out so hard I'm practically panting. My best friend's sister is not just off-limits, but off-limits to the second power because we've crossed the line once before.

No matter what my traitorous dick seems to think.

# CHAPTER FOURTEEN

## PIPER

My breathing is fast and jagged like I just ran a marathon.

"...smooth. Some of my best work," Sam mutters hoarsely.

Oh, to be wearing a sports bra. A tank top. Duct tape mummifying my torso. Anything but *this* lacy suggestion of a bra, more mesh than actual fabric.

I suspect he doesn't think I can make out the shape of his face, let alone track his gaze as it roves my chest. But my vision is clear enough, and he's not being discreet. Even as I force my eyes closed again, the heat of his stare singes its way across my skin, my neck, my face.

My balled-up dress hits my feet.

"A towel, please?" I manage, snaking my uninjured arm across my chest.

His tone is all business as he grabs one off a hook on the wall. "Right. Sorry. Let's get you cleaned up. I think you really did scrape a nail."

"Yeah, I slid for home base, coach." I wrap the soft towel around my chest and let my eyes flutter fully open. They sting, but not nearly as bad as before. I tilt my chin down and cringe at the crimson rivulets dripping into the basin. He rotates my arm so I can see the injury's full length.

He glances up, meeting my eye. "You'll need a few stitches."

"*Stitches?*" Bile rises into my throat.

"I'm a pro, Piper. You won't even feel it after the lidocaine."

"You can't— You aren't— Firefighters give stitches?"

"No, but I do. I took a few extra courses after Nico sliced his calf at Caleb's house a while back. Would you believe I've stitched three of your brothers at various times? Four, if you include Caleb."

My jaw falls open. "What the hell goes on at these guys' nights? Is it a fight club?"

He lifts my arm higher. "First rule…"

A strained whine escapes my mouth. "Do stitches hurt?"

"No," he says, clearly lying. "Can you straddle the edge of the tub so I can get to your arm?"

The indignity of this day knows no bounds. I swing my leg over the tub's side and lower myself down. Just another day in my bra and tights, draped over the side of a tub that looks like a crime scene.

Sam ducks into the hallway and returns a second later with a small bag.

I force myself to stare at the grout between two tiles so I don't pass out at the sight of his suture kit. "Are you just going to…dig in?"

Rubber gloves snap into place.

I suck my bottom lip into my mouth. "That's a yes."

"What's your favorite nineties hip-hop band?"

"Huh?"

A tinge of pain pulses up the back of my arm. "Ouch. What was that?"

"The sterilizing agent."

"It feels like I was doused in acid. Maybe I need to go to the ER."

Ignoring my complaint, he continues. "Here comes the pain relief."

"Let's stop—"

He swabs me with a viscous gel. It's cold, and then it burns. "In terms of distraction, do you prefer a song or my three-minute comedy routine?"

My heart pounds against my rib cage. "Oh God. Neither."

"You pick the topic, then."

He rustles in his bag for a while, and my pulse grows erratic. "What are you doing?"

"Waiting for the lidocaine to set in."

I saw my lip between my teeth as dull heat spreads across my arm. "Fine, I've got a topic for distraction. Why are you running for mayor?"

"Row, row, row your boat—"

"I'm serious. You have a job. One you are perfectly adequate at. If you win the election, what happens to your career?"

I feel fingers gather my skin into a tight hold. "I will keep working. Describe what you're feeling in your arm?"

"It feels weird. Kind of warm, but not stinging pain like it was. You'll work two jobs?"

"Absolutely. It's part of my platform, actually."

"How so?"

The second a needle hits my skin, he launches into an impassioned speech to drown out my moan. "Mayors, city council members, elected officials... they should relate to the people they serve. The people I'll serve as mayor work for a living, and so will I. I can scale back to every other weekend if needed, but I intend to stay active on the squad."

I whimper as the needle returns a second time.

"Is that the Piper seal of approval?"

"One belief does not a platform make," I grumble. The needle stings, but it doesn't unnerve me as much as the tugging. So much tugging. Maybe I should have let him sing after all. "What else you got?" I add, voice quivering.

He launches into a spiel about bolstering the community-school partnership by instituting mentorship programs at our alma mater, rent subsidies, investing in a new snowplow, and something about rezoning that's about as painful as the suturing.

"Who's your campaign manager?"

"Sam O'Shea."

"Treasurer?"

"Sam O'Shea, though I'm thinking about firing him."

"This is a lot to take on by yourself. *Why?* Why run now? You're so young. Why not run for captain when your dad retires?"

He goes still. "You don't think I can do it?"

"I didn't say that. It just seems like it would be easier to go for city council first. Build up to mayor."

"If I lose, I'll run for city council in the next election."

"Your logic—it baffles. If it were me, I'd start small and work my way up."

He looks skyward for a full ten seconds like he's summoning the strength to carry on. "I have a bachelor's in political science, Piper. I'm also a paramedic and hold an associate's in fire science. Not to mention kicking Model UN's nerdy ass all four years of high school and participating at the collegiate level. I've served this city in some capacity for the last few years and plan to for the rest of my career. Why *not* me?"

"Being qualified for a job and wanting it are two different things."

"Truth is, being a firefighter is the reason I'm pursuing this at all. I've learned every single second can be the difference between life and death. Emergencies are unavoidable, but when things work the way they're supposed to, lives are saved. A downed tree slowing ambulances because of a budget cut in city maintenance, an accident from unsalted roads because the city didn't make safety a priority, a house fire sparked from faulty wiring because working-class people can't afford an electrician—I can fix that as mayor. As a firefighter, I can only triage."

"That's…a great answer, actually." For the first time since he fessed up to his campaign—or extorted me with it, depending on your interpretation of events—I get the whole mayor thing.

His cheeks flush pink as he globs some medicine

over the center of an enormous gauze pad and bandages the wound. "Finished."

"You're already finished?"

"My favorite line out of a woman's mouth."

I groan.

"If you didn't like that, you would have *hated* my comedy routine."

His pants make a dissonant sound: the beep of my phone coupled with a curt *we be jammin*'!

I roll my eyes. "Your phone is busier than Grand Central Station."

He furrows his brow as he reaches into his pocket. "I have both our phones. I made sure yours wasn't on you before I shot you. Didn't want you to trash yet another phone." His mouth contorts into an unsettling *O* shape as he scans his screen.

"What's wrong?"

He trips over his words trying to get them all out. "It's a group text. 'Hello, this is Mona from Studio 7. I wanted to let you know the Gentrys are six minutes behind schedule. Expected start time: 3:06.'"

My body was not built for this roller coaster. I just got my blood pressure down, and now it skyrockets to a new peak. I scramble to a stand. "You said *four*. Contract signing at *four*. What happened to *four*?"

He's as still as a paint-splattered statue as he checks something on his phone. Without so much as an explanation, he abruptly lobs it into the bathroom sink and yanks off his shirt. The phone hits the basin with a decisive *clunk*.

I throw up my hands in case all thirty-seven of his abs plan to attack me. "What are you doing?"

He reaches for his waistband. "I'm taking off my pants. What does it look like I'm doing?"

"Gah, no, my eyes!"

"I'm leaving on my underwear, but I can't shower in my pants."

"Why—what—"

"I got the time wrong."

My vision of our uber-professional, life-affirming signing event flickers out like a dying bulb. "No. No, no, no. Not our *first formal business meeting*," I moan.

"We can still make it if we move fast." He lunges for the hot water handle, and his chest smacks me into the wall. Once again, I'm hit with a deluge of water as he turns the shower on full blast. I try to crawl out of the tub as he jumps in beside me and aims the showerhead at my my hair.

"What are you doing?" I cry. "Get out of my shower!"

"It's 2:03. I'm trying to get the rest of the paint out of your hair. Unless you want *this* in the publicity photo?" He lifts a matted curl into view.

I wrench my hand around his and attempt to

pry away the showerhead. All this gets me is another face full of water. "I don't"—*spit*—"need your help."

"We don't have time for this. It takes almost an hour to get to the studio, and with their *'they'll-be-six-minutes-late'* secretary accounting for their every second, I somehow doubt they'll be cool if we're late."

I can't answer him; there isn't time. I tilt my head to an unnatural angle to get my head under the water and attempt to rip my curls apart. A spasm shoots across my neck. Red paint streaks down my skin as I grope for the showerhead. "Gimme."

He relinquishes control for all of three seconds before snatching it back. "It's too low when you hold it. If I hold it we can *both* rinse off."

"*Whatever*, just rinse."

"What about your tights?"

My glare could melt the paint off his body. "Don't worry about my tights."

"Fine!" He tilts his head back and stares at the showerhead as his hand butts against the low ceiling. His free hand makes quick work of cleaning his body. His fingers squeegee paint and water off shiny, slick skin. Everything on his body is quarter-bouncing tight. I track the motion of his hand as it grazes his abs. The muscles near his navel are like arrows, pointing down…

*Gah.*

"Stop hogging the water," I snap. "I can't reach my side."

He lowers the sprayer and aims the blast at my hip. "This thing is really convenient. You can literally reach every single part of you—"

His eyes widen, and he snaps his mouth shut. The jet's noise as water slaps my skin is the only sound between us. His lack of blinking as he stares at the showerhead tells me he's aware of what he's implied.

Our gazes meet like two murderous felons across a prison cell. *Guilty.*

"I'm just gonna…" He places the showerhead delicately in my hand.

"Get out of my shower," I whisper, dangerously low.

"Yup." He skitters out of the bathroom, not even pausing when he rams the doorframe with his elbow.

The next few minutes pass in a blur. I grab my clothes off my bed and dress in the closet. When I finally emerge, brush tangled in my hair and makeup in my sweater pocket, Sam is waiting on the landing with my high heels. We are a cloud of shampoo and clean cotton as we run down the stairs.

He skids to a halt in the living room. "Wait."

"No time to stop."

His hand circles mine, pulling me back. "Piper, look."

I crane my neck to track his gaze. A crowd of people is gathered beneath the giant archway separating the living room from the kitchen. Dad's burly arms hold Mom in a supportive embrace. At this angle, I can see her tearstained face resting against his chest and the bright icing coating the cake knife in her hand.

They shift positions, and Mom meets my eye through the crowd. Even without hearing her laugh, her trademark trill rings in my head, clear as day. I rest my hand over the flutter in my chest, wondering if my frantic heartbeat matches hers.

It's a girl.

# CHAPTER FIFTEEN

## SAM

My tolerance for mess is pretty high.

Caleb spilled an entire Coke on my dash once, and I shrugged it off as he soaked it up with his hoodie. A guy from the squad bled all over the back seat last month after he sliced his hand, and I didn't flinch—though I did later disinfect.

However, as Piper's dusty makeup hitches a ride on the AC blast and spreads like shrapnel in every direction, I discover that fine, glittery powders are my breaking point.

"You don't need any more makeup, Pipes." I slam the gas pedal to enter the highway. "Your face looks basically the same either way."

"Aw, bet you tell that to all the girls."

She pulls a black tube from her bag of tricks and leans closer to the mirror. Her lips—freshly painted a deep red—part as she coats her lashes in what appears to be black tar.

I've always wondered if women do that open-mouthed move on purpose or if it's some sort of biological imperative. What would happen if she didn't? Loss of O2?

I can't help but look at her. The mouth move is irritatingly hot, and I can't afford to find another thing about Piper hot, as I just now recovered from the visual of her soaking wet in that see-through bra.

Damnit. There's the visual again, parked front and center in my brain. I don't need more gasoline to fuel these stray thoughts, but boy do I get it anyway. Perky, taut gasoline. The blood pumping south in my body informs me I was wrong. I have *not*, in fact, recovered from the visual.

Time to redirect.

I peek at her again from the corner of my eye. "You look nice. Like you weren't just slaughtered at paintball less than an hour ago, even."

She tilts her head slightly my way, and I catch a glimpse of the thick lashes framing her warm brown eyes. "I don't know if you're serious, but since this day is kind of a dream come true for me and I want to make a good impression, I'm going to choose to believe you. If we're late…" Her words melt into a nervous whimper before adding, "At least I can control my looks."

Interest stirs in my gut. It's rare for Piper to open up to me at all, unless it's in the form of a roast. I tamp down the urge to ask for more. But the more time we spend together, the more I find myself so fucking curious about what goes on in her head.

Now that I've told her about what I want out of my career, I can't help but think it'd be nice to even the score. To learn what's driving her toward this acting goal.

She wraps her hand around her hair and squeezes, dripping water on my center console.

An inhuman sound escapes my mouth. Glitter makeup and *intentionally* soaking my leather? Hard pass. "What are you doing?"

Her expression steels over. "I have to get the water out so I can put it up. What do you want me to do, roll in looking like a wet rat? They're going to take onboarding photos for our studio badge. This is the only way to salvage my appearance."

"You have to flood my car to put up your hair?"

"Don't be so dramatic. I'll wipe it up later. Besides, you're the reason we're late."

She has a point, and the guilt pricking my skin reminds me of that fact.

A quiet hiss escapes her mouth as she ties her hair in a low bun. She pulls a few tendrils of hair free on both sides of her head, near her ears.

"You okay? Is it starting to ache where he hit you?"

"It doesn't feel great. At least the bruise is mostly out of sight." She tugs another wave free as she consults the mirror, wincing slightly. "Completely, when I cover it like this."

I swerve and overcorrect the car, completely distracted by the curve of her neck.

She levels me with a look, equal parts sexy and smug as hell. "Eyes on the road, O'Shea."

I scowl, gluing my gaze to an ancient Dodge Neon three car lengths ahead. If I had to throw one back every time she caught me staring at her today, I'd be plastered.

It's not purely a testament to the way she looks. My eye is drawn to her the way it's drawn to flames in a hearth. You can't sit in a room with a fireplace and not acknowledge it or feel the ambient heat. Sometimes Piper spits pure fire, specifically when she's talking to me. Other times, when I see her interacting with others like I did today at Catherine's party, it's something softer. Warmth.

We pull into the parking lot with a minute to spare. I scramble out of the car and make it halfway to the door before I turn around and find Piper lagging. She's using the car for balance as she tugs on a heel. Her sweater slides off her shoulder, displaying her lightly tan skin. Her cherry red lipstick looks incredible, but I sure as shit won't tell her that.

My gaze travels a little south. God, the woman can wear a skirt. But I don't make the mistake of lingering like I did earlier. Not when there's a perfectly good parking lot to feast my eyes on. I zero in on a pothole a few feet left of Piper. In my periphery, I see her bend to grab the onboarding paperwork off the front seat.

"Do you need help?" I press impatiently. "What's the holdup?"

Huffing out a breath, she kicks it into high gear. "I'm going as fast as I can. Can you not stress me out further? I'm trying to savor this experience."

"Probably should've gotten here earlier, then. Hard to savor when you're so stressed."

"You're the one who got the time wrong!"

Not only did my joke not land, it exploded in orbit. I lift my hands defensively. "Sorry, Pipes. Savor away."

The truth is, I'm not sorry. Getting a rise out of her gets a rise out of me. If we can't have real conversations, I'll settle for the next best thing. And it lights me up when she takes everything I say so damn seriously. Even when her eyes go wide at my shitty jabs and she looks like a cartoon villain out for my blood, I still have her attention.

I hate that I want her attention at all. But it's an impulse I can't seem to shake.

She shoves through the studio door before I can open it for her. I follow behind, tugging at my collar. A woman named Mona, otherwise known as the woman responsible for my text-induced heart attack an hour ago, chats with Piper. I catch every other word— *onboarding, documentation, excited, signatures*—but my attention is mostly on how happy Piper sounds when she talks to literally anyone but me.

Mona leads us back to a tiny conference room. Darla and Damien are whooping it up about something when we file into two seats at the round table. Their good nature lightens the room, but Piper seems to be immune to *light* today. Her shoulders creep up to her ears, and she looks like she's holding her breath.

Darla flashes a thousand blinding white teeth. "How y'all doing today?"

The formality and the conference room setting calm me. This will be my favorite part of campaigning—conversations. Roundtables. *People.* I lean across the table and shake both of the Gentrys' hands. "Great. The traffic gods favored us today. And yourselves?"

"Oh, fine. Had a nice, busy morning. Some light technical issues, but that's the job," Damien adds, smoothing a hand over his beard.

Something tells me it was precisely six minutes' worth of technical issues. *3:06.*

"And you, Piper?" Darla asks.

"I'm well, thank you," Piper squeaks, sounding like her voice box is trapped in a choke hold, the tone a far cry from the honey she was spoon-feeding Mona at the desk. She's in her head, but why? We've already secured the gig.

"If you'll give me a moment, I'm printing extra copies of the contract. We just got the printer back online," Darla informs us as she busies herself on an iPad. Damien rolls his chair to the corner of the room where an ancient printer lurches at a snail's pace.

Under the table, Piper's leg vibrates as she bobs it up and down. Her nervous energy sets me on edge. I reach blindly under the table, and my palm lands somewhere on her thigh. I only intend to squeeze once so she knows I can feel her frantic legs about to take flight, but she stills at the contact and whips her head toward me, wide-eyed. A jolt shoots through my palm, zipping up my arm. I subtly retract my hand so as not to flag Darla's attention.

Touching her was definitely *not* the move, even with innocent intentions.

Piper has a catalog of looks, and the one on her face right now headlines page one—*what the hell are you doing, idiot man?* You'd think I typed in the nuclear code and smashed "launch" with the same damn hand.

She slides her chair away from me under the guise of needing to cross one leg over the other. Her cheeks flame red.

When the pages are finished printing and fresh contracts lay in front of us on the conference table, Darla invites us to follow along as she explains the high points. Unfortunately, I can't focus on a single word she's saying. I'm too busy taking my own pulse and wondering if Piper is going to cut off my hand later for touching her.

"Do you have any questions?" Darla asks after leading us through.

Piper looks to me, and I give her a reassuring nod. This is her arena. She runs this show.

"Er—I think we've covered everything I needed to know," she says with a hint of uncertainty in her tone. "My questions were mostly centered around timing, and we went over that in depth."

Darla leans back in her chair and shoots me a look across the table. "And you, Sam? Any questions or concerns we can clear up for you before we sign?"

Mona slides into the room with a camera in her

hand. "Ready for the first website photo, Mrs. Gentry?"

*Website photo.* That's more than an onboarding headshot.

Piper straightens even more in her chair, and her eyes do that *oh shit* thing.

"Sam?" Darla asks, this time with her brows raised. "Questions?"

The heat of several sets of eyes on me spurs me into action. Surely Piper read it through and wouldn't sign something that isn't fair. That'll have to be enough, since I can't concentrate to save my life today. "I'm good. Let's do this."

"Wonderful." Darla beams, gesturing for us to sign. "Mona, grab a photo of them making it official. Actors love that for the ol' scrapbook."

Piper reaches a shaky hand for the black pen in front of her. I follow suit, grabbing a matching one from a cup in the center of the table. I sign my name like I have hundreds of times before, carving cursive letters into the thick paper. When Piper finishes and peeks over at me, a bright flash fills the room.

The deal is sealed with a photo finish.

No turning back now.

# CHAPTER SIXTEEN

## PIPER

Of all the gin joints in all the towns in all the world, I'm spending tonight at my trash-hole alma mater, Hamilton Junior-Senior High School.

The Hamilton Hootenanny is the biggest fundraiser the Roseborough School System has ever held. The district is raising money for a new rec building with fancy indoor turf and state-of-the-art gym equipment. Holding the event in this ancient gymnasium seems like a calculated move to convince people of how badly the money is needed. On the fence about donating? Have a seat on the bleachers and experience the splintery wood beneath your thighs while you mull it over.

I arrive fashionably late with Nonna and five

of my brothers in tow—the ones interested and/ or old enough to attend something like this—and unleash them into the sizable crowd. Principal Bellini is manning this ship, and someone has given him a hands-free microphone to wear around his head like a half-time performer at the Superbowl. He's greeting people at top volume under a messy THIS DANCE FLOOR IS SQUARE banner hanging from the rafters.

Nonna and I lug our food contributions for the cook-off over to the contest table. My schedule the last three days has been recording shifts with Sam in the morning and laboring in the kitchen with Nonna in the evening. The Bellinis are entering five total dishes in the cook-off: Fra Diavolo for the bravest culinary adventurer, Italian Wedding Soup that makes Olive Garden's taste like dirty sock water, enough struffoli to feed an army, cannoli that turned soggy on us, and a metric ton of my secret-recipe eggplant parmesan. If we don't win at least an honorable mention on one of these dishes, Dad's going to be forced to revoke our Italian card and hide his face in shame.

After three straight days sidestepping Sam in the closet studio—while very much ignoring the shower we took together in our underwear—I'm just glad to be out of the house. And as always, I'm looking forward to a chance to spend girl time with Jane. She was volun-told by her principal at the elementary school to work the cornhole booth. Her text to me read, "At least I'll get a night out of the house" with sixteen emojis, so I don't suspect she's too broken up about the commitment.

Nonna carries the featherlight cannoli tray over to the food table while my wrists quake on either side of the stockpot. I deposit my burdensome load next to the other main courses.

In the time it takes to run to the parking lot, retrieve the rest of our dishes, and fill out the contest information sheet, a crowd has gathered at the gym's north end, where two giant tanks of water sit side by side.

I find Jane on the west end, collecting tickets in exchange for cornhole bags. "Hello and happy hootenanny. Didn't know dunking booths were still a thing."

Jane's gaze flits across the crowd before she greets me. "Apparently so. More importantly, how's my favorite Bellini sister doing this evening?"

"Only Bellini sister, until next month. You look nice. Where's your bandana and jean cutoffs?"

"I told you in the text." She smooths her silk shirt. A long and perfectly straight ponytail falls over her shoulder. "I'm treating this like a night *out*."

"As you should. Are you working this thing alone?"

As if on cue, two women run toward us, waving their arms and squealing.

"Here come the other second grade teachers from my school." Jane waves. "That's Melissa in blue and Shay in yellow. They're wild. *Especially* Melissa."

"They're almost ready to drop the hotties," a breathless Shay manages to get out as she slaps her hands on the table. "Melissa's kid is on the way to cover for you two so you can come with us, Janey."

Melissa, decked out in a risqué keyhole blouse and jeans, nods. "Yeah, he'll be here in a minute. It's *go time*, ladies."

I look to Jane for some kind of understanding and find her watching me carefully. "Piper and I will watch the booth. You all go ahead."

Jane's twitchy mouth sets off my radar. I narrow my eyes. "What's going on?"

Melissa, a cool foot shorter than me, grasps my shoulders. "Girl. RTFD versus RTPD. Hosers against Badges in the dunking booth. Every time they get dunked, they donate to the school. Hottest men in this crap town. I made my son teach me how to pitch for this." She mimics a surprisingly smooth baseball pitch, and I catch the waning gibbous view of her chest. Almost a full moon of cleavage.

The letters R-T-F-D prickle my skin. My panicked mind flashes to Sam in his uniform. If he were going to be at an event he knew I was attending, he would have mentioned it. No way he missed the fruits of my cook-off labor scattered on the counters every time he stopped to chat with Nonna after our recording shifts.

He won't be here. Must be some other "hosers" getting dunked.

"It's not only men on those squads; let's not pigeonhole," Jane says, her eyes still trained on me.

"Oh, totally. No pigeonholing intended." Melissa stands on her tiptoes and cranes her delicate neck toward the crowd. "Both squads have all kinds of hot people. But I'm saving *my* tickets for my future firefighter husband."

My gaze wanders back to the tank. "Your fiancé is a firefighter? What's his name? Maybe I know him."

"She's joking," Jane says in a warning tone usually reserved for silencing Caleb's antics.

Melissa's laugh is a shrill bark. "Oh, Sam's not my fiancé. Believe me, I've tried. And I'll keep trying for a date. Or I'll climb him like a tree—whatever he's up for."

A hoarse cough bursts from my mouth, the kind that makes your throat seize up. The only remedy is more coughing. My face heats as all four women watch me struggle.

"Piper, you all right?" Jane asks.

When I manage to recover some of the wind to

my lungs, I squeak out a reply. "Sure. Totally fine."

But I'm not. Every time I slip into begrudging acceptance that Sam is back in my life, I am confronted with a fresh hell.

Today's flavor: Sam, a local celebrity so hot, teachers want to *climb* him.

I crack my fingers at my side, one at a time. So what if Sam is genetically gifted? This isn't new information. I saw almost every inch of him in the shower, soaking wet. I know what he's working with.

*Don't think about the shower.*

A chubby teenager clutching three bags of Doritos in his fist strolls up to the table. "I'm here."

"Hallelujah." Melissa offers him a high-five. "Take tickets for cornhole, and we'll be back in twenty. Let's go, ladies."

Jane chews the inside of her cheek. "You want to, Pipes?"

I grit my teeth and pray it comes across as a smile. "No harm in checking it out, I guess."

We follow as Melissa sprints to the nearest dunk tank. At the start of what appears to be the first round, an officer in a navy-blue tee and basketball shorts climbs up the ladder on the left side of the massive tank. He scoots his scrawny bottom across the drop plank until he's dead center. Still waters lurk beneath him.

On the tank's right side, a firefighter materializes

from behind the tank in a black shirt and shorts. He takes his seat and folds his hands behind his head before winking to the crowd. No shortage of cocky firefighters in this town. I recognize this one from my visit to Sam's lounge.

Melissa whistles at my side. "Forrester is hot, but I'm waiting for Sam."

"Sam's not even here," I snap.

Out loud, apparently. Even though it wasn't my intention.

Melissa's brows raise to the rafters. "You know him?"

"Know him, I do." *Rein it in, Yoda.* "I mean, yes. We go way back."

Shay speaks over Melissa's head. "Forrester has a pretty long line. Someone'll dunk him, and we'll reap the benefits. That man is sinfully built." She pulls a metal water bottle from her purse and presses her berry-stained lips around the opening.

"Shay." Melissa extends a grabby hand. "Share the wealth."

I elbow Jane in the ribs. "Is that liquor?"

She snorts. "Spoken like a true non-educator. Rule number one: never ask what's in a teacher's bottle."

Melissa takes a sip, closes the bottle, and pretends to pitch it in slow motion at the dunk tank.

I don't know about the bottle rule, but I do

know a teacher who's *thirsty*.

"So what's the deal with you and Sam, Pipes?" Jane whispers.

"What do you mean?"

The first two pitchers position themselves behind a line taped on the ground. They toss their softballs at the targets in almost perfect unison. Both miss. The crowd offers a collective groan of disapproval as Forrester and the cop throw a few air punches in jest.

"C'mon, Caleb isn't here. We can talk freely about Ol' Hefty."

I cackle, immediately transported to our sweet-pea-smelling freshman dorm. "That nickname was some of your finest work."

She smiles in self-defense. "And if Sam ever asks, I'll deny it with my whole chest. That was before I knew the guy. Though Caleb would probably be way more mad about it. You know how those two are. Their friendship is the brototype."

"Caught in a rad bromance." Another shooter misses the target. The thud of a ball striking the tank's wall makes me flinch. "Things are eternally weird between Sam and me."

*Crack.* The perfect shot lands, and Forrester goes plummeting into the water. He flails behind the clear plastic wall for only a second before his body shoots to the surface. His shirt clings to his frame. A few feet away, Melissa hyperventilates.

"I know you were content to ignore him, but obviously that's out the window with you two working together. Give me the dirt. Is it different being around him after all these years?"

"Let's just say I miss the great separation of Sam and Bellini State. Simpler times."

"Do you? You can be honest. I've gotten to know him pretty damn well the last two years since moving in with Caleb. He's actually a good guy."

"Figured you felt as much." I work hard to keep my tone neutral. "You made him Kat's godfather, after all."

She worries her lip into her mouth. "I wanted to tell you sooner. But you haven't mentioned him in years, and Caleb waved it off like a nonissue."

"It is." I yank on her ponytail lightly. "A nonissue. He'll be *great* in that role."

And the unsettling part of this admission? I actually mean it.

She beams. "So we're good, right?"

Her sweetness cracks open the shell I'd like to crawl inside of. "Of course, Janey. Though it is a little weird, learning all this stuff I missed while I was still in the city. You know more about Sam than I do these days. Not that I care."

"Happy to answer any questions you may have."

She peeks sideways. "Not that you care."

Curiosity claws at me.

"Maybe *one*," I note in a would-be casual voice, if I could-be casual. "What does he do in his free time, besides being Caleb's emotional support peacock?"

The corners of her mouth take a devilish turn upward. "You mean does he *date*?"

After a long pause, I finally relent. "No. Yes. I don't know."

"He dated one girl seriously since I've been with Caleb. Alexandria."

Melissa—who I had no idea could hear us— invites herself into the conversation. "Alexandria? The Pats cheerleader Sam dated?"

Her statement hits like nails on a chalkboard. "Sam dated a *Patriots Cheerleader*?"

"Oh don't worry, she only cheered for like two seasons. Once she got into med school, she had to quit that shit," Melissa says.

"Good to know," I finally manage as Jane's stare forms a dent in the side of my face.

Melissa shrugs a bony shoulder. "He dumped her. And since Alexandria is a tall redhead and I'm blond and short, I choose to believe that means she wasn't his type, and thus I am."

Raucous cheers echo from the rafters. I drag my eyes to the tank in time to see my unreasonably tall, cheerleader-dating *business partner* mount the ladder.

"There's the future mayor, reporting for duty," Melissa hollers. Her voice cuts through the noise, and I can tell Sam hears it. Even from here, I can see the flush spreading across his neck. This man lives at the cross section of Commands Attention Ave and Easily Embarrassed Lane.

Adrenaline pulses through my veins as the crowd grows even noisier. I want to look away, but my eyes are too busy Mars-rovering Sam from top to bottom, exploring the snug fit of his black shirt and the shorts clinging to him like a glove. I study his long legs, the line of his calves, and the way he can't seem to make eye contact with anyone without breaking out in even more of a blush. He scoots into the seat's center and waves at a pack of kids pointing at him.

My breath catches in my chest, and the noise fades to a cinematic hum. It's like I'm seeing him through everyone else's eyes for the first time.

And it's *impressive*.

"Show time," Melissa squeals. Shay hops out of her way as she takes off for the line.

I grab Jane's wrist. "Give me your tickets."

Jane fumbles with her purse and pulls out a crisp strip of ten. "Oh hell yeah. Who needs to buy food when—"

"Thanks." I yank them from her hand and take off.

Some careful maneuvering gets me in line on Sam's side, five people deep.

At the front of the RTPD line, a woman leads her daughter forward and trades five tickets for one softball. The volunteer winks and gives the little girl three. The officer watching from his seat above the water laughs, googly-eyed for his family. He knows damn well his daughter isn't going to hit the target, but she'll look adorable trying.

Meanwhile, over here on the set of Girls Gone Feral, Melissa cups her hands around her mouth. "Oy, Mr. February!" She circles her arm a few times like she's warming up. "Ready to get wet?"

I bark out a noise somewhere between a laugh and a cry. I break away from the line and thrust Jane's tickets at the volunteer. "One, please."

I make the grave error of looking up as soon as the volunteer places the softball in my hand. Sam spots me, and I freeze, caught red-handed.

A smirk breaks out on his face that could be seen from space. He gives me a finger-wiggling wave before cocking his head to the side. "Hi, Piper."

How does seven simple letters incite violence in my gut? I close my fingers around the softball and squeeze. Melissa and the other girls duck out of the way as I stomp over to the taped line on the ground.

"Count down from three!" the volunteer chirps.

Sam's eyes haven't left me, which I know because mine haven't left him. I finally tear my gaze away—I can't dunk him with sheer will alone—and set my sights on the target.

"3...2..."

*A freaking NFL cheerleader.*

"1..."

The ball leaves my hand and sails way past the target, clear into foul territory. A volunteer lunges sideways to avoid getting hit.

I look down at my shaky hand and back up at him. How did I mess up so badly?

Melissa nudges me aside with her hip. "Pardon me, babe."

The crack of the ball when Melissa hits the target is louder than the shot heard round the world. The seat splits, and Sam's arms fly overhead as he falls into the water.

The catcalls as he resurfaces come from all over. Sam moves his hair off his forehead as his wet shirt creates a topographic map of his muscles. Melissa puts her fingers in her mouth and emits the perfect wolf whistle.

I turn on my heel, and I don't stop moving until I find Nonna in the bleachers. The only people who look more miserable than I feel right now are the square-dancing teenagers.

Her gaze is fixed on the food table until she spots me. "What's wrong, preferita? You looked piqued."

I plop down beside her, and the bleacher shakes in objection. "Have they called the cook-off winners yet? I'd like to get out of here."

"Soon, I hope."

I barely have time to collect my thoughts before Sam approaches, a towel wrapped tightly around his hips. Water drips onto his shoulders, soaking into the dark fabric of his shirt. "You all right? I got out of the tank, and you were gone."

"Sam! My goodness, you'll catch pneumonia. Do you have dry clothes?"

Sam drops to a seat on Nonna's other side, creating a human buffer between us. "I do, Julia, thank you for asking. Did you hear about your dishes yet?"

"Not yet."

"I'm sure you'll make a clean sweep of it. They'll have to change the rules next time to prevent you two from winning everything."

I stare numbly ahead, pretending not to hear his lavish praise.

"Pipes," Sam continues, peering past Nonna. "Would you like to come out with us tonight?"

Hairs prickle on my arms. "Who's us?"

"Me and the guys, Jane and her friends, Caleb if he can find a sitter. We're going to play pool at Jenson's."

"Jane didn't mention it."

"She probably didn't know. Melissa and Forrester set it up about twelve seconds ago."

"*Melissa*, eh?"

Nonna looks like she's watching a game of tennis, neck turning to keep track of the conversation.

Sam's left dimple appears. "Sure. Among others."

I lean back and plant my elbows on the bleacher behind me. "I can't. I've got to drive Nonna home."

"Nonna drives every day of her life," Sam reminds us both as he leans back to mimic my position. "Right, Julia?"

Nonna peeks at me over her shoulder. "Yes. The boys can help me get the leftover dishes back to the car. Piper, you should go out. You haven't had fun in—"

"Please don't finish that sentence."

Sam wipes a few fresh drops of water off his cheek. "Need a ride? Hey, maybe while we're there we can use a cue ball to practice your throw."

I narrow my eyes. "Moderately good looks, but with such a terrible personality…"

Nonna smacks me with her book. "Be nice."

Sam stands up, lips twisted in a smile. "Can't have it all, I suppose."

# CHAPTER SEVENTEEN

### SAM

Melissa passes out tequila shots for two straight hours at Jenson's, a cheap pool bar in Littleton. The smoky air and general dinginess of the place become less noticeable the longer we stay. Or maybe the more we drink.

Jane is the only one not drinking, on the grounds of being a mother allergic to hangovers. That hasn't stopped Melissa from trying to force-feed her drinks and yelling "pump and dump"—*the fuck?*—on a loop until Jane pries shots out of her hand and sneaks them to me. One man's trash is another man's tequila.

I've had a lot of tequila.

It's been a while since I've let loose this way. Outside of Roseborough city limits, away from potential voters or people who know my dad, I feed the urge to have fun for once. Energy courses through my limbs like I'm plugged in.

A few feet ahead under the glow of a low-hanging light, Piper leans her forearm against a vintage jukebox. The visual is very "1960s middle America." I half expect a waitress to bring her a malt sandwich or whatever it was the grease-lightning kids ate.

She looks calm. Much calmer than when she tried to drown me back at the dunk tank.

Calm is boring.

I drag my pool cue in her direction and thump the ground next to her foot. Her sweet scent is thick in the air. "Hi."

She cocks her head toward me. "Oh. Hi."

"*Oh. Hi.*"

"Come here to mock me, Hefty?"

I slide between her and the jukebox, knocking her arm aside. She stumbles and grabs my cue for support. My attention falls to her lips as she scowls and steps backward.

"If you wanted to play pool with me," I say, shaking my cue and squinting an eye, "you just had to ask."

She chews the inside of her cheek. "You're drunk."

"Am not."

"Good one."

"Play pool with me."

She exhales. "You want to play on my team?"

"That wouldn't be a fair game at all, hustler. We'd destroy these people."

A smile curves her lips. Excitement ripples through me at being the one to cause it. "What'd you have in mind?"

I cast a quick look at the nearest table, where our crew is congregating. "You and Jane, me and Melissa."

She shoves past me to resume her jukebox flipping. A Fleetwood Mac song wraps, and another begins. "Nah, I'm all set."

"You've been avoiding me all night," I point out.

"No I haven't. I've been avoiding Melissa."

"Why? What's wrong with Melissa?"

She pokes a button with her finger, and something mechanical happens on the other side of the glass. "Oh, nothing. She's bubbly, fun, and *desperately* trying to fuck you. What's not to love?"

My pulse kicks up a notch at the sound of the words *fuck you* on her tongue. "What did you say?"

"You heard me, Sam."

I study her, stuck on her fidgety hands as she jabs more buttons. Is it jealous jitters, or does she dislike Melissa for some other reason? The moment drags as I suss her out, examining her profile, trying to decipher what she's thinking.

Deciding if it should matter what she's thinking.

The tightening in my chest betrays me. It tells me I care *a lot* whether she's jealous. The feeling is strong and insistent. It toes a line I never planned to cross.

She tilts her head slightly my way, and her gaze meets mine for a fraction of a second before snapping back to the machine. Her body language is louder than her silence.

Seems I'm not the only one who's curious.

"Melissa likes to flirt," I explain. "She's like that with everyone."

"Charming. Anyway, no pool for me."

Melissa slinks through the crowd, heading our direction. When she calls my name, Piper huffs out a frustrated breath. I'm not proud of the way her irritation satisfies me.

"Hey, party people." Melissa loops her arm around my waist. "Are we having fun?"

"Tons," Piper mutters.

Melissa guides me toward the nearest pool table, where Jane, Shay, and three guys I invited from the squad are fighting over teams.

Melissa stretches her arms overhead. "I've got a proposition for you, Mayor O'Shea."

*Mayor O'Shea.* Hearing that thrills me, even though I feel more *Tipsy O'Shea* right now.

Piper materializes at my side, arms crossed. "He's not—he hasn't won yet."

Melissa either doesn't hear Piper or gives zero fucks. "I sink every stripe on this table in a row, and you take me out on a date," Melissa declares. "No strings attached; pure fun."

A hush falls over our group. Forrester hums a low whistle and rounds the table, plucking a cube of blue chalk off the edge. "Damn, Mel. You take no prisoners." He buffs the end of his stick and offers it to her, a mischievous gleam in his eye.

My brows arch skyward. Maybe there's a little truth to what Piper said about Mel after all.

I glance at Piper—who is staring at the green felt, lips pulled in a tight grimace—and back at Mel. "There's no way you can sink all those. Especially when you're floating in liquor. Sink…float…see what I did there?"

She bends over the table and sinks the nine without hesitation. "And do you see what *I* did there?"

Piper roars to life at my side. "*Wait*. It's no fun to play alone. How about a friendly competition?"

I nearly sprain my neck to look at her. "Competition?"

"If I win," she continues, "Sam babysits Kat one night so Caleb and Jane can have a date night."

I'm about to open my mouth to say I'd do that for free when the full weight of Piper's words knees me in the balls. She's cockblocking Melissa. A surge of energy grips me and squeezes. Piper knows she'll win—she's a fucking shark. My mind flies back to all those times she'd run the table in her aunt's basement. The same nights she'd tease me with kisses or touches when Caleb would run upstairs or turn his back. The days before he knew about us.

The energy morphs into pure heat, traveling south. My defenses are low from the tequila, and every word and look passed between us feels loaded tonight. I've got to stop drinking. With Piper, I need my wits about me.

Melissa flicks her short hair for no reason because it doesn't go anywhere. "Sounds like a win-win scenario to me. Someone's getting a date." She hinges over and sinks the ten with ease.

The eleven is awkwardly wedged between two other balls. She strikes it hard, and it ricochets off the wall and rolls into a side pocket.

My stomach twists into a knot. Maybe she's better at this than Piper realized.

Doesn't matter. Pipes will win.

"O'Shea, what're you going to wear on your date? Need to borrow something that isn't black or gray?" Forrester asks, sidling over to squeeze my shoulders.

I stroke my chin, pretending to consider. Forrester slaps the back of my neck.

I flinch. "Sorry, just thinking about which of your Tommy Bahama shirts would fit me best."

"Twelve," Melissa announces. The bright ball flies into the corner pocket.

Piper meets my eye across the table as Melissa attempts a trick shot, no lean, one-handed.

*Hustler.* I mouth it, almost letting it out as a whisper.

She rolls her eyes. I wink in response, and it earns me a laugh I can't hear in this noisy place. But in another sense, I *can*. The sound rings in my head, a memory that doesn't feel so distant. I want to box it and save it for when things are different tomorrow. When I'm sober and we're back to professional tolerance.

"Rats," Melissa cries. The thirteen ball misses the pocket by a narrow margin.

Shay drags her attention away from Forrester to tease her friend. "Got cocky, eh Mel?"

Jane shoves Piper forward. "You're up."

Piper rounds the table's corner, and I offer her my cue. Pinching a cube of chalk between two fingers, she puts on the fakest look of confusion I've ever seen and holds the chalk up to the light. "Does it need this?"

It does. And she damn well knows it.

I shrug a shoulder. "Might as well."

She fumbles it at first but manages to get a good dusting when Melissa looks away. "One ball, corner pocket." The ball dips into the pocket. "Oh my gosh, wow! Yay!"

I shoot her an ixnay at the overreaction. *Scale it back.*

She overcorrects by pretending to struggle to line up the two-ball shot. The perfect ricochet earns her a clap from Forrester. "Damn, Bellini. You're as good as your brother."

She taps her bottom lip. "Caleb is really good."

Forrester watches her with a spark in his eyes as the three shoots straight down the side into the corner pocket. I know that look.

I grind my teeth until I feel a hit of tension in my jaw. *Not happening, asshole.*

Forrester opens his mouth to speak again, and I cut him off. "Hey Pipes, what ever happened with the cook-off? Did Nonna call or text?"

Piper glances up, meeting my eye across the table as the cue slides through her fingers. *Four ball, corner pocket.* "She did. The eggplant parmesan won first place. Fra Diavolo took third..."

"Not a full sweep?"

The five flies into a side pocket. "...and the soup took second."

"Atta girls. No one else stood a chance."

Jane shoots me a look across the pool table, and all at once I remember myself.

*Relax, idiot.*

"Wait a damn second," Mel says, padding toward Piper with a full drink sloshing in her hand. "Are you less drunk than me or just really good at pool?"

Pipes perches on the table's edge and winds the stick behind her back. With a single glance over her shoulder, she runs the six all the way down the wall into the corner pocket.

Forrester and Shay yell out some variation of, "Oh shit."

She hops off the table and turns around, smiling softly. There are only a few balls on the table, but they're clustered, leaving only one good way to play the seven. The hairs on my arm jump to attention as she crosses to my side of the table. It's narrow on this side, no wiggle room with the wall behind us and the table in front of us.

Wordlessly, she taps the ground near my foot with the stick. I wait for her to verbalize what she wants, but she chews on her bottom lip and stares me down, apparently fine to wait me out.

I've got time.

"Are you going to move or not?" she finally snaps.

My lips curve into a smile. "Consider me a handicap."

"*Fine.* Stubborn ass."

A thrill of electricity shoots up my spine as she brushes past me and drapes herself diagonally on the table, her ass sliding against the side of my leg. As soon as she's steady, I bump her with my hip.

She glares over her shoulder. Her bent over in front of me is already destructive enough without her *looking* at me while she does it. My blood trips as I grasp to get a hold on my thoughts.

Her arm cocks back, and the cue strikes my ribs. Forced into motion, I fall forward against the table, bracketing her. "You're making it look too easy."

Adjusting her hold, she tilts her head to look at me as she takes the shot blind. "Guess I better make it hard, then."

The seven ball soars into the side pocket as I step away from her. Jane cheers like she's won the lottery.

Right. Babysitting. No date with Melissa for me. Relief wells in my chest. Though if the pent-up frustration fucking with my head lately is any indication, a no-strings-attached date with Mel—or anyone, really—is what I need.

Forrester's eyes are about to bulge out of his head. "Damn, Piper is a ringer."

Melissa strings a few curse words together. "There go my plans for us, Sam." She leans on the table, the line of her cleavage nearly swallowing the fifteen ball. "Though we don't need a pool game wager in order to hang out. You have my number."

"Speaking of numbers, how about giving me yours, Piper?" Forrester interjects. "You can help me improve my game."

I turn my back to Forrester, blocking him from Piper. "She doesn't have one."

Forrester pokes his head around me. "You don't have a phone number?"

Piper holds my gaze, her expression cryptic. Guarded. I stare back, irritation swelling as music pulses in the background. Does she *want* to give him her number?

"Yeah, what happened to my number, Sam? Did I gamble it away at the casino? Lose it in the war?"

I open and close my mouth, once again at a loss for words. My inability to form a response knocks me off-kilter. I'm usually quick on my feet—I'm trying to be a *politician*, for Christ's sake. But Piper brings out a side of me I don't know or understand.

"I'll give you mine, then." Forrester extends a hand. "Anyone got a pen?"

"I do," Melissa offers, practically hurling a Sharpie she rustled from her purse at him.

Forrester slides past me and reaches for Piper's hand. He scrawls his number in thick black ink on her palm. My fists clench as he blows a puff of air across it.

I tear my gaze from her, and it's like a suction cup releasing. "Classy move, Fore. Permanent marker. She's going to have to scrub that off to get rid of it."

"Why would she want to get rid of it?"

"*Why would she want it permanently on her skin?*"

"Guys." Jane's sharp voice cuts across the noise. "It's past midnight, and the forecast calls for hail by one a.m. We should settle up."

"Y'good to drive, Jane?" Melissa slurs.

Jane dangles her keys. "I didn't drink, and I have room for five of you party animals. Who's riding in the Katmobile?"

# CHAPTER EIGHTEEN

## PIPER

We tear through the parking lot like bats out of hell as lightning cracks across the sky. Sam and I are first to get there, with the girls lamenting their shoe choice in our wake.

Sam manhandles the van's sliding door as Melissa and Jane break away for the front seats. When the door finally relents, Sam pushes me in and dives in behind me. Shay brings up the rear.

It feels like my drunk body is hurtling through time and space. I stumble between the two captain's chairs in the middle row—one holding Kat's car seat—to reach the back.

"Keep it moving," Shay demands, ducking into the van. Sam climbs into the back row and slides into place next to me.

"Give me rain but keep your lightning and hail, Lord," Shay wails.

I click my belt into place. Jane and Melissa fiddle with buttons on the dash until heat and noise pour into the tiny cabin. The girls argue about playlists until finally settling on something loud and fast to drown out the sound of hail striking the ground. Jane exits the parking lot and drives carefully into the night.

Sam settles next to me, and his knee drapes over my lap. I shove it with my elbow, but it stays firmly put. "Stay on your side."

He points to the ground with a Vanna White level of flair. "I can't extend my legs because of all the diaper boxes."

"I think you're incapable of staying in your bubble."

Lightning flashes, and a sliver of light cuts across the cabin; otherwise, it's so dark I can barely tell where he ends and I begin. He reaches across my lap and grabs my right arm before I can react.

"Let me check on my handiwork," he murmurs as deft fingers roll up my sleeve. I tense as he runs his fingers parallel to the cut. "Damn, I'm so good at my job."

I peer out of the corner of my eye. His face is so close I can see the shadow on his chin, even in the dark. "Awfully cocky for someone who's scared of my sweet, gentle mother."

"I fear no one."

"Sure you don't."

He keeps his voice to a whisper, same as me. "Why don't you want me to go on a date with Melissa?"

I let out a huff of air. "Because."

"Because *why*?"

"Because you have no time in your schedule as it is." Heat flares in my cheeks. "I'm sure you have NFL cheerleaders on rotation who take up any limited free time you may have."

*Whoops.* The tequila truth serum I chugged before settling up is working extra hard.

He snickers. "Did you google me to see who I've dated?"

"*No*," I scoff. "I don't need Google to hear about your life. No one shuts up about you, and you're *everywhere*. Now kindly leave me alone so I can stare at the ice balls falling from the sky in peace."

"So you think I'm too busy, eh?"

A song from the nineties blares through the speakers, and the girls up front sing at the top of their lungs. I feel like I'm back at Merryfield skating rink in ninth grade while bubbly music assaults my ears. Sam spent that evening trying to get a rise out of me, too. "Yes, you're busy. As I am, finding myself a phone number. Apparently."

"You're welcome, by the way. Forrester doesn't need your number."

"Why not?"

"Because he will fuck anything that moves."

The word *fuck* out of his mouth drums up a primal storm inside of me. I need him to aim his low growl at someone else so I can think straight. "Good. Maybe that's what I want."

His eyes darken. "What did you say?"

"Don't look so scandalized. I like sex just as much as the next person." I pause and hold his gaze. "Probably more."

His face falls against the top of my head. His groan vibrates right through me, competing with a clap of thunder. "*Fuck*, Piper. You can't just say stuff like that to me."

"Why not?"

"Because I don't want to hear about your sex life." He lifts his head and brings his mouth to my ear. "You said you weren't seeing anyone when I asked at the studio."

"Stop remembering things."

He lets out a laugh as he moves hair off my shoulder. His fingers trace a lazy circle at the nape of my neck. "How long has it been since someone touched you here?"

I melt against the seat, and my eyes flutter closed, shutting out everything but the feel of his touch and his hot breath on my skin. "None of your business."

"How many men have you been with?"

"It sure *seems* like you want to hear about my sex life."

"Color me curious." He leans even farther until his lips graze the sensitive skin behind my ear and I go shock still. Just when I think he'll press in, he pulls back. "Do you remember when we went to the park off Fifer's Lane?"

I open my eyes before I get too lost in his game or whatever he's trying to accomplish here. "You're drunk."

He checks over his shoulder before dipping lower, brushing his lips down my jaw and back again. "Humor me. Do you remember that night?"

He's doing this to torment me; he must be. He knows exactly what my buttons are and how to push them. He discovered almost all of them, on those nights when we'd map each other's bodies like ravenous explorers desperate to get to our final destination. Satan incarnate could kiss me where Sam's lips are hovering right now, and I'd give him whatever he wanted.

"Which time?" I whisper, trying not to let him hear my jagged breathing. "We went there more than once."

He drags his lips across my skin, but only for a second before pulling back again. I shudder, incapable of hiding how it affects me.

This is not smart. We shouldn't be doing this. But he's so close and so warm and, damnit, I'm still thinking about the way he looks soaking wet.

He loosens my seat belt with a strategic tug, then does the same to his. My breath catches in my chest. I grip the tops of my legs to stop myself from touching him. It would be so easy to slide my hand up his chest or down the leg draped over my lap, but the girls and their scream-singing keep me tethered to reality.

He coils a finger through my belt loop and tugs. I only slide an inch across the leather bench seat, but it feels like a mile. "You know exactly which time. Have you done *that* with anyone else?"

*Don't bring up the past.* An unspoken rule between us, shattered. What does he want me to say? That I remember every kiss, every heavy-lidded look he's ever given me in a car? Of course I remember *exactly which time* he's talking about. We made each other see stars without losing a single layer of clothing, because that's how badly we had it for each other.

He's not the only one who knows which buttons to press to get a reaction. I slide my hand across his leg and stop when I hit the inseam of his pants. "I know what you're doing, Sam."

He glances at my hand near his knee. "What am I doing?"

"You're trying to distract me so you can get all the dirty details of my past." I push up against him like I'm telling him a secret. He's been in a dunk tank and a bar in the last five hours yet still smells faintly of shampoo.

"You're on to me."

I squeeze his leg, and his entire body tenses. "I'm not going to tell you what I've been doing for the last seven years. Or who. But I *will* tell you what I plan to do when I get home."

He sucks in a sharp breath as I move my hand an inch higher.

"I'll be tackling a two-person task all by myself. By hand."

I see the way this affects him in the tension of his jaw. Nothing frustrates Mr. Town Hero more than not being needed. His ragged breathing coaxes me to say more. "Or maybe by showerhead."

He's getting reckless with his body language now, burying his face in the crook of my neck, sliding his hand across my stomach. His voice is low and hoarse as he growls in my ear. "Keep talking." His warm fingers slip inside the bottom hem of my sweater. "Give me a step-by-step."

"First stop, Casa Bellini!"

Jane's voice is a gong, echoing through the van.

Sam snaps his head upright and looks around like he's misplaced something on the ceiling. I squint at the window as I try to catch my breath. I was so caught up I missed the turn into my neighborhood.

I climb over Kat's enormous car seat and thank Jane on my way out the door. At least, I think I thank her. I can't hear anything except my pulse pounding in my ears. It doesn't settle down as I race for my house, scrambling to make sense of my thoughts.

Sam's touch lingers on my skin as I unlock the dead bolt the front door. I catch a glimpse of myself in the mirror above the credenza and see little signs of what happened. Whispers of hair askew where he ran his hand, cheeks and neck flushed red, sweater sleeve still partially rolled up.

Didn't see this coming. Maybe I should have.

History suggests I am susceptible to his charm. He has so much of it, even when he's being annoying. Even when he's tormenting me, with his words or the brush of his fingers on my stomach…

My heart rate explodes anew. I could have pulled away, but I gave it right back to him instead. Making him sweat was as much a thrill as his lips hovering over my neck. *Fuck*. These thoughts can stay in the foyer with my shoes.

We did that in Caleb's fucking minivan, of all places.

I dart toward the stairs, socks sliding on the wood. Sam and I have barely found a foothold in this new landscape of working together. There's too much at stake to slip into old habits, no matter how good it may feel in the moment.

Knowing Sam, it would feel *better* than good.

My legs are wobbly as I move up the stairs. The impulse to turn around, like I left a burner on that might spark a house fire, tugs at me. This is the most on-edge I've been in…

A long time.

This thing happening in my body is a purely physical problem. Only one solution. I need to go on a date and get this energy out of my system.

I peek at the phone number inked on my palm. I could call Forrester.

The thought feels like a sucker punch in the ribs. I don't *want* to call Forrester.

My bedroom door is swinging wide open when I reach the top landing. Nova's voice is small and strained. "Piper?"

I find him wrapped in the duvet in the center of my bed, skin blotchy and eyes rimmed with red.

"What's wrong, little man?" I perch on the side of the bed. "Another nightmare?"

He shakes his head, and his eyes well up. "I don't feel so good."

I cradle his face in my palms. His skin is warm but not alarmingly so. "How long have you been up here?"

"I don't know." A whimper escapes his mouth as his crying picks up steam. "Daddy is helping Mommy because she threw up, and the basement is too dark, and I came up here and you were *gone*, and the wall makes noises, and it's so *scary—*"

*Stab me right in the heart, Nova.* It's a good thing I came home when I did.

For a lot of reasons. Getting-my-head-on-straight reasons.

I press my lips to his forehead the way Mom always did mine when she was checking for a fever. "I'm going to get the thermometer. Hang tight, okay?"

His fever is low-grade, barely a blip. I flip to a kids' cartoon marathon on the living room TV and build us a massive pillow fort on The Pit. As couches go, there's no better for when you're sick. Nova falls in and out of sleep as my thoughts drift to green pool table felt and eyes the same rich color. Absurd thoughts I have no business thinking.

Around a time when I'm not sure if I'm dead or alive, sleeping or awake, the sound of retching fills the room. I stir, studying my surroundings. Sunlight streams through the window, and Nova is snoozing on my lap, no traces of vomit in sight.

I whip my head toward the television.

The 7News logo on the screen's bottom right corner informs me the morning news broadcast has started.

But it's the grainy video of a black-haired, hoodie-wearing teenager projectile vomiting in St. Mary's church that informs me I'm *screwed*.

Royally, unforgivably screwed.

"*Local firefighter and mayoral candidate Sam O'Shea, lauded last week as the wunderkind to bring fresh perspective to Roseborough politics, brings something else to the table in new footage brought forth by an anonymous source—*"

The voice-over doesn't hide the video footage playing out on the screen; it simply mutes the drunken chaos of the original audio. My blood goes ice cold, and the television grows hazy at the edges. *No.*

How is this possible? How do they have my ancient footage? I sit like a limp sponge, absorbing the sights of St. Mary's red velvet carpet and Caleb's hairy arm flashing on screen as he attempts to snatch the phone.

The sight of the video zaps me right back to one of the worst nights of my life, when I was desperate to feel anything other than pain at the sight of Sam. I shouldn't have participated in the scavenger hunt, not when I was so fraught after the breakup. I shouldn't have allowed myself access to technology. He shouldn't have been so drunk. The list of *shouldn't haves* is a mile long.

Adrenaline spikes in my veins, and I cling to Nova's clammy arms as teenaged Sam lays down in the wooden pew. I know what comes next. I remember the phone's bulky feel in my hand as I circled the pew to zoom in on his face, aiming for the *perfect* angle as he passed out with his mouth open. I was somewhere between rage and grief that night. I thought the video would help me feel better—a taste of revenge. *He's not perfect like I thought, and everyone will see...*

But it didn't help. Nothing dulled the ache of losing him.

Nova's head lolls against my arm, trapping me as I watch teenaged Caleb attempt to lift Sam off the pew. But Sam was much bigger than my brother, even then. When Caleb finally managed to hoist Sam's arm over his shoulder and drag him toward the exit, the two of them collapsed into a messy heap on the ground. This roused Sam, who crawled away on his hands and knees, throwing up a trail on the carpet and then hurling one last time in a confessional booth.

It was the last time I saw him, until McLaughlin's.

I thought deleting my posts off social media days after posting was the end of the saga, but I failed to consider that anyone can screen record anything. I save videos all the time for the most random reasons. Someone must've saved it, thinking it was funny.

But for it to resurface *now*, and to be used against him?

Not funny at all. A certified disaster.

A hurricane of dread shuts my whole body down. He's going to blame me for the video getting out—not that I have *any* idea how it happened. God, he's going to skewer me.

And he's *absolutely* going to quit the gig.

The news cuts back to the morning anchors. "In a house of worship. That was certainly…a choice," one hedges.

"Pretty gnarly," the other agrees. "Think they had to replace the carpet?"

The first woman shakes her head, and disgust permeates her tone. "Today the candidates will speak at Roseborough Township Public Library about their visions for the city. I'll be curious what he has to say after all this."

"Makes you wonder what the poor kid was thinking, letting that video out in the first place."

"I'll tell ya what, Kit—I bet he wasn't thinking *'someday I'll run for mayor!'*"

# CHAPTER NINETEEN

### SAM

After a fitful night's sleep, I'm operating on adrenaline and fumes. My body isn't hungover, but my brain sure is. Thoughts of Piper hijacked my dreams last night, keeping me in a perpetual state of unresolved frustration.

I wake up hard after a particularly vivid one of her in those knee-high boots she wore to the station, but a glance at my alarm clock tells me I have no time to wrestle my conflicting thoughts on whether I should indulge the fantasy.

Because today is the day.

My first speaking event as a mayoral candidate. My speech is ready; clothes are dry-cleaned. *Game time.*

I grope on my bedside table for my phone and

come up short. My jeans on the ground are phone-free, too. A sweep of the house proves pointless. It's nowhere to be found.

Retracing my steps leads me right back to Jane's van. A place I both desperately want to return to and also can't think about without a chasm of anxiety opening in my stomach.

Despite what my body is screaming at me, Piper and I absolutely can't go there again. Caleb would kill us both, and I can't risk fucking it up by so much as holding hands with his sister. Our friendship is the most important one I've ever had, and we've already gone down that road, crashed, burned, rebuilt, and here we are. Him making me Kat's godfather symbolized that we're back to a place of trust.

And as Piper will undoubtedly point out, our working arrangement only works if we keep professional boundaries. So really, the reasons why *not* to give in to the mind-melting lust I feel when she's around are numerous.

I shouldn't be responding to her closeness like a horny teenager. Our jobs right now are hard enough without complication. And if anything were to happen between us, there's no way her mother would endorse me. It'd look like blatant nepotism. If we started officially dating, or got serious—

*Whoa.* The fucking leap my brain is capable of

when I'm wound up like this.

Maybe I think about kissing Piper, taking her full bottom lip in my mouth, gripping that soft space above her hips, and pulling her body against mine. *Definitely* thought about more than that last night, and she fueled it by feeding me that torturous showerhead fantasy. But dating isn't even a possibility. Anything that threatens that status quo has to be put out with the recycling.

My phone has to be in the van, but there's nothing I can do about that right now. I throw on my clothes and prepare a pot of coffee. While it brews, I flip on the television and plop down on the couch to pull on navy dress socks to match my pants. Diffused light streams through the window as the eight o'clock news returns from commercial break.

*"Local firefighter and mayoral candidate Sam O'Shea, lauded last week as the wunderkind to bring fresh perspective to Roseborough politics, brings something else to the table in new footage brought forth by an anonymous source—"*

I jump off the couch, and my socked feet fly out from under me. My ass hits the couch as a familiar video fills the screen.

No fucking way.

I don't have to watch it to know what happens. It's a moment from Sam's Hall of Shame, blasted for the whole town to see. A crappy memory made permanent by the media.

I stand up again, more carefully this time, and pace a few circles as my mind reels. This is a small-town race. It's Roseborough, not Boston proper. When I decided to run for mayor, I prepared policies, not plans for mudslinging.

It seems I've underestimated my opponent. Paul Stine, resident chauvinist and buzzkill, already has his team digging up dirt on me. Maybe I could've anticipated this if I wasn't so distracted lately. Could've done a deep dive on myself, searching the internet for potentially incriminating things.

Sweat beads my forehead. My speech is all wrong now. Everything I planned to say feels irreverent in light of this video. Respecting our town? Laughable. The clock on my cable box shouts *time is running out*.

Somehow, I have to stand up in front of a crowd in an hour and tell them about my plans to improve Roseborough, knowing they'll be thinking about me desecrating a historical *church*.

And the kicker? I deserve every bit of their judgment. It was exactly as bad as it looks.


At record speed, I tweak my talking points and hightail it to the library. Paul will speak first, so I have a few minutes to gather my thoughts.

The library's front lawn is crowded. I perform a sweep of the area as I find a spot off to the side to watch and listen. I'm not so much avoiding shaking hands as I am staying out of the fray, refocusing on what I want to communicate to these people.

The crunching of grass and the whistle of the wind are all I can hear as people shuffle around. There are ten or so rows of folding chairs facing the podium, and the crowd more than fills them, leaving the rest to stand. An American flag hangs off a flagpole jutting out of the library's entry archway.

I imagined this moment many times. What it would feel like to greet my first crowd. The idea used to fill me with helium. Instead, a lead weight in my stomach pulls me down.

I tug at my tie as I scan the crowd mingling between the front row and the podium. Paul Stine, his wife, and his four adult children form a loose circle with someone wearing a Roseborough Post badge around their neck. Paul's kids and wife throw adoring looks at him as he speaks. A blond woman entertains several kids in the roped-off front row. A sign on the end chair says RESERVED FOR THE STINE FAMILY.

Are all families so damn chummy?

I scan the crowd for my parents. Mom and Dad

have always avoided being at the same place at the same time—Mom works a second job just to get away from him—and today is no different. They're nowhere to be found.

I have no other family in the area, and no relationship, obviously.

My thoughts wander to the Bellinis. They'd turn up like this for one another, a battalion at Gio and Catherine's command. Caleb would be here if I'd told him about it. He's the only one I can count on.

My social circle is smaller than I realized if a married dude, his wife, and his baby are my primary social outlets.

Piper notwithstanding.

Not that I know where she stands. Or hell, where *I* stand.

I shake out my arms and refocus on the task at hand. If I win the election, I'll belong to this community. That's a social circle on steroids.

After this morning's news blip, I'll have to move mountains to make them see I'm the right guy for this job, not some irresponsible kid who doesn't care about his town or his reputation. I'll have to earn their trust back and show them I'll work hard to keep it.

Sweat gathers beneath my collar. Maybe it's the dimming crowd, settling in their seats, letting me know the time has come to start this thing. I maneuver through to the other side of the podium and shake hands with the event coordinator and a few others. My social engine roars to life, powered by adrenaline and a need to reclaim the narrative.

*Ready or not, here we go.*

Donna Lindale, head of the public works department, steps up to the podium and taps the microphone, code for, *do you see me up here, impatiently waiting*? She opens with a few words about the importance of supporting local politics.

When Paul takes his spot at the podium, he looks bored out of his skull. Dead behind the eyes. I try to parse his words as he drones on to find underlying themes, but it's word salad delivered without dressing. Boring. Dry. My thoughts wander to my own speech, and I zone out as I prepare.

Until I hear my name.

"—respect what candidate O'Shea is doing; I really do. To get out there as a kid and tussle with the big dogs? We respect it. It's great to see youth engaging in politics. When his time comes—twenty years or so from now, presumably—he'll make a great candidate. But today, Roseborough needs a seasoned leader."

Bile hits the back of my throat. He's leaning all the way in on the age thing. I anticipated this strategy, but it doesn't make it easier to stomach. As if being young means I can't do the job. If anything, it makes me more equipped to understand the unique demands of the changing political landscape.

My irritation spikes from the applause this generates.

When it's finally my turn, the crowd's excitement transforms into palpable tension. Or maybe that's what I'm giving off and they're mirroring it back.

Can't have that. I scan my brain for a happy, calming thought.

What comes to mind is a memory so random I hack out a laugh, from the night Piper came to the station. All I'd gotten from her was scowls and sarcasm until we ran that ridiculous practice dialogue. I read something about robots in the sack, and she giggled. It was light, airy, and unexpected. The first time I'd heard her truly laugh in years.

Whispers ripple through the crowd as I take my spot at the podium with a grin on my face. The smooth edges calm me as I squeeze the worn wooden sides.

I scan the crowd. I recognize more people than I expected to. The wind picks up, but it doesn't drown out the murmurs in the front row.

"—*firefighter kid*—"

"*He was in the calendar I shot last year.*"

"—*Catholic?*"

My ears burn hot. I wish any of these people could really *see* me. To them, I'm an immature kid, an extension of my job, a sacrilegious vomit comet streaking through town. I want to show them I care, that I'm competent. Trustworthy.

And then I see her.

Piper, four rows back.

I sure as hell didn't expect to—not after last night. We swam in dangerous waters, and I would've bet my car she'd avoid me until absolutely necessary.

But she's in the fourth row in a red coat, bright and bold, balancing on the edge of her seat like she hasn't fully committed to staying. My heartbeat kicks an erratic rhythm.

Her eyes are on me, wide and unblinking. Everything goes fuzzy at the edges.

She came here. Whether to heckle me or support me, I don't know. But she's here, and I'm hit with a hunger to prove myself.

Her mother's endorsement is important, but if I can earn Piper's support—a real belief that I can do this, not just a hollow promise exchanged in the heat of our pact—maybe I have a shot of convincing everybody else.

If she believes in me, I can believe in myself.

My voice mingles with the wind, crackling in the microphone.

"I'm Sam O'Shea, and I'm running for mayor of Roseborough, Massachusetts."

# CHAPTER TWENTY

### PIPER

My lungs are suddenly less functional than a McDonald's soft-serve machine.

Sam holds my gaze in the crowd, his lips pulled in a tight line, expression frozen. My mind spins as I try to pull a full breath.

What does that look mean? Is he panicked about the video and pissed I chose to show my face here? Nervous about his speech?

I side-eye the woman on my left. She's young, attractive—looks a lot like Melissa, actually—and seemingly unattached, if the older couple holding hands beside her is any indication. He could easily be looking at her. Or anyone else.

To make matters worse, my SOS texts from this

morning went unanswered.

*Please call me.*

*I don't understand how they got the video. I'm freaking out.*

*I'm so sorry.*

The anxiety of not knowing what he's thinking or feeling drives me to grind my teeth. But when he begins speaking, his calm baritone is void of even the slightest nervous shake. His composure is rock solid. A knot of tension unfurls in my gut. No matter how he truly feels, he sounds perfectly smooth up there.

It's a far cry from how he sounded last night, hoarse as his lips brushed my skin.

I shut that thought off immediately as heat blooms in my cheeks. That was a slipup. And now the stupid video took an already complicated situation and dropped it into quicksand.

As he segues into his history with RTFD and how it's shaped the way he sees community, a buzz of murmurs spreads through the crowd. The longer he talks, the more I relax. My fists finally release their anxious death grip when he hits the high points of his plans for Roseborough. He sounds confident. Articulate. Like maybe the video didn't ruin his plans.

All in all, he speaks like an optimistic man who

believes his dreams and visions are possible.

He sounds like...*himself*. But bigger.

A chill trickles down my arms. His voice is captivating—this isn't news to me—and it's a known fact Mr. February can turn heads. But to be able to compose a speech of this quality and deliver it with sincerity on top of everything else? God really penciled in a whole afternoon when it came time to make Sam.

I don't want his moment in the sun to end, but for selfish reasons. I don't want to face him and hear the excitement drain from his voice. Soon I'll have to reckon with his disappointment about the video circulating. His bitterness that it exists at all.

The longer I can postpone that, the better. We'll have to hash it out before we record this afternoon. But not showing up today wasn't an option. I had to hear this speech for myself, even if it's hard to see him, knowing my stupid video threw a wrench in the mix.

I wait for the cheesy promises politicians make, curious which trite line he'll spew. *Together, we'll ensure a brighter future*, or some such cliché.

"Finally"—he tilts his chin up—"I'd like to address the viral video clip circulating on local news stations. Unlike other public servants, I won't operate under a veil of secrecy, nor will I ever shirk responsibility for my poor actions."

Wind whips my hair across my cheeks as I suck

in a breath.

"To be clear, the events that transpired at St. Mary's resulted from incredibly poor decision-making on my part, and I am sincerely sorry. I cannot excuse what you saw. There's a difference between youth and immaturity—"

This time, when he tilts his chin and scans the crowd, I'm certain he sees me. His eyes find mine and hold me captive.

"—and that was pure immaturity. I was going through a hard time and made a mistake. But I offer you this assurance: that is not the man I am today. And I look forward to proving it."

A drumming in my ears picks up speed like a stampede closing in. A hundred people or more are here listening to him talk, yet it still feels like he's talking only to me. Taking full responsibility for something that never would've come to light if it wasn't for *my* immaturity.

His gaze lingers for a few more seconds before moving on to another member of the crowd. I know he says more words to close out his speech because the crowd goes wild. The applause is deafening even without walls to echo and amplify the sound. A few people with cameras in the front row snap photos.

Even without seeing those photos, I know how he looks.

*Accomplished.*

Sam should be here any minute for our session — if he comes. I wouldn't be surprised if he gets swallowed by the excited crowd and blows the session off entirely.

On top of everything, I now have to get into acting mode. I change into something indoorsy, a plain white sundress I yank out of my wardrobe at random. My closet gets warm when we are working so I try not to wear anything too heavy, lest I sweat to death before my first big audiobook project hits the e-stands.

The stairs' rumble alerts me to his arrival. I pluck a hairbrush off my old, whitewashed dresser and drag it through my strands to look busy.

Even though the door is wide open, he raps on the frame with his knuckles.

After hearing him talk at the event, it's almost strange to have access to him now. He looks so distinguished in his expensive clothes, leaning against the doorframe with one foot crossed over and a haughty tilt to his chin.

"Hi." The word rides out of my mouth on a puff of air, barely consequential.

He loosens his tie. "Fancy meeting you here."

My fingers tighten around the hairbrush. "I texted you. Several times."

"I just got my phone back. Had to swing by Caleb's after the event to fish it out from between Jane's seats."

Relief trickles over me. "Oh."

The space between us holds our whispered words in the Katmobile, the leaked video, the speech, and a hundred other unsaid things. The air is palpably tense, like I could get stuck wading through it.

He pulls down on the Windsor knot. The way he stretches his neck from side to side as his hand tugs the silk is hypnotic. Heat spreads across my cheeks as he unbuttons his top button.

"Well, that went better than I hoped, actually. But I'm not in the clear yet. There are still a few pissed-off, offended people. Some have questions about St. Mary's sanitation policies."

I bite back a tiny laugh. "They know vomit doesn't linger from seven years ago, right?"

He reaches up to grip the wood above his head, and his gaze hardens in concentration. "Your video doesn't have a time stamp. It's not clear that it was from seven years ago."

My hand grazes my stomach, but it doesn't tame the flare of nervous energy swirling inside of me. An apology on the tip of my tongue disappears with a swallow. "Right. *My* video."

"I thought the footage disappeared, never to be

seen again."

I cast my brush aside and stand. "I have no idea how the news got ahold of it. I've been trying to figure it out."

He takes two tentative steps into the room. "You have?"

"Of course, since the second I saw the news. The original video was on the internet for a few days. Someone must have saved it, thinking it was funny. But who? And why? I know people make compilation videos, so it's possible it was on a YouTube Fails of the Week or something—"

"Pipes."

A broad beam of sunlight bisects the room, casting a warm glow between us. Dust and particles dance in the air, stirred up by my frenetic pacing. It's easier to zoom in on those tiny fragments than it is to look at him, hovering near my closet door with his arms crossed. "Hmm?"

"Take a breath. You sound like you're going to combust."

"Right. Sorry." I take a deep breath to appease him. "Anyway, I've been thinking a lot about the... video."

*The video.* And nothing else. Not the feel of his hands slipping inside my sweater. Not the way he sounded in my ear when he was begging me to tell him more dirty things.

Just the video.

"I'm sure someone from Stine's camp is behind this," he offers. "It's Mudslinging 101. Figure out someone's Achilles' heel and target it. Mine is my age and therefore immaturity."

I meet his eye and linger there, pulling my lip between my teeth. "You were really drunk that night."

His lips curve into a wisp of a smile. "And you were really amused."

*Amused?* Unless that word is also German for miserable, I was *not* amused at St. Mary's. But there's no sense in telling him otherwise.

My pulse hammers in my ears. "So you aren't quitting the audio gig?"

He does a double-take. "What? Why would I quit?"

"Because it was my video. I nearly tanked your campaign before it even got off the ground."

"Unless you airdropped it to the press, I can't blame you for what I did back then, can I?"

I've spent hours waiting to hear those words, but somehow, I don't feel relieved. Instead, I'm hit with an acute awareness of how dependent I am on his help. How tangled our lives have become.

"Now that you've apologized for the video, is that the end of it? Or do you have to go sling some mud now?"

He runs his hand through his hair. "I don't want to bore you with shop talk, especially with your bedroom narcolepsy."

I freeze. He winces. Time immemorial takes a beat.

"Probably shouldn't have said that," he adds, Hulk-smashing the silence.

A noncommittal noise leaves my mouth. Getting bashed over the head with memories of all the times I fell asleep draped over his warm body while he stroked my hair and told me whispered stories is not the ideal way to break the leftover tension from the van.

He's the only person I've ever shared a bed with that made me feel safe enough to fall asleep first. When we found our groove as a couple, those dizzying early-relationship fears that used to keep me up at night—*does he think I'm pretty? Is he going to kiss me? Will he think I'm crazy if he knows how much I like him?*—faded into blissful silence when he held me.

I'm going to need a lobotomy before our contract is up. Or a sedative. Whatever rids me of these memories.

"Listen, we *did* decide it was okay to be open and honest, didn't we?" he asks. "It's silly to pretend those things never happened. Especially when we're in this room, Ground Zero for some of our best memory-making."

*Best.*

My stomach vaults into my throat. He's successfully rendered a voice actor speechless.

All I can do is dry cough like an elderly person jonesing for a lozenge. "We should get to work. We've got a long episode to record today."

"To the sauna we go. I'm ready."

With the storm brewing in my chest, I can hardly say the same.

# CHAPTER TWENTY-ONE

## SAM

Unfortunately for me—the person who is already sweating bullets—the closet is a few degrees warmer than Piper's bedroom.

Today we have a short line episode to record, heavy on fast-paced dialogue and short on internal monologue. Often, we take turns in the closet and Pipes smooths over any transition blips in editing. That makes it less of a sauna.

But with so much dialogue, we'll have to share the mic.

She brushes past me in the tiny space and turns on the floor lamp wedged in the closet's corner. I move the lone stool out of the way to create extra standing room, which requires ducking under the microphone crane.

Leftover excitement from my speech surges through my veins. Or maybe it's the thrill of another task at hand.

Maybe it's the overwhelming sensation of *her*. That damn fruity shampoo and the gloss on her lips. How the air feels charged between us.

The fact she hasn't said a word about the van, leaving me to wonder if it affected her, too.

Did she fall asleep as keyed up as I was? Did she make good on her promise to use that showerhead?

I shift, already needing to adjust myself after three seconds of being trapped in here. It's brutal being this close and not knowing what she's thinking.

To distract myself, I fiddle with the crane's arm. "Do you think we should invest in a second mic? I'm happy to supply the funds."

She narrows her eyes. "This microphone cost me a thousand dollars. Do you have a thousand dollars lying around, Sam?"

I flash her a smile.

"Never mind. Don't answer that. If we aren't fired for your amateur narration, we'll talk about a second microphone for the second installment."

I position the crane so she can't reach the mic, even on her tiptoes. "What was it Darla said in our last email exchange? *Sam oozes charisma?*"

She lunges for it, and I swat her arm down. "Why would anyone want to 'ooze' anything?"

"There are good ways to ooze, Piper. Or has it been so long you've forgotten?"

She storms over to the corner of the space—the only part of this closet serving its intended function of storing things—and pulls out a pair of high heels. I don't even bother to hide my stare as she slips into them. It feels like she *wants* me to watch. My gaze travels all the way down her legs and back up again. Twice.

I rub my chin as the room hums with static electricity. "All dressed up and nowhere to go."

She straightens, tugging the hem of her dress down. This does wondrous things to her cleavage. "Dress for the job you want, as the saying goes."

"What job is that?"

"A voice actress who can reach her microphone."

"Noted."

She shifts past me to access the desk and starts messing with the recording software. It whirs to life. Without bothering to warn me, she hits record, plucks her script off the desk, and takes her place beneath the microphone.

I fumble for my pages, which are tucked into my back pocket. The roll wants to stay coiled as I attempt to flatten it between my hands. It takes me a few seconds to thumb to the correct page. We angle our bodies toward each other so we can both access the mic. There's just enough room between us to fit our scripts, held close to our chests. I take a deep breath and lick my lips. She watches me instead of her script, bringing a buzzing awareness to my mouth.

Piper has the first line today. She tilts her chin toward the microphone and turns on her princess voice.

"*Last night was a close call. Too close. Your father always seems to know when I'm down here. What if we get caught?*"

"*We* won't *get caught, Vicky. I promise. And if we do, so be it. I'd rather be caught with you than anywhere without you.*"

"*If your dad had walked in a second later, he would have seen me in a most compromising position, unbefitting of royalty. And he would have told my mother, and, oh, I can't even bear the thought.*"

"*To be fair, it was I who was in a compromising position. I believe it looked…a little something…like this?*"

"*Laz, you tease me so. What* is *it about a man on his knees? It's a most powerful sorcery. Let it be me on my knees next time, in the interest of fairness.*"

"*To see you on your knees would shatter any resolve I still possess. God, just the thought of you, staring up at me with that doe-eyed innocence while you wrap those lips around my—*"

She lunges past me and pauses the recording function on the computer. "I don't like how any of that went. I—I don't think I hit the right beats."

I lower my script, more than happy for an interruption to my gutter thoughts. Talking about lips and Piper in any capacity would turn me on, but this scene is heading in a torturous direction. Her voice, gravelly and shot out from tiredness or overuse, hits me so right, like we're in a bedroom and tired for other reasons.

*Acting.* We're acting.

She's acting, at least.

I wave my script at her like a fan. "Are you all right? You look flushed."

"I'm fine." She finagles the tech and restarts the recording. "Let's go again."

The second time we record sounds and feels exactly the same as the first. Her words burrow into my brain after they fall off her tongue.

*Let me be on my knees next time…*

My skin feels too tight as she bends to pause the computer again. She tosses her script on the desk, knocking over a cup of pens in the process.

"Damnit." She grabs a fistful of the flimsy BICs and shoves them back into the cup, knocking it over a second time. "Oh, fuck it all!" The pens roll off the desk as I massage my temples with my fingers.

I inch closer to her, feeding off her panic. "Pipes…"

"Sorry. I don't know what's going on with me. My voice, my delivery—it's all flat. Especially compared to yours. What with all the *charisma-oozing*…"

I drop my script on top of hers. "You know I'm just trying to get your goat, right? We both know you're the professional in this arrangement."

"Where there's smoke there's fire, Sam. You know it better than anyone."

"What do you mean?"

She tilts her head back and lets out a groan that vibrates straight through me. "You're really going to make me explain this, aren't you? Darla and Damien called *you* first for this gig, remember? They delivered the news to you."

"Yes, because your voicemail was—"

"Damien fanboyed over you in the audition. Darla emailed you about tomorrow's dinner first, and I'm a plus-one, basically."

"That's not true, and she fixed it when I told her she forgot to add your email—"

She cuts me off again. "They compliment you every time I send them material. Charisma, the tone of your voice." Her head tips down, and her hair spills over her shoulders. "You do your third job better than I do my first. You're too…good."

Something like fury on steroids rips through me. "Look at me, Piper."

She lets out a soft grumble before glancing back

up. I risk a step closer, backing her into the desk. "I do not do this job better than you. I wish you could hear what I hear. See what I see."

Her words are a tight whisper as her eyes flash something raw. "I need this job, and I don't want to be the one to fuck it up. This is my last chance to make this career work before I told myself I'd give up on the dream, move on and find something more stable."

I hover my hands over her for a second before deciding what's safe to touch. They land on her upper arm. I wrap my fingers and squeeze her warm skin. "You aren't fucking anything up, and you are not giving up on the dream. Darla and Damien compliment me because they know I'm the rookie who needs to hear it. Do you think producers lavish Keanu Reeves with praise all day?"

Her gaze flits from my face to my fingers and back again. Her eye contact at this proximity nearly knocks the wind out of me. But she doesn't flinch. Doesn't pull away. Her reply is breathy. "Am I…Keanu?"

"You're in your head," I manage, soaking up the touch in my rough palms before I have to let her go. "Overthinking it."

Her exhale is dramatic. Warm, minty breath hits me. "I live in my head. I overthink *everything*, even though I don't always say things out loud."

"Believe me, I know." My hands slide down her arms, operating on their own motor, leaving goose bumps in their wake. My thoughts are so jumbled I can barely sort this physical contact into its proper category—sympathetic, comforting. The feel of her skin is dangerous, deliciously addictive. If I could touch her for real, I'd make it my goal to knock the thoughts right out of her head until she could just *be*.

My hands slip to her waist. She's frozen in her spot, her breathing all but stalled as she floats a hand over the muscles of my forearm. It falls away so fast I can't be sure she touched me at all.

*What are we doing?*

"Let's go again," she murmurs, sounding as strung out and desperate as I feel. "Another recording."

# CHAPTER TWENTY-TWO

## Piper

I grab my script. Sam doesn't move, forcing me to brush against him to reach the computer mouse. My voice is so affected by the nearness of him I already know the clip won't be usable. But if I don't walk over to the microphone and say these lines, I don't know what else I'll do.

He takes his position at the mic, tugging me with him as his hands tighten around my waist. I short-circuit at the touch, incapable of forming a response. Reading is the only thing I can manage to do. My script is almost resting on his chest. I don't know how I make it through my lines at all.

His tone is so loaded I feel the blood heating in my veins.

"*'To be fair, it was I who was in a compromising position. I believe it looked…a little something…like this?'*"

He puts his left knee to the floor, followed by his right. He's kneeling in front of me like he's worshiping at an altar, his head tilted up and lips nearly parted. I drop my arm to the side, and the script slips out of my hand. The pages flurry as they fall through the air until it hits the ground.

He slides his hands from my waist to my lower back. My body is so tightly wound up under his touch my skin might be vibrating.

All I can do is nod. *Yes.*

He drags his fingers over the sides of my hips, slowly passing over the fronts of my thighs before exploring down my legs. His eyes never leave mine, and I don't think I could look away if I wanted to. I'm transfixed. All I can do is watch as he exhumes this ravenous need for him I buried long ago. I had forced myself to forget the feeling of wanting him, and now he's on his knees, unearthing it with two bare, careful hands.

He reaches the spot just above my knees where my dress ends and fans his fingers over warm skin. Heat radiates from every touch point, sizzling up my legs. He must know what he's doing to me or he wouldn't be looking at me like that, with bottomless green eyes that are equal parts wicked and remorseful.

If he can stoke this kind of feeling in me with the brush of his fingertips, I don't stand a chance against his touch. But I want it so badly I struggle to stay still. I want him to grip. Press. *Push*.

"Say something," Sam says, voice scratchy and low. "Please. I need to hear your voice."

"Why?" I manage, my breathing jagged and uneven. "So you can hear what you're doing to me?"

"Yes," he growls. "*Hell* yes."

His words push me toward an invisible precipice. My thoughts are a hazy mess, but my body is prepared to form a silent coup if I don't get my hands on him.

"Tell me you don't think about this." He nudges the hem of my dress up a few inches. "My hands on you, doing the things our characters get to do." Heat spreads between my legs like a lit fuse. All I can think about is how badly I want him to touch me. I feel like Victoria at Laz's teasing hand.

"I think about it," I admit, breathless. I look down at his lips and feel a phantom pressure on my own. I take in the line of his neck, remembering the salty taste of his skin from when I used to kiss and suck until he bruised. He'd always do the same to me, and I'd secretly revel in the proof that our stolen nights together in my room were real. The impulse to taste him is so strong I bite my tongue. "I shouldn't, especially while we're working. But I do."

"What exactly do you think about? Don't hold back."

"I think about your hands. And your mouth," I whisper, a wild blaze spreading through the rest of my body. "You in my shower, paint running down your body." I run my hands through his hair and tug. He lets out a tiny groan that makes me want to forget all the reasons why I shouldn't touch him.

His hands slip beneath the hem of my dress, grazing the back of my thighs so gently it's painful. One more second of teasing might kill me. I grab him by the necktie and yank him to his feet.

He takes my face in his palms, and his mouth crashes into mine. His tongue brushes over my lips, gently coaxing me open. We deepen the kiss at the same second, and it's perfect friction as my tongue swipes his. He pulls my bottom lip into his mouth, and we descend into frenzied nibbling and sucking. There are not enough ways to consume his mouth. I want so much more from him. *Need* so much more.

Warm lips break away from my mouth and trail across my jaw and down, ghosting my neck, his ragged whisper muffled against my skin. "You smell exactly the same."

I melt against him as he runs his teeth along my collarbone and almost can't get the words out when he starts to suck. "It's the same…perfume…I've always worn."

"It's so *you*. So fucking good."

His growling affirmation breeds pure heat in my body. He grips the backs of my legs and lifts me like I weigh nothing at all. I coil around him as rough palms grip my skin.

I'm nearly sure he's heading out of the closet when he takes a turn and deposits me on the open stretch of desk next to my computer. I fumble my grip on the desk's edge, knocking the wireless mouse to the ground as I try to anchor myself. He drops down and nudges my legs open. His mouth finds the inside of my knee like a heat-seeking missile.

"Sam." The word falls out as he latches to my skin, sucking and licking a trail upward in painfully slow strokes. He's not even halfway up my thigh, and I'm already panting as my head falls backward. "Lock my door."

His mouth leaves my skin, but his hand replaces it, gliding all the way up my leg until his fingers skirt my most sensitive spot. I squirm in an attempt to make contact, desperate to feel the pressure of his touch. "Lock it," I repeat, barely able to speak.

He drags one finger across damp lace, and I let out a needy gasp. "Please," I beg, arching into his hand.

His tone is sinfully dark. "Please do this?" He lightly brushes a circle with his finger. "Or please lock the door?"

I moan, dangerously close to giving no fucks

about anything other than him, already imagining the slick slide of his touch when he nudges the underwear aside.

"Door *now*."

He stands up and plants a rough kiss on my mouth. "Don't move."

As if I could.

The microphone catches my eye as I watch him jog out of the closet.

*The microphone.*

*Damnit.*

I pull the keyboard into my lap and tilt the monitor toward me. The software has been recording this whole time. Panic seizes hold of my stomach. The last five minutes of footage do not need to exist, not even for another second. Dragging the cursor backward, I highlight everything and type in the command stroke to delete all.

Today's recordings disappear.

Along with the last session's.

"No!" I cry, smashing the keyboard desperately.

There must be a quick and easy way to undo this, but logic evades me. Did I back the last session up yet? Wrapping my head around anything but the throbbing between my legs feels like trying to reroute rush hour traffic on I-93. Why can't I remember basic job-related functions?

If we have to redo the last session, that's three

hours of lost work. Sam is already so busy with his campaign and work schedule, it'll be a pain to coordinate.

I slide off the desk, and my hands fly to my forehead. Panic hits me like a tidal wave.

*What are we doing?*

This is not good. One mind-melting kiss from Sam, and I am about to jeopardize everything. My mind is already catastrophizing three steps from now. Our working relationship in shambles. His campaign tarnished if something between us goes badly and Mom speaks out on her perception of his character. His friendship with Caleb damaged, *again*, because of me.

It was like this before. I was consumed, constantly caught up in the whirlwind of being with Sam. Now, with everything to lose professionally if we fall out and no better control of my feelings, I'm begging for his touch in the middle of a shift?

This can't happen.

He's taking a long time to lock the door. Dread pulses through me. Is he spiraling, too?

I walk out the door and find him in the doorway, his back facing me.

His voice carries across the space. "Thank you. That's kind of you to say, Mrs. Bellini."

*Mrs. Bellini.*

*Shit.*

Mom's voice is faint but still audible. "And you wrote the speech yourself?"

"Yes. Every word."

Her response comes after a pause more pregnant than her. "Interesting. Tell Piper I could use her help with the kids after you two are done working, would you? I don't want to climb any more of these stairs than I have to."

"Yes, ma'am."

The bedroom door shuts with a click, and he whirls around. "That was almost a disaster. Good call about the door." He closes the distance between us with four big steps and reclaims my mouth with renewed urgency, teeth mashing and hands tense around my waist as he backs me up toward the bed. Before the back of my legs hit the mattress, he pulls back and cracks a smile. "She listened to my speech on the radio and *liked* it. Maybe the seed you planted with her is starting to grow into actual approval."

I put my hands on his chest as he leans in, stopping his momentum. "I haven't exactly…"

But my resolve to tell him the truth falters at the last second. I haven't worked up the nerve to talk to Mom about Sam's campaign. The words cement in my throat every time I try. And now, with the perfect tee-up, I can't even admit that to him. My communication skills are as stellar as ever.

"It was a great speech." My voice is small, like

I'm lowering it to honor the hasty transition from day to night as darkness envelops the room.

His eyes soften. "Really?"

My heart stutters. It hurts the way joy sometimes hurts, to know I can make him feel something simply by showing up. What a bare-minimum thing, and yet he looks like he won a prize.

It hurts because this thing is snowballing, and I feel like I'm waiting at the bottom of the hill for the avalanche to hit me. When he looks at me like this, his eyes are even more dangerous than his hands, for completely different reasons.

How much this campaign means to him is written all over his face. I almost wish I didn't understand, but I do, because I know what my own dreams mean to me.

It is with razor-sharp clarity that I slide his hands off my body. "I think you should go."

"*Go?* Now?"

"I don't think I have it in me to record anything today. I just deleted a bunch of stuff by accident and need to fix it. I need time."

Concern streaks across his features, and he dusts his hand under my chin. "What's going on?"

I stare down, glimpsing the apples of my own cheeks. "Nothing. I just…can't."

His mouth sets into a hard line. "Don't do this, Piper. Don't shut me out."

"I'm not."

"I thought we were past this."

Anger flares. I reach down to peel off my heels. "Past *what*?"

"Past you shutting down every time you're worried about something. We need to have a real conversation about what's happening between us."

I let out an enormous sigh. "Fine. You want me to list all the things I'm worried about? Here we go. This three-book project is going to span well into summer, and we are going to be around each other constantly. If we can't...or even if we *can*...what if we—and then—*fuck*, why is this so hard?"

He rakes his hands through his hair, and it stands on edge, perfectly disheveled. "Imagine how much easier it would be to work together if we weren't constantly *frustrated*. I personally would be a lot more productive if I wasn't distracted thinking about all the things I want to do with you. *To* you."

He's stating a fact, but *God*, just hearing him talk about being as frustrated as I am makes me want to fall backward on the bed and pull him down on top of me. He'd blanket me in pure heat, and I'd suck the crisp cologne right off his neck. I'd curl up my legs on either side of his hips, arching into him, feeling his—

*Gah.* I put distance between us so I don't do anything stupid, like reach forward and rip the buttons off his shirt. "Then there's your campaign to think about, all the different ways I can screw it up if I'm incapable of holding up my end of the bargain. What if I can't convince my mom? Or more things like the video happen?"

"You're not going to screw up my campaign."

He's not even approaching me, and I still back all the way into my dresser, rattling the antique lamp. "What about Caleb? We can't do this to him again."

He dares a step in my direction. "I get it, all right? Believe me, I've thought about it, too. But *this*?" He gestures between the two of us. "This is a ticking time bomb. I don't trust myself to be fully professional with you. When I look at you, I don't see a friend or a coworker or my best friend's off-limits sister. I see the goddamn gorgeous woman I can't stop thinking about. In the closet, I asked you what you imagined when you thought of us. Right now, I want to lay you down on that bed and show you what *I* imagine."

Parts of me I didn't know were voice activated clench at the raw need in his voice. I grapple to keep hold of my resolve. "This ended badly before."

Again, he steps. Now he's close enough to touch. "Why did you ask for the break in the first place? What went wrong between us?"

Suddenly I'm sixteen all over again, frozen in my spot. Wanting him, denying myself, struggling every step of the way. I never felt in control of the way I felt about him. It was a reckless, 100-miles-per-hour-with-the-convertible-top-down,    soul-igniting feeling that never seemed to slow down. The more I had of him, the more I wanted.

We never had sex, though we did everything but. And I never told him that I'd fallen deeply, madly in love with him. I knew if I gave him that last part of me, he'd *stay*.

And that terrified me.

How could the larger-than-life, charismatic boy whom I'd grown up admiring give up his future for me? The fact that he liked me at all felt like I'd snuck a love potion into his Coke at a barbeque. I never thought it would last. There was a world of opportunities out there just waiting for him. Sam O'Shea was utterly out of my league, and I knew it.

Back then, I only knew how to be an extension of my family. Caleb's little sister, Principal Bellini's daughter, Mom's well-behaved golden child, Nonna's apprentice in the kitchen. I was an expert at filling roles. Maybe that's why I gravitated toward acting, so I could be someone else at the drop of a hat. Someone impressive, interesting, worthy. Whoever I needed to be.

The only thing I knew for certain was that I didn't want to hold Sam back. I wanted him to experience everything the world had to offer. He deserved that, and I wanted him to have it. It broke my heart to think about losing him, which was why I couldn't end it completely. It would've been simpler, but the thought of breaking up for good tore me in half.

A break was all I could manage. So that's what I asked for.

Of course, my stupid sixteen-year-old heart secretly hoped he'd refuse. If he fought me on the break, I might've given in, which was why I cut off communication. The day after I told him, I almost called him to take it all back, to tell him how much I loved him, to fight for us myself.

But then Sidney happened.

I orchestrated the break, suffered and sobbed and insisted on it because I loved him and wanted him to be happy. And he moved on so fast it was like we never even happened. Like I never meant anything at all.

And here we stand years later, in the same spot it all fell apart, chests rising in falling in perfect sync as he waits for me to speak. There's so much I could say.

*I was doing you a favor. Look at you, mayoral candidate, firefighter, cheerleader-dating, impressive O'Shea. Look at what you accomplished because I pushed you away.*

*And then you threw that act of love in my face.*

I bite my lip as I crumble in defeat. "It doesn't matter what went wrong."

"Addressing what went wrong is how you get things right, Piper."

"Maybe so." I brave a look at his face, and it crushes me to see the earnestness in his eyes. "But you and I both know we can't risk it again."

He fastens his top button and tightens his tie with an aggressive yank. My stomach clenches as his expression steels over. A tap turning ice cold. "I can tell I'm not going to get the answers I want. You want to leave the past fully in the past, fine. And you're right—why risk it now? Best we stick to business as usual moving forward. Starting with dinner with the Gentrys, tomorrow at eight."

My own logic thrown back at me stings something fierce. I nod—flinch—in lieu of speaking. By the coolness he leaves in his wake as he exits the room, I can tell I've already said too much.

# CHAPTER TWENTY-THREE

### SAM

Damien chose Gala Bistro for our work dinner, a Cambridge staple. Or put another way, a place for Harvard students to feed their big brains while sticking close to campus.

I race into the restaurant twenty minutes behind schedule. My interview with West Mass, a local independent magazine, ran much later than I was anticipating. The woman kept asking about my dad and the "other heroes of the station," to the point where I started to wonder if the squad was hiding around the corner in an elaborate gotcha move. *Psych, asshole, this interviewer is my cousin who I paid to troll you* has a distinctly Forrester ring to it.

Regardless, I couldn't exactly walk away in the

middle of answering questions. Piper may disagree, though. She's good at that.

My stomach turns at the thought of seeing her after yesterday. Our partnership is a rubber band pulled so tight it's bound to snap. I've lost the ability to compartmentalize and put work *here* and feelings *there*. Piper doesn't fit in a box anymore. She's infiltrated every part of my life.

Unfortunately, it doesn't matter how I feel. Historical data supports that fact. At the end of the day, her reasoning doesn't matter if the outcome is a rejection.

If only there was a way to forget the way she sighed relief into my mouth as she gripped the back of my neck. Or how she was so worked up she gasped from a brush of contact with my finger. I'd *love* to forget how warm and eager she was, because then I'd be able to convince myself she didn't want this, too. Curse this memory of mine.

A hostess directs me down a flight of weathered stone steps into a room that looks like a speakeasy. Hushed voices and clinking glasses punctuate the jazz piping through the speakers.

The Gentrys wave from across the room. Piper glances over her shoulder before snapping her head away. I can feel her irritation from here.

This ought to be fun.

Damien speaks first when I reach the table,

though both Gentrys rise to greet me. "Sam! Glad you could make it."

"I'm so sorry I'm late. A meeting ran over." I clasp Damien's hand. "I didn't mean to keep you waiting."

Darla waves off the apology. "No worries, sugar. We're glad you're all right."

I turn to my *business partner*, who gives me a weak half rise before plopping right back down in her chair. "Hello, Piper."

"Sam," she responds flatly, her gaze fixed on her glass of water.

"We were just mulling over the menu," Damien notes, flipping through laminated pages.

I slide into the chair next to Piper, and my leg butts up against hers. She can't slide any farther without hitting the brick wall, and my left leg already juts into the tiny aisle between the tables. It's a tight fit.

Darla flattens a linen napkin in her lap. "Busy day, Sam?"

"I was caught in an interview. Campaign events are so unpredictable, but that's no excuse for tardiness."

"Hey, whatever gets you to the finish line," Damien says. "I'd love to have an in with a mayor, especially with us spending more time in Massachusetts in the coming years. Wonder if you'll be able to help with some parking tickets, retroactively—"

Darla shoots him a look.

"Did I jump the gun?" he whispers. "Sorry, sweets."

Silence follows this. I've never been more grateful for a waitress interruption in all my life.

Shortly after we place our orders—mine being the first item I spotted on the menu I was too late to study—Darla clears her throat and straightens in her chair. She lifts her rocks glass in the air.

"Thank you so much for joining us tonight. I know with busy schedules it's hard to sneak away for an evening, but this is lovely. Though we would be remiss if we didn't talk shop." She leans back with a searching look on her face. Bangles on her wrist clink together as she gesticulates with her glass. "Once in a while I find myself in creative lulls. Usually when I'm overworked, sorting through too much content too quickly, that sort of thing. Life gets in the way."

"It's me. I'm life," Damien jokes, cheers-ing his wife before she's ready. The glasses clink noisily together.

Darla spares a pitying smile for her husband before continuing. "When I find myself feeling drained, I usually step away. I was ready to step away from this project and enlist the help of one of my assistants once it was cast. But you two have made that difficult."

Piper clears her throat. "Oh?"

"I've pored over the hours of footage you sent me and rewatched your audition a few times"—she shakes her head and takes a sip of her drink—"and I feel like I did when I first started on the voice-acting side of the business. You two are *electric*. The chemistry between you two is everything. The little looks throughout your audition, the longing in your voice, the way you step into Laz and Victoria so effortlessly—it's a treat. There's so much talent and potential there."

"You two put on a good show," Damien agrees.

Piper is stock-still at my side.

"I've been thinking." Darla lowers her voice, sounding like a conspiratorial teenager trying to talk her older sibling into buying her alcohol. "I have a project I'm working on. Writing it myself. Imagine a steamy time-traveling plot. Think *Outlander*, but bigger. Global. Intergalactic, even. Romance and adventure at every turn. I started it years ago, but as I'm writing it lately, I hear you two in the characters. How would you feel about an exclusivity deal when the Vic and Laz project wraps? I'm envisioning two years of work, minimum—"

My brain starts doing crunches.

*Exclusivity.*

*Two years.*

*Chemistry.*

At my side, Piper responds in gushing bursts,

gesticulating like she swallowed a pound of catnip. In my haze, I pick up on every other word. As it happens, every other word is *wow, impressive, flattered.*

"What would that entail, exactly?" I manage after a thick swallow.

Darla talks contracts, sponsors, and plans until the food arrives. I swiftly regret asking. This is the fucking Superbowl of voice acting, apparently.

It's a lot. More than I ever anticipated. It'd be nearly impossible with my schedule if I win the race.

But Piper's enthusiasm is so tangible I could hold it in my hands. And as easily, I could break it in half in a matter of words. The pressure lands on me all at once, settling on my body like a lead suit.

Letting her down isn't an option. But what choice do I have?

"Everything all right with your burger?" Piper whispers as the Gentrys dig into their meals.

I nod, neck so tight I almost can't swing it.

"That's it?"

Another nod.

She slides her phone off the table and starts smashing the keyboard with angry fingers.

*Can you at least pretend to be interested in this once-in-a-lifetime opportunity?*

I pocket my phone without responding. I have the length of a meal before I have to answer that, and I'm counting on the Gentrys' long-winded nature to buy me time to think.

Damien points at Piper with his fork. "You mentioned splicing footage in your email last week, Piper, and I've been meaning to tell you a trick with that. Fun fact about Adobe—something they don't advertise…"

Turns out Damien's social battery dies promptly at ten p.m. The Gentrys are gone before the ink is dried on the credit card slip, leaving Piper and me side by side under Gala Bistro's striped awning.

So much for time to think.

She whirls on me. Light from the restaurant casts a spotlight on her face. "What was that about? You totally froze in there."

"Nothing. I'm tired. We should call it a night."

Hurt flashes in her eyes. "Fine. I guess we'll just table this issue for now."

I nod once, no words left to spare. That table of our issues must be buckling under the weight. Apparently ignoring problems is our new MO, and I'm exhausted by it.

When we reach the stretch of sidewalk in front of my car, her cool hand encircles mine. She pulls me back. "You really aren't going to talk to me? Or even say goodbye?"

I soften for a second at the plea in her voice before schooling my expression back to neutrality. "I believe it was *you* who didn't want to talk last night."

"I never said that. We can talk."

"*Actually* talk? About us?"

She winces.

I throw my head back and exhale at the inky sky. "You don't want to talk about us. I'm too exhausted to talk about work. Maybe we just leave it at that."

She releases my hand, and I feel the loss of her touch instantly. "If that's what you want."

The desire to know what *she* truly wants builds to a dangerous peak. But I can't put myself out there again only to get nothing in return. I nod once.

"Fine." She takes a step toward my car. "Work question, then. Did something happen at your press interview today? You've been in a terrible mood all night."

"It just feels like a lot lately," I admit under my breath.

"What feels like a lot?"

"The campaign, managing public opinion, my job, our job, and now…" I rub the back of my neck and turn away from her. Looking in her eyes makes it harder to admit how overwhelmed I am. "Listen, I should get going."

"This is about the exclusivity contract, isn't it? You don't want it." She drags her hand across her reddened face. "I shouldn't have gotten my hopes up."

"I'm not saying I don't want it," I snap, my irritation rearing back to life. "I want *everything* at the same time. That's the problem. I don't see a way to make it all work."

She backs into the side of my car. "I get it. You upheld your end of the bargain. You don't owe me anything."

My thoughts are riddled with land mines. "We had an *arrangement*. A few months of work while I campaign. And with this new thing? It's way more time—years, it sounds like—that was never part of the deal! What am I supposed to do?"

"Right. A business deal. Tit for tat, partner."

I step forward and point straight at her chest. "Don't. *You're* the one who wanted to keep things professional. Uncomplicated. Now you're telling me you want to add *years* to that timeframe. Can you imagine years of being trapped in this limbo?"

"Damnit." The word slips out of her mouth like a quiet plea. She says it two more times and strikes the car with the back of her fist. With another curse under her breath, she shakes out her hand like it stings. Her eyes glisten with unshed tears. "It wasn't supposed to be this complicated."

I close the tiny gap between us and swipe her cheek with my thumb as the first tear falls. My body tenses, shouting at me to *fix it*. A tall order, since I'm half to blame. "Please don't cry."

When she speaks, it's so faint it almost gets swallowed by the wind. "I don't know how I'll look them in the eye and tell them no."

"Pipes." My left arm cages her against the car as my right hand grabs her chin and tilts it up. The contact zips through me like a tase. "You don't have to tell them no. You don't need me. Maybe they'll be bummed for a few minutes, but they'll find another male lead."

Her eyes well up, and it takes every ounce of self-control not to reel her in and hold her against my chest. Hot breath fogs the air between us as she gives in to her tears. She blinks up at me through thick, wet lashes. "They won't want me alone."

Her words hit like a punch to the solar plexus. "You are *more* than enough of a draw without me."

A siren blares in the distance as wind kicks up dead maple leaves at our feet. The rustle of foliage is as quiet as her whisper. "Remember what Darla said in there? They want our chemistry. Yours and mine."

Spurred by her words, my fingers slide from her chin to cup her cheek. Something inside me twists as she leans into my palm, accepting my comfort. I brush the pad of my thumb in a line across her bottom lip, back and forth in gentle, teasing strokes until her mouth relaxes open and her eyes suck me in. Charged energy flickers between us the longer we stare.

*Chemistry.*

What if we keep it for ourselves?

I want to pin her against the car and take that lip between my teeth, bad idea be damned. If this feeling surging through my body were a contract, I'd sign it in permanent marker without reading a single word. Knowing she wants it, too—seeing the frantic rise and fall of her chest, hearing her tiny whimper as I lean closer—is almost enough.

Our foreheads fall together. A parade could storm the street and I wouldn't notice. Seconds tick by as I wait for her to close that last inch between our lips.

Because I can't kiss her again. If she wants to do this, she'll have to initiate. I've made it clear where I stand.

She traps her bottom lip in her mouth. "I should…go."

"Should go or want to?"

"We've got our first two studio sessions next week, and we need to bring it like it's never been brought before. No distractions." She drags her gaze away from my lips. "Completely professional."

I put much-needed space between us. "I'll pick you up Tuesday morning. Driving two cars that far feels like a waste. And don't wear your perfume. I don't need to be tortured by you any more than I already am."

"Fine. Don't wear your cologne, then."

Her insinuation hits like a shot of bourbon, warm and potent. "No crying," I counter.

"No crying?"

"Yeah. Pretty sure I'm incapable of not touching you if you're in distress."

She opens and closes her mouth. For a stupidly hopeful second, I think she may cry again, giving me an excuse.

"Will you do me a favor?" Her face flushes red. "Will you at least not say no tonight? Give the idea of the exclusivity deal time to settle?"

I fix the sleeve that's slipped down her shoulder, my hand shaking. I'm learning that with Piper, no favor is off the table. Even if coordinating my schedule feels like a Rubik's Cube some days.

But this one is an almost impossible solve.

My words follow a resigned sigh. "I'll think about it."

Hope flickers in her eyes, and I hate myself a little more, knowing we're just kicking this conversation down the road.

Unless maybe, somehow, I can find a way to make it all work.

# CHAPTER TWENTY-FOUR

## PIPER

E.T. grinds to a dead stop overhead with a soft beep. The door opens, and Darla sticks her head into the studio, interrupting our scene for no less than the tenth time today. Every time we have to stop unexpectedly, my hopes of getting on the road before the storm we're expecting tonight hits die a little more.

"Sam, you're going to have to look at Piper when she's talking."

Sam blinks up from his script. "I—I'm sorry. I thought I was."

Heat sweeps across my cheeks as I busy myself with the water bottle I hid inside the podium. We've been in this dark studio for six hours. Already an hour past what we were scheduled. Apart from bathroom breaks, we've been shackled to our spots. My butt and legs are fully numb. With the camera off, I seize the opportunity to stand up and arch my back. Sam lets out a strangled huff when I bend over to stretch my hamstrings.

We're filming scenes out of order so we can capture the most climactic moments for publicity footage. Jumping between extreme emotions is exhausting work, but today and tomorrow are pivotal for launching this project.

Sam and I have spent most of today silently warring over the front seat of the struggle bus. Every time one of us finds a groove, the other slips into disarray.

Darla stopped the camera on me two scenes ago for being too quick to cut off Sam's reactions with my lines. Our gazes snagged until he mumbled that he needed a two-minute break and disappeared out the door.

She also stopped me during a sex scene to tell me I sounded like I was about to cry. Less-than-ideal feedback.

Prior to all of that, she stopped Sam mid–declaration of love because he was too rigid. *Grip the podium any tighter and you'll cut off the blood flow to your fingers, sonny.* I can't disagree with her there. He looked one step away from popping a blood vessel.

And now he's *back* in the hot seat. God help us all.

Darla offers him a sympathetic hum. "I know it's getting late and you're probably dog tired. For this last scene, it'll work best if you are *very* direct. Laz isn't scared of Victoria by this stage of the book, and he's not going to shy away from this interaction. Watch Piper say the lines, react accordingly, and then give her hell."

*Sorry, Darla. I'm already in hell.*

Sam massages the space above his right eyebrow. "Yes, ma'am."

We were supposed to wrap thirty minutes ago. The twins hate thunder, and I want to pick up storm treats on the way home to distract them. Skittles usually do the trick. Pure sugar is a surefire way to reroute their worries.

I try to meet his eye to give him a reassuring nod. We've made it this far, and the end of today's session is near. But Sam stares down at his script, doing everything in his power to avoid my gaze.

*Fine.*

"Resume at the top of the page, Victoria's line." Darla gestures at her husband through the glass and sidles out the door.

I clear my throat after E.T. beeps back to life.

"*What will it take to make Laz see that I'm smart and trustworthy?*

"'*Every single day of my life is the same, Laz. The trappings of royalty threaten to break me. Now* you *presume to tell me with whom I can fraternize, what topics I can discuss. How dare you?'"*

Sam levels me with a fiery glare. I know he's taking Darla's stage directions to heart, but damnit if my stomach doesn't lurch at the intensity behind his expression. If he's going for smoldering, it's working.

"*Victoria is maddening in her naïveté.*

"'*Be* reasonable, *princess. Your advisor, Simoan, cannot be trusted. I'm not going to stand idly by—'"*

I cut him off with a guttural cry of frustration as E.T. whirls to capture my face.

"'*Jealousy will be* your *undoing, Lazarus. Don't pretend you want what's best for me. You can't stand the idea of a male advisor in my ear.'"*

A crack echoes through the room as Sam slams the podium with open palms.

"'*And that's the* only *place he'll be.'"*

*Wow.*

I laugh my bitter, scripted laugh.

"'*Tell me: What exactly do you think we do in strategy meetings? You think Simoan lays me down on the table and spreads me open—'"*

The air between us is supercharged as we lock eyes.

"'*Don't you dare finish that sentence, princess.'"*

The lusty venom in Sam's tone is like a shot of electricity, spearing me awake from my tired haze.

"*Heat spreads through my core as Laz yanks*

*me closer by the ruffled fabric of my blouse. Even the thought of another man touching me makes him wild. I slap his hand aside and rip my blouse clean off, buttons skittering across the ground.*

*"'If you don't fear Simoan and me in the strategy meetings, perhaps it's the thought of us behind closed doors that sparks this jealous rage? Perhaps he serves as my escort, walking me back to my chambers after the sun has set. Maybe I let him inside.'"*

The camera swings back and wide until Sam and I are both in the shot.

*"Oh, she's a mouthy little thing. Her game is a mind fuck so thorough I want to fill her mouth with me just to get her to stop talking.*

*"I don't even have to unwrap her, tempt her, tease her. She's stripped herself bare. All for me. After a single lick, I tug her nipple with my teeth until she cries out and rips my pants down. I'm so hard for her I hardly think I'll fit, but I'll be damned if I'm not going to try."*

For the first time in the history of forever, I miss my cue.

I forget I *have* a cue.

I'm so lost in Sam's blown pupils I don't notice I'm breathing with my mouth open, digging my nails into my palms, hinging on his every word.

Too much time passes. He's finally looking at me, as Darla wanted. The problem is he's *really* looking at me and I don't know how to function. My body has turned into warm molasses. I don't know *how* much time passes because I am suspended in frozen animation. It could be a second. Could be minutes.

The camera swoops from me to Sam as his tone slips into something familiar, more him and less Laz fucking the princess in the barn. His improvised line yanks me back to the reality of the moment.

"'*Say something, princess. Or have you decided to stop running your mouth after all?*'"

I can salvage this. Darla wants me to embody Princess Victoria's essence right now.

Wants me to be super turned on by the stable boy about to rail me in the barn.

I can do that.

"*His hardness glistens in the moonlight. It's a heady thrill, knowing it's all for me.*

"*He tastes like the foamy salt water of l'Ocean de Boryonne on my tongue as I take my fill of him. I don't stop tasting him until his legs begin to quiver beneath my open palms.*

"*There's a mischievous flicker in his eyes as he watches me, like he may devour me whole.*"

Sam's response is like hot honey dripping down the side of a mug.

"'*Oh, princess. Did you think relief would be that swift after you teased me with that mouth of yours? This doesn't end until you beg.*'"

The camera shuts off, and Darla cracks the door. "That's a wrap for today."

I slump forward on the podium and bury my face in my hands.

Damien's voice crackles through the speaker. "Geppetto cut your strings, Piper?"

"Just tired."

"Well, not to be the bearer of bad news, but we need to get moving ASAP," Darla informs from the doorway. "The weather's taken a bad turn."

Sam straightens, white knuckling the edges of his podium. I can almost see the cogs turning in the disaster-readiness part of his firefighter brain. "What are we talking here, Darla?"

"Tornado watches for Middlesex and Worcester counties."

"I thought we weren't expecting the storm until later tonight."

Darla taps her watch. "It's already nine thirty. Didn't expect it to escalate like this."

In the span of a minute, as I gather my belongings, Sam has texted Forrester at the station, checked traffic reports, and pulled up the Doppler. "This is a mess. The road is littered with accidents in every direction. There was a small tornado that tore up some trees east of Roseborough." My hand flies to my chest as he quickly adds, "Not near your parents' house or Caleb's. Off Highway 13. There are downed power lines everywhere."

Damien lowers the glass. "That's May in New England. Weather's as wild as a bull seven seconds in."

Darla rubs her chin. "We're just up the road, but I don't like you kids hauling back to Roseborough in these conditions. Can we pay for a hotel? The main road has a Hilton less than a mile from here."

I chew the inside of my cheek. Mom is probably freaked out by the storm. "Are you sure we can't make it home?"

Sam rolls his eyes. "Piper. The roads are clogged. And beyond being dangerous, a forty-five-minute drive in these conditions could take hours."

Darla waves a black American Express card in the air. "Two rooms, whatever meals you require, gas. Keep your receipts, and we'll circle back on additional expenses as needed."

"Thank you, Darla, but we're fine," Sam insists. "It's my fault we made it out of the studio so late. I took us way over schedule with my reshoots. I'm sorry."

Darla tucks the card in her purse. "Never apologize for giving it your all, Sam. We better get going. Thank you for your hard work today."

We exchange quick goodbyes, and the Gentrys lead us out of the studio. Darla takes off into the storm, her bedazzled denim coat slung over her hair for protection. Damien trails behind his wife, shouting that she should have let him pull the car around.

We huddle under the overhang. Sam's voice barely competes with the howling wind. "I guess we should get this show on the road."

Lightning cracks across the hazy black sky. I count the seconds until it thunders to gauge how far away the bolt struck, a trick Nonna taught me when I was little. She always said ten seconds or more meant you were a safe distance from the center of a storm.

Only three seconds pass before the thunder rumbles.

Well, hell.

Primal panic spurs me into motion. I sprint across the lot with Sam hot on my heels. He unlocks his car, and I rip open the door, panting and wet as I climb inside. He's right behind.

"I'll call the Hilton." My teeth chatter as I locate the number.

"Fuck, what are we going to do about our clothes?" He cranks up the heat with the twist of a knob. "We'll have to run home early and change if the roads are clear."

I glance up from the phone. "We have to wear the same thing tomorrow on camera."

"I have another shirt this shade of gray. And plenty of pairs of black pants."

"Congrats on your depressing wardrobe. I, however, don't have another blazer or skirt exactly like this. And it's not washer or dryer safe, even if we do make it home. Damn you, wool-poly blend, pain in my ass—" I break off as another streak of lightning and near-immediate roll of thunder shake the vehicle.

The twins aren't the only ones who hate storms.

"Pipes." He pivots on his headrest, and his gaze lowers to my shaky hands. "Are you okay?"

"I'm cold. And lightning freaks me out."

"Don't worry so much. You're way more likely to die in a car crash than by lightning."

"You're not helping!"

Shutting him and the storm out, I navigate to the Hilton website. It takes me about ten seconds to determine they're at capacity. "We're screwed. They're fully booked."

Sam pulls out of the lot, brows furrowed in concentration.

I tug on my seat belt to make sure it's really locked. *Way more likely to die in a car crash...*

"Where are you going?" I ask, bracing myself for a stressful ride.

"I'm finding us a hotel, come hell or high water." The right side of his SUV tussles with a deep puddle on the uneven road. My hand vibrates as I clutch the oh-shit bar.

High water: check.

He sets his windshield wipers to top speed. "I remember passing something on the way in that looked like a hotel. Or a bed and breakfast. Or maybe it's a haunted house—who the hell knows. I'll try there first."

A horn in the distance punctuates his sentence. I tighten my grip. "I don't care if there are rusty knives for doorknobs and Lizzie Borden is the keeper of the grounds. I just want shelter."

# CHAPTER TWENTY-FIVE

## SAM

I bury my relief in a joke when the building I take us to is, in fact, a hotel. "I was right. Definitely a sleeping establishment. Hold your applause."

We sit in the parking lot of The Conquistador for a minute as Piper pulls up their website. The car heater purrs, and I try to focus on the warmth and not the unease in my gut as I sneak a look at the Doppler on my phone.

We're in the thick of it. But I'm not about to tell a worried, trembling Piper that. Instead, I silently pray for vacancy as I study the curves and arches of the building, terracotta roof tiles, and fussy iron railings outlining each balcony.

"This place looks stupid expensive. It has a

courtyard. With a fountain. I bet there's a fountain surcharge." She pauses her violent phone thumbing to shoot me a look. "You think this is our only option?"

Thunder cracks so loud it's like we're in the clouds. "Yes. And if you're worried about how much it'll cost, don't. I'm buying both the rooms."

"No way."

"Piper, please. Don't be ridiculous. It's late; let me take care of it."

"Damnit, this website doesn't tell me *anything*. Waste of a page."

I swipe the phone from her hand. "Let me try."

"What, you think I was making it up?"

"Just wanted to see for myself."

She harrumphs and crosses her arms across her chest. "Hurry up. I have to pee."

The website is as bad as she described. Seriously, they'd be better off with a 404: URL not found than this excuse for a landing pad. No room information, no rates, no nothing.

I toss back her phone and reach into the back seat to grab my duffel. "We'll just have to find out the old-fashioned way."

"Wait, why do you have stuff? I want stuff!" she whines.

"I basically live out of my car on my shift weekends, remember? You can have my spare toothbrush."

We trail moisture and mud into an ornate entryway flanked with floor-to-ceiling colorful tiles. Bet there's a surcharge for this foyer that looks like a shower, too.

Piper swerves into the bathroom on our left. By the time she catches up to me at the counter, my credit card is in my new friend Bill's hand.

"They've got a room. I'm finishing up here," I inform her.

"Room singular? As in one?"

"Yes. It's all they have."

"There's no janitor's closet you can squat in for the night? Or a carpeted elevator that moves nice and slow?"

I smile blandly. "Silly me. I forgot to inquire about closets for rent. I know how much you like me in a closet."

Her glare is lethal. She swivels and slams her palms on the counter. "We'll take the room. How much?"

"It's done." I take my credit card from Bill's offering hand. "Paid."

"It's a lovely room," Bill assures. "The Queen Suite, fourth floor."

She shifts her weight. "Two beds?"

"A spacious king."

Piper eyes Bill's nametag. "Is there a cot or a pullout in that bad boy, Bill?"

He presses his temple with two fingers. "I'm afraid we don't have *cots* at The Conquistador."

I tilt my head in her direction. Down, in other words. "We're lucky they have a room at all on such short notice. Or would you rather we brave the storm?"

"Thank you, Bill." She steals the keycard envelope and lumbers dejectedly toward the elevator.

When I catch up, she spares me a quick look and a faint, "I'm going to give you half the cost."

"Consider it a birthday present, four months early. Or belated, eight months late."

There's awkward, and then there's walking into The Conquistador's Queen Suite, which boasts a four-poster bed and one of those above-ground tubs with claw feet—out in the open. A chair would've been a more practical furnishing. I tug on a drawer of an ancient dresser, but it's fused shut.

"This place is an oven," I grumble, scanning the wall for a thermostat. "This radiator looks like it hasn't been replaced or serviced in decades."

"Settle down, grandpa. No one asked you to complete an inspection."

There isn't even a TV to drown out the silence.

"I'll sleep on the floor," I relent after we shuffle around each other for a few minutes.

"Don't be silly. You can sleep in the tub."

"That tub has you written all over it. I would

never fit in something that small."

"Good point, Hefty. Floor it is."

I study her wardrobe from top to bottom.

She pulls at her blazer's lapels. "Stop looking at me like that."

"My apologies, princess."

A cool chill passes between us.

*Princess.*

*This doesn't end until you beg.*

"Not like Princess Victoria," I add, sweat beading my forehead. "I meant the high-maintenance kind."

Heat flames in her cheeks. She stalks to the bathroom and shuts the door behind her. The nails-on-a-chalkboard sound of a hairdryer kicks on soon after.

Minutes later, after I've changed, hung my clothes to dry, and MacGyvered a bed on the ground from a spare blanket and a lone pillow I swiped from the bed, the bathroom door cracks open an inch. The racket gets even louder.

"How are you not done yet?" I holler.

She sticks her head out. "I'm trying not to die of heatstroke in here. And remind me never to wear a suit again. It's taking forever to dry."

I lift onto an elbow. "You're drying your suit? Why not just let it hang over night?"

"I told you! Wool-poly blend. That shit takes forever to dry on its own. I'm helping it along. It'll still have to hang dry."

"Well then, what're you going to wear?"

She narrows her eyes. "What do you think?"

*Right.*

Dumb question. She's in her underwear as she handles her clothes.

I jump up and retrieve my duffel before my dick runs away with the visual of her in barely-there scraps of fabric. Not that her traipsing around in a tight skirt and heels all day didn't inspire its own kind of mental warfare. Business clothes fit her so well it's a white-collar crime.

"Would you like a shirt?" I dangle an extra from my bag like a carrot. "Comfortable. Clean. Dry."

And more importantly, full coverage. Because if I get even a glimpse of a mostly naked Piper, I'll have to sleep in that janitor's closet or elevator to calm the fuck down.

Her lips twist, which lets me know she wants it and wishes she didn't.

I shake the soft cotton. "It's this or a shower curtain."

She disappears into the bathroom. I'm about to argue the point when the dryer switches off and an arm pokes through the crack.

*That's what I thought.*

I've resumed laying on the brutally hard floor, mulling over the merits of sleeping in the tub, when

Piper materializes above me.

My *god*. I don't know what I expected, but it wasn't the way Piper looks in my shirt, with her wild hair falling around her and her smooth legs begging to be touched. It wasn't how the fabric would fall against her curves and settle halfway down her thigh.

I can tell by her open mouth that she arrived with a comment locked and loaded on her tongue. I roll to my side to squash the visual of her directly above me. Dangerous angle. Too much fodder for my imagination.

"Get in the damn bed, Sam."

"With an invitation like that—"

"I won't be able to sleep with you rolling around on the ground. Too loud."

"As long as your motivations are purely selfish."

"You paid for the bed."

I shut my eyes and count to five. The woman is testing me. Sleeping next to her is a *horrible* idea. "I also paid for this floor."

"Please?"

I flip onto my back, stupidly, and try not to look up her shirt. She's somehow even closer now. I have front-row tickets to a show I can't attend. "What do you want from me?"

"If you don't sleep in the bed, I'll feel guilty, which will encroach on my REM cycle. Don't you want me to have quality REM?"

"You are the most frustrating woman alive." I force myself off the ground and cross the room to flip the overhead light, leaving the bathroom light and a bedside lamp to illuminate the room.

The bed is as pointlessly ornate as everything else in The Conquistador. I pull back the covers and fall in. For my own sanity, I shove a pillow in the bed's middle to create a barrier.

She flashes me a withering glare. "Really? I'm that offensive to you?"

"You kick in your sleep. Terribly violent stuff."

She chucks the barrier pillow on the ground. "No, I don't."

A grin of satisfaction pulls at my lips. I'm growing addicted to the flutter in her voice when she's trying not to react to something I've said. "How would you know? It happens while you're racking up your precious REM."

The fight seems to leave her all at once, and she shuts her eyes. "Good night, Sam."

I switch off the bedside lamp and stretch out under my side of the duvet. "Night, Pipes."

For being as exhausted as I am, my body is buzzing. My adrenals are working overtime with her so close. Sleep feels impossible, as my eyelids are suddenly spring loaded and refuse to say shut. I stare at the dim outlines on the printed wallpaper and count my breaths.

*One.*

*Two.*

Her every little movement sends vibrations through the bed. The duvet slides across my arm as she switches positions, and I'm certain I'm going to crawl out of my skin.

It shouldn't be this hard to sleep next to her.

After a few minutes of forcing my eyes to stay shut, my heart rate finally slows. As soon as sleep hovers within reach, the duvet shifts again as she lets out a long sigh.

Savage need bleeds through my body. I'm hanging on by a thread, and it feels close to snapping. She's *right there*, under the same blanket. In my shirt. Making noises.

I can't take it anymore. I need to at least see her. Throwing my own rule in the trash, I peek.

She's looking at me, too.

*Oh fuck.* Now we're looking at each other.

A thrill shoots down my spine, rippling across my back, snaking around my arms, and spreading across my chest.

I can't bring myself to do anything but swallow. Suddenly, the distance between us is not enough. Each second that passes with neither of us breaking eye contact feels like more chips laid on the table, upping the ante. Her dark eyes smolder like chocolate. It's all too easy to imagine what I'd do with melted chocolate dripped over her skin. All it takes is a look from her and I'm desperate, starving.

I grasp the blanket and lift the fabric, emboldened by the need in her eyes. All I see is my shirt flirting with her leg. I think my heart forgets to beat as I drink her in like it's my last chance.

Her expression is eager and pained all at once. She traces small circles on her thigh, and I want to push her hand aside and take over. I have to do something before I fist that fabric and drag her closer. "I'm going to have to sleep in my car. A man can't be expected to endure this kind of torture."

"I'm not torturing you on purpose," she whispers.

"Yes you are. You wore your perfume."

"You can't prove that."

I snatch her hand off her leg and bring her wrist to my mouth. One drag of my tongue across her hot skin, and I'm a goner. "The way you taste tells me otherwise."

She lets out a hoarse sound as her mouth falls open, spurring me on. I fasten my lips and suck. "Sam, please."

My heart tries to punch its way out of my chest. I replace my mouth with my thumb and stroke her wrist. "Is it for me?"

Her tone is as tormented as I feel. "What will you do if it is?"

# CHAPTER TWENTY-SIX

## PIPER

Sam slides closer. My breaths seem to leave my body at top volume as I wait to see just how close he'll get. When our chests are mere inches apart, he holds my gaze for a second.

Two seconds.

The air between us crackles. His eyes flash with unmasked frustration.

I point to a spot on my neck.

He leans forward and swipes his tongue over my skin. I know he tastes the perfume when he groans.

I pull back to meet his eyes. "It's for you. Since the first time you told me you love it, it's been for you."

He groans. "No more waiting, Piper." He covers

my mouth with his. His soft, greedy lips taste like mint and relief. My thoughts lose shape and form as he cradles my face in his palms, growling urgently into my mouth, "I can't take it anymore."

I melt into him, my mouth sliding across his as we take the kiss deeper. He traces my tongue with his in one smooth and perfect stroke. It makes me desperate for more, and I think he knows it because his tongue slips away the second I let out a little moan. Over and over he does this, chasing intensity and backing off, exploring my mouth with maddening softness and fleeting pressure.

I pull back to catch my breath. Panic flickers in his eyes. It's as though he thinks I'm pumping the breaks between us again, and the thought is as unbearable to him as it is to me.

*No way.*

This time I control the kiss, showing him what I want, biting his lip and urging his mouth with a few flicks of my tongue. I rake my fingers up and down his chest and stomach, feeling his muscles tense beneath me every time I dip lower. When I slide inside his shirt and run my nails down his skin, a sharp hiss escapes his mouth. He reels me even closer with a fist gripping my shirt until his hardness juts into my leg.

My heart rate explodes at the feel of him. "I want you. *All* of you."

His features come into full focus as he tilts his

chin down, all dangerous lines, carved cheeks, and lush lips. He threads his hand through my hair and tugs. The sensation is sharp and delicious. His lips travel up my neck, nibbling my earlobe, kissing a circuit until he lands on my collarbone. I gasp when he adds suction.

"Show me." He presses the demand into my skin. "Show me how badly."

I peel off my underwear and toss them aside. The muscles in his arm flex as I position his hand right where I want him. He's not even inside me— he's barely even *touched* me—and I am so wet his fingers slide with ease. I nibble on his neck as I rock into his hand.

"*Shit*." He forces his eyes closed for a second. I revel in the sound of his rapid breathing. "You are so fucking soft and warm."

My senses are completely overwhelmed by the gentle, circular brush of his finger as he explores me. It's slow, so painfully slow I groan into his chest and shift my hips to feel him at a different angle, greedy for more.

He moves lower, testing, still circling.

"Please." I grip his arms to hold myself steady. "More."

He slips a finger inside and exhales sharply as my muscles tense around him. "I always suspected you'd be the one to kill me."

I slide a knee over his hip so he can push deeper. "Is this how you"—he slides in another finger, and I let out a shaky gasp—"imagined death?"

His free hand sweeps the hair off my face. "It'd be a fine way to go."

Teeth graze my neck, and I whimper. He feels so good, even just testing the waters. The friction is incredible as his thumb makes slow circles over me as he slides in and out. My thoughts blur together, two rising above the rest.

*So good.*

*Too good.*

I want to slow it down and savor it. We've barely scratched the surface of what we can do while trapped in this room, the night stretched out before us like a lavish gift.

Against my body's wishes, I slide off his fingers and sit up. It's been an eternity since I've undressed him, and I'm bordering on desperate. I need to see him. Trace his abs with my fingers. Touch him everywhere.

"Off with these." I tug on the waistband of his shorts. "I want you in my mouth."

"No way I'd survive it. I'm barely hanging on just feeling you."

*Oh God.* This is what we get for waiting a hundred years to do this. We are both one right touch away from coming undone.

He pushes me down with an open palm against my chest and climbs on top, covering me with delicious weight and heat. I rip off his shirt and cast it aside. Miles of kissable skin tease and tempt me. I want to lick every inch of him. I plant my lips the first place I can reach, tight skin beside his shoulder.

Rough hands tug my shirt up and off.

"You wore *this* bra?" His expression darkens as he hovers above me with a knee pinned down on either side of my hips. He sweeps a finger over a black lace cup. "Thank God I didn't know sooner, or we wouldn't have made it out of your house this morning when I picked you up."

"Maybe I wear it when I want to remember you eye-fucking me in the shower." I slide my hand over the front of his shorts. My whispers make him grow even harder. "Maybe I wear it in the hopes you'll rip it off."

He lowers onto his elbows and pulls down my left strap with his teeth, devouring the skin of my shoulder, collarbone, all the way to the edge of the mesh cup with his hot mouth. My eyes fall closed as I zero in on the sensation of him nudging the fabric aside with his tongue. He teases circles around my nipple until I cry out in frustration.

"Do you know how many times this bra popped into my dreams? You in this see-through fabric, nipples hard like this?" I gasp as he drags pure heat over my peak with his tongue.

But then he stops. "Fuck, I'm probably saying too much."

I arch into him, gripping the sheets. "Don't stop." *Talking. Teasing. Any of it.*

He snakes his hand behind me and frees the clasp. Goose bumps ripple across my chest as he teases my skin, tickling me with mesh and wire until my nipple could cut glass. "I think about you all the time. It's constant. You aren't *always* naked in these thoughts. Just 90 percent of the time." He tosses the bra aside, and his mouth closes over me, dangerously warm. *Yes.*

"I think about you, too," I manage between labored breaths. "Whether you're safe during your shifts at the station. How good you look in a button-up. How"—I cry out as he sucks—"you'd feel inside of me."

He bites, and I whimper.

"God, I love your little sounds." He tugs with his teeth.

The sensation of him kissing a trail down my stomach fills me with immense conflict. I'm desperate for him, the things he can do with his tongue, but not giving him something in return makes me feel unbalanced and a little crazed. I grasp his hair and tug so I can see his face.

"Let me taste you," I beg. "I want to make *you* feel good."

His eyes flash with wicked glee. "Believe me, this does make me feel good. You can taste me on round two."

*Round two.*

I fall backward, fairly sure I'm hyperventilating as he passes below my belly button, coaxing my legs open wider with one hand. He kisses and licks everywhere *except* where I throb. He gets close—so painfully close—twice, before landing on a different spot. Both times I push off the bed, angling my hips. Pleading with my body. He's a masterful tease, laughing his hot air all over me, driving me to the brink. When he doesn't give in, I reach to touch myself.

He catches my hand and traps it against the bed. The heat of his breath as he speaks is enough to spark sensation. I feel him *there*. "Trust me."

And he hits the spot with his tongue.

Just once.

My entire body tenses, willing him to continue.

"You're the only one who's ever done this."

The words rush out like a caged animal let free. I don't know why I blurted that. There's a lot of things I could've said instead, like *my two exes skipped foreplay.*

Whatever the reason, the truth is out there. And it seems to spark his sense of urgency. His tongue returns with purpose. He licks and sucks with such authority I'm tempted to repeat *Sam parking only* simply so he won't stop. I'm terrified he'll go back to teasing and leave me like this, writhing in the bed with my hand clasped over my mouth.

Any coherent thoughts left in my head fall away as I chase a release hovering just beyond reach. I circle my hips as he picks up speed, my movements bolder and sloppier by the minute. He reaches up to brush circles over my nipple in time with the strokes of his tongue.

"Hand off your mouth, Piper. I want to hear you."

His growl rumbles straight through me. Desperation pools low in my stomach the closer I get, stretching and climbing until I'm holding my breath. I hover on the precipice, tensing, a chorus of *so close*, *don't stop* playing in my head.

His tongue does less and less the closer I get, until it's barely moving at all. He puffs hot air on my skin for seconds straight, exactly the kind of torturous sensation I need.

When his tongue hits me again, a single flick of pressure and warmth, I fall apart so thoroughly he grips my hips to keep me down and swears into my skin as I cry out into the darkness.

After the pulsing finally subsides, I'm no more than a puddle of mush with a skeleton. Rational thought creeps back in, the first of which being *damnit, he's good at everything*.

His hair is tousled from my hands, and his eyes are

nearly black, all pupil as he watches me come down from the high. When my breathing slows enough, he climbs over me, his abs deliciously contracted. I spread my palms over his chest, his arms, drinking in the feel of him. "Can I finally undress you now?"

"Please God, yes."

I don't need to be told twice. Down go his pants.

He rolls onto his side so I can pull them all the way off.

The part of me controlled by unrelenting lust wants to rip off his boxers with my teeth and lick every hard inch of him. But he's wearing those black Calvin Kleins like a glove, looking so unreasonably chiseled it'd be a crime not to soak in the sight.

This is not Sam the gangly teen of my past.

This is a man.

I trace him through the thin fabric, and he groans at my featherlight touch. The gruff sound he makes when I free him ignites something animalistic in me. He's steel in my palm. How many times have I wanted exactly this without letting myself indulge the thought? *Finally*.

Endlessly patient, he says nothing as I stroke him slowly from base to tip even though he's throbbing in my hand. As badly as I want him inside me, he must be circling the gates of hell waiting for relief.

I blink up and catch his gaze. His eyelids are heavy, and his lips are parted. Hooking my leg around his waist, I use him as an anchor as I scoot myself closer. "What are you waiting for?"

"You," he whispers, his breathing jagged. "For a very long time."

The words explode in my chest like a firework. Everything beyond his blazing stare is dull and hazy, like I'm suddenly nearsighted. I've never been more ready, more hopelessly strung out than I am right now.

Before I can say anything in return, he smashes his mouth against mine, all traces of patience gone. He climbs back on top of me and nudges my legs open with his knee. "Stay there, just like that."

He rolls halfway off the bed and pulls a condom from his duffel. He tears the package with his teeth and rolls it on in the blink of an eye. I reach between us and guide his tip to my entry, moving him in slow circles until he's begging my name into my mouth. "Piper, please."

I release his hand, and he pushes into me. It's a tight, nearly painful fit. We both look down at the same time, perhaps to confirm this is actually happening. At least that's why I look at first. The disbelief fades as I get lost in the sight of him, carved from marble, pushing in a little deeper each time.

My head falls back against the mattress, and he buries his face in my neck. He moves in rhythmic bursts, alternating slow and fast.

The slow is sweet torture every single time.

I kiss down the column of his throat, feeling the vibrations of every noise he's holding in. "You don't have to slow down for me."

"I want to make it last, but you feel so fucking good—"

Using the bed as leverage, I circle my hips faster, setting the pace. If he's not going to take it, I'm going to give it to him. His face is raw, starving need as I move beneath him, fast and wild.

He's close; it's written all over his face. I want to tell him how good he feels, but before I get a single word out, he sits up abruptly and shifts us into a position I've only ever seen in the barebones black-and-white illustrations of *Cosmo* magazine. *Face to face.*

Eyes aligned and chests flush, we're both in control. But with his hands on my ass controlling the depth and rhythm, I'm happy to let him take the lead. He can take whatever he wants from me.

It's so perfect, so thoroughly satisfying, to see him finish this way. He groans into my chest, my sweaty skin muffling the rugged sound, as the bedside lamp casts a warm glow on half his face.

He stills his movements, and the friction inside of me fades. I can feel him throbbing and pulsing so acutely it's as if it's happening to me. I never knew it could feel like *this*. We've melded into one single body, each wave of pleasure winding us tighter together.

How ironic that the sensations of his orgasm are the most arousing things I've ever felt. It's like a one-hour soap opera with a cliffhanger, guaranteeing you'll tune in for more. When he plants a gentle kiss on my lips and whispers that this night was worth every second of the wait, I'm ready to binge the whole series.

# CHAPTER TWENTY-SEVEN

### SAM

I wake in my usual state: startled, panicked I've somehow slept through an emergency call. Before I can fly off the pillow, a warm leg threads between mine, and an arm grazes my chest.

*Piper.*

My system surges to life at the feel of her body seeking out mine while she sleeps. Tiny bursts of hot air tickle my shoulder as she breathes. I bury my face in her hair and close my eyes, stealing one more second from last night.

The reality of her beside me—of what we did— sinks in as the sun casts a wide swath of morning light over the bed. It was better than my hottest, wildest fantasies because it was real but also because it was *us.* I've never deluded myself into thinking I wasn't attracted to Piper Bellini. But I'd done a pretty good job convincing myself I wouldn't fall for her again.

I miscalculated. Turns out, when I love someone, it lingers. And I've only ever loved her, even if I never got a chance to tell her. She dropped the break(up) bomb weeks before prom, totally blowing up my romantic plan to tell her that night.

Maybe it was for the best. My fears then are the same as they are now. Can you be *in love* with someone who doesn't feel it, too?

I can't be in love with her without knowing how she feels. It's a two-player sport.

If only I could get a window to her thoughts. The way she held me, gripped my back, cried my name, looked at me like I hung the fucking moon when I pushed deeper inside her felt a lot like love. But what was it Jane said in her shakedown at Little Gym?

*Our girl has a difficult time owning up to her feelings until they have her in a choke hold.*

Hard to forget something phrased like that. Even harder not to let it mess with my head.

All I know is everything shifted for me last night. Or maybe I just gave in to what was clawing at me since she walked into McLaughlin's. She cracked me open, and the pieces are scattered all over this room. The duvet on the ground, the sheet draped over her legs, her clothes everywhere. Her perfect sounds as she came on my mouth now live in the gaudy-ass headboard. They live inside of me.

I grope the end table and locate my phone. An avalanche of notifications buries my home screen.

*Twenty-three missed calls.*

I wince. Only a few more than usual. I was too distracted to check yesterday. When I see Caleb's name on the call log, I nearly chuck my phone. That is not a minefield I'd like to traverse right now.

*Seventy-four unread emails.*

My pulse kicks into gear. I scan the first few emails, looking for similarities. Seems everyone wants something different. A team of Hamilton High students asking to shadow me on the campaign trail, local colleges asking if I'd be interested in making an appearance, requests for a quote about St. Mary's, a silk tie company looking for a brand partner (what?). A lot of praising emails from civilians citing the library speech as inspiring (even more surprising than the tie thing). My breath catches in my throat as I scan further.

An email from city councilor Rhea Armstrong, asking for a lunch.

She's one of the undecided councilors who I thought for sure was a Stine-Hard through and through.

And then, interview requests. A lot of them.

*Whoa.*

The amount of stuff in my inbox is mind-boggling. Being busy is fun—addicting, frankly—but this looks like schedule gridlock in the making. The idea of saying no to an event that could boost my campaign pumps me full of dread. But Piper and I have recording shifts scheduled, plus my hours at the station, plus the publicity events I've already committed to over the next four weeks. Even without these new opportunities dropped like surprise gifts in my inbox, it's a struggle to do everything I want to do.

Piper stirs beside me. Her eyes bat open, and she glows like a damn goddess in the sun's spotlight. She lets out a grumbly morning sigh as she stretches her arms overhead, her naked body on display. A buffet ripe for the tasting. I can't drag my eyes off her hard nipples begging to be touched.

I make it five painful seconds before winding my arm around her and pulling her against me. My phone slips between us. I greet the sensitive skin beneath her ear with my lips. "Hi."

She shudders. Knowing her *on* switch comes in handy.

"*Hi*," she says, her voice thick with sleep. "You're awake."

"Once I'm up, I'm up." A vibration flutters between us. She wriggles in surprise, and I grab the phone.

*Incoming Call*

*Captain Dad*

I lob the hunk of metal and plastic at my duffel. "Sorry. Sixteen different duties are trying to call this morning. Campaign stuff and apparently station stuff."

She nods, and a sad smile creeps across her face. "Right. Busy guy."

*Damnit.* The last thing she wants or needs right now is a reminder of how busy I am. Especially when the exclusivity contract looms like a damn skyscraper in the middle of this room.

Her hand circles my chin, tilting my face back toward her. "You could've answered your dad. I know you have a million things on your mind."

"None of that matters to me right now," I tell her firmly, reeling her closer.

"Make sure he didn't leave a voicemail."

"Or..." I kiss her once beneath the ear, swiping her skin with my tongue, testing. Tasting salt and the faintest hint of perfume.

Her hands travel over my arms and land on my back as we explore each other, moving together in the silence. It starts slow and catapults into teasing. *Almost* kisses. *Almost* touches. Fingers grazing where I want them gripping. It's enough to make me forget what I saw on my phone, my middle name, our agenda for the day. I want to feel her everywhere at once, the heat of her body against mine.

She drags her palm over my hip. Her finger

traces my length with a delicate touch, once.

Twice…

"How much time do we have?"

The raw need in her voice takes me from *ready* to achingly hard. I take her face in my hands and stare for a beat. Her eyes don't leave my lips. The look is so blatantly transparent my composure snaps and I climb on top of her. My hips pin hers as I answer with my lips to her throat. "Enough."

"Sam." My name on her tongue in the morning sounds like pure sex.

Possessiveness grips me, hot and demanding. I claim her with a rough kiss, and she claims me right back, sucking my bottom lip in her mouth like it's hers. Her knees slide up, bracketing my waist, changing the angle of contact. The hard press of me against her makes us both suck in a breath.

I want to jot mental notes of all the little things I'm noticing—how her dark hair spills across the crisp white sheet, how comfortable this feels, the gravelly sound of her just-woke-up voice—but her hand moves lower until she's gripping me inside my boxers, and my thoughts funnel into one word. *Need.*

My hand skates to her lower back, and I grip her skin, tearing a whine from her mouth. She grinds against me, lifting her hips off the bed as I nibble at her jaw, her throat, her lips, kissing and relishing. Her skin is warm and soft as I kiss my way past her collarbone.

"These are fucking perfect," I groan into the swell of her breasts, squeezing one of them with a greedy hand, teasing her nipple with a gentle swipe of my thumb, a stroke of my tongue. I'm learning that gentle drives her wild as she arches into my mouth, whimpering at the faint trace of contact.

I look up, meeting her hooded stare. "More?"

Her mouth falls open, but no words escape. Eyes still glued to hers, I puff air over her skin.

"Harder?"

She digs her nails into the back of my neck, communicating wordlessly. I graze her with my teeth. A cry escapes her mouth when I finally bite.

She pulls away abruptly, shimmying down the mattress. My groan fills the room as she hooks her fingers on my boxers and slides them off. "Pipes—"

My ability to form a sentence disappears the second her tongue hits my shaft, tracing from base to tip. I make the mistake of looking down and find her watching me, expression so goddamn playful and sweet I tighten even more, harder than I thought possible.

"More?" she whispers into my skin, obliterating me with my own word thrown back at me.

My hips move reflexively, jutting off the bed. She laughs as she takes me deeper, her hot breath making an already intolerable bliss that much more. The fingers of her left hand spread over my stomach, anchoring me as the other works in tandem with her mouth. I try to stretch the seconds into minutes, but it feels impossible, not with her white-hot tongue doing *that*, and then *this other thing*, and then *her lips*—

"Pipes, I—"

She pulls off with a pop, and my synapses misfire at the loss of contact. I grab underneath her arm and try to yank her up to kiss me, but she reroutes, shoving me backward, maneuvering until she's straddling me, palms on my chest. An angle so dangerous I have to squirm so I don't slip inside of her. Fuck do I want to. I'm losing my mind at how close she is, how hot and ready.

With a smile, she takes me in her hand and teases me against her slick skin, stopping shy of letting me in. She moves the tip higher and lower, circling, tempting fate. She's swollen, and any humor slips out of her expression as her hungry eyes focus on where we touch. And separate. And touch again. Wetter. And lower. One slipup and I'd be inside. The mere temptation ratchets me higher. My orgasm takes shape at the edges.

I'm wrecked. My voice is wrecked. "I need you. On the ground, my bag—can you—"

She jumps sideways off the bed and finds a condom in my duffel.

When I'm sheathed and she positions herself this time, inches above me, I buck off the bed. Her lips curve into a smile as she jerks away from me. I lift my head off the pillow and take her nipple in my mouth, skipping straight to teeth and tugging.

I urge her hips closer, the skin beneath my hands burning inside my tight grip.

Her hands clamp the headboard, and she lowers onto me with a force that makes us both gasp. Gravity, the tight fit—all of it works together, and it's perfect, impossibly good. She sets the pace, fast and furious, slamming into me over and over until we are both losing our shit, wild as she cries my name and I dig my fingers into her skin.

I want it to last longer, but the sensation overtakes me, heat barreling down my spine as I moan into her chest.

"Come for me."

The three hottest words imaginable, and she bosses them right into my ear. My muscles jump and freeze, everything tensing until I give in. My orgasm grips me, disassembles me from the inside out.

I stroke her hair as she falls motionless against me, struggling to catch my breath. The aftershock is dulled when I realize she wasn't finished.

"*Damnit.* You weren't done."

"Trust me; it was amazing." She silences my objection with a kiss before reaching over to check the time. Her skin is still flushed, her nipples still hard. "We've got about an hour until we need to be back at the studio, and I'd like to hit a drugstore, at least."

I roll her over and kiss the hollow of her neck. After what we just did, she needs to finish. "An hour is *plenty* of time to take care of you and still make it to the studio on time."

She runs her hands through my hair. "As much as I want that, we need to get moving *now* if we want to get camera ready and make it to the studio on time. Especially when I look…"

"Freshly fucked?" I offer with a smile.

"Freshly fucked," she echoes. "Now put away the dimple before I make an irresponsible decision."

Obliging, I remove my mouth from her skin. "Fine. But this isn't over."

As soon as I say it, silence lands between us. The heaviness of my words hangs in the air like a canopy over the bed.

This can't be over. What we did—what I feel for her—is so beyond a one-night-only (plus morning) situation it's laughable. This is Piper we're talking about.

But then, this is *Piper* we're talking about, a woman who likes to keep me guessing as to what's going on between us. I have no idea what she's thinking. The great wide expanse of what comes next seems to loom outside. And asking right now, when she's calm in my arms, doesn't feel right. I don't want to burst the bubble.

"Rain check?" I study her face. Search her reaction for something to hold on to.

"Yes," she whispers, planting a soft kiss on my temple.

For now, that will have to be enough.

"That was some kind of magic," Darla says, grasping Piper's elbow as we exit the studio. "You were steady yesterday, don't get me wrong, but *today*..." She waves her hand in the air like she's trying to summon the words. "Fabulous performance. Piper, love the little extra umph you brought today. So dynamic. Keep it up, you two."

Piper and I exchange a brief look before she drops her gaze to the concrete. Her cheeks flush pink. "Thanks, Darla."

The storm of last night is all but a memory as the bright sun beams overhead. Darla pauses in the doorway on her way back inside. "Be safe getting home. Keep me up to date on your home sessions. Hey—any thoughts on the upcoming project we discussed?"

Piper makes a noise distantly related to the "*uh*" family.

The politician in me rears to life. *Noncommittal. Enthusiastic.* "We're excited and interested. We're working through some scheduling things, but hopefully we'll know soon."

"It is a big decision!" Darla says with the chipperness of someone who doesn't have to make a big decision.

The conversation ends with a "talk soon" I'm only moderately sure I said out loud.

Pipes is giggly and borderline delirious the entire ride back to Roseborough. I want so badly to feel it, too, but the longer we drive, the more Darla's words sink in.

*Big decision.*

Inaccurate. It's more impossible than big. I can't say yes, because if I win the race, I won't have enough time to commit. I'd have to quit my job at the station or clone myself. The latter is more realistic. I love being a firefighter, but more pressingly, my father wouldn't let me hear the end of it. I can practically hear his Irish lilt through time and space. *Four generations of O'Shea firefighters, and you're just going to quit?*

I steal a look at Piper as she lowers the windows and sticks her head out like a golden retriever catching wind.

Saying no would crush her.

My stomach roils. I'll have to figure it out, but not today. Not when she looks so fucking happy.

"Your version of a cold shower?" I ask, poking

her in the ass.

She drops back into her seat. "You wish you had that effect on me."

The second we hit a red light, I lean across the center console to kiss her. She presses her thumbs in my dimples, and I taste the fruity gum she stores in her purse.

"I've wanted to do that for the last six hours." She bites her lip. "Don't let this go to your head, but you're good at the whole voice-acting thing."

"Yeah?" I whisper.

She pulls back, eyes alight. "Honestly? You're good at everything."

My heart grows two sizes, pressing against my ribs. I'm so fucked.

# CHAPTER TWENTY-EIGHT

## PIPER

It's terribly inconvenient timing, Caleb's game night.

A few days before Sam Conquistador'ed me and things grew complicated, Sam and I agreed we could do things like play *Monopoly* without insult or bloodshed. *Anything for Caleb*, we said. *It'll be tolerable*, we said.

We did not bargain for eye-banging across the coffee table. I didn't plan for his excellent banking skills or keen real-estate intellect to turn me on in a major way. Thank goodness we have so many buffers. Caleb suckered Luca, Enzo, and two of the nurses he works with into playing. The noisy brood provides enough distraction from my wandering thoughts.

Jane's here, too, but she's the opposite of a buffer, watching me like a hawk. I swear she can smell the lust on me.

"Are you all right?" she asks under her breath as Caleb, Sam, and Enzo argue about the rent due on Sam's railroad conglomerate.

*Confused. Overwhelmed. Consumed.*

"I'm good." I sip my cold cider to show how *good* I am.

"I saw you in the back of my van the other night, Handsy McGee. I have a rearview mirror. '*Good*' is all you've got for me?"

I choke on my drink and whisper a frantic, "Please don't—"

"I won't tell. But I have questions."

Yeah, Janey. Me too.

Last night, after Sam rendered me stupid with his sexy voice in the studio, he proceeded to tease me the whole way home with a hand slipping in my skirt and fingers toying with me at red lights.

He also left me high and (metaphorically) dry. His dad called the second he pulled into my driveway. Before I could invite him upstairs, I was subjected to the business end of an argument. He left me panting on my front porch as he zipped off to the station for a work crisis.

Toward the middle of *Monopoly*—or beginning or end; who can say—I excuse myself to the kitchen. My Angry Orchard cider is empty, but it's mostly because I need a breather.

The kitchen is quiet and dark, a reprieve from the living room noise. I toss the glass in a recycling bin, spin on my heel, and stop dead in my tracks.

Sam eclipses the narrow kitchen doorway. He glances over his shoulder and back at me before approaching.

My pulse quickens. "What are you doing?"

He snakes an arm around my waist and whips me around. Wordlessly, he walks us backward until my body is pressed against the pantry door. My heart beats wildly in my chest.

"We can't do this here," I whisper, voice shaky. "If Caleb walks in…"

"He won't. He's busy." He leans in and hovers his mouth above mine. Those deep green eyes blaze like someone set the forest canopy on fire. "Tell me to stop."

It's like we broke some kind of seal. Now that I've touched him, kissed him, it's all I want to do. My resolve slips like sand through a sieve as we lock eyes for three…

Two…

"Don't stop."

His hands cup my face as he presses into me, driving my back into the hard wood as his mouth covers mine. I give it up quickly, tongue sliding over his, showing him with my kiss how needy I feel. How much I crave him.

The *keeping our relationship professional* to *unintelligible horny thoughts* pipeline is slick. Wanting him like this makes me feel out of control. I've thrown all my carefully constructed boundaries out the window, and what's terrifying is I can't seem to care right now.

"Can we go?" I mumble in his mouth. "My house is closest."

He pulls back to look at me, then glances at his watch. "What about the plan? Your family's dinner is in an hour and a half, and we're all supposed to head to your house at the same time. Nonna's cutlets, remember?"

"I can't—" My mouth clamps shut.

But it's too late. He already gleans my intent before I've said it out loud. A wicked grin spreads across his face. "Say it."

"Never mind."

"Say the word, and I'll tell them we have a call with our producers. Whoops, they moved the time up, that kind of thing. Then we'll hop in the car and go. When they get to your parents', we'll be wrapping up studio work."

He has me up against a wall in more ways than one. Because if I don't say something, we'll have to endure three more hours of no touching, minimum. And Caleb loves to shoot the breeze with my parents after family dinners, so it could be even longer than that.

I dig around in my reserves for a shot of courage and find it in his clean-shaven face, tight black shirt, and snug jeans.

Three hours isn't going to work for me.

"I can't wait. I want you now. But can't we go to your house?"

"We can't go to my house because if *Monopoly* wraps early, they'll show up at your parents' and discover we aren't there. We'll have no alibi whatsoever. At least this way we can work when we're done."

I nip his bottom lip. "I'm going to need every last minute until dinner with you."

Still pressed against me, he adjusts himself, an erotic tease that makes my mouth go dry. "You go first. I need a second." I glance down, ogling, and he gropes my ass. "The sooner you walk, the sooner we get out of here."

Only Jane, who watches me with a critical eye as I breathlessly gather my belongings, makes me question the strength of our work excuse. Mercifully, Caleb is too busy fighting with our brothers to care all that much.

He is a problem for a later day.

We're ten minutes from my house, but it feels much farther as Sam's hand slides up my dress the second we hit the road, trapping my panties between his fingers. I encourage him with a tilt of my hips. He slides them off and flicks them into the back seat, eyes never leaving the road. The next three minutes are a game of chicken. I rub him outside his pants. He grips my thigh, forces my legs open, slides his hand up my leg—

And returns his hand to the steering wheel at the last second.

The third time he pulls this move, I smack his arm. "You're an infuriating tease."

He smirks. "Safety first."

"We can't have sex in my driveway," I inform with little conviction in my voice when we pull onto my road.

"Who said anything about sex?"

I sit there for a second, deciphering his meaning.

"You okay, Pipes?" He steals a look at me. "You look flushed."

"You took off my underwear, took me home, and you aren't even planning to have sex with me?"

He shrugs a shoulder as he parks behind my car in the driveway.

And proceeds to say nothing.

"What's your angle?" I ask, swiveling to face him.

He hits me with intense eye contact, head-on, hands now folded in his lap. "No angle."

"Are you trying to make me touch myself?" I press my fingers to the throbbing heat between my legs.

"Jesus, Piper." His pretense slips away, and his eyes nearly pop out of his head. "*No*. I was just teasing you. But now that you've said it, *yes*, I would very much like—"

I lean forward and cut him off, smothering his words with my mouth. He slides his tongue against mine a few times, a mere suggestion of what he did to me two nights ago. The memory is like an electric shock. I can't get enough of him fast enough.

I slide into his lap and reach down to recline his chair.

"You're going to get us caught," he says with a breathy laugh. His hands slide up the backs of my legs and don't stop until they're hiking up my dress and kneading skin.

His pulse drums against my lips as I suck his salty neck. It's so easy to find a rhythm with him, grinding against him as he groans into my hair. Even through his pants, his hardness pulses against me.

"Inside," he says, voice shaking.

"Here," I counter. "Now."

He shifts my weight until I nearly hit the horn with my ass. "I want to take my time." He pulls down my dress. "I'm taking you upstairs, and this time I'm not stopping until I get the job done."

Wild heat radiates through my core. I fall back into the passenger's seat and check the mirror. After a quick swipe to remove the smudged lipstick beneath my bottom lip, I practically fall out of the car.

Sam catches up to me as I weave through vehicles, squeezing my ass and gripping my waist. When we hit the front door, I stop him with a palm to his chest. "We have to relax before we go inside."

He arches a brow.

I demonstrate the correct posture for deep belly breathing, my hand making a small circle over my stomach. He does not follow suit but instead destroys me with the sexiest smirk I've ever seen as he takes a step toward me like he's about to pounce.

*Fuck.* I'm going to blow a fuse and fuck him against my front door if he keeps looking at me like that.

I race through the foyer, snickering as he stumbles over a sneaker behind me. The living room is empty. This feels too good to be true, but I do not go out of my way to locate a stray Bellini. I charge up the staircase and don't stop until his arm slips around my waist near the top steps.

"You are so fucking beautiful." He kisses the back of my neck as we trip up the last few stairs. Heat explodes beneath his lips, trickling across my shoulders. "I love seeing you like this, completely possessed."

I grope behind me blindly, grabbing his hips, murmuring *come here* as if we aren't already touching. Without the light of my landing, no one would *really* see us unless they were looking. I crowd him into the banister, kissing him as he sneaks a hand inside my shirt.

I'm the first to break away, because I might actually collapse if I don't get him inside of me. We fall through my door, shushing each other like teenagers as he kicks it shut with his foot. It's a reckless rush, the thrill of knowing we shouldn't do this here but are *1,000 percent* going to do it anyway.

His hands circle my waist, and he lifts me against the wall. A framed picture near my head rattles at the force. My dress rolls up as I wind my legs around his hips. Leather cracks through the quiet room as he whips off his belt. The metal buckle clanks against the wood floor.

"What do you like?" he asks, eyes flashing dangerous intent.

*You.*

"Let's try everything so I can decide."

"Fuck, that's hot."

I suck his lip into my mouth, and he shuts up.

He reaches into his pants and frees first himself, then a condom from his pocket.

"You had that in your pocket the whole time we played games?" I whisper, incredulous.

He works it over his length. "I'm tired of pretending I don't want to fuck you, Piper."

*Holy shit.* I'm a goner.

He's inside in one hard thrust. The pressure is unreal as he pushes me one way and the unrelenting wall pushes back. I clamp a hand over my mouth to keep from crying out.

He pulls my hand away and covers my lips with his, tasting all of my frantic little sounds. The rhythm of his thrusts matches my tight gasps, building speed. Warmth builds in the base of my stomach, dizzying and unstable.

I want it so bad I can taste it. The orgasm is there, within reach. But I also don't want this to end.

This circular thought pattern takes over my brain for a second, completely derailing me. So many years of my life were marked by wanting and not getting this exact moment, and now that it's here I'm afraid it's a fluke.

Turns out I don't want *one more time*. I want so much more I could break in half.

The more I crave release, the more my body fights it.

*I'm taking too long.*

"You're thinking." He slows his movements as he traces my chin with his thumb. "What's wrong?"

"I…" I move my hands from his shoulders to the back of his neck. "This…*us*…" I pinch my lips shut before I can add any more disjointed words to that nonsensical string.

The problem is there *aren't* words to describe

what I'm feeling. But still, I want him to know. I need him to know.

He stills his hips and moves his mouth to my ear, tickling the skin with his breath. "I think I'm much less surprised than you are."

I uncoil my legs, and he lets me slip down the wall. Clasping his hand, I guide him backward to the bed. Clothes hang off our bodies in disarray. The slowness of our walk helps me reset.

We reach the edge of my bed, and he holds me steady as I step out of my clothes. He kicks off his pants.

We had sex in a bed two nights ago, but it wasn't *this* bed. It wasn't mine, the place where it all started between us. The heat of a blush flares in my cheeks. Despite the things we've already done, this feels like a monumental first.

He perches on the mattress and leans on his elbows. His little half smile wrecks me, quickening my pulse yet again. I'm in so fucking deep I could drown.

So much has changed in seven years, but the same question still hovers on the edge of my mind. *Will he think I'm crazy if he knows how much I like him?*

I slide between his legs, and his arms wrap around my waist. His chin rests against my chest as he blinks up at me. "Tell me what you want, and it's yours."

The Piper he dated in high school would have

deflected with a question of her own. *What do* you *want, Sam?*

But I'm not that girl anymore. I take his hand and put it exactly where I want it, showing him the pace and pressure I need. "This. Even when you're inside me, I still want your fingers here. And I like your voice. I like it when you talk to me."

He exhales sharply against my skin. "I like it when you talk to me, too."

He pulls me to the middle of the bed and centers me underneath the cathedral window. Burned tones of twilight play off his tan skin as he climbs over me. It's hard to imagine a more perfect sight.

The minutes melt together as he whispers in my ear, filthy and reverent things in rapid succession. He tells me I'm the only one who's ever made him suffer in a way that felt like pleasure as he pins my knees against my shoulders and pushes deep inside of me.

That I'm so soft and sweet as he strokes me with his thumb.

That the first time I opened my mouth in our audition, he imagined fucking me right there in the studio, as I stifle a moan in his sweaty chest.

And finally, something unintelligible as we come seconds apart, me first and then him. As though he really was waiting for me.

# CHAPTER TWENTY-NINE

## SAM

"We should put on clothes," I murmur into the back of Piper's neck.

Our bodies curve together like quotation marks. Her back vibrates my chest when she grumbles in displeasure. "Five more minutes. You wiped me out."

I run a hand through her hair in slow strokes. "I feel like I could run a marathon."

"Simmer down, Energizer Sammy."

I reposition her on her back so my head can hover over her stomach. "What do you think about politics?"

She peeks down at me, brows raised. "That question isn't going to wake me up."

"Ha." I press my lips to the soft skin above her

right hip. "Have you ever considered running for office?"

"I was thinking I might run for mayor. Will you sign my petition?"

"You'd be a worthy competitor."

The streetlamp across the street switches on, bathing her in golden light. I trail kisses in a circle around her belly button, mostly dragging my lips across her soft skin, tickling her until she laughs.

She grazes the side of my face with her fingertips. I want to tell her how perfect this feels. I want to be honest. But honest for me means coming on too strong, showing my entire hand. It means telling her I think about her more than I should, seeing her face when I close my eyes at night. Thinking of her first when I open them in the morning.

I swallow the words. I'm not sure how much longer we can postpone a real conversation about what this means.

"I'm talking to my mom tonight," she whispers.

I perk up. "Oh?"

"Yes. I have praises to sing. The conversation is long overdue." She props up on an elbow. "I won't be mentioning that you can't keep your hands off me, though. I don't want her to think I'm biased in my assessment of your political prowess."

I plant my lips on her shoulder and kiss a sloppy path until I reach the hollow of her neck. "I'm fine being your dirty secret for now, as long as I get to do this."

She hums, and her throat vibrates my lips. "Maybe someday I'll run for city council."

"I think you should." I glance up and catch her eye. "We'd be a Roseborough power couple. I'd use you to peddle my more unpopular agendas."

It's the perfect opening, and I deposited it right in her lap. *Power couple.* Not a question of what we are but a suggestion of what we could be. Blood surges through my veins, pumping hard as I wait for her to give me something back. A crumb of insight into to how she's feeling.

Her thumb traces my jaw. "I love a good conflict of interest."

"Yeah?" Reckless hope swells inside of me, setting my skin on fire.

She pulls my hand over her pounding heart and holds it there. Her skin heats beneath my palm, and for a stretch of time, it's like she's showing me a feeling she doesn't want to name. We breathe in tandem as her pulse races, gazes locked. It's the first time I've ever felt silence all the way to my bones. The first time I've ever felt satisfaction and desire so powerfully at the same time. The two feelings don't compete; they coexist.

I wind my hand behind her neck and guide her face to mine. She dusts one of my cheeks with a kiss, then the other, then my nose. Finally, her lips brush mine in a soft lingering kiss. Her eyes stay open, and I'm afraid to blink and miss out on the tenderness in her stare.

I'm afraid to miss *anything* with this woman. It's why I can't say no to a job, a favor, a party, a round of pool, a game night. Ache spreads through my chest and radiates outward, and, fuck, I *am* in love with her.

One kiss turns to two, and then they spiral.

*I'm in love with Piper.*

She hasn't said where she stands, but it doesn't change the way I feel. Love may be a two-player sport, but I'm all in anyway.

Her soft lips grow hard and urgent, sliding and sucking. Taking. *Good.* Right now, all I want is to give.

Rough with intention, I pull her legs apart and center myself on top, biting and licking my way down from her mouth, taking charge. She stretches her arms behind her to grasp the metal headboard. Her perfect skin is even more delicious when it's pulled tight.

I drag my tongue from one hard peak to the other, and her back arches, asking for more. Her mouth falls open in a sinful *O*. I fasten my lips around her nipple and suck harder and harder until her head falls to the side and she lets out a sharp cry.

"Are you okay?"

The question comes in a high-pitched voice across the room.

Piper screams and shoots upright.

Nova is standing right outside the cracked bedroom door.

I roll off her and fumble with a pillow, trying to cover Piper with it. "Here, *here*!"

She jumps up to a sitting position, clutching the fluffy mass against her chest. "I'm okay, Nova. Go downstairs, and I'll be down in a minute, all right?"

"Did you get hurt?"

"No, Nova. Downstairs!"

He turns on his heel and scurries away, his curls bouncing.

I collect my clothes off the floor. "Should I talk to him? Man-to-man?"

"He's a little young for the birds and the bees talk. Catch him after pre-K."

"Do you think he'll say anything?"

"What would he even say? He's four. He had no idea what we were doing."

"Maybe he thinks I'm a vampire."

She shields her chest with her arm. "Aren't you, though?"

A few seconds after Piper and I hit the kitchen, Caleb storms in the house, loudly announcing his presence with a melodramatic, "Can one of the fifty warm bodies that live here help me before I implode?"

He barrels through the living room, Kat strapped to his chest like a bomb.

I wince at the matching father-daughter misery on their faces. "Where's Jane?"

He ignores my question, laser focused on Piper as he unstraps the apparatus. "Take this. She's your daughter now."

Piper wrestles Kat to her chest. Kat answers with a bloodcurdling wail. "She was fine when you were carrying her, Caleb! Why'd you take her off?"

"I love my daughter more than life itself, but she woke up from her nap *miserable*. I might accidentally auction her on eBay if I don't get a break. Jane's laying down with the early stages of a migraine."

Piper jumps to action, strapping the baby to her body. "Okay, Kit Kat. You're with Auntie Piper for dinner."

We filter into the red-walled dining room right at six and settle into our seats. Catherine arrives home in time to throw her purse on the counter and sit down near the head of the huge table, next to Gio's empty spot. My back straightens, and I lace and unlace my hands.

*Get it together, dude.*

Knowing Piper is going to talk to her *tonight* is both thrilling and scary. But the Stine councilors have already vocalized their support. It'd be a huge boost to get Catherine's this week, especially when I'm already gaining traction. I've accepted six interviews in the next three weeks from press outlets, specifically focusing on those interested in different facets of my platform. Diversifying the narrative. It'd be even better to get it before my lunch with Councilor Armstrong. Rhea and Catherine are aligned in their core interests, and the support of one could push the other over the line.

"Mom, why don't you take Dad's seat so you have more room?" Piper suggests gently. Civility slips from her tone when she addresses her brothers. "Nico, Raf, Georgie, over there where I've poured water. No trading. Everyone's water is exactly the same, I assure you."

She attempts to sit. Kat immediately hollers, and Piper jumps back up. I hide my laugh in a cough. Pipsqueak is Pavlovian-style training my girl.

"Ay, asshole. Did you hear what I said?"

I swivel my head toward Caleb. "Sorry?"

"I said, we thought Enzo won *Monopoly*, but the little shit was smuggling money under his seat. Must've swiped it from under your nose. As the banker, you should've caught that."

"Sorry. I was distracted." Piper's laugh flits across the dining room. "Work stuff."

Gio strides in the room, arms outstretched. "Greetings, Bellinis. And Sam." He offers me a curt salute.

I salute back, because what else?

"Ma, your cutlets smell amazing, as ever."

Nonna beams proudly at her son.

Gio plops in an empty chair and casts a cursory glance at the table. "Where's the wine?"

"I'll get it, since this one is determined to keep me upright," Piper offers, padding through the doorway.

Gio pokes his distracted wife with the blunt end of his fork until she stops shoveling food in Davie's mouth to pay attention to him. He proceeds to pepper her and the rest of his family with questions.

When his gaze lands on me, my nerves kick up a notch.

"How's it going upstairs, Sam? Soundproofing working out for you two?"

I splutter like an old car choking on fumes. "*Sir?*"

"The studio," he continues, sawing his cutlet. "Are you able to get your work done up there with this noisy clan downstairs?"

I lean back in my chair, my appetite now a vague memory. Piper has me so thoroughly wrapped around her finger that I fucked her senseless under her parents' roof and didn't even have the decency to worry about it. "Er—yes, it's fine. No background noise coming through on our recordings."

Thoughts swirl in my head as he moves on to interrogate Caleb. Cart-before-the-horse-type thoughts. Yes, Piper and I agreed this thing between us needs to stay under wraps for a while. But I'd be lying if I said I wasn't thinking about the future. Being involved with Piper means being involved with her family, whether she lives in this house or not. I need to tread lightly. Respectfully.

The sensation warming my chest confirms I am exactly that: serious about Piper.

Sweat gathers at my collar. If she's on the same page and it's as real for her as it is for me, we'll have to tell Caleb. If we're doing this, we'll have to prove to him we're not going to fuck this up twice.

A knot forms between my ribs as I consider the weight of those *ifs*.

Kat's cries gain steam in the kitchen until more than one of us turn our attention to the archway separating the two rooms. Piper returns with an open bottle of cabernet and pulls a few glasses off the antique hutch as Kat's chubby arms and legs flail. "Caleb, do you have a bottle I can feed her? Is the diaper bag in your car?"

Caleb's flatware clinks as he drops it on his plate. "*Fuck*."

"Caleb," Catherine says in a warning tone. "Little ears."

Caleb leans forward and brings his forehead to his hand. "I forgot the breast milk. I was in such a hurry to get out of the house, I didn't even pack the diaper bag."

Nova points at Piper with a piece of chicken. "Sissy can feed him!"

"Kit Kat needs special milk from his mommy, sweet boy," Piper explains. "Her daddy can run home and get some."

"But you fed *him*," Nova says, thrusting the same piece of chicken at me. "He drank your mommy milk. Why can't you feed Kat, too?"

# CHAPTER THIRTY

## PIPER

It is at this exact moment my soul leaves my body. I can almost see it escaping through the AC vent on the ceiling.

My mother spits water everywhere, spraying her plate and the side of Georgie's face. Caleb's mouth twists into a disgusted frown as he turns to face Sam. Luca and Enzo, who had just entered the room, mumble a chorus of *nope* before getting the hell out of dodge. Nico and Raf laugh and point at Mom's ridiculous spit take. Nonna cuts her chicken cutlet, unperturbed.

Kat ratchets up the noise, probably because of the misery radiating straight from my core and into her back.

"I was not… That's not even a thing that… would happen," I sputter.

Nova narrows his eyes. "I saw you. In your room. Feeding him milk like Baby Kat eats."

*Words.*

*Sequence words.*

"I was not feeding— That's *not* what we were doing."

I realize a second too late I should have kept my fat mouth shut. Nova is four years old and almost exclusively talks about boogers and butts. He has zero credibility. I should have let the moment pass, since what he's saying sounds like gibberish anyway. No one would have thought twice about it.

But I had to go and say *words* and draw attention to it.

Sam is watching me like I'm a loaded gun that might fire off at any second. I am focusing all my energy on not looking at him. If I look at him, I'll give something away. My mother can read me like a book. So can Caleb.

"What on earth are you talking about, Nova?" Mom asks, dabbing the side of Georgie's face with a napkin.

"He's a kid. He's being silly," I insist.

Caleb's jaw twitches. "Are you two together again? Oh my *God*, is that why you left my house early?"

"Caleb, *stop*."

"Answer the question: are you two together?"

"Who?" Sam asks, blinking one hundred and seven times in the span of a second.

I bury my mouth in the back of Kat's head to keep from answering.

"Come on. Give me some credit. I was there the first time this started." Caleb pauses until he meets my eye. "I was also there when it ended."

The words hit me like a punch to the gut. My stomach clenches, and all I want to do is disappear. Sam and I haven't even put a label on what we are.

But what we did upstairs felt like more than a label.

When he felt my heartbeat and stared into my eyes, it was more than words.

I open and close my mouth. "It's complicated."

Caleb blows out air. "Complicated *how*?"

I desperately wish my brother could read my mind. Because as much as I don't want to do this with him, I doubly don't want to do this in front of my mother. I needed time to talk to her, to scaffold back her trust in Sam. He may need her approval, but I need it just as badly, for totally different reasons. My family is everything to me.

I swallow thickly. "Caleb." My voice is firm. "This time is different."

"'Different' my ass. It was never supposed to

happen in the first place, and then I had to choose sides when you broke up. Every time I spoke to him, you freaked out."

"I'm sorry. I was hurt, all right?"

Caleb's sharp laugh slices through me. "That's my best friend, and we didn't speak for six years. Because I was trying to be a loyal brother. Do you understand what I lost?"

Guilt batters me so hard I clutch my stomach. Of course I know what Caleb lost. I had a front-row seat to their entire friendship, endured their bromance on every family vacation Sam attended with us, heard them cackling clear across the house at SNL every week. Witnessed Sam talking Caleb off of a ledge about his fears over moving for college, making plans that never came to be about how they'd rule UMass Amherst as roommates. Neither even went there in the end.

And don't I fucking know how wonderful and supportive Caleb was by taking my side in the breakup, and how much I hurt him by letting my pain overshadow his? As if I could forget all the ways the fallout for my bad decisions haunted him over the years. Caleb refusing a bachelor party for vague, made-up reasons because he wouldn't admit *it's not the same without Sam*. Caleb not visiting my parents for months at a time because he was trying to make new friends on campus at BU to fill the void.

Pressure builds behind my eyes. "I was heartbroken. I made mistakes. I regret those mistakes to this day."

"You weren't the only one," Sam interjects. "We both made mistakes."

We lock eyes across the table, and my heart seizes. So much for our little secret.

"Kids, that's enough," Dad commands, competing with Kat's cries for volume.

"I can't take the drama," Caleb groans. "I haven't slept enough. I can't believe you're doing this again."

"We've matured, Caleb. The past is in the past."

Caleb laughs darkly. "Until history repeats itself. Until you decide you're still mad about what happened. You were mad for *years*, Piper. It took this long for him to come to our damn house, which I'm now seeing was a mistake."

"We've moved forward," Sam insists. "*We.* Two adults making the decision here. We *both* want to make this work."

"Caleb," Mom barks, "get your ass in the car and go get your daughter's milk before I feed her formula."

He turns to her, scandalized. "*Formula?* But Jane will—"

"Then you better move fast."

Caleb skulks out of the dining room with a pout on his face. The rest of the family watches us, shoveling food into their gullets. Dad sips his wine, staring daggers at Sam.

Mom expels a long sigh. "What exactly is going on between the two of you?"

I look to Sam, but his gaze is fixed on my mother. "Piper and I are seeing each other. And working together as well. I'm sorry it had to come out this way."

An impossibly long silence follows this declaration. "And Nova...?"

*Damn.* Mom is going for the jugular.

"Nova saw something he shouldn't," I answer. "Simple as that."

I silently award myself props for not adding *because he's always coming up to my room at random times for emotional support, and you're welcome for me providing that to your son.*

But I'm thinking it, and I hate that I'm thinking it.

Mom sighs. "Sam, you should go."

He salutes, because apparently that's a thing he does now. "Yes, ma'am."

"Sam, you don't have to—"

"It's okay, Pipes. Talk to your family." His chair screeches against the wood floor as he backs away from the table.

I nod once before he disappears. Oh, to be the one fleeing this scene.

The dark bags underneath Mom's eyes and her

unusually pale complexion make me inclined to do whatever she says. "*Piper*. What are you thinking?"

I wrap my arms around Kat, my plush little human shield. "Things are different now, Mom."

"You know who says *things are different now*? People who were hurt when things weren't different."

This statement drives a wedge into a tiny crack I thought was sealed. "I didn't plan for this. I can't help the way I feel."

"Why didn't you tell me you had feelings for him?"

I wince. "I've been waiting for the right time."

She reaches for my hand. As I slide mine in hers, the invisible rope that tethers a mother's heart to her daughter's twists, the tension pulling us closer. "I've never seen you in as much pain as when you two broke up."

"I pushed him away," I admit. "I can't be mad that he let me."

"And now? Everything is magically better?"

My heart drums violently in my chest. I know it's a trap, but I don't care. "Yes."

"You forgive him?"

The question hangs in the air between us.

Nonna taps her fork against her plate. "Catherine, maybe we should give her a break."

Mom releases my hand, shaking her head. "My two cents? He's playing you like a fiddle. And you are letting him. It's awfully convenient he pops back into your life months before an election hinging on making nice with city council, don't you think? Maybe I should endorse him, since he obviously knows how to charm people into doing what he wants. A true politician."

"Not *Sam*," Nonna objects.

"He's using Piper! It's so obvious."

"I forgive him." My voice is almost gone, and my throat is raw. "You think I haven't thought about our past already, had those talks with him? And as for the future—he's not the only one who needs something here. My entire career is tied up in him now. I'm screwed if this goes badly."

"All the more reason why this is a terrible idea! Tying your career to a man you're sleeping with…" She braces herself on the table and closes her eyes for a second. "What happened to my practical Piper?"

"Practical Piper is exhausted from helping raise all of *your* kids, because you don't have the time for it anymore!"

The words tumble out of my mouth and free-fall through the air. I want to reclaim them instantly before they land.

My mother is my idol and my best friend. As a little girl, I lived to strut around the house in her high heels until the fronts of my toes blistered. She blasted Shania Twain while she cleaned, so I memorized every word to Shania's songs. I relished being her only daughter, the person she entrusted with her secrets. The one she laughed with when "boys would be boys." Our bond is as distinctive and powerful as the floral notes of her Elizabeth Arden perfume.

And now I've thrown our closeness in her face.

Mom's gaze falls to her stomach as she tucks her short brown bob behind her ears. "Take a break. Before we both say things we'll regret."

*Too late.*

I unstrap the baby and pass her to Nonna before racing to my room, feeling every bit like a scolded kid again.

Mom doesn't come knocking, and I don't seek her out, choosing instead to cocoon in my duvet and stare at my ceiling fan. The adrenaline and high of my evening with Sam plummets to a new low. His crisp cologne lingers on my pillow. My stomach twists in a knot. I should've talked to her sooner. I could've avoided some of this mess.

When I drag myself out of bed the next morning, I manage to sweet-talk Nonna into joining me at the Roseborough Rec Center for Sam's campaign event. The Globetrotters are doing a demonstration and meet and greet, and Raf, Nico, and the twins are off-the-charts excited to attend.

Nonna's more than happy to break out her disposable camera and tag along, so long as I don't try and upgrade her to a digital. She's the perfect companion for this outing; it's kid-centric, and her entire life is being available to kids.

Sam struck a deal with the rec center manager—an old friend of his dad's—as well as the event manager of the Globetrotters: he can high-five all the kids in line to meet the athletes and talk politics with the parents, so long as he wears a name tag identifying himself as a political candidate unaffiliated with the Globetrotters organization. Win-win.

I dress Nova and Davie in matching striped basketball shorts, mostly-clean white tees, and the well-worn Jordans I bought secondhand for Christmas last year. My mother and I won't be braiding each other's hair anytime soon, but I know she'll love to see the photos of the twins in their very official, not-at-all-stained sportsball outfits.

The parking lot of the rec center is hopping with young families. Dark clouds swirl overhead, and I curse under my breath. Charlie Williams of Channel 6 Weather warned of an impending category 1 hurricane, but we've got a little time before it hits. It'd be nice if Mother Nature took a nap, but she seems content to torture Massachusetts this season instead. After the last storm, I'm not going to be caught off guard again. I'll be hunkered down at home and ready.

Nonna spots Sam the second we hit the gym. He's standing about fifty yards ahead of us near where two Globetrotters are posing for pictures in front of a colorful backdrop.

"Preferita, so *sneaky*, coming to see Sam! I won't tell your mother." She can barely contain her glee as she fluffs her hair. "Oh, he looks so *handsome* in blue."

That he does. Seeing him across a crowded space is like being plugged in. My mood brightens instantly.

Sam is effortlessly social, smiling and laughing in a way that looks sincere. He's chatting with two men as their children stand by, eyeing a dribbling Globetrotter. The sight sets off tiny flutters in my chest.

The twins sprint toward the action, their tiny shoes scuffing the linoleum. Nova nearly face-plants three steps in as I yank him up by the back of his shirt.

Nonna is bobbing on her toes watching Sam. My heart swells with affection, but I have to lay down the law. "I know you'd love to tackle Sam, but let him do his thing. We'll say hello if there is a lull in his campaigning."

Her thin lips turn downward. "But I want to snap a picture of him with the boys."

"No ma'am, we will *not* be snapping a photo of Mayoral Candidate O'Shea with my little brothers. I'll thank you not to embarrass the crap out of me today."

"You're a grown woman, Piper. You can't seriously be embarrassed over a simple photo."

"That feels too couple-y."

"Aren't you a couple?"

I reply with the eloquence of a drunk parrot. "A couple? Not a couple. Well *yeah*, a couple…"

She throws her hands up, silencing me and my ramblings. "All right, fine. Let's get in line, then."

By minute fifteen of waiting, most of the kids in line have gone off the rails. I'm in the middle of slipping the twins my tablet as a distraction—to Nonna's immense dissatisfaction—when I spot Sam stepping away from a group of police officers. He cuts through the line, offering smiles as a form of payment to pass the tolls.

He wraps me in a hug the second he sees me. Public physical contact with him—especially when he's campaigning—zips through me. His touch still feels brand-new, stirring wicked and warm thoughts.

"Hello, gorgeous," he whispers in my ear.

"Hello, Mr. Mayor."

"Bad luck," he reminds me as his hand brushes my lower back. He turns to Nonna. "You look lovely today, Ms. Julia. That sweater is becoming. Have I seen it before? It looks great with your pearls."

It's the little things with Nonna. She'll be talking about this for a month.

"Sam, you ol' flirt," she blusters.

She's in the middle of her next sentence when I catch a piece of the conversation happening behind us.

"That's the guy. Right there, in blue."

I tilt my ear toward the source, trying to pick up the rest of what he's saying.

"—on the radio on the way here. Yeah, *filthy*. Yeah, definitely him. The one running for mayor."

I tug on Sam's sleeve. "Don't turn your head or let him know you are looking, but there's a guy in a black shawl-neck sweater speaking to a guy in a Pats hoodie a few feet back. They're talking about you."

His gaze flickers between me and the line behind us. "Oh? What's he saying?"

"I'm trying to listen."

That's a difficult task, considering the noise of dribbling basketballs echoing through the gym. Sam looks down at his shoes and strokes his cheek as he attempts to concentrate.

"—looks like the type. I had to turn the radio down in the car on the way here so the kids wouldn't hear."

"Maybe that's the girl he was talking to."

"I don't know. She looks a little prim and proper, no?"

"It's always the ones you least suspect. She could be a closet freak."

"I mean, he *did* say he'd go back to jail if it meant he could fuck her in that barn again. *Back* to jail. Can you even run for mayor if you've served time?"

# CHAPTER THIRTY-ONE

## SAM

The world goes red at the edges.

"Sam, don't." Piper grabs my wrist as I try to turn around. "It's probably a misunderstanding."

"Piper, he's quoting our stuff," I growl under my breath.

"There's no way. That stuff hasn't even been released. He must think you're someone else."

"It's our stuff. No doubt. *The barn?*"

Our urgent whispering gets Julia's attention. "What are you two talking about?"

Piper throws a look over my shoulder at the men, then scans the gym. "Nonna, can you watch the boys? Sam and I need a minute."

"Of course. You kids go ahead."

I swallow air as I try to calm myself. "You can stay, Pipes, and I'll just—"

"—lucky him if she is the barn chick; she's a tight little package—"

—*disassemble them limb from limb.*

Piper yanks me back by the arm. "Ignore it. Let's walk. Your face is beet red."

"He's talking about you."

"Think like a politician."

My vision reduces to a pinpoint. *The campaign.* The implications unfurl in my head as we sidestep our way past all the people in front of us, mumbling apologies under our breath and picking up speed until we are nearly jogging. She guides me to a door leading to a hallway and comes to a stop between locker-room doors.

"I'm googling you to see what's out there." She digs her phone out of her pocket. After a pause, her furrowed brow relaxes a bit. "Nothing unusual comes up. Just stuff about the station— *Oh shit.*"

"Give it to me straight, Pipes."

She blinks up, and her troubled eyes land on mine. "This is on Eagle Eye's website under *New and Newsworthy.* Local Mayoral Candidate Sam O'Shea Delivers Another Banger of a Speech." She clears her throat. "Subheading... *And it's not what you think. Hashtag not safe for work.*" She pokes the screen, and my voice fills the narrow hallway.

*"I would do anything for you. I'll go back to jail if it means one more night with you in the barn.*

*"I'd fuck you until you forgot who you are and why we aren't supposed to do this. This relationship may be against the law, but nothing can stop me from loving you. I'm lowly scum, and everyone knows it, but you want me anyway.*

*"You let me wreck your perfect life, and you loved it, didn't you? Loved it when I fucked you like a dirty commoner until you forgot your status. Loved how your family didn't approve, because it meant you called your own shots for a change. You get off on breaking the rules."*

Panic shocks me still. "Is that it?"

"Yes."

"No follow-up explanation or any context whatsoever?"

She nods, her eyes filling with tears. "I'm so sorry."

*Double fuck.* I grip my hair and pull until it stings. On top of the utter shitstorm this is going to cause for me, Piper's—*our*—project has leaked. Of course she's crying—this stuff is supposed to be under lock and key.

I can't pile on with my campaign panic. I need to get out of here and figure out my next steps before this escalates.

My pocket sounds with my dad's assigned text tone. I peek at the screen.

*We need to talk. Now.*

*Fuck.*

It's already escalated.

"I have to fix this," I manage, my voice hollow.

"Sam, we should talk it through."

"Damnit, now Dad is *calling*. Let me deal with this, all right?"

I stride for the exit to the parking lot and shove open the door.

Pouring rain. Nowhere to run.

When I swivel around, Piper is sitting against the wall with her head between her knees.

With a sigh, I slide down beside her, my shirt scraping the uneven cinder blocks.

"The hell is this, Sam?" Dad says by way of greeting. "I'm getting call after call, wanting to know what sick shit my son is up to. Requests for a statement."

"I can explain—it's *not* how it sounds. There's a shit ton of context—"

"*Everything* is how it sounds in the press. This is what I've explained to you time and time again. You give yourself to the public, and they own your ass. In what fucking *context* are you out there recording crap like that?"

"It's a gig I worked with Piper. She's a voice actress, and we recorded an audiobook. A copyrighted audiobook, but that's another problem."

"Right now, your problem is explaining to the Good Lord and everyone else in this nosy town why you were spitting filth like a goddamn sailor. It's disgraceful, son. Not just for a politician, but for a member of *my* squad to be caught talking about illegal barn fucking."

"It's fake! They are just audio clips. Christ, you act like I wanted this."

"You obviously weren't wise enough to prevent it."

"*I get it*, all right? I'm going to fix it."

"How?"

"I don't know!" My voice echoes down the hallway. "I just found out two minutes ago. I need time to think."

"Step one will be separating from whatever this project is. Publicly sever ties—immediately. I've got John Bromwell at *The Post*'s number if you want to make a statement. In fact, I can conference him in right now—"

"No. I have an obligation. I'm under contract."

"You signed a contract? With whom?"

"With the producers of the audiobook."

"That was your first mistake. They're obviously incompetent to let his happen. How do audio clips just up and walk themselves to the press? You'll need to reach out to a lawyer who specializes in defamation."

My stomach roils. "I'll handle this my way."

He hangs up without a goodbye.

A frustrated groan leaves my mouth as I shove the phone in my pocket.

Piper pulls her head from between her knees. "What did he say?"

"Pipes, you encrypt the files before you send them, right? Is it a cloud server? How do you share the files with Damien?"

She tilts her head, and I glimpse her tearstained cheeks. "It's all in a cloud server. I email Damien a link when I finish compiling new content so he can get straight to the most recent recordings without having to dig in the server. I don't know what kind of encryption is on it, if any." Her face falls. "This is my fault."

"I'm not looking for someone to blame."

"I do what Damien tells me. I wasn't expecting something like this."

I massage my temples. Her sadness makes me feel guilty, and I can't stomach even more pain right now. "We need to call them. They've got to know something. What happened or how to fix it *fast*."

Piper dials with a shaky hand, opting for speakerphone.

Darla answers on the fourth ring with a "Hi, sugar!" Her voice is barely audible over the sound of a loud announcement blaring in the background.

"*Flight 1669 to Cabo, now boarding Zone 1.*"

We exchange looks of horror. The Gentrys are on their way out of the country. Of all the fucking times.

Piper pinches the bridge of her nose. "I have some potentially bad news, and I wanted to tell you before you hear it from someone else."

"Is everyone okay?"

"Everyone is fine, thanks. It's about the Vic and Laz project. It seems—and I have no idea how this happened—some of the audio clips have gotten out."

More silence.

Piper clears her throat. "I called because I need to know what our next steps are. In terms of what we can share about the project with the press."

"The press?" she repeats.

"Sam will need to make a statement for his campaign. We need to be able to share the nature of the clips with the press. Otherwise it sounds... Well, you know the project better than anyone. Out of context, those voice clips will ruin his reputation."

"Wait. They are playing the clips on the radio? Who has the clips?"

"97.9 is playing them. You can play it through their website, and I heard people at the rec center saying they heard Sam's voice on the radio. They're out there."

"97.9 broadcasts all over Boston."

Piper exhales in a sharp burst of air. "I know. So, I

was thinking if I could *call* the station, let them know the clips need to be pulled for copyright reasons, and explain what they're being used for, this can blow over."

"I'm afraid it's not that simple, sugar. First of all, if they've got one clip, they've got others. I don't know if they accessed your server or took them straight from file share software, but either way they've likely taken more footage. And if someone took it to the press, it sounds like they have an agenda. I need to get our copyright lawyers involved. This isn't an overnight fix."

"Please, let me call *someone*. I'll do whatever I can."

"There's always a fix. It just takes time."

"Why can't I call the station now and tell them it's a voice-acting project?"

"Imagine you wrote a book and someone went on air and read all your lines before your release, before any editing, completely out of context. Wouldn't you want professionals handling it?"

"Of course, but every second we aren't in control of the narrative, Sam's reputation suffers."

"I'll take it to the appropriate channels. It'll get handled. Let's circle back with Damien about encrypting your home server. Not much we can do now—everything already on the server has likely been copied. Let's circle back end of next week, to give me time to contact the lawyers and the rest of our team to figure out a plan. Don't record anything until you hear from me. All right?"

Piper stares at the phone in defeat.

"Don't talk to the press," Darla urges. "Stay off the internet. We'll get this sorted as soon as we possibly can. Tell Sam to hang in there."

Piper clutches her phone to her chest, and her eyes flutter shut. "*Damnit*."

Panicked thoughts swirl in my head. There's nothing we can do right now.

There's nothing I can do.

Stillness.

I don't know how to be still.

She drops her head on my shoulder. I can't relax, even at her touch. How do I get around a gag order from the Gentrys?

How do I solve this problem without creating an even bigger one for her?

"Come back to my house," she mumbles into my shirt. "We'll eat and we'll figure something out."

"I can't. I have to head home after this. I need to work."

A white lie.

Really, I need to think.

# CHAPTER THIRTY-TWO

## PIPER

My heart rate picks up, drumming in a staccato beat, like I'm in some kind of danger if this conversation ends without a solution. I want him to relax into me and tell me it's fine. Face pressed against his shirt, I peek up at him, grappling for any reassurance. "Please be careful driving. Don't listen to the radio."

He cracks the smallest smile as he pulls himself to a stand. Or maybe it's an involuntary twitch of his mouth. "The damage is done. Might as well listen and critique my performance, no?"

"Sam, don't—"

"Here." He extends a hand. It's cold around mine as he helps me up. "Tell Nonna I said goodbye, okay?"

I nod, throat tight. He's gone in a flash, without

so much as a kiss goodbye, leaving me alone to stare at the darkened hall.

After my sobbing subsides, I find Nonna and the boys in the main gym, buzzing from their meet and greet with the Globetrotters. The only thing keeping me together on the drive home is the steady drum of rain, forcing me to stay focused on the road and not the fear and guilt swirling in my head.

At the house, Mom is curled up on the couch, clutching her stomach. The dim glow of the television casts soft light on her furrowed brow as she takes deep, labored breaths.

"I don't remember contractions like this at thirty-three weeks." Her hand curls into a fist next to her belly button as she exhales.

Nonna shoos the twins into their bedroom and turns to Mom. "It's all right, Cat. It's just Braxton Hicks. You've had them with the others, no? You'll be just fine with a little rest."

Mom's expression softens as the pain seems to subside. "I guess."

"I'm going to make you grilled cheese," Nonna insists, hobbling for the kitchen. "You too, preferita. Nothing a sandwich can't solve, for the both of you…"

I drop down on the couch beside Mom as Nonna's muttering fades. "Are you sure you're all right?"

Her gaze flits over my face. "I could ask the same of you. That's a lot of mascara streaking your skin."

My eyes well under her knowing stare.

Wordlessly, she accepts me, opening her arms and letting me collapse into her. My head comes to rest on her shoulder. Relief softens me, letting me breathe easy again. We sit quietly for a while, the only noise in the room the hissing and spitting of the fire dancing in the hearth.

"I messed up Sam's campaign," I whisper.

"Ah. I heard about the clips."

My stomach drops, Tower of Terror style. "You did?"

"Dawn called after she heard from Rita. Who heard about the 'horny felon mayor' from someone else."

I groan.

"This isn't your fault. You two were doing a job, and things always have a way of spiraling out of control in politics."

"You think Paul Stine is behind this?"

Mom doesn't speak for a few seconds. When she does, it's with resignation. "Probably. His campaign manager is a little shit. Tucker Tooberry."

I choke out a laugh. "*Tucker Tooberry*. What in the Nickelodeon hell is that name?"

"Who knows. But he's got eyes everywhere. I can see him digging around for dirt on Sam. Have you two been out together in public?"

"I visit him at the station once and a while. We

sat by each other at McLaughlin's." I trace my chin as little flashbacks from the last few weeks pop into my head. "We went to the pool hall with Jane and a few others. Then there was his speaking engagement. Dinner with the producers in Cambridge…"

*Wow.* We've been together more often than not. Somewhere along the way, I lost track of time. Seeing him stopped feeling like work and became second nature.

Now it feels vital, like he grounds my day-to-day life. Like I'm hurtling from a plane and he's my safe landing place.

How did it happen so fast?

I press my eyes shut. Did it really happen fast, though? Or was falling for Sam a second time the slowest-moving inevitability that ever was?

"That's a lot of togetherness," she states plainly. Waiting. Searching.

My throat locks up.

Sam has been in our lives longer than half of her own children. He was a kid she cared for long before he was my anything. There's no hiding who he was or what we've been through.

If only she'd see past our mistakes as a couple. I want her to know the incredible person he's become.

She brushes her fingers through my thick hair. "I'm sure one of Stine's connections saw you, did a little research. Figured out your job. You kids make it so easy with your social media pages. It'd be easy from there to deduce what Sam's up to. Paul was shaking in his boots last week, telling anyone who would listen at City Hall that Sam has no idea what he's doing, can't be trusted at his age, et cetera. The Stine camp is nervous, and they'll do anything to sow seeds of distrust."

I sigh. "I'm sure you agreed with him, as far as Sam is concerned."

"I didn't say anything because I mind my own business."

"Sure you do," I mumble.

"But I'll tell you this, Pipes. Anyone who pulls a stunt like this is not someone I can throw my support behind. It's one thing to drag a candidate for their lack of experience. It's another thing entirely to drag their character. Whoever is behind this—that Tooberry twat, most likely—has no idea what kind of damage he's potentially doing to Sam's character. And, by extension, yours. It's unacceptable behavior."

My gut unclenches at this somewhat indirect show of support for Sam. This feels like progress. Maybe she'll endorse him after all.

*Maybe it'll be too late.*

My anxiety pendulum swings.

Seconds later, my phone vibrates in my pocket. Maybe it's the Lord himself to tell me he fixed everything.

Maybe it's Sam, ready to talk about his feelings.

The name "Dollar Store Tom Brady" flashes on the screen.

Caleb.

*Did you and Sam break up already? Why did I hear him doing voice porn on the radio? He's not answering my calls. WHAT THE HELL IS GOING ON?*

Dollar Store Tom Brady asks a lot of valid questions. I don't respond to any of them.

"Can we watch something mindless for a while?" I pluck the remote off the coffee table and jab the *search* button. "I want to forget today happened."

The Real Housewives of Wherever the Heck, paired with Nonna's grilled cheese, is almost enough to make me forget the look on Sam's face when he nodded goodbye at the rec center. Mom's amusement at the show helps, too, as does her insistence that *people like this don't exist in real life.*

By the time the episode wraps, she's snoozing with her head on my shoulder. I gently reposition her and jog to her bedroom to grab her favorite quilt. As I return to tuck her in, the tail end of a loud commercial blasts the quiet room.

"'*You get off on breaking the rules.'*

"*Straight from the mouth of Sam O'Shea.*

"*A drunk and a pervert serving as mayor? Not in my town.*

*"Paul Stine for a respectable Roseborough."*

The devil works hard, but Paul Stine's camp works harder. They've already packaged a new commercial with the voice clips.

My first instinct is to yell "Jesus Christ" at the top of my lungs, but I'm fairly sure he'd want nothing to do with this mess.

My second instinct is to curl up and die. Let the earth reclaim my body.

When it rains, it pours.

This month, the storm never lets up.

• • •

Sam doesn't answer my before-bed phone call, nor does he reply to my are-you-okay midnight text. When I roll over the next morning and check my phone, the lack of response is a gut punch.

Massaging my eyes, I check the time. *7:45 a.m.* That explains why I want to drown myself in a vat of Dunkin' Original Blend. Or Folgers.

Anything works as long as I drown, really.

Nonna rolls into our bustling kitchen an hour later, rocking a poncho and rain boots. "Happy Sunday, i miei amori."

"You shouldn't be driving in the rain," Dad barbs. "I could've at least come for you."

She waves this off. "Well, I'm not going out in it

again, so you're stuck with me."

"I've told you time and time again to move in."

"And I've told you I'll move when I'm well and ready."

The steady hum of noise and chatter helps fill the growing hole in my chest. My family has a way of distracting. For a blissful stretch of time, I don't worry about whether Sam is okay. Whether *we're* okay. Instead, I bicker with my siblings and laugh with my parents over fried eggs and espresso.

As I wash the breakfast dishes, my phone vibrates in my pocket. I squeeze the sponge in surprise, shooting foam at my shirt. My brain immediately jumps to Sam, and my breakfast rises in my throat. So much for distraction.

The phone slides in my wet hand.

A text from Jane.

*I have a confession to make.*

The three bubbles keep me waiting.

*When I was at the house last week, I left a present in the trunk for you. Wrapped so Caleb couldn't see. You're going to want to open that in private. It's not a Bellini-family-friendly thing…*

I tilt my head and try to imagine what could fit in a box that she'd want to keep private from the family. My brain makes some comical leaps of the batteries-not-included variety.

The rain looks like it has no plans to chill, but

my curiosity gets the better of me. I jog out to my car, submerging my UGGs the second I hop off the front steps. The frigid wind shocks my body.

The "something" she hid behind the baskets is perfectly square and easy to spot, wrapped in black-and-white polka-dot paper. I hug it to my chest and hightail it back inside and don't stop until I hit my room.

My heart gives a tiny little flutter when I turn it over in my hands. It's almost too pretty to open. A sticky note pokes out from beneath a frilly bow. My fingers brush the curly tendrils aside to get a good look.

*When this thing popped up on eBay, I had to buy it for you.*

*Didn't want to miss out on something great. Something tells me you'll feel the same.*

*Love, J*

The flutter in my chest accelerates to a full throttle as I lift the corner of the wrapping paper. Smooth plastic peeks out, and I lose all restraint. The paper falls off after one big tear.

THE FIREFIGHTERS OF MERRYFIELD COUNTY

I squeak out a tiny laugh. Oily, chiseled torsos, red suspenders, khaki pants… The cover is everything I pictured when I first heard about Sam's calendar. It's delicious and campy, all dramatized lighting and smoldering looks.

It's *amazing*.

Sam is wedged between Forrester and another guy I vaguely recognize. Sam has one hand wrapped around a suspender and the other behind his neck as he smiles at the ground. It's the ultimate camera-shy pose. He must've done crunches right before this photo was snapped because his abs are shiny and perfect. A vision of him oiling up makes me weak at the knees.

My fantasies will fantasize about this. I want to snap those suspenders and hear them crack.

I tear off the plastic with greedy hands.

*Mr. February.*

I was prepared for lusty thoughts. Maybe even filthy ones.

I'm not sure what to do with the longing that flares as soon as I see his face. His face is everything, those eyes that always find mine in a crowded room and take hold. An eternally snarky smile that makes me come undone. Jet black hair I want to tug and fluff. And perhaps the hottest thing of all: the quiet confidence he wears like a second skin.

In the photo, he holds a heart-shaped box of puppies in his hands.

The same way he holds my heart.

He's fucking perfect. He's been shades of perfect his whole stupid life.

This should not be a revelation, but my brain

is firing at rapid speeds, as if it's trying to assimilate brand-new information, altering everything I know to be true.

I love him.

I'm *in* love with him.

It was true seven years ago when he first defined the word for me. He etched it in my dictionary, taught me what it meant. I couldn't tell him and tie him down, and I fought tooth and nail to force the feelings away after it all fell apart, but it was true.

And it's true now. I love him with an acute clarity that dismantles my heart and reassembles the pieces into something better. Stronger. *Whole.*

A flair of possessive energy curls around my torso and squeezes until I'm breathless.

I dial his number and saw my teeth against my lip until he answers. I don't know what I want to say. There will certainly be no declaration of love. I have no idea how he's feeling, and the pressure of those three words amidst this crap basket of a week is the last thing he needs.

His voice in my ear will be enough for now.

After four rings, the voicemail kicks on, and I press the end call button. I wasn't prepared to leave a message.

I switch to text and fire off a message with shaky fingers.

*Are you okay?*

One nap, two cannoli, and three moody outbursts at my brothers later, I finally receive a response. I'm in the middle of chopping onions for fajitas when the first text comes through.

*Paul put out a billboard.*

Cold sweat peppers my forehead. I didn't hear this update, but I can imagine a little too vividly what that billboard features.

The time stamps on our texts show a nine-hour delay in his response. Either the station is busy today or he's mega pissed about the clips. And by "clips" I mean the clips, the commercial, the entire foundation of our arrangement that got him in this mess in the first place.

And by all of that, I mean *me*.

He must be angry at me.

*I'm sorry about the billboard. Are you okay? How's work? You went in this morning, right?*

He types and erases on a loop. I can tell by the three little dots on the screen as they pop up and disappear. The onions on my cutting board are suddenly so small they qualify as minced. My eyes sting and water. I force myself to still the knife until he replies.

*Hard day.*

My sense of doom surges. A two-word response. He clearly doesn't want to talk. I probably deserve it, but it doesn't make it any easier to stomach.

I lob one more pathetic attempt at contact into the void.

*I'm free if you want to talk about the press stuff. Or anything else.*

He types in fits and starts. It takes a full two minutes for him to send the message.

*Another time. I have a lot on my mind.*

Frustration tugs my lips into a hard line. Something is wrong when Sam shuts down communication. He usually never stops talking.

My indignant rage—*what about the intense few days we just shared?*—squares up to fight my fear that his problems are entirely my fault. I should've been a paralegal. Paralegals don't accidentally fuel campaign ads.

I throw my phone across the kitchen counter, and it knocks over an empty plastic cup.

My weighty chef's knife helps me take out my aggression on a flank steak. Each chop soothes my haggard soul.

"Something wrong, kiddo?"

I startle at Dad's question. How long has he been standing in the kitchen, staring at me with his bushy eyebrows aloft?

"No."

"Really? Because it *seems* like something is wrong, given you're destroying a perfectly good piece of beef."

"I'm chopping this for fajitas."

"You threw your phone."

He has me there.

He plods up beside me and leans an elbow on the counter. Aunt Dawn (*fondly?*) calls him Loud Luigi, and when he wears this green polo the likeness is unsettling, right down to the uptick of his mustache. "Talk to me."

I should keep my mouth shut, since this family has enough Sam ammo to last a lifetime, but if I don't talk about it I'll throw more than a phone. "Sam's campaign is screwed, I feel responsible, and he doesn't want to talk about it."

I fail to mention that I've fallen hard, that I'm in over my head. It's too much to share with anyone, especially the man who's expressly stated his intent to marry me off to a wealthy, unproblematic, Italian-American landowner in line to inherit a throne.

"Sam doesn't want to talk? You're telling me the chatty peacock who talked our ear off on road trips…" He clears his throat and fiddles with the saltshaker. "That's unlike him."

"I know. It's making me anxious." I pick at the skin around my thumbnail, wondering about the Gentrys' lawyer and how quickly this could go away. Thinking about what I could've done differently. How I could fix it. I blink up at the ceiling, fighting a swell of tenderness in my chest. "I wish I was more like you or Mom. So competent at *everything*. You run this small army and have impressive day jobs. Even Caleb is halfway to two kids and a white picket fence, and he'll arrive with an advanced nursing degree in hand. And Sam…"

I sigh. What can't that man do?

"I think you see perfection in the people you love, Pipes. But we all have hard days—hard seasons, too. Don't be distracted by how things appear on the outside. Your mom and I have had our struggles. Hell, I missed half you kids' school functions because I was working. I couldn't even tell Nova and Davie apart for a few weeks after they were born."

I snort. "Dad."

"Mom's a superhero, though. I'll give you that. She gives everything to our family. And now the city, with her work. Always putting others first." He eyes me for a second. "Not unlike someone else I know. It may serve you well to let others step up."

He proceeds to uncover a cake platter and slice into a half-eaten pound cake, as if his comment was a perfectly benign thing to say over pre-dinner dessert.

"What do you mean?"

"Pipes, until next month, you are my only daughter. It is my job to make sure you are set up for success in the future. That includes men, dating, all that jazz. Which means it's my life's work to know exactly which bloodhounds are sniffing around—"

"Ohmigod, I am *begging* you to stop—"

"Let me finish. It's my job to know which men are after your heart so I can vet them. And which men you're most interested in. You've made that easy. It's only ever been Sam."

"I dated other men in college."

He flashes me a wry smile. "And you never brought a single one of them home."

I drop the knife and brace myself against the counter. "So what if it's always been him?"

"So, nothing. It just means you know the man very well. He's a smart guy. Maybe it's time you give him a little credit. Instead of trying to fix his campaign and solve his problems, give him the space to choose how he wants to proceed. Let him handle it." He shrugs. "He agreed to do the job with you. He signed the contract and pocketed half the money, didn't he? Didn't have a gun to his head at any point?"

I blink up at him. "Yes to the first, no to the second, but—"

"No buts. He's an equal partner in this. It may have been your job first, but he's a big boy and knows what it means to commit to something. If he can't handle the fallout from that decision…well, that's not the Sam I know."

A powerful protective impulse rears in my chest.

"Being mayor means everything to him. He didn't know the audiobook was going to be so explicit. How could he have expected this? Pretty sure if he'd known he wouldn't have signed on. And now that he has, and we're in this mess, if I could just do something—"

"You said it yourself. He *did* sign on, lovebug. He committed to it, and that's the way it is. You have to trust people to do what's right for them. He *chose* to work with you. He knew what he was doing. Take a step back. Let him make his own decisions. That doesn't mean you can't give him advice or tell him how you feel about the issue. Communication is important. It just means you can't solve the problem for him and shouldn't take on that pressure."

My stomach roils. "I haven't been the best at giving Sam a choice in things, historically."

Dad's smile is soft. "What would happen if you did?"

I stare at the chopped meat. I tried to give Sam what I thought he needed before, and it backfired on both of us.

Maybe the best thing I can do is let him handle this his way.

# CHAPTER THIRTY-THREE

## SAM

The howling wind outside my bedroom window is oddly soothing, like the Earth is just as miserable as I am. I stare at the message Piper sent me hours ago as my bedroom's electric fireplace spits weak heat.

*Don't know why they call it a hurry-cane. This storm is slow-moving as heck.*

Even now, when I've been sent home from work for the first time in my career and can't bring myself to get out of bed, she still manages to draw a laugh out of me. The sound dies on my tongue.

She's correct about how slow-moving the storm is. We've had nonstop calls. Everything from houses hit by fallen trees, to car accidents in rising waters, to medical emergencies. The longer it lingers, the worse the calls seem to get.

And my head was *not* in the game. Not at all. I was so distracted my dad had to call in another firefighter so he could release me. Fucking sucks. In another world—one where my dad is capable of empathizing with despair in others, instead of hoarding it all for himself—I'd believe he sent me home to do me a favor. But in this world, it was a punishment, done in front of the squad to prove a point.

*If this team isn't your top priority, we don't want you here.*

His follow-up text simply said, *Sleep it off. We'll discuss this when my shift ends.*

Pretty telling of his personality that he found that sentiment too personal to say aloud.

If possible, Dad is even more mad at me now than he was when the clips leaked two days ago because I keep dodging his questions. Fact is, I'm dodging everything. Staring into space when I should be working or brainstorming solutions to my problems. But it's like I'm only half present in every room. Body only. That's why he sent me home in the first place.

I've never hit the elusive "wall" before. I thought I never would. Logic tells me if a person does enough, moves enough, schedules enough, they'll stay in motion.

But for the first time in my life, I'm completely frozen. Helpless. Overwhelmed with problems I can't solve.

Piper's picture pops up on my phone screen. Even if I wanted to avoid a conversation—because talking will inevitably lead to me disappointing her—I can't resist her. "Pipes?"

Her voice comes out in a breathy rush. "Sam. I'm—oh *shit*—"

My sheet falls away as I bolt upright. "What's wrong?"

"I was driving to get Mom something from the drugstore because she has been feeling terrible all day. There was a deep puddle I didn't see, and I hydroplaned and— I'm on the side of the highway now. There's a ditch—"

Pure fear shocks my body. I can hear the shake in her voice. "Where are you, exactly?"

"The water is rising really fast. Should I— I could try to back up, but it's coming down so hard I can't see."

"Tell me where you are, Piper," I urge, already halfway to the door.

She spits out a stuttering response, describing the nearest exits and landmarks as I run out. My screen door whines and rattles in the wind. I don't slow down to lock it.

"Stay on the phone with me, baby. I'm ten minutes away."

"I feel like if I shift positions or even talk too loud my car will slide into the ditch, and it's full of water. I'm going to drown."

I talk her through a series of questions to understand but also to distract. *What position is your car in? Do you feel movement beneath your tires? Stay calm; I'm almost there.*

Her car is nose down in at least a foot of water when I arrive, the front of her car dipping into the ditch more than I think she realized.

I kick my door open and trudge to her car as the water spreading across this part of the highway laps at my legs. The haze of my diffused headlights guides my way. This stretch of road has given us endless trouble over the years, with its short shoulder and steep drop-off. When we get hit with rising floodwaters like this, it's downright dangerous.

If the water catches and carries her car…

Not on my fucking watch.

The wind howls as I yank the handle. Through the glass, her face contorts with effort as she pushes back. Stupid fucking matchbook Ford, too small, too low to the ground. I'm buying her a tank of a truck. Great heaving droves of rain drown out my frustrated groan as I rip her door open. Water rushes over her floorboard.

"C'mon." I grab her hand and yank her out of the car as my feet sink into wet earth. The water level is near my knees and climbing.

"I can't leave it here—it'll slide in!"

Every second on the side of the road risks another car hydroplaning and knocking us out. "I'll call a tow!"

I shield her from the road with my body as we trudge through the water. My pants drag, and my eyes blur from the onslaught of water. In the distance, white light cracks in the sky.

She grasps for the oh-shit bar above my passenger's seat. Her hand slips, and she stumbles. Her knee strikes the floorboard. I boost her from behind and practically throw her up into the seat.

My tires spin and spin as I attempt to gain traction. They finally catch, and I lurch onto the road. Until we're in the clear, I'm too tense to speak, driving down the center of the road where the water is shallowest.

As we hit my suburb and I exhale in relief, Piper hisses "*fuck*" under her breath as she fumbles for her phone.

"What's wrong?"

"Mom's blood pressure cuff. I was on my way to the store to pick one up before all this happened. That's why I was out in the first place."

"There's a cuff in the drawer of the coffee table. I left it for her to keep at brunch, remember?"

"*Really?*"

"You didn't hear our fight where I insisted she keep it and she insisted she would never need such a thing, despite your Dad complaining *but your blood pressure, dearest* in the background the whole time?"

"I was busy trying not to notice you at brunch," she mutters, retrieving her phone. "It was a struggle."

If only she knew how hard I tried not to notice her, too. From the minute she stepped into the bar and every time I saw her after. "Please don't say cute shit when I'm operating heavy machinery in a storm. Makes it hard to concentrate. Call the tow company, let them know where to find your car so they can grab it once the water goes down, and then call your mother."

As I drive us the final stretch to my house, she chats with a tow company, then her dad, telling him about the cuff in the drawer and checking on her mom. The last thing out of her mouth, delivered with hesitation, is "I don't know when I'll be home."

My heart leaps ahead of my brain, and I plant my hand on her leg, squeezing.

I want her to stay with me, and not just because of the storm. I want all of her to myself. My hand moves of its own accord up and down her leg, anchoring me in the reality that she's okay. The accident could've been so much worse. Nausea wells in my gut, thinking about her car in the ditch, rolled, with her trapped upside down in the water.

"This is me." I throw the car in park.

She drops her phone in the center console and

glances toward the windshield as rain pelts the car. "Nice house," she says, even though it's barely visible in the storm. "I can't believe I've never been here before."

I want to smile, joke, *something*, but my skin feels too tight. My heart feels like it's trying to claw its way out of my chest.

Her gaze finds mine, searching. "Should we make a run—"

I lean across the dash and claim her mouth. She startles for only a second before her lips come alive. She sighs into me, and I both calm down and stir with urgency in the same breath. "I'm so glad you're okay," I murmur into her mouth. "You could've…"

The words fall away as her hands coil behind my neck. She pulls back only long enough to say, "But I didn't."

The sound of her shallow breathing unlocks something primal in me. My lips glide across her jaw, down her neck, up to her ear as my hands gather a fistful of her wet hair. It escalates until I'm ready to rip the center console out and throw it into the storm to get closer to her. We're both soaking wet, clothes dripping, but her skin is hot to the touch from the heat piping through the car vent. The windows fog around us as I groan into her mouth. My instincts take over, silencing the part of my brain that knows we have things to discuss. I tug at her sweater, pulling it up and off. Her shirt clings to her skin. I want here, now, *more*—

She yanks back, breathing fast. "You haven't been texting. You didn't call. I thought you were mad at me."

Lightning streaks across the sky as her words sink in. "*Mad* at you?"

"What was I supposed to think? The clips happen, and then you all but disappear."

I go still, feeling her breath on my lips. I'm so many things at once—frustrated, overwhelmed, out of my depth with work—but mad at Piper isn't one of them. It's the opposite. She's the only good thing in a sea of disaster.

But the reality of our situation means my every decision could hurt her. I'm crumbling under the weight of the pressure not to fuck this up. The stress manifests in my body. My muscles are tight and tense. But I don't want her to know any of it until I've figured out a plan. I stroke the soft skin next to her mouth. "No, baby. I'm not mad at you. Not even close."

A smile tugs at her lips. "I like it when you call me that."

Her whisper is like a caress. My muscles pull even tighter. I'm almost vibrating as she glides a soft finger over my mouth, exploring. I ache for more contact. It's dizzying how fast she takes me from zero to one hundred.

"I need you." My hand floats to the waistband of her pants. "Now."

"Can't get my wet clothes off in here. We'll have to move."

I cast a look over my shoulder at the back seat, sizing it up.

Her gaze tracks mine and flits back to my lips. "Inside. Race me."

I fumble with the car handle and make a mad dash for the house. She splashes and stumbles ahead of me but rights herself before she face-plants in a deep puddle. We hit my front porch, and I usher her through with rough hands on her waist. An automated night light flickers to life as I kick the door shut.

"You are so beautiful." I crowd her against the door and peel off her shirt. What's left is a soaked white cotton bra, so fucking see-through I mutter a string of curse words as I palm her with a greedy hand.

She stares down at where my thumb slides over her stiff nipple, mouth open and panting like it's the hottest thing she's ever seen. "Harder," she whispers hoarsely.

I pinch her, and she throws her head back, knocking the door. "Again."

Blood thunders through my veins at the frantic sound of her voice. It's so sexy to see her unleashed, to hear her tell me what feels good. I spin her so she's bracing the door. Her fingers spread for balance as I break the clasp of her bra and tear the whole thing off. Coiling an arm around her torso, I pull her against me and pinch and cup and knead until she cries out.

"What else?" I beg as she arches into me.

"Pull my hair."

Her command rips through me. I grasp at the root and tug so I can reach her mouth. Her kisses are desperate and sloppy. I've never wanted to give and give as badly as I do with her. I want to deliver her demands on a platter until she's full.

*Full.*

Once the word is in my head, it takes over. Fuck, I want to fill her. The savage thought drives me as I work her pants down her legs.

She kicks them the rest of the way off, and goose bumps cascade down the backs of her legs. I falter. I can't let her stand here shivering in my cold house.

Inspiration strikes. One surefire way to get her warm—and wet, and *slippery*—sits down the hall.

I turn her toward me and scoop my arms beneath her ass. Her legs wind around my waist, and she leans into my ear. I expect a whisper but receive her mouth on my earlobe, tugging with her teeth before she moves lower, nipping and sucking so hard I'm sure she'll leave a mark.

I want the marks. To be claimed.

She takes a fistful of my hair and yanks, tearing a grunt from my mouth. I stumble into my bedroom doorframe, overcome by the distraction of her. I want every version of this woman, but Wild Piper is a goddamn revelation. I'm impossibly hard, and I've never been more grateful for my boxers, the only thing keeping me from losing my mind and fucking her raw, mid-walk to the bathroom.

"Go start the shower," I mumble into her skin, reluctantly letting her slip from my hold in my dark bedroom. "I have to get a condom."

Illuminated by the glow of my television's neon home screen, she bites her lip as her chest rises and falls with each heavy breath. "I'm on the pill. Had my annual last month. I'm good on my end."

*Oh.*

I choke on a mouthful of words. "I, uh…I get checked every six months. More if I've—" I clear my throat. Let's just say I haven't *needed* a check in the last six months. "I'm good to go."

The air changes between us. Frantic static gives way to a steady current of white-hot electricity as we step onto the tile floor of my bathroom. She slides the glass door and cranks the shower to life.

I let her undress me as the shower fills the bathroom with steam. When my boxers hit the ground, I'm naked.

But when she whispers my name with her palms flat against my chest, a breath of calm in the middle of the storm, I'm stripped bare.

The words *I love you* rise in my throat.

Warm caramel eyes, searching my face. *I love you.*

Flushed cheeks I brush with my thumbs. *I love you.*

The first lips I ever kissed. *I love you.*

*Say it.*

My breathing stalls. What if this thing between us is just about what we can do for each other, and isn't more to her? If we do this again—if I go all in and lay my heart on the line—and it doesn't mean as much to her as it does to me, I don't know how I'll recover. Not again.

The moment stretches longer and longer until she wraps a hand around my length. Steam wets our skin and makes her grip warmer, wetter, more consuming than it's ever been. It's so tight and hot my words fall away. She strokes once, testing. Twice, firmer. I groan.

In every way, this woman has me in the palm of her hand.

I walk us into the shower, concentrating all my energy on not coming at her touch. The warm water rains over us, and I force my eyes shut. The sensations are so good I need to shut off the visual stimuli, the water running down her creamy skin, tracing a path over her perfect body. But without her to look at, the slide of her hand is heightened, slick, unreal. Heat and pressure climbing up my spine.

I jerk backward.

*Too close.*

My arm clears the shower bench in one clean sweep, knocking half-empty bottles to the ground. They rattle at her feet as she falls into the seat. I spread her open and pull her all the way to the edge as water pelts my back. Color blooms across her stomach, down her legs, over where she's so swollen for me. My tongue sets her off like a starting gun. Her moan reverberates in my core as she grips my hair in a possessive hold.

I get her close and back off.

My gaze flits up, drinking in the view. Her expression as she stares down at me is ruining. "So good," she murmurs.

Her encouragement kicks me into high gear. I suck until she cries out and pulls up on my hair. Not the *more* kind of pull. Something else. "What's wrong? Do you want to stop?"

"Sam, I think I…"

I rise and pull her up with me. Steam and water blur my eyes, and her words blur my brain. *Tell me.* I'm not sure it comes out of my mouth. I don't hear anything but the steady slap of the water.

Something soft flashes in her eyes, and she blinks down as she reaches for me. "I want us to finish together." Her eyes widen. "Is that…? I'm sorry, that's cheesy. Forget I said it."

Inside me, something shatters at her tender

request. The kind of shatter that could never be pieced back together. Her arms circle my neck, and I lift her, desperate to get her eye level. "I can't forget anything you say."

When I bend to kiss her, the brush of her lips is soft. For all the frenzy, this thing we're doing has never felt more like making love. I pull back to savor the look in her eyes, surrender and desperation.

"Please?" she whispers.

With a slow slide, I'm halfway in. The wet heat of her sends me to another plane. The sensation is magnified tenfold, softer than silk. I have to stall so I don't finish, it's that good. Nothing has *ever* felt like this. Or ever could, with anyone else. This woman makes me want to earn it.

"Oh," she gasps, eyes falling closed. "*Oh.*"

"Look at me. I need you here with me."

Her eyes flutter open, and she meets my gaze, holding it. "It's never been like this."

"I know, baby." I kiss the soft space beside her open mouth. "I feel it, too."

Another push and I'm all the way in, buried in her. I move slow at first, languid strokes to help keep me off the edge. But as her gasps come faster and faster, I increase my speed and power to rhythmic bursts to match her need. She tells me everything with her body, circling her hips and nodding to let me know *yes, closer, almost there.* Fiery pressure pools low in my back, spreading as we move together.

She grips my back with her nails as her legs tremble, and I can feel how close she is. I've been on the edge for minutes, holding on for her. Three circular brushes of my thumb and we both unravel in a fit of breathy yells. Her *ohmygod* rings in my ear: *Sam, I love you.*

Startled, I loosen my hold, and she slips down my body. Her feet hit the ground as my orgasm pulses. Did I imagine those words out of her mouth? It's hard to trust my ears or any of my senses while I still throb so acutely.

I meet her eye, and she nods back and forth, brows knitted in fear. "I'm sorry. I shouldn't have said that. Not like that."

I wipe the water from my face. "Wait, what? You love me, you're sorry, you shouldn't have? Which is it?"

"I shouldn't have said I love you during sex. The most cliché thing I could've done."

"Do you, though?" I swallow thickly. "Love me?"

She steps toward me, hair obscuring her face, her eyes fixed on mine. "I..." She purses her lips, and her gaze drops to the floor.

A voice carries through the crack in the bathroom door. "Sam, the fuck are you doing in there—drowning?"

*Dad.*

Piper stumbles sideways. "Oh shit. What is he doing here?"

"What were you going to say?" I tilt her chin toward me. "'I…' *what*? I need you to finish that sentence."

She flails her arm toward the cracked door before hugging her chest and turning to face the wall, as though convinced my dad is going to bust in here.

"It's my house. He can wait."

"Sam, *go*."

I smash the shower handle. My shift comes flooding back, one shitty part at a time. Then the week. Everything hits me at once, full speed.

Resigned, I lower my voice to a whisper. "Stay here. I don't want you to have to listen to this."

I snap a towel off the wall hook and shut the bathroom door firmly behind me.

Dread and dry air cool my scorching skin. I think I'd rather deal with the crushing reality of my work problems, getting sent home, whatever my dad's about to throw at me than listen to Piper tell me her *I love you* was a heat-of-the-moment mistake.

Because that's exactly what I'm afraid she was about to say.

# CHAPTER THIRTY-FOUR

## PIPER

I said I love you. Out loud. How could I let it slip out when we were both barely able to breathe, let alone converse?

My insides clench as I hurry out of the shower. Who says *I love you* for the first time mid-orgasm? I was so relieved he still wanted this—me—after the clips, I got lost in it all. Lost in us.

I love Sam. So much I couldn't keep it inside. But what if love isn't enough or he's not on the same page? What if we can't make it work, and everything falls apart all over again?

Our working arrangement won't survive it. His friendship with Caleb won't survive it.

Losing him once was hard enough. I can't go

through it again. Rushing him with an *I love you* before he's there—if he's ever there—isn't smart.

I ransack his closet for clothes. The grating, unsettling voice of Captain O'Shea is loud and clear, even with the bedroom door shut.

"I told you I'd be by after my shift. Not that you ever listen."

I wince. Whatever Sam says in return is much quieter than his dad's response.

"I'm not talking to you as your father. I'm talking to you as your boss. You may call the shots with this mayor crap, but at the station, it's *my* rules. You would do well to remember that."

*Your boss.* My heart misfires at his clinical tone. I crack open the door so I can see but hopefully not be seen.

The captain stands in Sam's living room, arms crossed over his chest. He didn't even take off his hat.

"Show me where it says I can't do both," Sam demands. "Where is it written? Stevie bartends on the side. Don sells real estate Monday through Thursday. You're telling me I'm the only one—"

"Once again, you fail to see how your actions affect me. This is an embarrassment to the entire station. They're blasting your name—the O'Shea name—from here to Montpelier."

"It's a temporary setback. When I can explain the nature of the clips to the press, this will blow over. As I explained to you before, I was able to get a lawyer on the phone again this morning to discuss damage control. It should only be a few days, then I'll be back to my regular campaigning."

*Lawyers.*

His words hit me like a physical blow. He talked to a lawyer without me and didn't think to mention it?

"I don't give a *shit* about the campaign. You shouldn't be running in the first place. I entertained it because you've always had this ridiculous idea that you could run for office, but you should have waited until it was your time."

Sam's voice hits a high key I've never heard out of him. "So, it's Paul fucking Stine's time? I have to defer to that asshole because he's older—is that your point?"

"Doesn't matter now, does it? Your foul little side project cost you the election. The radio is blasting your voice, the commercial plays every twenty minutes, there's a billboard off Prior Street… A week will be too late to fix this. I hope it was worth it. This is going to be a blight on our family name forever. All my work as captain of this precinct is now tainted—"

"This has *nothing* to do with you," Sam growls.

"The hell it doesn't. Being captain of RTFD is my life. And the job will be yours in a few years if you'd toe the fucking line. You have a responsibility to this precinct, in case you've forgotten."

"What about your responsibilities as my father?"

His dad scoffs. "You shouldn't be mixed up in this bullshit in the first place. Seems like something my son would know without having to be told."

"Sorry to disappoint, *captain*."

The venom in Sam's voice jolts me, and my knee knocks the door.

The captain jumps at the noise. "The hell was that? Is someone here?"

I've never wanted to run away from a confrontation more in my entire life. My legs itch to carry me through Sam's window, across the city, into the heart of the storm. Anywhere but here.

But the hurt shining on Sam's face draws me down the short hallway. This is my fight, too.

"This isn't Sam's fault." I ball my hands into fists to stop the trembling. "He couldn't have seen this coming or prevented it. It was a security breach."

The captain glances at me, expression sour, lips downturned. At once, every cell in my body feels exposed. *Sam's shirt. Sam's shorts. Wet hair.*

"All due respect to your little project, but Sam shouldn't have gotten mixed up with it in the first place. Piper, if you need respectable work, I am happy to line something up for you."

Before I can process that he'd say something like that out loud, Sam's voice goes dangerously soft. "Don't you fucking *dare* imply what she does isn't respectable."

The captain stiffens. "It's an embarrassment, is what it is. If that's what Piper wants for her life, fine. But is it what you want for yours, Sam?"

Red-hot humiliation slaps me in the face.

"Dad, *stop*."

The captain shrugs and straightens his cap. "You need to take the out, Sam. Sever ties and move on. And if and when Piper is ready, I'll make a call to Deidre over at Shalvis and Associates. A nice nine to five without any of the stress—"

I step toward Sam as the rest of the captain's words fade to fuzzy background noise. "What *out*? There's no 'out' in our contract."

I'm fairly sure it's Christmas by the time Sam speaks. "Can we talk about this later?"

My brain feels like an hourglass, his words slipping through before I can catch on. "What is there to talk about? It's a three-book deal, and we're not even done with the first book."

He angles his body toward me, and his gaze flickers between my eyes. "Please?"

"Please *what*?"

The captain is oblivious to the doom swirling inside of me. His tone is all business. "Tell her what the lawyer said. She may want to exercise the same option."

Sam glares at his father but softens as he turns to me. "There's a clause in our contract that lets us out between books…at a penalty. It's a big penalty and prohibits future work with the Gentrys, but it keeps things clean. It'd allow you to move forward without me."

In a flash, the fragile house of cards we'd built for ourselves comes crashing down.

I always thought it'd be louder when things fell apart. Cinematic, even. Instead, it's quiet and still. A searing draft blows from an overhead vent, boiling my skin. I feel the ghost of his hands on me in the shower, movements so tender and loaded I couldn't imagine anything more wonderful. Was his mind on quitting the whole time? When his mouth was on my neck, his hands in my hair, was he plotting the best way to let me down easy? Thinking about what a massive wrench I've thrown in all his plans? "Oh."

Sam leans against the living room wall, eyeing the ground. "I didn't plan for any of this. I don't *want* to quit."

I hug my chest. "But you are. I understand. I should never have dragged you into my work when you had so much on your plate. This is my fault."

"Don't say that. You didn't drag me into anything I didn't want to do. It's not exactly a simple situation."

I didn't expect this. My dad encouraged me to step back and let Sam handle his crisis—and *I* wanted him to have the freedom to do what he needed to do to save his campaign—but I thought it'd be a conversation with the Gentrys where he begged permission to speak out sooner. I thought maybe they'd supply some talking points that don't breach our contract so Sam could make a speech. I imagined some kind of creative fix.

It didn't occur to me that he'd walk away completely.

This feeling is worse than a sting or an ache. It's a bruise being pressed.

The captain clears his throat. "I didn't realize you had company when I stopped by. I'll let you two talk. Call me when she leaves so we can make a plan."

My nails dig into my palms. "No need, captain. I'll leave now." I take three steps, remembering abruptly I *can't* leave. I'm trapped in this hellish conversation.

"If you want to go, I'll take you," Sam offers, defeat audible in his every word. "But it's safer to stay put."

The captain is already distracted by his phone as he walks toward the door. "Told you to invest in a bigger vehicle, Sam. We'll finish this conversation tomorrow when you've had time to think. Piper, nice to see you."

His dad disappears out the door without a backward glance.

Sam presses the space above his eyebrows. "I'm sorry about that. About him."

The beige walls feel like they're closing in. "Why didn't you tell me you were planning to quit?"

Sam reaches toward me with fingers outstretched but seems to change his mind at the last second. His arm falls. "I *don't* want to quit. It kills me to think about walking away and letting you down."

"But you are. You talked to a contract lawyer. Without telling me. You must've felt strongly you needed an out."

"I'm looking at all my options to see what makes the most sense." He ransacks his already-mussed hair with his hand. "My reputation is on the line. The attack ads prove this project directly conflicts with what I'm trying to accomplish. I'm trying to prove I'm trustworthy even though I'm young. The lawyer felt stepping away from the project and making a statement as soon as possible is my best option to salvage my career."

"Of course." I silently curse my shaky voice. "This is what you need to do. For your career." I brace myself, hands splayed on my stomach. "So that's what you're going to do?"

His silence screams so loud all of New England could hear it over the merciless rain.

I don't think I breathe for an entire minute as I process what this means. "Okay."

"*Okay?*" His voice is pleading. "It's obviously not. *I'm* not. None of this is."

"It's fine." My heart lurches. "I just wasn't expecting it. It makes sense."

Nothing could ever be less fine, in my career or my heart. I'll never keep the Gentrys' interest without Sam. Books two and three won't sell as well with a different male actor at the helm. They'll yank back the exclusivity offer, too, since nothing has been signed for that.

I was so close.

*We* were so close. But this wasn't his dream.

And I'd do well to remember that.

Sam pulls in a breath and holds it for several seconds. His body language is so unfamiliar, his limbs tense. "The Gentrys love you, Piper. If I take this out—*if*—nothing has to change for you. Your career will be fine. Better than fine."

I step back, my heels butting against a stone fireplace. It's not his fault he doesn't understand how fraught these arrangements are, how much my success hinged on us as a team.

I'm not going to tell him that and make this any harder. His exhaustion is visible in his slouched shoulders and heavy eyes. He's crumbling under the weight of all this. Something's got to give.

My job got us in this mess, and his job can carry him forward. Into a better life, with or without me. At this point, I don't know. It hurts to consider. I ache thinking about the end of our work, of being so thoroughly left behind.

I'll be back to square one, gig hunting. He'll be the goddamn *mayor*.

He deserves that.

He steps toward me, making up for the distance I put between us. My gaze drops to the ground.

"Piper…"

I force myself to meet his eye. He sways slightly, like whatever he sees in my face changes his mind about coming any closer. I feel too hollow to touch, like I might crumble at his hand.

"You can barely look at me." His tone is flimsy, a rubber band already snapped.

"I just need a little time."

His jaw clenches. As soon as I've said it, I know how it sounds. *Time.*

He flinches like he's been lashed by a whip. I've never seen him look so gobsmacked, face twisted in confusion. "Are you *kidding* me? After everything we've been through, how can you say that?"

The hurt in his voice makes me second-guess my instincts. It makes me weak enough to almost take it back. "I'm being honest."

"No, you're disengaging. It's written all over your face."

"Because there's nothing left to say."

His expression, stuck somewhere between a glare and panic, cuts me to the core.

I can't do this. I can't fight anymore.

"Please, Sam," I whisper. "I'm tired."

After a long beat that spirals me deeper into the hollowness billowing inside me, he schools his expression into something neutral. He lets out a strained sigh and plucks his keys off the ground where he threw them. It feels like hours have passed since we tornado-ed through his house, tangled in each other.

He sweeps a look across the living room. "I'll take the couch. You can have my bed. I'll drive you home in the morning."

I'm halfway down the hallway when the question comes.

"What else were you going to say in the shower?"

I slow to a stop, feet sinking into the rug, willing myself to turn around and tell him.

*I was going to tell you I love you.*

*Of course I love you.*

"Nothing." My voice is small enough to box up and stow away.

And it's the truth.

# CHAPTER THIRTY-FIVE

## SAM

I pace the dark, newly paved street in front of Caleb's house with nothing but my racing thoughts to keep me company. My head throbs in time with my steps.

*Ten paces, turn.*

*Ten paces, turn.*

*Ten paces, turn—*

My heel catches on a patch of slick tar, and I nearly eat pavement. I flail like I'm failing a field sobriety test. The spike in my adrenaline fuels me to keep going. Movement is the only thing I can tolerate right now.

I should be sleeping. I haven't since I last saw Pipes on Sunday. Whenever I hit the pillow the last three nights, I saw the hurt in her eyes all over again.

What the hell am I doing?

My whole body tenses. I hate the sadness that was in her voice and the fact I caused it by considering walking away from the gig. I let her down and made her feel like our work isn't important.

I also hate that *she* shut down and pushed me away. Really hate that.

Face-planting on the road would feel better than this. I crave the tangible kind of pain that can be fixed with swipes of a sterile cloth and stitches.

I miss her so fucking much I feel it in my body.

I miss her so much I'm a wild animal stalking circles outside her brother's house, seeking some sort of clarity I don't deserve, from him of all people.

A dull ache spreads through my core. In every other area of my life, I anticipate problems and solve them. Obstacles are only obstacles if you don't see them coming and swerve. But this mess knocked me for a loop.

I should've known this thing with Piper and me would come at a price. That I'd have to sacrifice something to make it all work. But she's always been my Achilles' heel. I never see clearly when it comes to her. She consumes me. Issues creep up unnoticed because she eclipses my vision. From the minute she walked into the station last month to ask for my help—looking sexy as hell, and acting so sweetly nervous it was all I could do not to pull her down on my lap and whisper in her mouth that she could have whatever she wanted to calm her down—I should've anticipated that I'd make a mess of juggling things.

But damnit, if I can't be the mayor, keep my job, and belong to her—I should've chosen *her*. My commitment to her, the gig, all of it. And I should've done it loudly, to her face.

Nothing I can do or say now will erase the fact that I hesitated. I made her feel second-best to my goals, which now feel like the pointless ceramic knickknacks on my mother's shelves. They mean nothing if the whole house burns down.

And worse than hurting her, I have to look Caleb in the eye and own up to my feelings and the mistakes I've made, when I assured him our troubles were all in the past.

Caleb's porch light flickers to life, casting a warm glow on lush grass. He steps out, arms crossed over his chest. "O'Shea?"

I squint and turn away. Maybe it's not too late to run—

"The fuck are you doing out here?"

I grip the back of my neck. "I've been trying to reach you about your car's extended warranty."

A few new fossils form as he processes my dumb joke. "Get in here," he finally mutters.

I jog up the path. He leaves the door open a crack, and I nudge it open.

I usually feel clumsy and large in Caleb's small living room. But today, as I step into the space, I feel hugged. Hugged by the frilly curtains hanging in the window. Held by Jane's vintage poster collection lining the walls. Surrounded by the warmth of a crackling fire. Smothered by the familiarity of it all.

At my house, the fireplace never gets used, and the walls are bare. This place feels more like home than my own.

Caleb clears his throat. I look over and find him tunneled between crumpled blankets on the couch. He grabs a striped throw pillow to hug. "Have a seat."

I shuffle to the chair opposite him, nerves poking me between the ribs. "*Have a seat.* This a job interview?"

"Maybe. Did you prepare anything besides jokes?"

"You wore a matching pajama set to this interview, and I can't tell jokes?"

"*O'Shea.*"

I gesture at the pillow he's clutching and all the fluffy blankets around him. "Marriage really suits you."

He scowls. "I have a wife, baby, mortgage, and a full-time job to take care of. Let me have my fleeces. Now tell me why you're really here."

Pressure builds behind my eyes. My fuck-ups are sure to damage my friendship with Caleb, *again.*

Hurting Piper means hurting him. Yet another thing I should've anticipated and swerved.

Sweat beads at my forehead.

"Start with the yard pacing," he offers.

"Technically, I was pacing the road." I sigh and begin again. I barely recognize my own voice when it comes out timid. "I screwed up, dude. I've made a mess of everything."

"And?"

I blink twice. The surge of fear inside me crests and diffuses.

*And.* That's it?

My shoulders slump. "What do you mean, *and?*"

"I mean you fucking up was an inevitability when you decided to date my sister, while *working* with my sister, without consulting me."

"Why would I consult you about a relationship with your sister when that's the last thing you wanted?"

"You have no idea what I want. Can't blame you—you are historically awful at asking my advice in this arena until it's too late."

"Because you don't want to talk about it!"

"Did I want to talk, at great length, about the ways my best friend and sister ruined each other's lives in high school? No. Do I want a repeat of the past? Absolutely the fuck not. She was wrecked after your relationship. You both were. *I* was. But if you're serious about her now, *that* I need to know. Preferably from you. We aren't kids anymore."

"Technically you *don't* need to know any of this, Caleb. Because you're right— we aren't kids. How Piper and I feel about each other is our business. Period. No matter how badly things are going or how complicated it is, it's about *us*. And that relationship has zero to do with you and me. Our friendship is separate."

I didn't come here to say any of that—I fully intended to grovel—but I know as soon as it's out that it needed to be said.

And no matter how important Caleb is to me, my loyalty lies with Piper. Even in the middle of this fucking mess. Loving her means things will never be the same. And they shouldn't have to be.

He sits up a little straighter. A wry smile breaks out on his face as he strokes his chin. "Fair enough."

I raise a brow. "Fair enough? That's it?"

"I'm married with a kid. I know what it means to put my woman first. Honestly, I respect the fuck out of your answer."

I blink a few times. "Oh."

"Do you love her?"

I've never answered a question faster. "Yes. I do."

"Then we need to fix whatever has you pacing outside my house like a fucking Labrador off his leash. If you're willing, I'd like to help you turn this shit around."

"I—wow. Okay. Thank you. Seriously."

A smile breaks on his freckled face. "Underestimate me a little less, asshole."

I didn't know how badly I needed to hear him say that until now. Not the asshole part—though, *fair enough*—but the tacit permission to love his sister. I didn't need it, because I love her regardless, but damn am I glad to have the blessing. The relief of it warms me to my core. "Will do."

"Now about you messing everything up," he continues. "I need more than that. Start with actually telling me what's going on—your side of the story."

I lean back and let my head fall against the chair. It's easier to confess to the ceiling. "I was so sure being mayor was what I wanted. Keeping my job, too. The voice-acting stuff... It all felt manageable when this thing started. It never occurred to me that I couldn't do it all."

He throws his pillow at me, and it bounces off my chest. "That was your first mistake. You always think you can do it all. Remember when you tried to do Model UN and the debate team at the same time? During soccer season?"

I chuck the pillow back, aiming for his face. "So maybe my time management needs a little work. But the bigger mistake was how I handled it with Piper. It was fucking brutal when she found out—from my dad, of all people—that I was looking for loopholes in our contract."

He *tsk*s in disapproval.

"Believe me, I hate me, too. I can't pretend I didn't think about quitting, but it was a panic reaction, a Hail Mary type of thing."

"Okay, so are you quitting the gig or not?"

"Well, she's so hurt I may not even—" I grumble into my hands. "Right now, I'm a mess. I can't make a coherent decision."

His tone shifts from leader of the Spanish Inquisition to normal Caleb. "I don't get it. You committed to doing this thing. Yeah, those weird clips leaked—and I *don't* want to hear more about those, gag me with a goddamn spoon—but is bailing on her really going to help?"

"When they leaked, I felt like I had to *do* something. Before Piper and I talked, I thought it wouldn't matter all that much if I quit. She's the professional; I figured they'd find her someone else to work with."

"You are a master of bullshit."

I lift my head. "What?"

"You tell yourself she doesn't need you so you don't have to feel guilty when you disappoint her. But she does need you. She'd never tell you that, but it's true."

"She barely acted like she wanted me, let alone *needed* me during our fight the other night. She told me I was right, completely shut down, and pushed me away. Just like in high school."

He stretches his arms overhead. "Put yourself in her shoes. The gig is ruining your campaign, or so she thinks. That's her passion project, her *thing*, and now she thinks it's fucking up your life. Of course she's going to push you away, so you can go fix your reputation and have your dreams. Remember when you told her you got into UMass and UC the same day, and suddenly she asked for a break a week later? Ring a bell at all?"

I straighten in my chair. "Wait...was it really a week?"

The reality of what he's saying sinks in slowly.

Several years too late.

It was a few days after I told her about those acceptances that she asked for the break. I never connected the timing before. I almost snap at Caleb and ask why he didn't bring this up before, but I stop myself just in time. Because it wasn't his job to spell that out for me. But I'm damn glad he's doing it now.

He casts the pillow aside and perches his elbows on his knees. "She doesn't want to stand in your way, Sam. She wants you to be happy and will do whatever it takes to make it happen. My sister is good people."

Guilt feels a lot like heartburn, shooting up my throat, forcing me to swallow. "I don't deserve her. I'm just some asshole who never left Roseborough.

Piper is one of a kind. Funny. Nurturing—does anyone care more about their siblings than she does? She's so talented. God, when she gets going in the studio, it's amazing. And of course she's stunning—"

"Okay, okay, I get it; you like my sister. But the bottom line is you don't *have* to deserve her. That's on her to decide."

He leans back and stares daggers into my face, so much so I turn my gaze to the fire in the hearth. "I can't sleep, knowing I may have fucked up her work. This is not how it was supposed to go."

"Just because things aren't going to Mr. February's overly ambitious plan doesn't mean all hope is lost." He glances at a framed photo of his family on the mantel. "Surely you can fix this?"

He makes it sound so simple. "You didn't see her the other day. I don't know if she wants to fix this."

"Of course she does."

"How do you know?"

"Because I know my sister, and she loves you, even if she shows it in confusing ways sometimes. She loved you when you were a dumb-ass kid, and she loves you as a dumb-ass adult. Job crap isn't going to change that. Apologize, grovel, prove to her that she's your priority. The ball is in your court."

I grip the tops of my thighs. "Even if that's true, my life is a mess. Half the town thinks I'm a scumbag because of the clips. My dad thinks I need to quit the

gig and back out of running for office. Piper thinks
I'm bailing on her and that she's not important to
me. Your parents must think…" I trail off as a lead
weight settles in the pit of my stomach. "If this were
a debate, I'd have trouble arguing my worthiness for
anything right about now."

"Put all the other people out of your mind for a
second. You're the most qualified, competent guy I
know. Assuming anything is possible, what do *you*
want? You wake up tomorrow, clean slate, what's your
first move? Is it quitting the gig? Writing a speech to
the town? Blocking news alerts on your phone?"

I try to do what he says, but there's one person
who won't get out of my mind, even for a second.

Piper's shower *I love you* rings in my ear. My
pulse skitters as if she's saying it right here and now.
The moment hits me all over again, her leg over
my hip, nails digging in my back as she moaned the
words in my ear.

I jump up, adrenaline coursing. I should've yelled
*I love you* back right then and there. I've been saying
it for weeks. I whispered it in her ear in the back
of Jane's van. I murmured it into the soft skin of her
neck after she kissed me in her closet. I said it through
clenched teeth the first time she touched me in the
hotel. I haven't stopped saying it, but only to myself.
So what if she could break my heart all over again or
if she's not on the same page? I should've told her,

because it's the truth.

And now, I might have missed my chance.

"Dude, are you all right?"

I glance from Caleb to my legs. The thought of losing Piper has me pacing a groove into the carpet.

"I need to grovel. I have to show her she's the most important thing to me."

"Well, yeah. But is she?"

"Of course."

He grunts. "Well, from where I'm sitting, your quest for world domination is the most important thing to you. Your job, campaign, your father's approval…all that seems to come first."

The words land like an anvil. I stop pacing and fist my hands on my hips. "First of all, you're sitting in a nest of blankets, so that may not have been the best way to couch your argument. Second, I do not need his approval. He wants me to be a one-trick pony and take over as captain when he retires. I've gotten very good at doing the opposite of what he wants, and I plan to keep it that way. As for the rest, I planned to do it all until this got out of hand."

The first time Piper and I didn't work, I figured out a way around the pain by filling the void. I buried myself in college, then my career, setting goals. Chasing the high of achievement. Everything I wanted, I went out and got for myself. Maybe I got a little addicted to the grind.

Maybe I'm trying to prove to *myself* I'm worth it. Worth *her*.

No job will ever make me feel the way Piper does. No job is more important to me than protecting her heart. In another world, being mayor might've been an impressive start to the rest of my life.

But in this world, it's the very thing standing in my way. I've never had something I'm this afraid to lose, but now I do. And I am worth her love, if she's willing to give it to me. And I don't need to keep trying to prove that to anyone but Piper herself.

"I'll quit the race."

Caleb lets out a low whistle. "You've been obsessed with this campaign since the start. You'd be willing to quit, just like that?"

The rush of certainty floods my body. The answer is so obvious.

Sometimes a direct question begets a direct answer.

"Yes." I voice the word aloud, fortifying my intention in steel. She's my priority now. I want to voice so many more promises.

Just not here. And not to Caleb.

I'm ready to make a plan.

# CHAPTER THIRTY-SIX

## PIPER

Wednesday morning brings a fresh wave of nausea that coffee only intensifies. The day does not improve from there.

The last few days have been about as fun as chauffeuring Aunt Dawn home from a dive bar. I refresh my phone for hours, waiting for some kind of update. An update from the Gentrys about whether they've touched base with the lawyer and/or fired me. A text from Sam saying he's bailed on the contract or released a statement to the press. *Something.*

Nothing comes.

Once he officially quits, I'm screwed. Darla could love me like a daughter and still choose not to look past someone terminating a contract between books.

My future with them is in shambles. I just know it.

I miss Sam, but I don't want to call him. He'll hear the sadness in my voice. I can't have him feeling sorry for me when he's got a race against that shriveled old raisin of a man Paul Stine to win.

And yet, I *do* want to call him. Or I want him to call *me*.

This merry-go-round has no exit.

My family tiptoes around me like I have some kind of communicable disease. As if moping is contagious. You'd think between a hurricane and Mom's roller coaster of pregnancy mood swings, they'd be too distracted to fret over me.

Nonna's offered me tea and grilled cheese multiple times today, even though I always say no. It's pushing sunset, and I can't bring myself to eat. Nova stays glued to my hip all day, an emotional support Bellini at my beck and call.

I feel empty. Hollowed out.

Sam's absence is like a heavy weight I can't shed. I still feel the warmth of words pressed into my skin as he held me in the shower, still see the mingled panic and determination in his eyes when he rescued me from the side of the road like his whole world was at risk. I ache for his touch, his arms around me.

And with that, I need a breather.

Shooing Nova to the basement, I drag myself to

the backyard in pursuit of fresh air.

My hand clasps the doorknob when my father's voice drifts out of his bedroom. "I know. It's all right. I'm here."

I shouldn't listen, but his gentle tone strikes a chord in my heart. A few side steps position me outside their cracked door. Back flush against the wall, I press my eyes shut.

"It's never been like this before. I can't eat. I can't sleep. It hurts." The tension in Mom's voice triggers the same in me. My fingers dig into my arms as I hug my chest. "I don't know if I can do this again. It's too much. I think I'm...scared."

An ache blossoms behind my eyes. Mom *never* uses the word scared.

"C'mere, sweets." In the lengthy pause, I visualize Dad wrapping her in his trademark bear hug, as best he can with the size of her belly. "You aren't doing this alone. I won't let you do *anything* alone, as long as I live. You understand that? I'm here for you. We're a team. This isn't all on you to handle. You can't take care of everyone all the time. Let me take care of you."

"You have so much on your plate, Gio. I ask so much of you—"

"So I'll buy a bigger plate."

"Be serious."

"I'll take an early retirement."

"You wanted to go after superintendent next year. That was the plan."

"Plans change."

"I'm sorry, Gio. I didn't want to *need* more help. But I do."

"You only ever have to ask, my love."

When I hear Mom's muffled sobs, the leaden heart in my chest shatters. Shards of pain and longing radiate from my core, feelings so intense I have to brace myself against the wall to keep from buckling.

I want what my parents have, but time and time again I stand in my own way.

Everything I know about love, I learned from my mother. She is the blueprint of putting others first. She stayed home for years to take care of the kids, even when I know she longed to work. She wanted to run for city counselor long before she pulled the trigger, and she only did so after my father's insistence that he'd set better boundaries at work to help pick up the slack at home.

But he never would've done that had she not *asked*. I'll never forget the way she sat the family down at the dining room table and made her desires to have a purpose outside the house known. And now, when she's asking for help, he's ready and willing to give it.

Maybe I haven't always been the best learner, but the lessons were there for the taking. They're the perfect example of balance. When one is in need, the other gives. Adapts. Sacrifices.

I never gave Sam a chance to be that balance for me. I didn't tell him what I want from our partnership, neither in the studio nor outside of it.

Things could've been different if I had.

They still could be.

I ache all the way to my bones, but avoiding pain doesn't feel like the ultimate goal anymore. Maybe my heart needed to break completely so I could empty it, releasing the painful memories and misbeliefs once and for all.

Sam and I are not who we were. I'm no longer the girl so afraid that loving her boyfriend would hold him back in life. He's not this perfect man I've created in my head, destined for great things if only I'd let him go.

He's just Sam, and I'm just me.

We've made mistakes at every step. And this week, I made another one. I pushed him away, closed myself off because I was afraid of being the reason his hopes and dreams imploded. Even if pushing him away upended my own dreams.

Yes, I want him to be happy. But I want him to be happy with *me*.

I want him to work with me, and I need to tell him that, but more than anything, I need to show him I'll fight for *us*. I need to have the hard conversations and open up in a way I never have.

He can't be there for me if I don't let him. Or know what I'm feeling if I don't tell him.

If it's not forever with Sam, I don't want it for another second. And to get to forever, I'll do whatever it takes to show him I'm in this. Fully.

I don't ever want another "break."

I race back up to my room and dial his phone number. It rings and rings as I perch on the edge of my bed.

Finally, an eternity later, the voicemail picks up. The sound of his chipper recorded message makes me grin like a fool.

Clearing my throat, I manage a breathy, "Hi."

I pause, trying to mold several days' worth of anxiety and emotion into a single coherent thought.

"I've been thinking a lot lately. About work. Us. Everything. Other politicians delegate, and you took on this whole mayor thing yourself. I don't know how you manage it all. It's *so* much. And then my project on top of it…all in the hopes my mom would rally behind you? That's dedication. I wish I was half as dedicated as you. You're kind of my hero."

I suck in a breath. My throat is tight, and I've barely scratched the surface of what I want to say to him.

"There's more. I promised myself I'd start telling people how I feel and being honest about what I want.

So, here goes. The job we're doing—it's my dream job, and I knew it would change my life, but I didn't realize *how*. Your voice, whether you think so or not, is an integral part in the success of it. I told you to quit like it was no big deal, like it wouldn't crush me, but that wasn't the truth. I don't want you to quit. Working with you on it has changed *everything*. But even if—"

A curt *beep* cuts me off.

And then there's nothing.

"*Fuck*." I glance down at the black screen. What does that mean? Did the message go through, or did I run out of time? There's so much more I want to say, the most important piece.

It doesn't matter. I'll tell him in person. I'll track him down and show him in person just *how* ready I am to fight for us—for what I want.

I race to my dresser to find something other than baby pink leggings and a sleep shirt. An outfit that screams, *I'm here to speak my truth, take it or leave it, but preferably take it, and then take* me *in your bed—*

A pounding at my door as I'm unfurling a pair of jeans throws off my momentum.

"Pipes? Pipes!"

Dad's tone is all wrong. I halt in my frantic prepping. "I'm here. Are you all right?"

"Your mother. She's bleeding."

# CHAPTER THIRTY-SEVEN

### SAM

"For an entry-level setup, the Scarlett Solo and the AT2020 will get you there, assuming your space is already outfitted. If not, we need to talk about an acoustics treatment."

I nod as if a single thing out of this store associate's mouth makes a lick of sense. The last time I heard this many unfamiliar words and brand names strung together in a row was Piper's makeup tutorial.

The dude runs his hand over a box. "What questions can I answer for you?"

*Uh.* I'm thinking I don't even know enough about this to ask a coherent follow-up question. The problem with surprising Piper with a big "I'm in it to win it" gift is that I need her and her expertise here to tell me what would make her studio better.

I rack my brain for something to ask. "Is it flammable?"

He pauses. "Which item?"

"The uh—the Scarlett. That's the mic, right?"

"The AT2020 is the mic."

I squint into Best Buy's fluorescents. "Right. That's what I meant."

"And you want to know if it's flammable?"

Suddenly this question feels as ludicrous as me thinking I could pick out equipment. "Never mind. I'll take them both."

He piles the boxes in my arms. "Make sure you tell them Nate helped you out."

I swerve through the aisles. As I fall in line at checkout, my pocket starts singing. Forrester's ringtone—which he programmed in my phone while we were bullshitting at the station, and I forgot to change because he doesn't call me—draws immediate attention from the gaggle of girls queued up behind me. The high-pitched cry of Olivia Rodrigo grates my ears.

"—*Guess YOU didn't MEAN what you WROTE in that SONG about ME—*"

I fumble the boxes in my furious attempt to rip the phone out of my pocket. My greeting is tepid at best.

"Hey man, glad you answered." Forrester's tone

is devoid of his usual sarcasm. "We're leaving for an assist on Avebury Boulevard."

The road name expands like a gas in my chest, pressing and pressing until I can't catch my breath. That's Piper's street. My vision narrows to a pinpoint, and I can only manage a weak, "Who?"

"Female, forty-four."

Catherine.

He runs down their response, how she presented, assuring me that the paramedics had her stable before they loaded her for transport. As stable as any pregnancy emergency can be, at least, which is not good enough until they rush her into the ER for scans and next steps.

Fear clogs my throat. "Oh."

His voice lowers. "Your girl's here. She's…well, she's upset. I think you should come."

I'm already halfway out the door, boxes abandoned on a shelf. "I'm on my way."

Avebury Boulevard is quiet and still, as if nothing monumental just happened here. All response vehicles are off scene by the time I pull in Piper's driveway.

In the living room, I find her kneeling with her back to me, a squirt bottle aimed at the bloodstained carpet. The smell of cleaner burns my nostrils as she sprays.

And sprays.

I kneel at her side. "Pipes, are you all right?"

She stares a hole into the ground. "How did you know?"

"Forrester called me."

Another spray.

I lay a steadying hand on her forearm. "Please stop. Let me take care of this."

Her voice is high and sharp. "The longer the spot sits, the worse it'll stain."

"Talk to me. Are you all right? Do you feel queasy? After a trauma—"

"Sam, don't. I *can't*." Her voice breaks on the word. With a rag wrapped around her right hand, she leans forward and scrubs. Red liquid bleeds into the cloth. The taste of copper coats my tongue.

I rub her back. "It's okay to stop."

"I can't stop!" She leans away from my touch and pushes all her weight into the ground. The solution grows more potent in the air the more she scrubs, mingled bleach and blood. "Not until it's clean."

"They are going to take good care of your mom," I whisper.

"You don't know that. You didn't see her." She rips the lid off the bottle and pours it all over the carpet.

I remove the bottle from her hand. "I know it's scary, but you're going to get sick off these fumes. Take a few minutes. Go upstairs."

"What about the kids?" she asks wearily. "They're all awake. They saw her on the ground, bleeding—" Her mouth snaps shut, and her face flashes an unsettling shade of green.

"I'll check on them and meet you upstairs in a little while, all right?"

Eyes fixed on a point in the distance, she nods and rises on two shaky legs.

Thirty minutes later, after I've checked on the boys, learned more about their mother's scare, and touched base with both Gio and Caleb, I find Piper sitting on her closet floor, wrapped in a towel.

My arm floats toward the light switch.

"I want the darkness," she says, her voice hollow. "My head hurts, and it helps. Plus, the carpet in here is soft."

"Can I get you anything? Something for your head?"

She slides forward and pats the ground. I enter the closet—our sacred spot, it feels like—and lower beside her. She opens my legs and positions herself between them so her back is flush with my chest.

Her body relaxes, notching into mine.

"The boys are all back to sleep," I whisper. "Your dad is going to call me with any updates. They're running tests."

Silence follows, giving way to her quiet sobs. She cries until her voice fades into nothing.

I remove the elastic from her wrist and sweep her wet, dripping hair into a ponytail. "You must be exhausted. You should sleep. I'll wait for updates."

"I'm not going to be able to sleep. What if the baby is born right now? What if Mom…"

I pull her tight against me. It's never safe to tell someone their loved one will be okay. I can only tell the truth. "She's one of the toughest people I know."

"One minute, she was resting; the next, she was bleeding and unresponsive. I've never been so scared in my entire life. I still don't even understand what happened. I think I was in shock. Did Forrester tell you any specifics?"

I trail my hand in gentle strokes up and down her back. "From what he told me, it sounds like a hypoglycemic emergency, potential placental abruption. But she was stable in transport, and that's promising. The next few hours will be about the baby and running tests."

"If anything happens to her, I don't know what I'll do."

The thought of something happening to

Catherine turns my blood cold. "I know."

Eventually we stand, first her, then me. She leads us into the light and wanders to her dresser.

I turn away, facing the wall to give her privacy, remembering reality all at once. I feel so many conflicting things I could combust. Fear for her and her family. The crushing weight of the last few weeks. Sadness and longing so heavy they bear down like weight on my shoulders. A desire to be the man she needs, especially right now.

My mind flits to the promises I planned to make tonight. But decisions and declarations must wait, since disaster doesn't know how.

Piper's phone sounds, and we both jump. Mine follows suit a half second later. Gio texted us both, and Caleb, at the same time.

*Mom is stable. We need to talk. Bring everyone at nine a.m. for visiting hours. Don't worry.*

A strangled cry of relief escapes Piper's mouth. Tears stream down her cheeks, but her voice stays steady. "She's okay."

Instinctively, I move to her, brushing away her tears with my thumbs. I cradle her face for a few seconds longer. "Are *you* okay?"

"Why would he write 'need to talk' and 'don't worry' in the same text? Dad is a menace."

I perch on the edge of her bed. My forearms come to rest on my thighs as I watch her step into a pair of shorts. "I don't think he'd write 'don't worry' if he didn't mean it."

"Maybe. I still have this awful feeling there's bad news he's not saying."

"One minute at a time, Pipes. Lay down, all right? You've been through a lot."

She climbs into bed, collapsing on her pillow.

Tension balloons between us as I look down at her. I'm sure the question is written all over my face. *Do you want me to go?*

But when I consider actually leaving this room, I can't bring myself to say it. My tired, stupid heart can't handle being away from her. "Is there anything else I can do for you?"

She watches me, unblinking. A decade ticks by until she pulls her lip between her teeth. "Will you stay with me?"

A relieved gust of air escapes my mouth as I slide into the space beside her. I'm content to let her set the tone, happy to be here however she wants me, but when she twists her hand in my shirt and pulls, I'm drawn all the way in. I feel like the goddamn moon to her planet, hopelessly bound.

She burrows her face in my neck, and we move together, soft and seeking. Cuddling and comforting. It's as vital as breathing that I touch her everywhere, soothe her with the palm of my hand on her back or my closed mouth pressed to her shoulder. Her knee slides over my hip, and her hands rake my hair. Our eyes keep meeting. Finding their way home.

Her hands skim across my chest. "Did you get my voicemail?"

I narrow my eyes. "What voicemail?"

Her gaze is shot with relief. "I left you a message. About our jobs, and"—her cheeks flush a rosy pink—"life. I thought maybe you got it and didn't like what you heard."

"I didn't get any message."

I can tell she's suppressing a smile by the way her full, perfect lips twitch. "Okay. Good to know."

"What did you say?"

She takes a deep breath like she's preparing to dive underwater. "A lot of things. First and foremost, I don't want you to quit the gig." She pauses, and the words settle between us. "I'm sorry I wasn't honest up front. I was trying to leave space for you to do what you need to do, but I never told you how I feel. Which is that I want us to finish the rest of the contract. Together. Do what you want with that information, but I had to say it."

I open my mouth to respond, and she presses a finger to my lips.

"And there were some things I *didn't* get to say in the aforementioned voicemail," she continues. "Important things I want to tell you."

"Oh yeah?" I gently slide a fallen tendril of

hair from her face. This is new, Piper sharing her feelings voluntarily. It feels important. "What kinds of things?"

"I want you to know that I love"—she plants a tender, lingering kiss on my cheek—"working with you. No matter what you decide, just know it's been the best weeks of my life, sharing the studio with you. Being in the closet with you. Going everywhere with you."

My heart drops into my stomach. "I—"

"*And* that I love"—her mouth moves to my neck, where she hovers a second before dragging her lips to my ear—"your ambition. It intimidates me, but it inspires me even more. You're going to do incredible things in this life."

"What I *want* to do—"

"And *you*." She pulls back to search my face. "I love you, Sam. Not just that, but I'm *in* love with you. I'm not going to hold back how I feel or what I want anymore. I want *us*."

My heart stutters, and the timeline of my life resets at her words. Without a shadow of a doubt, this moment beats every other that came before it. It feels like a beginning.

It feels like *everything*.

I pull her on top of me, reveling in the warmth of her body. When she looks down at me, I pinch her chin between my fingers. "Say it again."

She doesn't even blink. "I love you. Like, a lot. I'll say it a million times. As many times as you can stand to hear it."

"Good. Because I love you, too." I stroke the apple of her cheek. "I'm *in* love with you, I *fucking* love you—all of it. Every iteration. And I'm dropping out of the race. I don't want to quit the gig or do anything to compromise our work with the Gentrys. It's important to you, and therefore it's important to me."

She opens and closes her mouth twice before whispering, "You're sure?"

"I've been thinking about what I want, what I *need*. Work—firefighting, mayor, whatever—meant everything to me for a long time because I didn't have anything else. I didn't have *you*. I almost put the campaign before the most important person in my life. That was a mistake. What I want is a life with you. You're my priority now."

I almost can't bear the tenderness in her warm whiskey eyes. They strike me dead in the light of the full moon beaming through the window. "I like the sound of that."

The brush of her lips against mine, slow and wet, evolves as her palms slide behind my neck.

I roll us sideways as soon as we start to get sloppy. "There's something else I have to tell you. I spent my only day off this week negotiating with

Darla and Damien."

Her brows furrow. "Oh?"

"Hammering out a new contract. For the exclusivity deal. One with more freedom for me. Since I plan to continue my employment with RTFD, I needed to make sure there was a clause allowing me to work in a government-related field. We took out the minimum number of hours requirement, and voila, a new contract was born. Easy peasy."

Her lips twist into an adorable scowl. "I'm not surprised it went smoothly. The Gentrys love you. They'd give you whatever you want."

I lean in and speak into her lips. "Jealous?"

"Nah, I get it." She nips my bottom lip. "They're not the only ones."

# CHAPTER THIRTY-EIGHT

## PIPER

The Bellini clan tornadoes their way into the labor-and-delivery lobby as soon as it opens for visitors. Our unmitigated chaos awakens the quiet room.

"Did she have the baby?" Georgie asks, clutching Raf's shoulder. "Is it still a girl, you think?"

Raf shrugs. "I never believed it was a girl, even for a second."

"Ten bucks says she's here and still a girl," Georgie bets.

"I've got twenty that says Mom popped out another set of twins," Caleb goads.

Dad enters the lobby through a highly secure door, eyes rimmed with red. His thin, greasy hair stands on edge.

None of us were sitting, but I see a few of my brothers stand up straighter from the corner of my eye. Sam's hand circles mine and squeezes once.

"She's here. Poppy Quinn Bellini, born at 4:59 a.m., weighing in at a formidable six pounds, three ounces. Poppy had a little jaunt in the NICU but is now sleeping peacefully in Nonna's arms. Not sure she'll ever let her go, actually, but the kid has to eat eventually. Mom is doing fine."

Relief washes over me, warm and soft. I step aside to recalibrate. Sam follows me to a wall of windows showcasing a cloudless blue sky.

He tucks a strand of hair behind my ear. "Poppy, eh?"

"So it seems."

"Sounds like they are riffing on the name Piper."

"You're right. They are pretty similar."

Cloaked in sunshine, he hugs me, lifting me so high my toes leave the ground. "I don't blame them. They struck gold with their first girl. Makes sense they'd want to copy-paste."

"Poppy-paste?"

He lifts a playful brow. "Piper-paste."

I bury my face into his unbearably soft skin. If this is a NyQuil-induced dream, I don't want to wake up. "I'm glad you're here. It wouldn't be complete without the whole family. Strange as it may sound coming from your girlfriend, you're kind of an honorary Bellini."

He blinks a billion times in the span of a second.

"Just because…you know. Growing up together. All the memories."

He drops his face into his palm, and I immediately want to retract the sentiment. Maybe I creeped him out.

Caleb wanders over. "What's cracking?"

"I think I might've broken Sam." Just when I'm about to force him to move his hand and apologize for making it weird, he pulls Caleb and me into a bone-crushing group hug.

"I love you guys. You know that?"

"Okay, okay," Caleb huffs. "You're such a softie, O'Shea."

But when Caleb pulls back, his smile is as bright as the sun beaming through the window.

The brothers visit Mom in reverse-age order, and the visits get progressively longer. Nonna stays in Mom's room the entire time to play referee, in case the boys get too rowdy for Mom. This is Nonna living her best bossy life.

I swear I see Luca wipe a tear on the tattered sleeve of his hoodie when he comes out.

"*What?*" he growls as Caleb elbows him in the ribs. "I like Poppy."

I hold Kat while Jane and Caleb go back for their visit. As they reenter the lobby, I distinctly hear Caleb mumble *back here soon enough* under his breath to Jane.

I will *definitely* be following up on that statement when the dust of the day settles.

"Excuse me, would you mind holding my perfect niece? I want to see Mom," I say, thrusting Kat into Caleb's scrawny arms.

He kisses his daughter's fuzzy, jet black hair. "I'll allow it."

Sam attempts to sneak away from me, but I clamp my fingers around his wrist and yank him toward the silver double doors.

"I'm not trying to give your mother a heart attack on her big day. Why don't I wait out here?"

"*Because I said so.*"

"Wow, the Catherine Bellini jumps out."

This is my favorite compliment in recent history. "C'mon. Do it for me."

We cross through the doors and pass a few rooms before reaching Mom's. The words "Poppy Quinn" are written in massive bubble letters on a whiteboard outside the door.

We see Nonna first, perched in a chair outside a large curtain blocking Mom's bed. She's holding a sleeping Poppy close to her chest. My heart does a tap dance.

"Preferita, she's as perfect as you were," Nonna coos, never taking her eyes off Poppy's face.

Damnit if I'm not already about to cry again. It's all I do these days. "Can I hold her?"

"When I'm good and ready to let her go," she barbs.

"So never, then?"

"See your Mom first."

Sam nods me forward and slips into a nook next to the sink. "Go ahead. I'll be right here."

"Sam? Piper? Come over here."

The Great and Powerful Oz has nothing on Mom.

I drag Sam past the drawn curtain.

Mom is clutching a plastic mauve mug and sipping through a straw. Her bed is lifted so she can sit upright. I want to rush over and bury her in a hug, but I know she's barely able to handle sitting by the strained look on her face.

"*Mom.*" The title has never felt more reverent.

"Hi, honey. Stop looking at me like that. I'm *fine.*"

Sounds like a blatant lie to me, but I'll play her game.

Sam waves his arm in a big, sweeping arc like he's landing a plane. He's never not weird around my mother. I'll never not find it endearing. "Hi there, Mrs. Bellini. Congratulations."

She watches him for a moment with a critical eye. She'd be a lot more intimidating if she wasn't in a dressing gown with a nub-sized ponytail on top of her head. "Thanks for taking care of Piper and the family last night."

Sam looks to me before answering. I kick him in

the calf. "Er—of course. Ma'am."

She flashes her rarest smile, one only the closest to her get to see. "Your squad was first on the scene. Thanks to them and the paramedics, Poppy and I are okay. I'm grateful for what you all do."

His lips lift, and I spy a hint of pride in his smile. "I'm so glad you're doing better, Mrs. Bellini."

"Call me Catherine."

I stroke the area between his shoulder blades lightly, and he relaxes a smidge.

"How's the mudslinging? What's the latest on the campaign trail?" she presses.

"Mom, you just got out of surgery. Do you really want to talk politics?"

"Do you know me even a little?" She winces as she adjusts positions in the bed. "That's *exactly* what I want to talk about."

Sam clears his throat. "Actually, Catherine, I've decided to drop out of the race. It's interfering with our other commitments, and I've done enough damage to the O'Shea name for the time being, I'd say."

Mom's expression morphs from confused to resolute. "No."

Sam and I share a confused look.

Mom's tone is all business. "If you drop out now, in the midst of scandal, you look like a coward. It'll give validity to the claims you have secrets, skeletons in the closet, et cetera. Your future campaigns will be tainted. Don't drop out. You need to see it through to the end. There's no chance you'll win with voters hitting the polls in a few weeks, but when the press clips finally drop and explain all this away, you can slowly rebuild your reputation and run for office in the future."

"I never thought of it that way. Future campaigns," he echoes, his brows knitting together. "That's a great point."

"I didn't win a city council seat my first time running because of my good looks," she deadpans.

Nonna peeks around the corner, Poppy bundled up in her arms. Nova comes skidding into view. Dad barrels in after him.

"You may say goodbye and that's it, Novie Bear. Poppy needs to eat soon."

"That's our cue!" Sam says, practically lunging for the exit.

"Not so fast." Mom lifts a hand. "Piper, grab me a phone charger out of your van. And Sam, I need a second more of your time, please. There are a few things we need to go over."

I hover at the curtain's edge for a second. What could she possibly want to talk to Sam about? Me? The idea makes me sweat. "Okay. Is there anything else I can do for you?"

Her chocolate-colored eyes find mine and hold me captive for a moment. I snap a mental photo of the way she looks right now: fierce yet fragile. Happy. Whole. That invisible rope binding us seems to loosen. It feels like slack I've never had before. Letting me go—not completely, but just enough.

She blinks away and swipes one finger under her eye. "That's all, Pipes. Thanks for everything."

• • •

When one is essentially housebound helping with an infant and bedridden mother for a few weeks, video games are the only feasible way to pass the time.

Said Caleb three hours ago, when he hooked up his PS4 in our living room against my wishes.

When Nonna and the twins go to bed and the rest of the boys play their own games in the basement, Caleb and Sam switch from some racing game to *Grand Theft Auto*. An hour passes of Jane and me pretending to care about the game before my and Sam's phones sound in unison.

He ignores it, but I check immediately.

*I know this took longer than you wanted, but I think this will help Sam's campaign. It's already trending.*

Beneath Darla's text is a YouTube link. I click, and video overtakes my screen.

"Holy shit. It's here." I shake Sam's arm. "Babe, look at this."

He peers over. "What am I looking at?"

"What are *we* looking at?" Caleb interjects, eyes still plastered on the TV screen.

"You're looking at a pimp stealing a car. I'm looking at the first press release for our audiobook project."

Sam drops the controller on the coffee table. "Oh *shit*. Cast it on the television so we can all see."

I press a button, and the video populates the TV screen. A glossy-haired and sultry-eyed Piper leans into the microphone, the Studio 7 paint colors providing a dark and familiar backdrop.

I deliver my lines like any seasoned professional would. But damn it if I'm not *impressed*. The audio quality is fantastic, I'm not breathing heavily into the mic, my hair is working for me, and my lines are smooth.

"I can't believe that's me."

Sam wraps his hand around my knee and squeezes. "See why I kept this job? My costar is sexy."

His image pops up next.

*Sweet fancy Moses.* My boyfriend is hot as hell.

We watch in collective silence as Sam feeds the mic his voice like he's doing it a favor.

Turns out the microphone and I have something in common. I also need Sam's mouth close to me when he whispers those wicked little lines.

My thoughts are quickly forced back to neutral,

unsexy territory, given my brother is going into cardiac arrest across the living room listening to this ad.

The video is enough to tease our project and *more* than enough to demonstrate exactly what we've been up to for the last few months. And it's on YouTube, which means it's public.

When it ends, I flop back on the couch in relief. "Hallelujah. Time for the public to know you aren't trying to fuck your way back to prison!"

Caleb groans. "I need to gouge out my eardrums *and* my eyes. Thanks a heap, guys."

Jane fans herself with her hand. "Holy smokes. Is the whole book that hot?"

Sam and I share a loaded look. When he winks, I'm smacked with a strong impulse to drag him upstairs to reenact the barn scenes.

"*Jane*, ew," Caleb whines. "We are never listening to that book. Or watching any more footage."

"Speak for yourself."

My eyes fall to the bottom of the screen. "Wow. This video has over seventy-five thousand views already. How did it climb that fast? It says it was uploaded this morning."

Sam shrugs.

I fire off a text to Darla asking her the same question. Her answer comes a minute later, and I read it aloud to the group.

*Seems to be a case of reverse marketing. Sam is*

*kind of a local celebrity, even if it's not for the reasons he wants. Damien tagged the video with the keywords "mayor," "candidate," "Roseborough," and of course your names and the identifiers for the project. This ad for the project already has more views than any of our past projects. Tell Sam thanks!*

Caleb snorts as he returns his attention to *Grand Theft Auto*. "'Tell Sam thanks.' 'Local celebrity!' Mr. Fucking February strikes again."

# CHAPTER THIRTY-NINE

## SAM

When your smoke-show girlfriend texts you *I need you NOW* from a bar, odds are high her mimosa brunch took a hard left into liquor territory.

As enticing as her request sounds, drunk Piper is far too noisy to fuck in the bathroom of a Roseborough bar—we'd absolutely get caught by someone we know in this small town—so she'll have to settle for a ride to my house instead.

Since the mayoral announcement last week, Piper's been walking on eggshells around me. I forced her into brunch with Jane to lift her spirits. She's taking my loss harder than I am. My primary emotion when Paul took the title was relief. It wasn't my time.

And honestly, I'm grateful. More time for

projects with Piper.

I hop in the car and shoot Caleb a text that I'd give Jane a lift as well. Lord knows she's a lightweight. If Piper is drunk, Jane will be rolling on the ground.

There's no open parking near McLaughlin's, and I would obviously never idle in a fire lane, so I park a few blocks down and hoof it.

I hover outside the door for a second, soaking up the early summer sun. Massachusetts hasn't had a proper rainstorm in weeks.

Feels like a fresh start.

I pull open the door, and a bell jingles overhead.

The room erupts.

The word *surprise* ripples through the packed bar like a wave, people echoing one another.

I've never seen so many familiar faces packed into a space. Caleb and some of our old friends from high school mingling with a few of the nurses from his program. My squad—all the guys who aren't on shift. Jane and her friends, most notably Melissa, who's hanging on my coworker Brent's arm.

My parents, standing on opposite sides of the room but still both present.

Bellinis—a lot of them, even the young ones, circling Catherine's feet like sharks.

And Piper at the center, arms in the air, wearing the brightest smile in the place.

A banner hangs limply behind the bar,

haphazardly strung between two pendant lights.

*FIRST RUNNER-UP*

"Oy, asshole," Caleb calls across the bar, lifting a pint of beer in the air. "Congrats on second place."

A chorus of congratulations follows, and suddenly I'm shaking hands with people and fielding well-wishes as if I won the actual race.

I scrub my chin, looking to Piper as she closes the distance between us. She rifles through her purse and lifts out a single silver medal.

A smile threatens my lips. "And here I thought you texted me for a booty call."

"You didn't think I'd let your second-place victory go uncelebrated, did you?" She places the medal around my neck and ruffles my hair.

"Technically I was last place," I point out.

"Mr. February, you don't mean to suggest that anything other than first place is unacceptable? You're not going to be *that* parent, are you?"

My heart stutters. "Wait, you're not—are you—"

Her head falls back as she laughs. "No way. Despite your commitment to daily practice, I'm still very much on the pill."

I pull her close and plant a kiss on her temple. "Gotta get it in daily. Muscle memory and all that."

Caleb wanders over on the tail end of that family-unfriendly statement. Jane's not far behind. With Kat strapped to her back in a complicated apparatus, she looks like she stopped at McLaughlin's for a pint on a rigorous through-hike.

"New harness for Pipsqueak? You usually wear her on the front."

She and Caleb exchange a panicked look.

"Ohmigod," Piper gushes. "*I knew it.*"

Their panic intensifies.

I stare blankly. "What? I don't get it."

Piper punches her brother in the gut. "How have you kept this from me?"

He laugh-wheezes, clutching his skinny excuse for a gut. "My mistake. I forgot everything is about you."

"Is anyone interested in telling me what's going on?" I press.

Jane, who has watched Caleb and Piper with a look of mild amusement, turns to me. Her lips curve into a smile. "It's been a few minutes since the last Bellini boy was born. Couldn't let that stand."

We celebrate quietly so no one hears, exchanging hugs—Kat pulls my hair over Jane's head—and talk timelines. The fertility of this damn family makes me wonder if Piper's pill stands a chance. A thrill trickles down my spine. Maybe she won't need it much longer.

Maybe we'll have a family of our own.

"So, what's next, Mr. February?" Caleb asks, crossing his arms. "You won silver in this mayor race—are we trying for a bronze in senate?"

"I thought maybe I'd focus on the projects I

have for a while. These audiobooks and fires aren't going to sort themselves out."

Piper tosses me a look. "No city council run next year?"

"Nah."

The noise fades away when she looks at me. "Are two full-time jobs going to be enough for you? I know how much you like to stay busy."

I hover my lips over her ear and drift my hand over the curve of her hip. "I'd like *you* to be my full-time job. If I'm a good little employee, will you promote me?"

"I could use a right-hand man."

"Get a room," Caleb grumbles.

Abruptly, I remember we're surrounded by people. *Our* people.

I always wanted to be part of something bigger than myself. To belong. I've felt it in bits and pieces along the way. In the camaraderie of my squad. In the whirlwind of a campaign crowd. At the Bellinis' full dinner table. And, on those rare but memorable days, in quiet moments with my parents. I've spent my life doing the most, chasing a feeling.

In Piper's arms, I've finally found it.

# EPILOGUE

## PIPER

The day we officially christen the last room in our new house—guest bedroom, hello temporary futon—Sam reminds me of a recording appointment on our joint calendar. I cannot for the life of me remember scheduling it.

We load into his car, camera ready. "You know, I'm still confused by this whole thing. You're *sure* Darla said we're filming book-two promos today? It seems too early for that."

Sam unbuckles his seat belt and kisses me across the center console. He nips my bottom lip once before pulling back. "She's the boss. We are her willing little puppets. If she wants to film extra stuff, so be it. At least it gives us a reason to dress up."

I can't say I hate the opportunity to get camera ready, especially since my wardrobe lately has been of the moving casual variety. He ushers me into the lobby of Studio 7 with a hand to the small of my back. Darla meets us at the hallway entrance in a distressed Biketoberfest shirt and studded jeans. The outfit either cost her hundreds of dollars or was assembled from swag-bag freebies. There's no telling.

"Right on time!" she chirps, waving for us to follow.

I stretch my arms overhead as we cruise to the recording room. "Morning, Darla. Book two already! I can hardly believe it. We still have footage from book one to record."

She fluffs her bouffant hairdo. "Oh, these things are on a funny time schedule—lots of moving parts. You know how it is."

I pretend to know how it is.

Damien is in his usual spot, seated behind the glass wall. He waves but doesn't lower the glass.

I wave back. "No takeout containers? Damien must be sick."

Darla's laugh is a light trill, but something feels off. "He had a big breakfast. Biscuits and gravy... that sort of thing."

We approach our spots, and I begin to sweat. The thrill of being here never subsides.

Our pages are already on the podium.

*One.*

*One* as the title of a second book in a series? Strange, but I don't want to yuck on anybody's yum. I position my microphone and take a calming breath. Slowing my heart rate is a challenge when Sam's smirking like he's just said something exceedingly clever, his left dimple out in full force.

If only his hotness took a day off so I could concentrate.

Darla lowers the lights, and the door snaps shut.

E.T. springs to life, holding wide.

I open my script to the first page.

*Blank.*

Without reacting—the NOW RECORDING sign above the door is alight, and the camera is running—I leaf to the next page.

*Blank.*

I lift my gaze to Sam and open my mouth to speak, but he cuts me off.

*"Ten. That's how many years it's been since our first kiss. It was like an explosion of Technicolor and sound in my black-and-white little life."*

My heart climbs into my throat. He's holding his mark and speaking into the microphone, but his words sound like they were written for me. "Sam, what are you doing?"

*"Nine. The time on the clock when you wandered into McLaughlin's the night we remet. I was sure every*

*sip you took was going to be your last, because why would a beautiful girl like you spend even an extra second of her time with a nerd like me? It doesn't compute. You've been too good for me your entire life."*

What a lie. If my mouth wasn't glued shut, I'd tell him he's dead wrong. I'd tell him just how *good* he truly is.

I glance over at the window. Darla's head rests against Damien's shoulder. When her hand comes over her chest and her lips press together like she's trying not to cry, I feel the weight of what's happening all at once.

*"Eight. How old you were the first time you broke a bone. I know that because your mom let me bring Gatorade up to your room so you wouldn't have to come downstairs. Do you remember how many damn drinks I brought you?"*

I speak through quivering lips. "A lot. You brought a lot of drinks."

He smiles, the corners of his eyes crinkle, and he leans back into his mic.

*"Seven. Your jersey number when you played flag football that first and only summer. You'll recall I destroyed anyone who came near you, under the guise of sport."*

He destroyed a lot of kids that summer.

*"Six. The number of kids I want. This is up for*

*discussion, as I am willing to consider seven."*

I snort. A crooked smile plays across his lips. In that moment, the camera spins a circle around us, holding tight on my face. He takes a step sideways, no longer blocked by his podium. Every cell on my body switches to high alert. In this quiet, insulated space, I hear his steps, the swish of his pants, his uneven breathing.

*"Five. The number of minutes it took me to list the things I love about you on paper. I could've filled a novel. Your kindness and composure. The way you show up for family. The brightness of your smile. The tiny birthmark above your left hip. Your ambition. God, your sometimes infuriating* humility, *despite the breadth of your talent. Your legs. Your ass. Every part of you…"*

My giggle seems to reset his train of thought. He winks and continues.

*"When I look into your eyes, it feels like something snaps into place. Yours feel like the only pair I've ever really seen.*

*"This is by no means an exhaustive list, but parts are far too scandalous for this video, so I thought it better to write them down."*

He pulls out a rolled-up piece of loose-leaf paper from his back pocket. The camera pulls back as he slides it into the pocket of my blazer. His hand lingers at my side, like he's trying to decide if it's the right time to touch me. I guide his fingers to my waist. We step into place, chest against chest, my head resting below his collarbone.

"*Four.*"

His hand brushes beneath my chin and tilts my face toward his.

"*The maximum number of seconds I can look you in the eye before I kiss you. Every time I think about the hours we spent together recording in your studio or hanging out and not touching, I award myself a medal of restraint. I am now a world record holder: Most medals held by a human being.*"

My lips crave his, but I don't dare interrupt. He brushes his cheek against mine, flooding my face with warmth.

"*Three. The number of people I told about this little plan. The trifecta: Gio, Catherine, and Julia. When I left your dad's office that day, my shirt was soaked through with sweat. Julia cried.*

"*And your mom gave me her endorsement in the hospital. Not for the campaign. For us.*"

He lowers his voice, barely a whisper skating across my skin. The mic would never pick it up, but I don't need it to. I could never forget the way he sounds.

"*Two. The number of chances we needed to get this thing right. The second time's a charm, for us. I can't do life without you, Piper Bellini. I'm tired of trying to.*"

I soak his shirt with my silent tears. His body pulls away from mine, and he slides to the ground. On one knee, he's the most handsome man I've ever seen. My breath hitches as he opens the black velvet ring box.

Nonna's heirloom diamond glints, bathed in the spotlight.

*"One question. Will you marry me?"*

I melt at the tenderness of his tone. I don't want to keep him waiting, but I can't stop staring into his eyes. They glint with hope and promise. They say *I love you* at a pitch only I can hear.

There's always been only one man for me. And now, there's only one word.

"Yes."

# ACKNOWLEDGMENTS

*Write a book*, they said. *It'll be fun*, they said.

They were correct. Writing this book is the most fun I've ever had.

I still pinch myself daily that this book is in the world, and I cannot thank the people who helped me enough. I couldn't have done it without my village.

First, to the team that made this book possible. To Heather Howland, whose keen editorial eye saw straight to the heart of these characters. You changed my life in an instant when you gave me the yes. This book wouldn't be here without you, and I'm forever grateful. I cannot wait to cook up more cinnamon rolls with you. And to my agent, Barbara Collins Rosenberg, who supported me at every step of the publication process. You keep me grounded and on track, and I'm grateful every day for your expertise.

To Rochele, who plucked me out of the Author Mentor Match slush pile and taught me all the romance tricks. Piper and Sam thank you for your service. You are a great mentor and an even better friend.

To my CPs, who scooped me up when I was a lost baby writer and taught me how to share my work. Sarah T. Dubb, Jessica Joyce, and Risa Edwards—you've taught me more than you'll know. And to our larger romance matrix, Alexandra Kiley, Maggie North, Jen Devon, Sarah Burnard, and Ingrid Pierce, thanks for being the best betas in the game.

To the group chats, vast and varied. My DGIAB sisters, Rachel, Kate, Brittany, Brooke, Cat, Hannah, K.C., Libby, Lindsay, Morgan, Kenn, Katy— I can't explain what you all mean to me but please know I think about you, ghosts, and PowerPoints every single day. And Olivia and Skyla, thanks for letting me live in your DMs rent-free.

WTS writing squad, thank you for being the first friends I had in the publishing space. For the sake of anonymity I can't list you all, but you know who you are. You believed in me and this book when it was nothing but a seedling. I'm lucky to call you all friends.

And to those who know me outside of writing and support me in this wild endeavor, you mean everything to me. My incredible husband, Corey, and our sons, Theo and Link, you make my world spin and are only allowed to read this page of the book. Mom, with your Boston influence. Faith, Carl, Nina, Karen and Bill for all you do. Lauren, Austin, Jordan, Josh, Melina, Raymond, Rachael, Connie, Shannon, Megan, Megen, Ashley— you motivate and inspire me endlessly. Shanda, Brad, Hilary, Ryan, Tyler, thanks for playing *D&D* so I could sit at the table and write this book.

To my grandma, who made me the writer and person I am today. The Nonna blueprint. And Juno, for reading every version of every story, no matter how rough.

And to you, readers, an extra thank-you. First books are special because you write them for yourself, never knowing if they'll be shared. To know that Piper and Sam found their way into your hands is the greatest gift I've ever received.

# ABOUT THE AUTHOR

Romance author Livy Hart has two children, too many Funko Pops, and a husband who's workin' on the railroad—literally. She currently resides in Dallas, Texas where she enjoys long walks on the concrete and people-watching at malls so big they have their own zip codes. When she's not writing, she's bickering with her KitchenAid stand mixer, road-tripping to her sleepy Florida hometown, or sipping espresso on her Nonna's porch.